THE CURSED CROWN

ELDRITCH HEART BOOK #2

MATTHEW S. COX

DIVISION ZERO PRESS

The Cursed Crown

A novel
By Matthew S. Cox
© 2018 - All rights reserved
Cover by Amalia Chitulescu
Interior art by Ricky Gunawan

ISBN (eBook): 978-1-949174-84-7
ISBN (paperback): 978-1-949174-85-4

This novel is dedicated to anyone who has ever needed to hide their true self from a world burdened by antiquated ideals and hatred cloaked as virtue.

- -

Also, it's rather difficult to disregard a sequel request from a young woman in a hospital bed.

CONTENTS

AUTHOR'S NOTE

This novel is a continuation from the events of book one: *The Eldritch Heart*. Reading *The Cursed Crown* first will smother you in spoilers.

Sharp spoilers.

The kind of spoilers that creep out of nowhere like a Lego brick on the floor at three in the morning when you're trying to sneak barefoot to the bathroom.

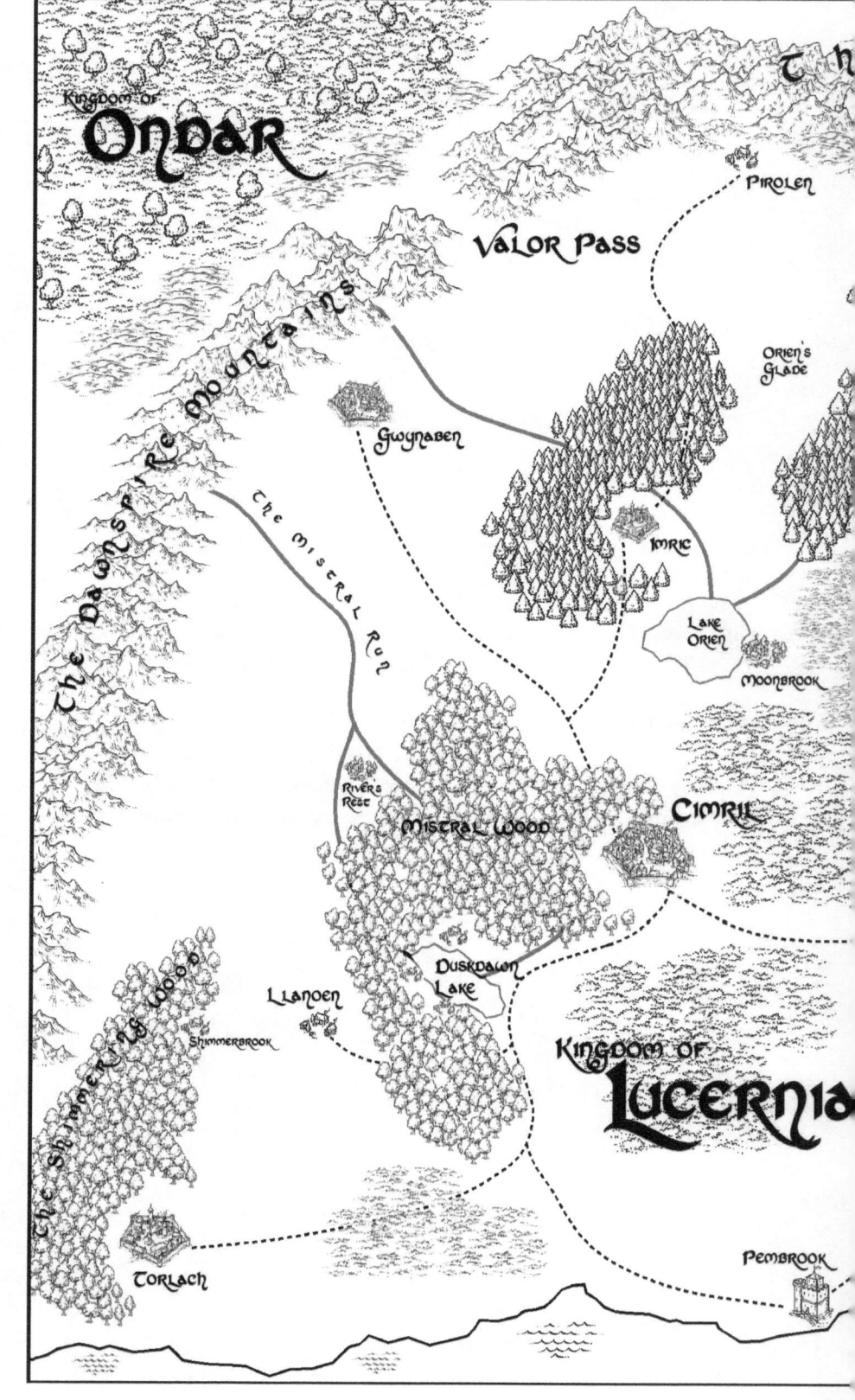

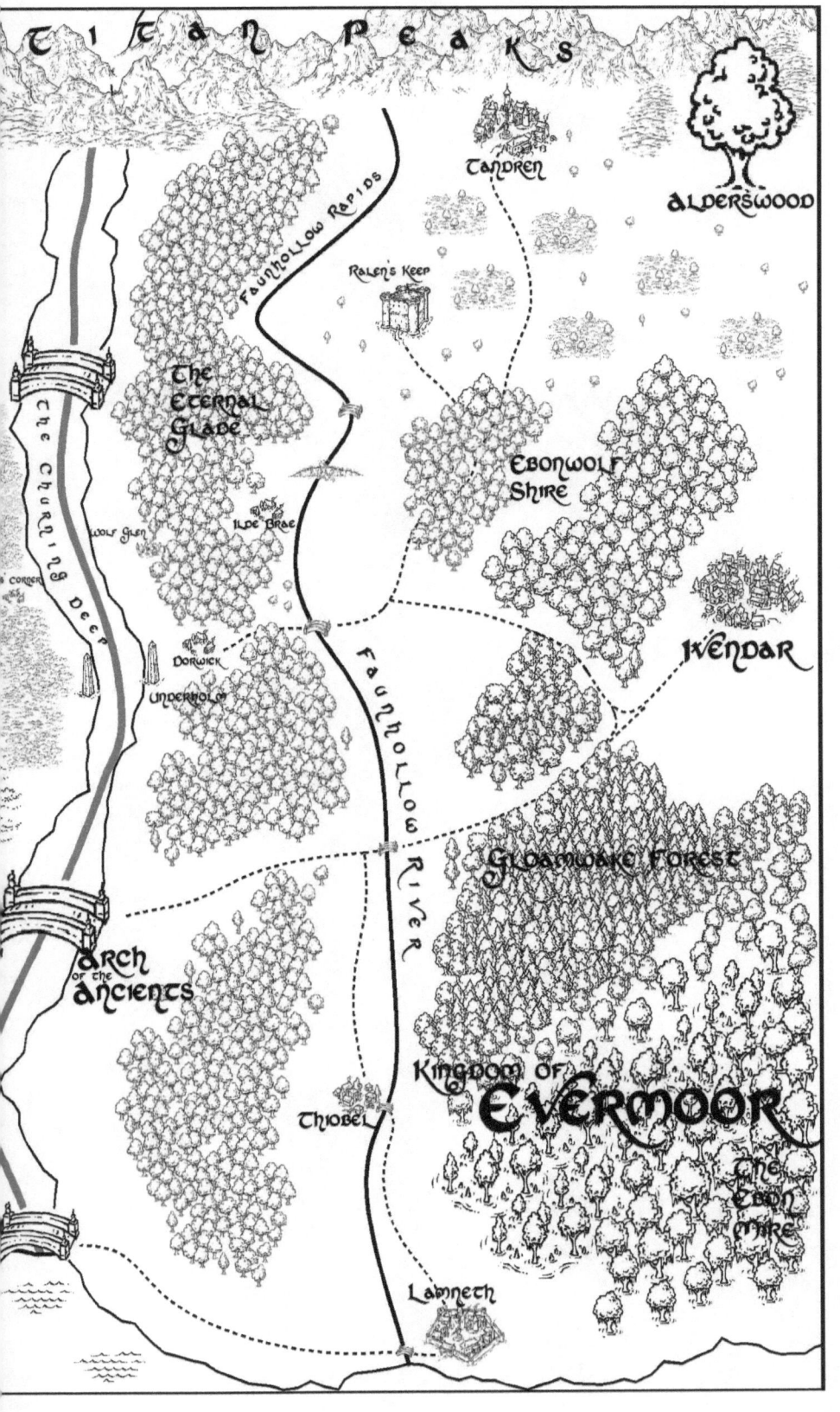

A FINAL MOMENT

OONA

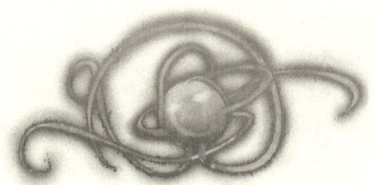

Turmoil kept Oona's eyes open and her mind wandering. Her luxurious bed offered physical comfort, but no relief from her worries.

The same bed she'd slept in for thirteen years made the black-walled cell she'd spent days confined in feel like something out of an awful dream. Try as she might, she couldn't dredge up even a tiny scrap of memory of her life before the castle. Ruby, her actual mother, had told her she'd accidentally lit fire to one of the chickens at the age of three. Magic being rare among the people of Lucernia, word of the event had found its way up to the king.

And overnight, she'd gone from peasant child to princess.

Evie, her seven-year-old sister—who everyone agreed looked like a smaller version of her—lay asleep beside her. Other than a nine-year gap in age, they had two distinct differences: Evie had green eyes instead of blue, and the girl slept *hard*. Another assassin could kick down the door, engage in a fifteen-minute sword fight, and the girl likely wouldn't stir. She had a room of her own, though the vastness of the castle—especially at night—frightened her. Had the king not taken Oona as a decoy, she would likely have shared a bed with her sister until being married off, so she didn't mind having her close each night.

Oona gently squeezed her sister's hand under the covers. *Soon, you will be a princess and this will be your room.*

She hated thinking it, for it made her dwell on what Kitlyn said. The Council of Lucen, the six leaders of the temple, prepared to strip King Talomir of his title as high priest. Initially, she expected they did so due to his acceptance of her love for Kitlyn—another girl, and the king's true daughter—though much to her surprise, they objected to his causing a twenty-year war, thousands of deaths, and spending the past twenty years lying to the kingdom more than who she'd chosen to give her heart.

I am being dramatic. She sighed to herself, unable to quite pin down the exact moment she *knew* her feelings toward Kitlyn had changed from dearest friend to something more. But ever since that moment, she had become acutely aware of how the nation, a people devoted to Lucen, God of Purity, viewed such unions. Despite it being utterly ludicrous to even place a girl in love with a girl on the same significance as King Talomir's crimes, years spent in dread fear had conditioned her.

She would have gladly suffered the scorn of a kingdom to admit her love, but she had feared Kitlyn's potential rejection most of all. To calm her mind, she closed her eyes and thought back to that moment on the shore at Duskdawn Lake where they had finally admitted the truth of their feelings for each other. With such a great burden lifted, the triviality of people expecting her to destroy an entire kingdom didn't bother her much. As long as she had Kitlyn, she could handle anything —even a stupid foretelling.

But all that had passed—and not in the way anyone had hoped for, or dreaded. Perhaps in light of the people of Lucernia learning that their beloved king had caused two decades of war, all the while feeding them deceptions as if from the tongue of Lucen himself, the revelation that the princess had fallen in love with a girl wound up an insignificant bit of news on the side. Not even the elevation of a peasant girl to the Baroness of Gwynaben elicited so much as a raised eyebrow. Then again, the people had been used to thinking of her as the princess already.

And Lady Tenebrea gave us our blessing.

Oona tried to project her gratitude up to the goddess while picturing the apparitional form that had drifted across the courtyard. King Talomir had challenged the gods directly, stating if any god had issue with who his daughter had chosen to love, let them say so in person. This, of course, had drawn a collective gasp of horror from all assembled, including several priests. Surely, even the High Priest of Lucen dare not speak with such irreverence, *demanding* anything of Lucen.

Though, Tenebrea had listened—and answered with a smile. Oona had long felt a sense of solidarity with her as a fellow outcast. Most people avoided even looking at paintings of her. She had no more choice in being the goddess of death than Oona had in who her heart chose to love.

Somewhere between the ensuing discontent sweeping over the kingdom and a nod from Tenebrea in person, it seemed as though everyone (at least in her near vicinity) had decided to either accept or ignore the two of them without comment. Whispers had reached her that a handful of castle staff departed quietly over it, though no one Oona could recall meeting often enough to recognize. Even Elsbeth, as awful as the girl had been to Kitlyn through the years, didn't take any issue with them... only with their social status. She'd hated Kitlyn for being 'a peasant above her station.'

Ugh. The girl is so fixated on who she can feel superior to.

Elsbeth had been quite unhappy that Kitlyn had promoted Piper, the kitchen maid, to be Oona's handmaiden, but didn't complain about not receiving the post herself. Considering her cruelty to the king's actual daughter, she likely had expected much harsher reprisal and contented herself to remain as First Maid.

Oona opened her eyes, gazing over her sleeping sister at patches of blue moonlight on the wall. She wanted to have Kitlyn close, in the same bed, even if only to find comfort in her presence so she could sleep. King Talomir forbade them from sharing a room before a wedding took place. No one made mention of all the times they had done so before anyone knew they loved each other, albeit nothing romantic had ever happened between them. And, he would no doubt have issued the same decree if she had been betrothed to Prince Lanwick of Ondar. She would not have been allowed to share a bedroom with him either before a wedding.

She suppressed the urge to roll her eyes at the notion two people in love would be considered 'impure' for being alone together before some priest could officiate their union. As much as she revered Lucen, the pointless ceremony of it struck her as an invention of mortals. After all, for many years, everyone thought he forbade women loving women and men loving men, and that turned out not to be the case, merely the overreach of mortal priests taking 'purity' the wrong way.

Also, Oona's magic still worked. If she ever displeased Lucen, he would rescind his gift.

She stared up at the ceiling, annoyed at no one in particular for her inability to fall asleep. Without the constant worry of figuring out how she'd wind up wiping out all of Evermoor before her people died, she'd assumed she might no longer suffer such sleeplessness. A new trouble plagued her, one that would—mercifully and horribly at the same time—not remain for long.

The priests would publicly declare King Aodh Talomir a heretic and cast him out from the temple of Lucen.

Kitlyn expected he would take his own life before suffering such a public humiliation. She'd told Oona as much, and that she assumed the priests warned her of their plans specifically so word would reach him and he would do just that, sparing the kingdom the disgrace.

How can she be so distant about her father's death? Oona choked up, tears gathering in her eyes. Despite everything that happened, she still thought of the man as her father. She *had* a real father, but the man hadn't seen her since she'd been three years old, and he had died six years ago to the war. She couldn't remember him at all, nor anything of her home in Llanoen.

No. Not my home. Again, she squeezed Evie's hand. Her 'mother' had been harsh on the little one. Quick to slap her around, quick to shout at her for mistakes. Though, somehow, the child had retained her cheery disposition and innocence. Oona couldn't help but spare her more of that woman's treatment. Offering Ruby money in exchange for the girl staying here had only proved her instinct correct. No real mother would *sell* their children. *Both* of them.

She fumed in silence.

I have to do something. I can't simply lay here while the man I think of as my father dies.

No sooner had Oona started to sit up than a soft knock broke the stillness. She jumped and grabbed the handle of the longsword beside her bed, frozen in a stare at the door. A few seconds later, she remembered the war with Evermoor had come to an end and no more assassins would sneak in to harm her—at least none from a foreign kingdom.

Also, assassins didn't usually knock.

Assassins *might* come for Kitlyn, depending on how various arguments no doubt going on in cellars and taverns around the land played out. Would the people accept two queens? Would they accept the heir of Aodh Talomir after what he did? Advisor Beredwyn seemed quite confident in his statement that the people loved (or at least respected) both of them. Oona had the admiration of Lucernia, and Kitlyn had won over the citizens of Evermoor. Then again, saving an entire population from a withering death tended to put you on their good side.

Who would possibly call on me in the middle of the night?

She blinked twice before the thought it might be Kitlyn sprang into her mind. Again, a knock came from the door. Oona pulled the bedding aside and slid to her feet, swallowing a soft whine of alarm at the coldness of the polished stone floor. She left the longsword be and padded over to the door before whispering, "Who's there?"

"It is I," said the king. "Forgive me if I woke you."

Oona undid the lock and pulled the door open, peering up in mute horror at the man standing in the hall.

King Talomir's cheeks held little of their usual color and more wrinkles creased his face than his age should imply. His eyes had sunken in and possessed a distant quality, his hair wild. If not for his expensive nightclothes, he could've been drunk in an alley outside a tavern in Cimril, screaming incoherent gibberish at passersby. He looked as though Tenebrea had already touched him.

"Father…"

He bowed his head. "Please forgive me for how I have treated you."

Oona edged out into the corridor and tugged the door almost closed. A whispered conversation would likely not wake Evie, but words unfit for the ears of a seven-year-old would surely draw wakefulness where the explosion of a magical fireball could not.

"You have not treated me poorly, father. My greatest grouse had always been that you permitted everyone to behave so cruelly to Kitlyn. That and not permitting me to waste my coins at the shops in Cimril. Such a trivial, petty thing to be so upset about." She gazed down at her pale toes, peeking out from under the hem of her nightdress. "Everyone called me spoiled, and they had been right."

"Oona…" King Talomir grasped her shoulders, trying to look her in the eye as one might try to lock stares with a specter they couldn't see. "I took you from your home, your rightful parents."

She pressed her hands to his chest, unnerved at hearing his every breath rattle around as though it took great effort. "That woman is not my mother. You gave me a better life. Because of you, I found Kitlyn."

"You lived with the burden of a station not your own for years. A burden too great for a mere child... and my fault." King Talomir bowed his head.

Oona blinked, realizing he no longer wore a crown, not even his simple one. Of course, he likely didn't wear it to bed. But the man had been terribly proud of his station and never went anywhere without it. "You look exhausted." She gently pushed at him. "You should retire. Are you sleepwalking?"

He managed a faint smile, still not quite looking right at her. "No, child. I am awake. More awake than I have been in many years. For everything I have done to you, I am truly sorry."

"You have nothing to apologize to me for. It's Kit you should apologize to. You have always been like a father to me. You *are* my father."

"I stole you from your family." He sighed. "I stole your father from your mother, and from the realm of the living."

Oona pivoted to the side, arms crossed, studying her toes again. "That woman would have disowned me eventually. Who I am is not of your doing. I would have certainly been drawn to another woman, and Ruby would not have accepted that either. Because of you, I met Kitlyn."

"You are too quick to forgive." He pulled her into a hug, mushing her cheek against his chest. "I have never known anyone so pure of heart. I have caused much needless death and suffering."

She clutched at his nightclothes, clinging as though she'd never see him again. "Please don't..."

"I must."

Oona sniffled. "So many needless deaths. What good will it do to add one more?"

"Lucen knows my soul, and the sorrow I now feel for everything. Perhaps he holds me yet in contempt, for I regret what I did to my daughters more than speaking falsehoods under the guise of his name."

"You can atone. Work to aid those who have suffered. Dedicate your life to undoing as much of the damage as you can."

He let out a long, weak sigh. "I shall soon make it right with him."

What! She tore her gaze off the floor and stared up into his eyes. The dawning realization of what he meant washed over her like a slow seep of icy water. *He means to... This is his last farewell.* Overcome with grief, she clamped her arms around him and burst into tears. Despite all he had done, she still couldn't bear the thought of losing the only father she'd ever known.

King Talomir patted her back and made an attempt to comfort her, though moved much like a giant marionette worked by strings.

He's already halfway to Tenebrea. She gathered up her tears and pushed herself out to arms' length, again looking him in the eye. "Please, father, you mustn't do what you're thinking. Disappear into the hills of Gwynaben..." A suggestion to disguise himself formed, but she pushed it aside—too close to lying. "...or something."

"Oona..." He brushed a hand across her forehead, chasing a few loose blonde strands away from her eyes. "I have done many things wrong. Perhaps selfishly, my treatment of Kitlyn bothers me the most. To have her look upon me like a stranger is... the worst punishment."

She clenched two fists in his robe. "Then live with that punishment. Don't do this. Please. I forgive you for dressing me up as a decoy."

"I never intended for you to be harmed." He gingerly grasped her wrists, plucked her fingers from his nightclothes, and pressed her hands together, holding them. "It is Lucen's honest truth that I did everything in my power to keep you safe, foolishly denying to myself that the danger had been entirely of my own making. And with what little power I still possess, I still wish you safe. Do not betray who you are for my benefit. Do not repeat my mistakes and tarnish your connection to Lucen. I see it in your eyes that you wish me to deceive, to flee, to pretend to be someone else. I cannot place that burden on you as well. No, child. Events are set in motion that will bring about my end one way or the other. I have accepted there is no avoiding my fate. For the sake of the kingdom... I cannot allow the people to suffer even more. It was for the sake of the kingdom that I protected Kitlyn with ignominy."

Looking at him made her want to scream and throw the phrase *for the sake of the kingdom* back in his face. *If you cared about the kingdom, you wouldn't have stolen the Eldritch Heart to begin with!* She balled her fists, bracing to whirl into the same sort of tantrum she often resorted to on the rare occasions he denied her wants. Images of men's insides spilling out at the end of *her* blade flashed through her mind as well the stench of foul poison and the overpowering elation when she had been reunited with Kitlyn. Somewhere amid all that, she had changed. Scream-whining wouldn't help. It never had accomplished anything beyond earning contempt from the castle staff. The more she thought, the more she dwelled on Kitlyn being made to toil endlessly... and worse, never knowing the warmth of a father's arms around her.

For a brief moment, she found herself more furious at him for the abandonment Kitlyn must've felt than anything else he did.

A wave of sorrow lapped upon the beach of her anger, smothering it.

Oona bowed her head, feeling selfish all over again. Kitlyn's torment paled in comparison to the thousands who had perished for his greed, or the suffering of widows and orphans left in the wake of the war—on both sides. She couldn't tell if Lucen would be displeased at her for placing so much weight on Kitlyn's bleak life compared to all the rest of the suffering King Talomir had caused, but she couldn't help her heart. Perhaps because she kept the thought to herself, he would understand.

"It offers me some small peace to see you safe and happy." The king brushed a hand over her cheek. "Though it is time for me to go."

"Please, don't," whispered Oona, shocked at the coldness of his hand. "There must be another way."

He held her for a few minutes in silence before kissing her lightly atop the head. "I shall think on it."

His voice sounded so hollow, whispery, and lifeless, Oona didn't even need the magical sense that Lucen gave her to detect his lie. In the brief moment grief paralyzed her arms and mouth, he slipped away and glided off toward the main stairwell, silent as a wraith. His nightclothes flashed blue each time he crossed a patch of moonlight, and for all the lack of sound he made, she wondered if he had *already* died.

She watched him go until the curve of the hallway blocked her view. At the moment he disappeared, it seemed he faded away as much as stepped behind stone. Oona's heart weighed down inside her chest. She slipped into her room and eased the door closed behind her. Evie remained asleep in bed, as though nothing at all had happened.

Back pressed to the door, Oona debated running after the king, but if she *had* been visited by his ghost, it wouldn't matter. Something *had* seemed woefully off about him, so sickly and unfocused as though his mind roamed elsewhere. Perhaps the burden of his guilt did that, as he hadn't given off any dread or sense of chill. But Oona had never seen a spirit before, especially one who loved her.

A long, slow sigh escaped her lips. She eyed the bed, but couldn't take even one step before grief pulled her down.

Curled up on the floor, arms wrapped around her legs, she bowed her head against her knees and wept.

2

WHERE ALL ROADS LEAD

KITLYN

A dream of being little again, running around the castle with Oona took a strange turn.

They ducked into the library, giggling the whole way to the secret passage. Miss Harper came out of the darkness with her enormous wooden paddle, her teeth twisted to demonic triangles by the paintbrush of imagination. Kitlyn pulled Oona up to a sprint, racing down the rickety stairway and out across the kitchen toward the castle gardens. The mean governess chased them over the field, swinging the huge wooden horror every few steps, but missing every time. As soon as they neared the ivy-covered wall, Omun plucked them up like a stable boy catching a pair of tiny mice, then stepped on Miss Harper. The stone ancient set the girls down on one of the winding paths inside the garden. A short run around in laughing circles ended with Oona tackling her— and in an instant, they both grew to sixteen.

Dream-Kitlyn opened her mouth to say something, but couldn't find words upon realizing their clothing had disappeared. She stared down at Oona, not entirely sure how to start doing 'those things' that Ruby accused them of already having done. She grinned mischievously, as did Oona, but the awkwardness of lying in the grass together with only a thin layer of perspiration between them boiled over into laughter.

Oona grabbed her shoulders and rolled over on top of her. She started to lean down to kiss her, but began shaking her instead. "Kitlyn…"

"What?" asked Dream-Kitlyn.

"Kit, wake up," said Oona.

Sunlight glimmering through wavering branches overhead blurred into a swirl and faded to darkness. Kitlyn found herself awake, in a large guest room like one Prince Tristan had been staying in. Oona straddled her, shaking her by a hand on each shoulder. Unlike the dream, two nightgowns, a sheet, a blanket, and a comforter separated them.

"Oona? What's wrong?" asked Kitlyn, trying to push sleepiness aside.

"Your father…. He's going to…" She broke up into sobs.

Kitlyn sat up and wrapped her arms around Oona, knowing full well what the man would most likely do. That she felt so little about it seemed like the sort of thing she ought to be ashamed of herself for. Still, she couldn't summon much emotion about his loss either way. Beredwyn had been far more of a father to her over the years… holding her when she'd had scary dreams as a little girl, sometimes reading her stories at night, and more recently, always there with kind words when she needed it. True, he'd somewhat distanced himself from her as she'd become more of a castle servant than a child who lived there, but he always took whatever opportunity he could to offer warmth. Sixteen-year-olds didn't really need bedtime stories after all, nor did they often require comforting for thinking Grengwylf might be lurking under their beds.

King Talomir, though… she'd always been frightened of him, wondering if at any moment he might grow tired of the 'peasant girl' being around the castle. She still couldn't quite reconcile herself with the idea of being his daughter. For everything he'd done to the people of Evermoor and Lucernia, he probably deserved more disgust or anger than she showed him. Perhaps her sense of familial loyalty had played out in a lack of feeling anything for him. Any love she might've felt for having a father negated her anger for what he did. She understood how the people could hate him enough to plot rebellion. All those families ruined by his greed. Of course, her family counted among those ruined —a mother she never knew, killed by assassins. A father ever distant, refusing to acknowledge her, pretending another to be his daughter… but she couldn't find a scrap of self-pity anywhere. What he had done to her, to her mother, didn't hold a candle to the near-death of everyone and everything in Evermoor… or all the people in Lucernia who died.

"You're angry," whispered Oona.

Kitlyn sighed. "Every time I think about him, I have a storm in my heart. Anger, disgust, grief, sadness… mostly anger. But not for what he did to me."

"Most of the servants were all so mean to you, but you never complained." Oona squeezed her tight. "I don't want him to die. Please help me stop him."

"I don't think we can." Kitlyn rested her chin on Oona's shoulder, rocking her side to side. "It's not as though I like it either, but it will happen one way or the other. What message would it send to the people if a king could nearly destroy an entire nation only to seek power for himself and not answer for it? And all the while making a mockery of Lucen's teachings."

Oona sniffled. "It is so strange to hear you speaking of the gods."

"Well, I certainly don't think about them as often as you do, but I also don't carry Lucen's gift." She sighed. "And, well, perhaps I had been somewhat cross with them when I thought they had taken my parents away and left me to suffer here. The servants never really bothered me. It only proved how petty they are."

"I'm so sorry." Oona leaned back, wiping her eyes. "I tried and tried to make them stop tormenting you, but they wouldn't listen to me."

Kitlyn smiled. "I know. They will now. You're not a spoiled little princess screaming her head off because someone put the wrong color sheets on your bed. You're a woman."

A sad laugh slipped from Oona. "I don't think I was *that* bad."

Kitlyn pinched her fingers in a 'little bit' gesture.

"Was I?" Oona smirked.

"You had your moments… but it's not entirely your fault. They pampered you."

"The king felt guilty. They all expected I would die to an assassin." Oona stared down into the narrow space between them.

Kitlyn kept quiet for a moment, captivated by the sight of Oona's long, blonde hair spilling down her front onto the bed. The moonlight made her delicate face practically glow blue, and grief gave her the look of a brittle porcelain doll. It struck her as odd to think of this girl sitting in her lap as the same one who had killed Evermoor soldiers for trying to poison her. This *woman* before her didn't seem entirely like the same laughing little girl she had spent so much time with growing up.

It almost felt wrong to be happy with her, after all the pain her father had caused.

But happy she was.

"He came to me," said Oona in a half-whisper. "He had the look of death upon him already…" She spoke of his visitation, working herself up to tears again by the time she finished.

Kitlyn tried her best to be comforting, talking about some of the better times they'd had as children before the foretelling stole Oona's ability to be happy. For the past two years, simultaneously watching her dearest friend in a perpetual state of terrified sorrow while trying to figure out why 'dear friend' had changed to something entirely different left Kitlyn little time to feel sorry for herself. Being treated like a servant didn't bother her anywhere near as much as seeing the once giggly Oona reduced to a mournful specter of worry.

She couldn't quite find it inside herself to forgive her father for doing that to Oona, and it infuriated her that he again made her suffer. *Her heart is too big and soft. Even a man like him, she cannot stand to lose.* Kitlyn clenched her jaw, for a moment wondering if she simply couldn't comprehend what it would be like to have a father. Did that make it easier or even possible to forgive him for what he did to the kingdom, to so many people? Oona sounded more upset with him for the life Kitlyn had than all the suffering he caused.

Kitlyn had no idea how a daughter *should* feel toward her father… though when she thought of Beredwyn locking her in the dungeon, she somewhat understood.

He'd done that to protect me from assassins.

"We can't stop it." Kitlyn gathered Oona's hand in both of hers. "The priests intend to sever his ties with the temple of Lucen. He has the blood of thousands on his hands."

Oona sniffled. "I know. But he doesn't have to die."

"For no consequence to come of his actions would only serve to further weaken Lucernia. The people are already restless. Many of the soldiers feel betrayed. Faith in Lucen has been shaken that he allowed such deception to continue for so long."

"Now you rather sound like him." Oona wiped her eyes with her left hand. "Do you hate him?"

"No." Kitlyn shook her head. "I… have too many different emotions toward him that I feel nothing really."

Oona looked down.

"It isn't your fault." She brushed a hand over Oona's cheek. "Is it selfish of me to think the worst part of all of it was to see you these past few years so joyless. You used to laugh so much, always smiling."

Oona slid off Kitlyn's lap and sat beside her. "I hadn't known of the foretelling then. How could I be happy thinking I would bring about the end of so many lives?"

"I understand why you lost your smile, but that doesn't mean I cannot hold him in contempt for doing it to you. He has much to answer for."

"But why does he have to die?" Oona buried her face in a handful of nightdress. "There has been enough death."

"The man cannot tolerate the humiliation of being cast out of the temple. I suspect he also wishes to spare the kingdom the task of removing him." Kitlyn listened to Oona sniffle for a moment, hurt that she could do nothing to take away that pain. "Kings who betray the trust of their people leave power only in death… whether by their own hand or at the ends of pitchforks."

Oona spun and grabbed her. "Please, Kit. We must do something. Can we at least try to convince him to go into exile? There has been too much death from this war."

Though unable to summon much sympathy for King Talomir, it pained her to see Oona weeping. "Alright. We shall try." Kitlyn pulled the bedclothes aside and stepped out onto a rug quite like the one she'd been summoned to clear a wine stain from.

"I fear we may already be too late," whispered Oona, clinging to Kitlyn's arm on the way to the door.

The frigid floor in the hallway startled a gasp out of Kitlyn. A seconds' concentration called to the stone beneath her bare feet, magic lending warmth. They hurried to the other side of the castle and the royal wing, where the curving hallway led past Oona's bedchamber, two unused chambers almost as large, and the tiny closet Kitlyn had once slept in. A pair of grand double doors carved from Mistral Oak capped the end, bearing a bas-relief of Lucen and Navissa.

The door with the likeness of the Night Goddess hung ajar.

Kitlyn grasped the edge and pulled it outward, revealing the vast bedchamber in which the king slept. Straight ahead lay a study where bookshelves surrounded a desk. To the right, a few divans sat among tables. Creeping shadows and glowing swaths of moonlight danced upon the wall. The room continued via an archway to the left wherein a thick burgundy curtain hung. Lush carpeting cushioned Kitlyn's steps. She padded up to the curtain and pulled it aside, peering in at a massive four-poster bed with a canopy, still undisturbed and perfect. Great wardrobe alcoves on the left held clothes, but no king. To the right, past more chairs and tables, three narrow arches presently covered with heavy curtains led to an outdoor balcony.

Kitlyn crossed the room, opened one of the tall doors behind the curtains, and peered outside. No sign of him.

"He hasn't slept." Oona traced her fingertips over the bed.

"Come…" Kitlyn hiked her nightdress up past her knees and ran out into the hall.

Oona followed close behind, the two of them moving too fast to keep quiet. The patter of their feet on stone echoed, seeming as loud as a castle siege in the otherwise dreadful silence. Here and there, they passed a guard standing post, noticeably fewer than had been around during the war. While they all questioned why the girls ran around in the middle of the night, not one knew anything of the whereabouts of the king.

The closest man to the royal hallway *not* seeing him set Oona off weeping again. Kitlyn put an arm around her, and offered a silent prayer to Lucen for her father's soul. *He would have had to walk past this guard. For him not to see my father visiting Oona's bedchamber means only one thing… we are too late.*

Still, Kitlyn pressed on, dragging Oona to the last room she had seen the king alive in, where she had left him sitting slumped like an abandoned prop from a theater production. Upon finding no sign of him in that room, she circled back and checked several sitting rooms and finally the war room she had dusted the shelves of so many times.

Kitlyn stopped two steps in from the door, her toes at the edge of a moonlight patch in the shape of a tall arched window. The grand map remained as she remembered it, all the tiny figurines representing troops still set up. It had been almost two weeks since Prince Ralen had left Lucernia with the Eldritch Heart, and as far as she knew, no one had been back in here since. What need had they of a war room without a war?

Seeing the map and shelves covered in dust made her feel like a servant all over again.

She stood in silence, gazing at the small wooden men arranged around a ten-foot-square map upon the giant table. *How many died due to words spoken in this room. Argh! How naïve I was to think of Evermoor as rife with demons and savages.*

Oona shuddered, wrapped her arms around herself, and sank to her knees.

"This room is filled with suffering," whispered Kitlyn, squatting beside her with an arm around her back. "And it is too cold for you to run about at night."

"I'm not cold." Oona fought back a sob. "It's too late. He's gone."

"What?" whispered Kitlyn, biting her lip. *Didn't she already suspect she'd seen his ghost?*

Oona leaned into her, clinging. "I don't know how I know... I just... *felt* him go."

With that, she burst into tears.

A twinge of sorrow at losing him needled at her, but anger at never knowing a father crashed into it, leaving her feeling only the mild sort of distaste that often accompanied an unpleasant task that had to be done. Seeing the woman she loved in so much pain hurt far more. Kitlyn shifted to sit on the floor, holding Oona close. Anything she tried to say would probably come out harsh, so she kept quiet.

While she hadn't wanted him to die, the inevitability of that outcome only mildly dampened another wave of disgust at him for hurting Oona yet again. The priests may or may not have called for his execution. If they didn't, enough generals, soldiers, and some citizens demanded his head that she suspected a revolution already brewed. At least this way, the disruption to the people would be minimal.

"He protected you," whispered Kit.

"What?" Oona looked up, her eyes bright red and running with tears.

Kitlyn pulled her close. "Lucernia teeters on the brink of another war, an internal one. The people would have tried to overthrow him, and a mass of furious citizens could easily have been caught up in the fervor and slain us both as well. He knew that might happen and wanted to protect you."

"You as well." Oona wiped her eyes. "Not that he showed it much."

The door behind them creaked. A glint of blue moonlight flashed from the polished helm of a castle guard. "Pardon, your highnesses, is something amiss?"

Kitlyn drew in a breath, gave the man a 'one moment' nod, then pulled Oona to her feet before facing him. "I fear something has happened to my father. Have the castle searched. Lucen has told Oona of his passing."

At the calm, commanding tone in her voice—no trace of grief or confusion—Oona bowed her head and squeezed her hand.

The guard's cheeks paled. "Right away, your highness." He hurried off.

"I don't understand how you can hide your feelings from your voice. You will make a good queen," whispered Oona.

Kitlyn lifted Oona's face with a hand at her cheek, staring into her eyes, their noses almost touching. "As will you."

3

GRIM TIDINGS

OONA

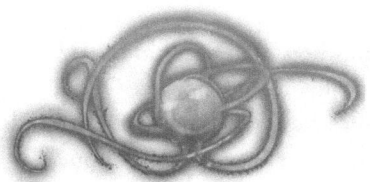

ear and grief took turns raking their claws at Oona's heart.

King Talomir's death meant more than the loss of a father. Worry gnawed at her: with him no longer standing between the kingdom and Kitlyn, some new wave of objection to their upcoming marriage might rise. Given the man's clear betrayal of Lucen's trust, having his approval might hurt more than help, though she much preferred him being alive to speak in their favor. The absence of his voice to defend them made her feel as vulnerable as if strolling across Cimril in her smallclothes.

She sat at the table in the private dining room she'd always eaten in when not required to attend a larger gathering, acutely aware of three major differences: Kitlyn sat across from her, the king's chair remained empty, and little Evie sat beside her. Quiet servants glided around the periphery of the room like phantoms, though not for the same reasons they had done so while the previous queen had lived.

It seemed the entire castle already suspected what Oona knew, though no one had returned to bother them all night with news. Kitlyn spent what remained of the night in the princess' bedroom, the king's decree be damned, and woe be to the first person to suggest anything more inappropriate than weeping occurred.

Evie kept trying to smile in hopes of cheering them up, and it helped a little. While debating the finer points of wondering if providing less than the full truth of what happened to a little child offended Lucen, Oona had explained the king had become ill and may not survive the night. A seven-year-old didn't need to be burdened with the agonies of politics. She hadn't known the king enough to have formed much of an opinion of him beyond 'he seemed nice' and saying she hoped he didn't have any pain.

Kitlyn teased her fork around a half-finished meal of eggs and sausages. Though somber, she hadn't hesitated *that* much at eating, but slowed upon noticing the almost untouched plate in front of Oona.

When Evie finally picked up on her older sister barely eating, she set her fork down and wrapped herself around Oona's left arm.

Between the two of them staring at her with pity and concern, Oona relented and forced herself to eat. Silence hung over them for a while, save for the scratching of silverware. A *click* came from the left, and one of the double doors leading out swung inward, revealing Advisor Beredwyn with Piper right behind him.

The slender brown-haired girl had taken enthusiastically to her new role as Oona's handmaiden and looked altogether like a new person in a white-and-pink dress with matching shoes. Plain, the garment fell short of nobility, though the fourteen-year-old could pass for the daughter of a wealthy family. A bit of red rimmed her eyes, though whether the girl had wept for the loss of the king or simply felt bad for her, it didn't matter. The show of sympathy eased Oona's stomach.

"Come then, Evie." Beredwyn lifted the little one out of her chair and set on her feet by Piper. "It is time for your lessons."

"Okay." Evie scurried back to hug Oona, ran around the table to hug Kitlyn, then dutifully marched over to stand beside Piper.

Beredwyn ambled around the table and took up a position behind the king's chair, an equal distance to both Oona and Kitlyn.

Tense awkwardness lingered. Oona managed a feeble smile at Evie, who waved before following Piper out, holding her hand.

As soon as the door closed, Beredwyn bowed his head. "King Aodh Talomir is gone."

Kitlyn nodded.

"I felt his passing," said Oona, lip quivering. "I-in what manner did his death come to pass?"

"They found him then?" asked Kitlyn.

"Indeed." Beredwyn took and released a deep breath.

The men had been close friends, perhaps even somewhat of a father-son affection had grown between them. Oona leaned forward, resting her hand atop Beredwyn's where he gripped the back of the king's chair. His gaze flicked up, meeting hers. The grief etched within the wrinkles of his cheeks drew tears from her eyes. They shared a moment of silently comforting each other before he looked down at the table again.

"He drank poison in the tomb of Queen Solana." Beredwyn heaved a sigh. "Perhaps he finally allowed himself to believe that her blood stained his hands."

"Did you know?" asked Kitlyn.

Beredwyn shook his head ever so slightly, making his long beard wobble. "Your father and I shared many secrets, but he kept that one from me. Had I known the true cause of the war, I would have hounded him to no end to do the right thing… and he knew it. Perhaps I am at fault for never suspecting the man could carry such deceit for so long."

"It is not your fault." Oona squeezed his hand.

Kitlyn leaned back in her seat, flicking her thumbnail at the stem of her water goblet. "I do not think it would be wise for me to accept the crown."

"What?" gasped Oona.

Beredwyn's sorrow faded to concern. "Nonsense. The people — of both Lucernia and Evermoor — need you." He glanced at Oona. "Need *both* of you."

"By now, everyone knows the way he treated me. I expect to be accused of murdering him by noon."

"No…" Oona stared at her. "How could anyone dare to even suggest such an awful thing?"

"I can think of several reasons," muttered Kitlyn.

Beredwyn appeared to momentarily consider sitting in the king's chair, but thought better of it. "There is quite a clear reason why few would take such an abhorrent suggestion seriously: Oona."

"Me?" She blinked.

"Of course." His grandfatherly smile returned, deepening the wrinkles shrouding his eyes. "The whole of the kingdom knows what sort of person you are, and that you bear Lucen's gift. Had Kitlyn poisoned him, you would not remain at her side."

Oona's cheeks rushed with heat. "She would not be capable of such a thing!"

He raised his hands. "I do not mean to suggest such. Merely that you would know the truth. And…" He again smiled, lowering his arms.

"Several of the castle guard observed the two of you searching about last night prior to the king entering the tomb. The guards there observed him entering alone, and none followed him."

Kitlyn nodded once. "I still think this may be unwise. The resentment people feel toward my father might color their perceptions of me. And, I am sure many still silently disapprove of *us*." She sent a longing stare across the table.

"I don't care what anyone thinks." Oona's heart thudded, her emotions swaying wildly between love for Kitlyn, grief over the king's death, and renewed worry that the whole kingdom may turn on them for being abominations. "Nothing will change how I feel about you."

"Well." Beredwyn stood straight, eliciting a *creak* from the chair he'd been leaning on. "A people do not have to *like* their leaders—though it helps—they must respect them. And, the people do respect you both for bringing an end to the war and the truth to light."

"Am I ready for this?" asked Kitlyn. "All I know how to do is scrub floors and do laundry."

"And arrange troops"—Oona made a ticking-off motion on her fingers—"and deal with a foreign prince, and cross deep into 'enemy' territory on your own, and talk to people, and… oh, a mess of other things."

Kitlyn managed a bashful smile. "I'd hardly call riding atop a forty-foot stone giant 'alone.' He's rather persuasive."

"Yes, but you didn't have him the whole time," said Oona.

"You will make a fine queen." Beredwyn offered a reassuring smile. "You have your advisors, a strong mind, a strong heart, and Oona beside you."

"It is so much for people all at once. The king's lies, doubt in Lucen for not stopping it sooner, their feelings about us together." Oona briefly daydreamed about running away with Kitlyn again.

"It's all right," said Kitlyn in a soothing tone. "Don't work yourself up into a panic again. We'll not be going off into the woods in the dead of night."

Oona giggled.

"I think you'll find Tenebrea's nod most persuasive as well. Certainly as much as that stone ancient's presence." Beredwyn fussed at his beard. "However, if I may offer a small bit of advice…. As loathe as I am to suggest this, perhaps you should refrain from overt shows of physical affection in public."

Oona cringed, feeling scolded.

"The people would gasp and fret over that from a king and queen as well," said Kitlyn, sounding unbothered. "But I am not my father, nor am I my mother. The crown does not elevate me above the people, but bears the weight of their fortunes. I would hope that seeing us full of love would lift their spirits as well. What use is staid pageantry? Everyone always frowned."

"Hmm." Beredwyn continued stroking his beard.

A scrap of hope slipped out from under her sorrow. Oona kneaded her hands in her lap, wondering what the future might hold for them. King Talomir had been responsible for so much… evil. The word in her thoughts made her flinch. As much as she hated to admit it, the man she'd thought of as her father had been exactly that. Though he may not have taken delight in—and may have even been horrified at—the casualties, he hadn't let any of it stop his lust to steal power from the Heart.

She shuddered at the realization he could have ended it all at any time, but chose not to.

"It is natural to feel nervous." Beredwyn moved around the table to put a hand on Kitlyn's shoulder. "Though you are not the youngest to do so, you are quite young to assume the throne. Worry not. You have me beside you, and the other advisors."

"Speaking of which…" Kitlyn narrowed her eyes. "What of Fauhurst?"

Beredwyn's white caterpillar eyebrows crept up his forehead. "The man hasn't been seen in over a week."

"Probably still under a table at the Owl and Cask," muttered Oona.

The old advisor smiled the sort of smile he often did when laughing would be inappropriate.

"Is it too soon for me to make decrees, then?" asked Kitlyn.

"Depends on the significance of it." Beredwyn nodded. "Anything of consequence should wait for after the official coronation, though with Aodh's death, the crown has already legally passed to you as his only living heir."

Kitlyn shot a glower across the room; the hardness in her emerald eyes so reminded Oona of the former king that she momentarily worried becoming queen might change the girl she loved into someone else. "Master Fauhurst is no longer an advisor. Please locate a suitable replacement for me to consider."

Beredwyn nodded. "Of course."

Kitlyn held up a hand in a 'wait a moment' gesture, glancing at Oona with a sparkle of delight in her eye. "I would like *two* new advisors. One shall be the new High Priest of Lucen, whoever they name. For the other, please find a farmer, crafter, or commoner regarded as wise by the whole of their town or village."

Oona grinned. A priest of Lucen as she would have wanted, and someone from humble origins—like Kitlyn—to lend a grounded perspective. Already, the Kingdom of Lucernia seemed destined for significant changes.

"An excellent thought." Beredwyn smiled, then leaned toward her, casting aside his formality. "I am here for you as I have always been, albeit without the need to keep mum as to who you are."

Kitlyn momentarily ceased being a new queen, and leapt into his embrace like a frightened granddaughter. Oona fidgeted until Beredwyn invited her with a nod. She sprang to her feet and hurried around the table to accept his arm around her as well.

Perhaps we shall find a way after all.

4

CHILDREN

KITLYN

itlyn sat in the grass outside the castle gardens, gazing past her bare feet at Evie and Pim running around. Oona's little sister and the head cook's six-year-old son had made fast friends, and watching them laugh and play took some of the heaviness from her heart. The past few hours had been difficult, dealing with the removal of King Talomir's remains from the tomb as well as discussing it endlessly with priests, advisors, members of the royal court, the mayor of Cimril, and seemingly everyone with any scrap of title within a hundred miles.

Distancing herself from the truth of his death had been far easier prior to seeing his dead face. As angry as she had been with him, the sight of his body slumped against the side of her mother's sarcophagus, as if he had been begging her forgiveness, hit her unexpectedly with tears. She mourned the loss of whatever future relationship they would never have more than the man himself.

Oona sat to her right, on the other side of a cloth holding a tray with a few small pastries as well as a sliced ivenberry. She attempted to snack on a sliver of said berry without dribbling juice on her dress. This, of course, resulted in a somewhat comical pose of leaning forward over the tray while stretching out to nibble. If not for the somberness of the past several hours, Kitlyn might've laughed at her... though she did smile.

"They're having the time of their lives." Oona nipped off a hunk of ivenberry.

"Yes. Reminds me a bit of us at that age, before life became complicated." Kitlyn swished her feet back and forth in the tickling grass.

"It would be nice to be small again, I think. To have no cares beyond if we'd turn our noses up at dinner and no worries but bedtime coming far sooner than we liked."

Kitlyn considered one of the small pastries, but decided against it. She hadn't said a word to her father after leaving him in that room, though he placed a wax-sealed letter on her nightstand while she slept. She hadn't noticed it last night. He evidently visited her before Oona but didn't wake her. His farewell letter repeated his apology for making her live as a servant, not showing her the affection a father should have, and for the war. Reading it caused such a tangle of emotions she pushed everything aside and settled on being annoyed with him for dropping the crown on her head way before she considered herself worthy of it.

Maybe in a few years I can shed tears over his loss, but how can I mourn a father I barely knew?

Pim zoomed by, Evie chasing him. He 'tripped' and she caught him with a tag, then proceeded to chase her around not quite catching up.

Kitlyn grinned. "Well, at least we don't have to worry about destroying a whole kingdom anymore."

"Ugh." Oona rolled her eyes. "Stupid old men. Why does anyone listen to them?"

"Well, they weren't technically wrong." Kitlyn shrugged one shoulder. "We *did* end the war. But it would've been nice for them to be a little clearer as to the how of it."

Oona tossed the last bit of ivenberry in her mouth and wiped her hands on a napkin before reclining flat in the grass, gazing up at the clouds. "Oh, they just write down the most minimal thing so whatever happens, they can say they got it right."

Evie and Pim ran by again, giggling, and darted into the garden out of sight behind the ivy-covered wall.

"Don't go too close to the pond," yelled Kitlyn.

Answering shouts came from the kids that sounded close enough to "okay" that she didn't get up to chase them.

Oona wiggled her toes. "Shall we run about like children?"

"If you like."

"You don't sound as though you want to." Oona rolled on her left side, facing Kitlyn. "It's all right. We really ought to both be sad for a while. It would only be proper."

Kitlyn smirked, but wound up chuckling. "I barely knew him, but seeing him there by my mother's grave was just..."

"Yeah."

"I don't remember her at all," said Kitlyn.

"Nor I."

She glanced over at Oona. "She died before they brought you to the castle. They brought you here *because* she died."

"No, I meant Ruby. I don't remember any of it. Even lighting fire to the chicken."

Kitlyn laughed.

"I can't for the life of me imagine why I would've done that."

"It probably chased you or something. Chickens can be nasty, especially to kids not much bigger than they are."

Oona raised her arm straight up, summoning her little light ball. Two pale spots resembling eyes rotated around to fix on Kitlyn. Despite not having a mouth, the tomato-sized thing gave off a sense of smiling. "It would be nice to frolic like children again, but even without the war, we will have much too much to worry about."

"We could run off into the woods and forget it all."

"Alas, we cannot." Oona sighed into a chuckle. "That was rather foolish of me to run off like that. I'm sorry for getting us captured and putting you through all that worry."

"We've been over this." Kitlyn moved the tray aside and pulled Oona over, resting her head in her lap and stroking her hair. "I could have dragged you back straight away to the castle and didn't."

Oona smiled up at her. "I feel like such a fool. No wonder everyone thought me a petulant brat."

"But you're an *adorable* petulant brat." Kitlyn tapped her on the tip of the nose.

Oona stuck out her tongue and raspberried her.

"We could take holidays. Perhaps once a month, we leave the kingdom in the care of Beredwyn and frolic the day away like children. At least until we're too old to frolic without breaking bones."

"Oh, stop." Oona giggled, but it turned somber. "Children..."

"What of them?" Kitlyn perked up, listening for signs of the kids. "Evie? Pim?" she called. "Are you two still alive?"

Two small voices yelled "Aye" from the garden.

"Oh, we would make such wonderful parents, wouldn't we? Letting them go clear out of our sight. They'll drown in the pond."

"I told them not to go near it." Kitlyn twirled a bit of Oona's hair around her finger.

"And at their age, what would we have done?"

Kitlyn smirked. "Gone straight to the pond, thrown off our clothes, and jumped in." A bit of warmth flooded her cheeks at the thought of doing that now at sixteen rather than six. At the time, they'd thought only of not ruining their dresses by getting them wet. She hadn't seen Oona naked since the last time she'd attended her bath before they'd run away. That moment had been awkward, but mostly because she didn't know how Oona would react to learning the truth of her feelings. With that fear well and truly dead, she had no idea what might happen the next time they had no clothing between them. The thought terrified her as much as it thrilled her.

"Indeed. We should keep a closer eye on them. And my... you are as red as an ivenberry. What is going on inside your mind?"

"Thoughts I should not dwell on until we are married," said Kitlyn. "But back to playing like children. I think we should take a day or two a month and forget about everything but sharing company and having fun."

"Ahh yes. But speaking of children... Do you think the people will accept Evie as our heir? Or..."

Kitlyn rolled her eyes. "The only child I'm interested in bearing would be yours, and that is... well..."

Oona laughed. "That would truly be the work of the gods."

"It would at that." Kitlyn grinned.

"Ooh..." Oona squirmed, wide-eyed.

"I have not touched you in any way worthy of making that face."

"Oh, you didn't, but... I just felt the strangest tingle sweep over me. As soon as you mentioned the gods."

Kitlyn shook her head, gazing at the clouds. "Stop teasing me."

"The children are still in the garden unsupervised," said Oona.

"As were we many times."

"Yes, but we were what, ten? They're still a bit young."

"If you want to go into the garden, you have but to say so."

Oona reached up and traced a finger over Kitlyn's forehead. "You're not wearing a crown."

"Nor are you."

"I don't feel particularly royal today."

Kitlyn kept stroking a hand over Oona's hair. "Well, for one thing, I have not been officially crowned. For another, my father was quite proud of being king. He never left his bedchambers without it on, preening and strutting about as though it made him superior to others. I suffer from no such illusions. A heavy ring of metal upon my skull would serve only to remind me of how much I have suddenly become responsible for."

"But you are the queen…"

"Not quite yet I'm not. And… yes. I understand that. But I shan't dwell on it. What need have I of fancy gems on my head? However, I suppose when need be, I shall yield to tradition."

Oona sat up. "Shall we go into the garden then?"

"Yes, let's."

"Shall we try climbing the tree?" asked Oona with a raised eyebrow.

"You'll become frightened and scream for help."

Hands on her hips, Oona blinked. "After sitting on Omun's shoulder, I doubt a tree will bother me at all anymore."

Kitlyn poked her in the stomach with one finger, tickling. "I suspect you will still be frightened."

"Eep!" Oona grabbed her finger. "Stop that!"

"You're so ticklish."

"You are as well!" Oona pounced.

They rolled around in the grass for a little while trying to tickle each other, though their moderately heavy gowns got in the way. Eventually, Kitlyn wound up draped over Oona, both of them out of breath. She pushed herself up, staring down into her love's bright blue eyes. Their noses hovered less than an inch away from each other.

Kitlyn started to lower herself into a kiss, but hesitated at soft gasps of surprise. She shifted her eyes up, catching sight of three small faces watching them over the half-height wall separating the walkway along the castle from the field—the same one she had so often been made to sweep seed pods from.

Mary, Laura, and Rowan, the three youngest maids, watched them with wide eyes and expressions like they'd found an adorable abandoned kitten. Rowan appeared to notice Kitlyn had spotted them and blushed. She grabbed the other two by the shoulders, and all three twelve-year-olds ducked out of sight.

For a moment, Kitlyn didn't entirely know how to process their reaction of 'aww!' to watching her about to kiss Oona. She'd expected most everyone to cringe away in disgust or pull a Fauhurst and scream at them. The sight of the young maids finding them cute choked her up with joy.

"Kit?" Oona leaned up to give her a peck of a kiss. "What's wrong?"

"We have an audience," whispered Kitlyn, then explained what she saw.

Oona grinned.

A startled yelp came from Evie.

"Oh, no," muttered Kitlyn, before springing to her feet and pulling Oona upright.

"I think that's distinctly a 'Pim shoved a frog in her face' scream."

Kitlyn raised an eyebrow.

"Come on. I wish to walk in the garden anyway." Oona hurried toward the garden arch.

Kitlyn took a step, but glanced back at the garden walk. Again, three small faces peered over the wall, but only enough for their eyes to see over it. She smiled at them, hiked up her dress a bit, and trotted off after Oona, intending to pick up where they left off with the kissing.

Alas, she found her crouched between Pim and Evie, telling them about the faeries that 'lived' in the garden. Pim held a tiny brown frog in both hands. Kitlyn ducked behind a tree, grinning to herself that Oona had been right about the scream. She sent a bit of magic into the earth and raised a handful of small stones surrounded in emerald green light, which she levitated in the approximate shape of a human figure six inches tall before sending it on a long circular flight so it came into view some distance away in front of the children behind the trees.

Evie gasped at the moving glow, then pointed. "Faerie! I see one!"

Oona's eyes gleamed with childish delight as she whirled around to look. While she and Evie squealed, Pim twisted back, scanning the trees until he spotted Kitlyn. He grinned at her, but kept quiet. Evidently, she had amused him often enough with her dragon-shaped rocks that he'd recognized the glowing energy.

She amused Evie for a little while, teasing her a bit like waving a feather at a cat, until Oona finally got a good look at the 'faerie' and let out a sigh of disappointment.

"Aww, it's just rocks." Evie stopped trying to chase it and let her arms hang limp.

Kitlyn burst out laughing, losing concentration on the magic. She abandoned her hiding place and joined the others, spending the better part of the next hour with Oona entertaining the kids until the first signs of a weakening sun announced it time for the children to go inside.

Once the kids had run off out of earshot, Kitlyn took Oona by the hand. "Shall we visit the pond?"

"Ooh. Yes, let's." Oona grinned. "Though we won't have too much time before dinner."

They wandered the meandering footpath across the garden to the large pond built at the corner of the wall. Kitlyn clenched her jaw at the sight of it, remembering Fauhurst ruining their moment. She decided not to dwell on that since the man would never plague her again, and led the way over to the bench, sitting with her feet ankle deep in the chilly water.

"Ooh!" squeaked Oona. "It's so cold."

"It will be autumn soon."

"Yes." Oona turned her head to look at her, sapphire-blue eyes wide with nervous anticipation. "Are you sure we should be alone here? We're not married."

Kitlyn leaned closer. "Quite sure. This place brings you peace. I'm sorry if I'm not more visibly upset over…"

"I understand." Oona kissed her on the lips for a long moment, then shifted to rest her head on Kitlyn's shoulder, content to hold her. "I don't know that I could bear this without you."

"This?"

"Losing… well, not my father." She sighed. "It's hard to think of him as anything else, despite why I came to be here."

Kitlyn rested her head against Oona's. "I don't think you have it in you to hate anyone."

"I rather detest Fauhurst."

"Hah."

Oona sighed. "I'm not fond of Ruby either right now, but I don't think I hate her. I hate the way she treated Evie, and I hate the ease with which she gave us both away."

"I will never understand how she could do that." Kitlyn frowned at the water. As they sat in silent contemplation, she briefly wondered what her life would be like had not some poor random chicken ignited in blue flames thirteen years ago. Before she could decide if she'd have been spoiled and 'princess-y' or simply locked away somewhere assassins couldn't get to (and likely gone mad) she pushed it all aside and offered thanks that things had happened exactly the way they had.

She squeezed Oona close. *It was all worth it.*

"Umm…" A timid woman's voice broke the quiet behind them.

"This place is evidently cursed," said Oona in a calm tone tinged with amusement. "We are always interrupted here."

"At least it's not Fauhurst," muttered Kitlyn.

They turned together to find Meredith standing a few steps away.

"Will you be having dinner at the usual time? 'Tis almost ready."

Kitlyn smiled at her handmaiden, then at Oona. "Yes, thank you, Meredith. We shall be in shortly."

"Very good." Meredith offered a small curtsey and whisked off into the trees.

"No 'your highness'?" asked Oona, grinning.

"Only in public." Kitlyn sighed. "Are you all right?"

"Not really, but there's little to be done about it but mourn."

Kitlyn stood, hiking her dress away from the water. "I hope you are more interested in supper than you were in lunch."

"*You* didn't eat lunch either." Oona gave her the side eye.

"That"—she stepped up onto dry land and let her dress fall—"is precisely why I am hungry."

Oona gathered her gown in one hand, reaching for Kitlyn with the other to hold steady while navigating the muddy bank. "I think I shall eat as well."

Arm in arm, they headed back to the castle.

Two guards by the door snapped to attention as they passed.

Once inside, Kitlyn let out a soft sigh. *I will never get used to that.*

5

OBLIGATION

OONA

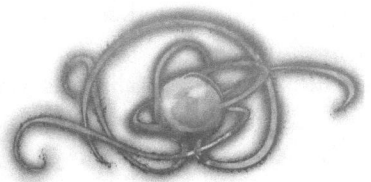

One week after King Talomir's passing, black engulfed the full length mirror at the corner of Oona's bedchamber.

Two pale spots broke the darkness, a pair of faces that could be the same girl ten years apart. Oona fidgeted and grimaced while Piper did up the back lacing on her new dress, something she would likely wear once and forget about entirely—until the next time someone important died. Evie stood beside her in a somewhat simpler but similar gown, playing peek-a-boo with herself in the mirror by lifting and dropping the veil.

Her little sister had wound up proving both Kitlyn and Oona wrong. Oona thought the girl would loathe being made to wear shoes, having grown up to the age of seven without any. Kitlyn assumed she'd adore them and turn into one of those people who had entire closets devoted only to shoes.

As it turned out, Evie reacted to them with ambivalence. She went barefoot when she wanted to and wore shoes when she wanted or had to, not once seeming to care either way. Oona suspected Kitlyn still disliked shoes, something about her magic, but the Queen of Lucernia could hardly traipse about like a peasant girl.

At least, when not visiting the garden in private.

The priestesses of Tenebrea had prepared the king's body, though given the circumstances of the war, the deception, and everything associated with it, he had lain in state at the Tenebrea temple as would any normal citizen. Neither Kitlyn nor Oona dared ask the priests of Lucen to afford him the honor of the grand cathedral, nor did they feel it appropriate to conduct the usual great ceremony of welcoming all the citizens of the land into the castle to pay their respects.

Few had any respect to pay the man.

Oona smoothed her hands down the front of her dress, stifling the urge to wince whenever the younger girl behind her pulled too hard on one of the ties. Piper had only a week's worth of training under Meredith, and still hadn't quite gotten the hang of dealing with the more elaborate pieces of wardrobe. Still, at fourteen, the girl had plenty of time to learn, especially with Oona more than happy to tolerate the process. After all, that girl had lost both parents to the war, even if she had been born in Evermoor.

"Forgive me, Lady Oona," whispered Piper. "The loops are small and the ribbons protest being moved."

"It's all right. And please, you don't need to be so formal when we are alone. Bad enough what my fath—I mean the king did."

Piper tugged at the next set of ties, securing them into a decorative bow knot. "Milady, please stop apologizing. I don't blame you for it. You hadn't even been born when the war started. I still can't believe you forgave me for what I came here to do."

Evie looked up with a questioning head tilt.

"There's nothing to forgive. You didn't *do* anything but wash dishes... and okay, perhaps snoop around."

Piper chuckled.

Evie shifted her gaze to Oona. "What did she do?"

"Some people took advantage of her and sent her here to kill me. But she also thought foretellings are foolish."

The child's eyes widened in shock.

"I couldn't simply poison a girl not much older than me without *knowing* she was as evil as everyone told me." Piper tied the last bow and fidgeted at the gown here and there.

"Oona's not evil," said Evie in a small voice. "How could you think that?"

"I don't." Piper patted her on the head, and adjusted the child's dress. "It is easy to think bad things about a person who is far away and you had only ever heard people speak ill of. As soon as I came here and saw her, I had too many doubts. I decided to learn as much as I could about her, but even I didn't realize she wasn't the king's daughter until Kitlyn became angry in the kitchen that night."

Oona managed a weak smile, remembering the story. "She does look quite a bit like him when she's furious."

"Aye. 'Tis her eyes. But I am sure you will give her many reasons to be happy instead. That man always had a scowl on his face. And…"

"It's all right. I don't hold it against you that you find comfort in his passing." Oona sighed, finding the dress more comfortable with all the air out of her chest. "My real father died because of the war, so I should feel the same as you, but there have been so many lies…"

"Lyin's bad," said Evie. "Lucen depests…" She bit her lip. "Umm. Doesn't like liars."

Oona made a silly face and flipped her little sister's veil down. "Yes, Lucen does detest liars." *And we are about to bury a great big liar. Lucen forgive me.*

"All done." Piper took a step back to appraise her work.

"Thank you." Oona smiled at the girl before twisting left to right, examining herself in the mirror. Having a handmaiden that the castle staff actually allowed to function as a handmaiden made her hate the elaborate dresses and gowns somewhat less, though she still disliked being confined in them. However, some events—such as the funeral of a king—did demand a certain degree of protocol.

Piper crouched to help both Oona and Evie into their shoes, also black but simple since no one would see them under the heavy gowns. She had expected the girl to ask to be excused from the funeral of the man responsible for her parents' death, but Piper made no such request. *She likely wants the satisfaction of seeing him in death.*

Her grey dress signaled a lack of mourning, but she'd chosen one dark enough not to give off disrespect. Oona envied her the simpler garment that wouldn't make breathing a chore.

She took Evie's hand and led her out into the hall, Piper following them close behind. They met Kitlyn, also in an elaborate black mourning gown, in the grand foyer. Some of the castle staff with any status of note joined the foot procession, though it hardly seemed like a significant portion.

Oona suppressed the urge to look around and take note of faces, despite feeling the group quite small. Kitlyn showed no sign of noticing or caring either way. They walked side by side with Evie at Oona's left out the main gates into the streets of Cimril. Two rows of ten soldiers marched on their left and right, forming a veritable wall of armor-clad bodies. Citizens occasionally looked at them, some offering hand signs of respect to the gods, a few ignoring them, and a handful scowling.

Unable to tell if the scowls came from people unwilling to accept her love for Kitlyn or if they merely expressed contempt for the king, she kept her head bowed until the procession reached the entrance to the Tenebrea temple some minutes later.

Beyond a pair of large black gates, a modest courtyard held a life-sized statue of the goddess. It depicted her as a girl of about fifteen, barefoot in a simple dress, perched upon a rock and reaching down as if to help a struggling skeleton climb out of the ground. The uneducated often mistook her for the patron of necromancers, a comment that could enrage one of her faithful. Tenebrea *hated* necromancers for they abused the dead. She ushered the deceased into her realm to protect them.

Oona looked up to make eye contact with the statue—the only person in the entire procession of fifty or more to do so. Almost no one ever dared outside of her priesthood. Despite gazing at a sad-beautiful face molded from dark stone, she felt a brief note of awareness in the statue's eyes. To almost anyone else in all of Lucernia, such a sensation would have caused instant panic, expecting it to be an omen of imminent death. However, Oona returned a grateful smile and bow of respect.

A pair of black-robed priestesses flanking the temple doors took note of her not shying away from the statue's gaze and also offered shallow nods of respect to Oona.

"My thanks for offering my father his final rest." Kitlyn bowed her head.

"You are most welcome," said the priestess on the left, a woman in her later thirties, most of her face hidden beneath a voluminous black hood. "Everyone is welcome in our lady's arms."

A subtle shift of unease swept over the castle staff and guards.

Each priestess grasped a handle on one of the double doors, pulling them aside and holding them for everyone.

Kitlyn and Oona led the way in. Outside, the air carried a trace of late summer warmth, but the temple interior could've been a winter day. Black walls bedecked with lamp holders shaped like the upper halves of tiny twelve-inch skeletons passed on both sides. Here and there, paintings or statuettes of Tenebrea decorated small alcoves. Evie, eyes as wide as saucers, clung to Oona's arm, shivering while gazing around.

Another priestess, her face also concealed mostly by a hood, met them at the midway point of a hundred-foot-long corridor. Pewter-colored hair hung down the front of her robe to her belt, and she wore a fancy cloth shoulder mantle the other priestesses lacked. The woman greeted them with a nod, then turned to lead them down the hall and around a corner to a wider passage with a curved ceiling. Four enormous black curtains, two per side, blocked giant archways except for one where the curtain had been pulled open wide enough for two people abreast.

Inside, the remains of King Aodh Talomir lay out upon a dais. He'd been dressed in the garb of a nobleman with a rich blue cloak. Kitlyn had not wanted to offend Lucen by burying her father in his priestly regalia, nor did it seem appropriate to bury him with his crown.

The procession moved around a bank of wooden bench seats, stopping in the aisle. Kitlyn approached the dais, stood in silence for a moment, then headed to the center bench facing it. Oona walked up next, her throat tightening at the sight of her 'father' lying there dead. Most alarming, he appeared healthier than he had the last time she'd seen him alive. As much like a ghost as he'd seemed, he couldn't have been one at the time.

Evie stayed close, still holding her hand, but shied away from looking at him.

"I will never understand what led you down the path you took," said Oona in a low tone. "I don't know whether I should think of you as my father or as something else. I know you grew to care for me in some way more than you likely expected to. I grieve for all that cannot be because of your actions, but for anything you did to me, I forgive you. May you find in death the peace you never knew in life."

Evie tugged at her arm, clearly wanting to move away from a dead person.

Oona guided her over to the bench and sat beside Kitlyn. One by one, Beredwyn, Advisor Lanon, Margaret, Elsbeth, Meredith, and those of the castle staff who'd decided to attend approached the dais before taking seats. A handful of the guardsmen did as well. Piper didn't go near the king, heading straight over to sit beside Evie. Few stayed long near the body, most making the common hand sign of Tenebrea's blessing: bowing the head to touch the fingers of the raised right hand, then turning the palm outward with a slight pushing gesture.

Almost no one showed any emotion in their expressions.

They've all come out of obligation. Oona held her head high, deciding to ignore their brevity despite a small sense of insult. True, the man *had* caused a war that claimed countless lives, but he had been their king. *That only makes his betrayal worse. I should be thankful they are here at all.*

Evie fidgeted, but didn't make noise or stir too much.

Eventually, the procession took their seats and the entire room sat in total silence for at least an hour before a priestess walked out to address those assembled. Oona glanced around at the mostly empty benches. *A commoner would have more in attendance than this.* She slipped her hand into Kitlyn's, trying to hold back the tears that wanted to pour out of her. *We should content ourselves with quiet indifference instead of overt rebellion.*

"Welcome to the Temple of Tenebrea," said the priestess. "We gather to send Aodh Talomir into our lady's arms, may she guide him peacefully in the Shadelands."

Oona's jaw tightened at her omission of any title. *Like a commoner.*

Soft murmurs came from about half the people.

"The Goddess of Dusk welcomes all, from the poorest peasant to the wealthiest noble. From the most virtuous to the most despised." The priestess looked around. "Would anyone care to speak?"

No one stirred for a moment. Right when it seemed the priestess would continue, Kitlyn rose to her feet and stepped forward to stand beside the woman in the black robe, then faced everyone.

"I, as do many of you, have fairly mixed feelings for my father. It's no secret anymore that I spent most of my life not even realizing he *was* my father. In truth, some of you knew him far better than I. My world was entirely different from his. I dare not offend Tenebrea by speaking poorly of those who walk with her in the Shadelands, nor shall I offend Lucen by giving voice to that which is untrue. Out of tradition, we pay respects to those who have crossed. I thank you all for being here with us today. May Tenebrea guide him."

Most of the room repeated the phrase.

Oona swallowed the lump in her throat. *She cannot say anything good about him without lying, nor will she speak badly of him. Surely, the Lady of Dusk would not have cast him into the Pit. He had not cavorted with demons. Is that why he looked so deathly? Did he expect an eternity of torment?*

Kitlyn bowed her head to the priestess and returned to her seat.

The priestess raised her arms wide, giant sleeves draped nearly to the floor. "We shall now prepare his remains for interment. Those of you who care to are welcome to join us for the ceremony at the tomb."

Six figures in black robes, two male priests among them, emerged from a shadowed alcove and transferred the body to an ornate casket. Some people in attendance left, not bothering to wait for the second portion of the funeral. Oona listened to them shuffling down the rows of benches, refusing to look.

Piper approached a nearby priestess, head bowed, hands clasped in front of her. They spoke for a moment before the woman nodded at her. A desperate gasp escaped the young handmaiden, and she clasped her hands at her chin while asking, "Please" perhaps a bit too loud for the inside of the Death Goddess' temple.

The priestess walked with Piper to the side of the room and chanted a few brief lines. Eerie whitish light glowed from within her hood. Piper again conversed with the woman, though this time, spectral vapors leaked from the priestess' mouth as she answered. Soon, an emotional Piper bowed several times while muttering teary thanks. The priestess nodded to her once again, then glided across the room to assist the others in preparing to move the body.

Piper hurried back over to the bench and sat, barely containing tears.

"What's wrong?" whispered Evie.

"Piper?" Oona reached around her little sister and grasped the girl's shoulder.

"I heard rumors," whispered Piper, "that Tenebrea's priests can talk to the dead. I asked her if she can speak to spirits in the Glimmering Vale."

"And?" asked Oona.

Piper wiped at her cheeks, nodding. "She can. I spoke to my parents through her. At first, I didn't know if I should believe it since no one in Evermoor talks about Tenebrea, but they called me Pip. Only my parents even knew that. They're together in the Glimmering Vale, and they're happy I have a home now and didn't... umm... you know. I miss them."

Oona pulled Evie into her lap, scooted left, and hugged Piper.

"Please don't apologize again. It isn't your fault." She sniffled. "But at least I know they're in a good place. They wouldn't tell me how they died, only that it happened during a battle."

"I can't say what I want to say, for I'd speak unkind things about a dead man in the house of Tenebrea." Oona tried not to scowl at the casket. "What your parents said is correct. You do have a home. As often as you need me to be a sister, friend, or… well, I'd say mother but I'm only two years older than you."

Piper sniffled out a weak chuckle, relaxed, and wept on Oona's shoulder for the remainder of the time it took the priests to arrange the casket on a litter and form up to carry it out of the temple. Evie bounced to her feet, eager to escape the gloomy confines of the temple of death. At a pat from Oona, Piper gathered her composure and stood.

Barely a word broke the silence as the procession exited the temple and wound through the streets of Cimril to the rear of the castle grounds and the royal cemetery. Some had suggested it unwise to inter him there, though Kitlyn refused to separate him from Queen Solana's tomb, stating that even condemned killers are granted a final request within reason. Aodh's had been to be with his wife. No one offered serious protest to that.

None of the castle staff beyond the advisors proceeded to the tomb. Oona nudged Piper to return to the castle, as the girl needed time alone and had no interest in visiting the tomb of the man who indirectly caused her parents' death. The girl bowed gratefully, and hurried off.

And so, the priests of Tenebrea bore Aodh Talomir's remains into the underground sepulcher that held the remains of three prior kings all of the Talomir bloodline: Iastor the eldest (and his wife Moeth), his son Branok—who wore the crown for about a week and hadn't married— then his youngest son Eoim, father of Aodh, (and his wife Glema).

A pair of stone doors guarded the entrance to a plain corridor decorated only in carved writing invoking either Lucen or Tenebrea to watch over those who rest here. The second opening on the right led to the chamber which held Queen Solana's grave. Workers had already opened the tomb beside it in preparation for his casket.

Oona followed Kitlyn to stand near the stone box on the left side of the room, watching in solemn silence as the priests hefted the litter up on two long poles and set it atop the open sarcophagus. Four of them took hold of the casket itself, lifting it enough for the others to withdraw the litter, then they lowered the former king into his final resting place.

Green light bathed the room. All eyes went to Kitlyn, who held her arms out, swirls of energy coiling around them. Stone shafts extended from the ground, lifting the massive lid into place before receding.

Did the workers refuse to seat the lid? Or is she sparing them the toil? Oona pulled the fidgety Evie close, sharing her little sister's desire to be done with the dreary affair as soon as possible. A week after the man's death, she had days ago cried the last tears she would likely shed over him.

The Tenebrea priests conducted a simple rite, standing in a circle around the casket while beseeching their goddess to welcome him to the realm of the dead. They blessed the room and also the queen's tomb before everyone stood for the customary six minutes of silence.

At long last, the priests performed the closing chant, then walked by in single file. Oona thanked them each in turn for their help. They invoked Tenebrea's guidance upon her… then repeated the entire process with Kitlyn before walking out.

Once the last priest exited the chamber, everyone else left with no small amount of haste.

Kitlyn put a hand on the king's tomb, and a wisp of green light swam over her arm.

"Kit?" asked Oona.

"I fused the lid. His burial vault is one solid piece now. No one will desecrate his remains… at least not without having to smash the entire thing open first."

Oona's eyes widened. "Do you think anyone would dare?"

"Perhaps not if it is too difficult." Kitlyn faced her. "Are you all right?"

"As fine as can be expected. Are you?"

"I've made as much peace with him as I am able." Kitlyn managed a weak smile. "Come on. I know you can't wait to be out of that dress."

"Oh, this?" Oona glanced down. "It's all right. I'm quite used to barely being able to breathe."

Evie bounced on her toes.

Oona glanced back at the stone box encasing the king's casket. "Goodbye, father. Rest well." Head bowed, she squeezed Evie's hand and walked at a brisk stride for the door, eager to escape such a dreadful place.

6

AT LONG LAST

KITLYN

Three days after the funeral, Kitlyn stood in the throne room facing a strikingly tall man with long, flowing hair the color of fresh-cut hay and piercing green eyes. Except for a slight tint of age to his features, he looked much like she had imagined the Anthari, or elves as most people called them—not that any had been seen in Lucernia for several centuries.

The new High Priest of Lucen, Balais Aldin, had served at the grand temple in Torlach, having been their most senior priest. After a twenty-hour period of meditation, prayer, and reflection, the council of elder priests announced that Lucen had selected him for the title of High Priest. His long, angular face, perfect nose, and gem-like eyes regarded her still with a mixture of uncertainty. Though King Talomir had only been thirty-seven years of age, and this man was a year short of fifty, he appeared younger than her father except for faint wrinkles around his eyes and thin vertical lines down his cheeks.

A traditionalist, he had initially been aghast at Kitlyn's love for Oona, but upon conferring with the priests from the temple in Cimril who told of Tenebrea's visitation and that Lucen had not taken away Oona's gift, he had accepted them with guarded caution. She could not call him overjoyed at the prospect of two queens, but he at least did not seem hostile. He had also warmed to her somewhat more upon her insistence that he become an advisor, inviting the eyes of Lucen into the court.

Kitlyn resisted the urge to fidget at the burdensome formal gown and massive, heavy cape draped over her shoulders, the train going some thirty feet behind her. Fortunately, no one expected her to actually walk anywhere while wearing it. She considered it more of a ceremonial carpet resting on her shoulders. *How did my father stay upright with this burdensome thing on... he was only eleven when crowned.*

Balais held aloft a new crown, a fairly plain ring of silver with crenelations, each one set with a square emerald. "As Lucen gazes down upon this proceeding, Lady Kitlyn Talomir, Princess Regnant of Lucernia, do you swear before him that you shall ever act in the furtherance of purity and in the best interests of those over whom you govern?"

"As Lucen watches, so do I swear," said Kitlyn. *Lucen guide me. I hope I am able to bear this burden.*

A brief flash of bluish light danced across Balais' eyes. The corners of his lips picked up in a faint smile. Seeming pleased, he offered a brief nod. "Lady Kitlyn Talomir, Princess Regnant of Lucernia, please kneel."

Kitlyn took a knee.

Balais lowered the crown upon her head. "And arise as Queen Kitlyn Talomir."

The added weight—albeit not that much—of the crown on top of the ridiculous cloak made rising difficult, but she managed it with a minimum of wobbling. The throne room erupted in a deafening roar of cheering. All the castle servants who could fit lined the two upper balconies on either side of the main room filled with nobles, merchants, and as many commoners as squeezed into the hallway beyond, a crowd that spilled well outside into the streets.

Oona, close by her side, beamed with pride and wiped a tear of joy.

Guard Captain Lorne approached, handing her the ornate broadsword once carried by her father. Her eyes bulged at the weight of it, though she didn't falter. She would not, however, carry that particular blade into battle should the need arise—at least not without some magical enhancement to her physical strength.

"Thank you, Lightbearer." Kitlyn offered a slight bow to Balais.

He responded with a nod and stepped aside.

Emitting a faint grunt at dragging a hundred pounds of cloak plus a sword she could barely lift, Kitlyn took four steps to the edge of the second set of stairs leading down from the throne dais.

"Thank you, everyone," said Kitlyn, trying to project her voice over the room. "Lucernia is at the beginning of a new age of peace. As I stand before Lucen, I give you my word I will do everything in my power to secure the safety and prosperity of every citizen. We have seen too much war. Yes, I am young. Except for the past few weeks, I have not been alive in a time without constant war, constant stories of loss, hardship, and suffering. Now it is time to *live*. I ask you all to set aside whatever animosity you may have had for the people of Evermoor. Let us re-establish trade and prosper together as allies once again."

A somewhat less enthusiastic cheer followed.

"Now what?" whispered Kitlyn while glancing sideways at Beredwyn.

"Now," replied the elder from beside her, "we feast."

"Excellent." Still smiling at the crowd, she leaned closer to him. "Can I take this damnable cloak off yet?"

Two weeks following the coronation, Kitlyn paced anxiously around her bedchamber perhaps an hour before dawn. Sleep had proved elusive, and though near exhausted from nerves, she couldn't sit still.

In less than six hours, she would *finally* be married to Oona. Finally able to share a bedchamber... and possibly do some of those 'unseemly things' Ruby mentioned. Assuming, of course, they ever figured out exactly what they were.

Frustrated, she flung herself on the bed and closed her eyes.

A knock came from the door.

Kitlyn popped fully awake, noting the sun had started to come up. *Oh... I must have dozed off.* She attempted to speak, but made a noise like a reanimated corpse.

"Your highness?" asked Meredith from behind the closed door.

"Come in." Kitlyn shifted her eyes down to the pillow her face presently lay mushed into, lacking the strength to push herself up.

"Oh, my." Meredith hurried over. "This is going to take a lot of work."

"Sorry," mumbled Kitlyn into her pillow. "Didn't sleep well."

Her handmaiden pulled her upright and guided her across the room to an alcove where a bathtub already waited with steaming water. Despite not being even half the size of the giant swan-shaped tub in Oona's bedchamber, it still offered more space than seemed necessary for a bathing vessel. Meredith peeled Kitlyn out of her nightdress and proceeded to help her bathe. The over-warm water plus anticipation and nerves shocked her awake.

Soon, she stepped out of the water, smelling of floral perfumes. Once she dried off, Meredith hurried her over to the wardrobes. After putting on her underpinnings, Kitlyn stood there in a daze while her handmaiden scurried about the cabinets gathering the various pieces of her wedding gown.

At some point, one handmaiden became nine or so women all buzzing around her like a flock of hummingbirds assaulting a helpless flower. When tugging at her hair started, she tried to grab and swat the nuisance away, but something trapped her arms and pulled them out to the sides. Kitlyn emitted a weak grunt of protest along with a feeble struggle, but couldn't pull her arms back under her control.

The tugging at her hair continued.

It eventually annoyed her to full consciousness and she realized a pair of attendants manicured her nails while two others fussed at her hair and Meredith plus three more assembled the dress on her. *Oona adores this attention... I'd just as soon be married in my peasant tunic and breeches.* She gasped as the corset cinched around her, then glared down at shimmery white fabric with floral embroidery and little pearls stitched on in clusters here and there. Some degree of finery needed to come with her station, but this dress made her feel greedy. Its cost could likely feed an entire small village for a month. Then again, Lucernia didn't presently have any serious issues with starving towns. More like large numbers of widows and orphans from the war, along with a relative scarcity of laborers as most able-bodied young adults had been swept up into the military.

Kitlyn sighed at her reflection in the tall mirror. The current political climate offered enough security that reducing the size of the military wouldn't threaten the kingdom, but it might make the senior commanders reconsider their support of such a young queen, especially one with a wife. But the nation needed to rebuild and didn't need so many soldiers sitting around with nothing to do. And so, she thought on it while the swarm of attendants poked and prodded and pulled and tweaked.

She felt ridiculous, like a child's toy doll… but it would make Oona happy, so she offered no more protest than the occasional 'help me' stare at herself in the mirror.

By the time they finished weaving a floral circlet into her hair and putting it up, she had an idea of what to do about the bloated military: declare a quarter of them 'reserves' and allow them to return home to pursue trades rather than sitting around at garrison. That way, they could do productive things while technically remaining in the military so as not to make the generals feel she tried to weaken them.

Elsbeth knocked purely as a matter of forced courtesy, barging right in without waiting for anyone to answer the door. "Your highness, it's almost time. Are you ready?"

"Yes. Yes. Quite ready." She took as deep a breath as the corset allowed. *To get out of this dress.*

"Almost," chimed Meredith, holding up a pair of glittery white high-heeled shoes.

Kitlyn narrowed her eyes at them, wishing she had a sword in easy reach. "Must I?"

"Oh, my lady," said Meredith with a hint of a chuckle. "You're not a small child anymore. You can't simply run about barefoot all the time."

"Oh can't I now?" Kitlyn raised an eyebrow. "I am the queen. If I can decree law, I can plunge my toes into the grass whenever I see fit. But those things… they're not shoes. They're a devious rogue's trap designed to break my neck."

The attendants all exchanged glances of surprise.

"You've never…" Meredith held the shoes up at her.

"Of course I've worn shoes." Kitlyn sighed. "Just not ones like that with the stick on the heel end. I shall not stumble down the aisle looking like a baby stridefowl." If she dared try to wear such things on her feet, she would surely wobble about like one of those lakeshore birds. A fluffy, cottony body perched upon tall, narrow legs. While the adults moved with grace, the chicks could barely stand upright and often fell face-first into the mud.

The women all giggled.

"Well, we shall have to do our best to keep up appearances." Meredith crouched, lifted the hem of the elaborate gown, and proceeded to attach the demonic things to Kitlyn's feet. "You will ruin your hose without shoes."

Kitlyn flailed her arms, her body teetering back and forth on the verge of falling over. "How is it that I am queen, yet have no say in this?"

"Tradition." Meredith secured the tiny buckle.

"Oh, I'm going to break my nose." Kitlyn swung herself to the side and clamped onto Meredith, surprised to find herself slightly taller than the woman. She tried to stare down at her feet but couldn't find them under the billowy skirt. "Ooh… Whoever invented these infernal things, I shall send to the dungeons. If you let go of me, I will wind up on the floor."

"You'll do fine." Meredith winked.

Kitlyn smiled to herself. A wedding with two brides had thrown the castle court into a frenzy of questions. Who stood at the altar? Who strolled down the aisle? Did someone have to 'give away' *both* brides? They'd decided to both walk in, with Beredwyn escorting Kitlyn—as he'd been more a father to her than the former king. Oona asked Guard Captain Lorne to escort her, as she had no surviving male relatives.

The attendants fussed over her for a while more, the whole time she clung to Meredith to avoid falling over. Piper and a few of Oona's entourage popped in and out to coordinate things, all of them grinning and trying not to giggle. For a moment, Kitlyn felt like the least enthusiastic person in the entire kingdom for her own wedding, but blamed it on a mixture of minimal sleep and frustration at her outfit. If she could dispense with all the formality and merely spend the day with Oona somewhere quiet, she would.

But the kingdom needed a statement, and Oona rather enjoyed the fanciness. After all, a wedding day was supposed to be the high point of one's life. With a resigned sigh and a scowl of determination, she heeded Meredith's prodding and practiced walking back and forth around the bedchamber in heels.

"This is thoroughly pointless. No one will ever see these shoes under all this gown… until I'm flat on my face in the middle of the temple with my underpinnings blooming like a white rose for all to see."

The attendants gasped, blushed, and laughed.

Meredith squeezed her hand. "You're getting the hang of it already. It is only for a short while, and it will make Oona happy."

A long, slow sigh slid out between her teeth. "It would be less unpleasant to bring about an end to another war than wear these torturous thi—" She yelped as her left ankle wobbled, spilling her over to that side.

Fortunately, Meredith caught her and two women on her right side pulled her back to balance.

"I cannot believe you've never worn fancy shoes," said one she wanted to call Ivonne.

"The poor thing barely had shoes at all," grumbled another, perhaps Elaine. "Certain parties kept stealing them."

While the attendants erupted in a flurry of fretting over how poorly Kitlyn had been treated, Meredith continued walking her around in circles. By the time she *had* to make her way over to the temple of Lucen, she felt reasonably competent at walking in high heels—as long as she kept a hand on someone for support.

Castle staff holding flowers lined the corridors and rooms, forming a road to the main gates. Kitlyn climbed up into an open-topped white coach with rose-hued seats, pulled by two horses—one black to match her hair, the other white for Oona's blonde.

Citizens of Cimril City had turned out in large numbers to wave and throw flower petals as she rode by on the way to the temple. One or two (both older men with sour faces) tried to throw tomatoes, but missed. Their hatred hurt, but Kitlyn forced herself not to show it on her face. She couldn't expect everyone in the kingdom to abandon centuries of misunderstood dogma overnight. Some people, likely a lot more than let on, still objected to her marrying another woman… though between the goddess Tenebrea herself making an appearance and the temple of Lucen officiating the ceremony, public dissent had been minimal.

They know they speak not for Lucen but for hatred. In what way could who we love possibly affect them at all? She barely managed to resist scowling off in a random direction. *Well, perhaps since I am the queen, having no king to give me a child may affect them… but we have Evie.* Kitlyn blinked away the annoyance. *I shall not burden myself with such thoughts today. This is a day of joy.*

The coach arrived at the temple of Lucen, rolling through the grand white gates and around the great statue of the God of Purity. Soldiers formed a human wall at the forefront of the crowd, keeping an open passage for the coach to travel to the temple stairs.

Meredith hopped down first and helped Kitlyn navigate the small ladder, then supported her arm on the way inside. They followed an acolyte to a well-appointed sitting room… and yet more waiting. The same coach would go back to the castle to retrieve Oona, who would soon find herself in a similar sitting room elsewhere in the temple.

Some of Kitlyn's attendants entered and resumed fussing around with her gown. An agonizing few hours (actually, only half of one) later, the acolyte returned and bid her to follow. Kitlyn forgot herself and tried to walk unassisted after him… and wound up flopping on a divan when her right shoe twisted out from under her.

All the attendants gasped.

Meredith hurried over and helped her up.

"That was my fault." Kitlyn waved her arms for balance. "I forgot I've been hobbled."

Clinging to her handmaiden's arm, she walked out into the corridor and followed the acolyte to an antechamber where Beredwyn waited in his finest advisor's robes of deep loam green. A white tabard hung down the middle bearing the crest of Lucernia. Flared shoulder pads trimmed in emerald and gold glittered in the sun filtering in from the high windows along the cathedral wall. She couldn't look directly at his tall hat, nearly two feet high, the top sloped forward like a hatch that might let out a tiny goblin.

As a small girl, she'd adored asking the advisors questions that would make them nod since their hats made the gesture utterly ridiculous.

"You look lovely, child." Beredwyn smiled so broadly his eyes disappeared to narrow slits trimmed by bushy white brows. After a moment, he glanced about as if about to share a matter of state secrecy, leaned close, and whispered, "And I am sure you cannot wait to be rid of that gown."

Kitlyn pressed her palm into her stomach. "I fear the most difficult part of assuming the throne is that I spend most of my days barely able to breathe."

"Ahh yes. Starting or ending wars is a simple matter. Changing tradition, not so much." He offered her an arm.

Meredith leaned in and whispered to him about her unsteadiness on elevated heels. Beredwyn nodded to her. Kitlyn looked away from the wobbly hat but still snickered. He led her down a narrow side passage that led to a foyer at the far end of the main cathedral chamber, where three small girls—no doubt children of dukes or barons—greeted her with giant smiles, all holding baskets of white and pink flower petals. The girls swarmed, oohing and ahhing over her gown.

"Are you really going to marry a lady?" whispered the youngest, about five, with dark blonde hair in ringlet curls.

The other two, each a year or two older, stared at the little one in horrified shock.

"Yes, I am." Kitlyn smiled.

"You love her?" asked the little one.

"More than anything."

"That's nice." The tiny one beamed up at her.

Kitlyn grinned back.

"My father says you won't be able to make a rabbit," said the five-year-old.

The other two kids blinked in confusion.

"W-what?" asked Kitlyn.

Beredwyn covered his mouth to hold in a laugh.

"He said the kingdom needs a hare and you can't make one," said the little one, dead serious.

The older girls giggled, then blushed at Kitlyn with wide eyes as if they expected to get in trouble.

Kitlyn laughed. "Oh, I'll figure something out."

Beredwyn collected the flower girls and guided them left toward the cathedral a few paces, arranging them in a vee formation, leaving Kitlyn to teeter in place. She stared at the floor threatening to fly up and kiss her. Sitting upon Omun's shoulder hadn't been as scary.

Before she careened over, Beredwyn returned to take her arm and guided her up behind the flower girls.

High Priest Balais stood some hundred yards away on the altar, flanked by the red-haired priestess and the prematurely-grey priest who had warned her of her father's imminent dismissal from the church. Fortunately, all three Lightbearers appeared in high spirits.

Soon, a small army of minstrels in a balcony directly above her launched into the royal march, the same song that always played whenever the king went out in public. At the onset of the music, Kitlyn steeled herself and let Beredwyn tug her along. A room of several hundred people all twisting around in their seats to stare at her unnerved her ever so slightly more than Evermoor soldiers coming after her with swords.

With the music blaring around her, Kitlyn made her way down the aisle in a slow, deliberate walk, squeezing Beredwyn's arm so tight it had to be uncomfortable for him, though he showed no sign of minding. The girls tossed bunches of flower petals around as they advanced in single, synchronized steps. Upon reaching the altar, she scooted to the right, but refused to let go of him.

Beredwyn and the priests exchanged a momentary confused glance.

"I do not wish to fall," whispered Kitlyn. "I have never worn shoes of this type before."

"Ahh." Balais nodded.

The music wound down and stopped. A din of soft murmuring filled the cavernous room. A moment later, the minstrels started up again with a formal sounding piece that had somewhat the cadence of a march.

A grinning Evie zoomed down the aisle tossing flower petals by the handful. She made it about a quarter of the way before skidding to a stop and twisting back at someone making a hissing noise from the foyer. The girl looked at Kitlyn with an 'Oops! Sorry!' expression, then hurried back out of sight.

Soft chuckling swept over the crowd.

Evie reappeared, struggling to walk at a controlled pace in front of two other flower girls near in age to her. Kitlyn fixated on the willowy figure in a gleaming white dress beside Guard Captain Lorne, her face hidden under a veil. Oona's dress bared a wide swath of her neck, the tops of the lacy sleeves adhered as if by magic to the outsides of her shoulders. Her lower body vanished under the same sort of fluffy, billowy gown that Kitlyn wore, though she moved with the grace of a being from the gods' realm.

Guard Captain Lorne held her hand in a ceremonial manner, clearly not supporting her weight in the least. If anyone noticed that the queen could barely stay upright while the actual girl born a peasant glided as if she'd come out of the womb wearing expensive shoes, they didn't let on. Entranced by her approaching love, Kitlyn daydreamed of the only other time she'd touched a shoe with such a high heel. They'd both been about eleven, and Oona let her (risking punishment by doing so) try on a pair. It didn't last long, and ended with Kitlyn's face bouncing off a bedpost.

She reached up and rubbed her nose at the memory.

Oona arrived at the altar and took a place beside her, their sprawling gowns making it a bit of a task to stand so close together. She appeared to be crying under the veil, but couldn't possibly smile any wider.

Kitlyn huffed at her own veil, annoyed by it as well—but nowhere near as much as by the torture devices on her feet.

Some murmurings swept over the people in the front rows. Kitlyn caught a few words here and there, people finding it unusual to see two women about to be wed. One or two replied with 'well, she *is* the queen' or 'the gods permit it.' Of course, a handful of 'the gods are punishing us for Aodh's betrayal' and 'this is unnatural' happened as well, but mercifully few.

Oona took Kitlyn's hand.

High Priest Balais welcomed everyone to the cathedral and announced the wedding of Queen Kitlyn Talomir to Baroness Oona of Gwynaben. He spoke of Lucen's light for a time, and how that light had guided them together and allowed his kingdom to emerge from the shadow of deception and betrayal.

"The desires of Lucen and the gods are occasionally twisted by men to suit *their* wants and desires," said Balais, to murmurs of agreement from the crowd. "Many of you may be wondering how or why Lord Lucen permitted such things to go on, but yet, I have come to an understanding. He means to teach us by example. The word of one man is merely that—the word of one man. To truly know the will of Lucen, each and every one of us must look inside ourselves. How easily we accepted Aodh's deception as truth."

More, louder murmurs of agreement came from the crowd.

Oona glanced over with a 'what is he doing?' stare.

Is this a wedding or a political speech? Kitlyn tightened her grip on Beredwyn for balance.

Sensing her confusion, Balais made eye contact with her and offered a knowing nod.

"For as long as everyone here has walked the land, it has been our belief that purity had a certain definition. The teachings of Lucen require purity in thought, in deed, and in word. And we... humans, took that in a certain way." Balais raised his hands over Oona and Kitlyn. "I have seen a form of purity that many in the kingdom would struggle to accept. The love our queen has for this young woman is the very definition of purity."

Kitlyn's eyes widened. Oona squeezed her hand.

Mixed murmuring came from the crowd.

"Ask yourselves." Balais swept an arm across at the crowd. "Look inside. For the past twenty years, most of us believed those in Evermoor had been taken with demons based solely on the word of one man. We priests are human, as are you. We are subject to flaws, and can only do our best to follow Lucen's teachings."

The red-haired priestess and the priest beside Balais both appeared shocked. Never had anyone—especially a priest—spoken in such a way, implying that the priesthood could be anything but infallible, their words as if from Lucen's lips.

"These past two decades have been a difficult lesson. I believe Lucen meant to show us that we must seek his truth from inside more than outside. While he has chosen us as priests to bear his light to the kingdom, he has welcomed all of you as his children as well. As you set aside the deceit you were fed in regard to Evermoor, set aside the deceit you were fed regarding the love our queen has for this woman."

Evie clapped, stirring another ripple of soft chuckles from the crowd.

With that, the high priest took a step back and raised his hands. "Great Lucen, we call upon you to witness this day a declaration of love and commitment." A standing column of white fire formed in front of him, roughly a foot wide and as tall as the ceiling. It gave off no heat, only light and a tingling sense of awe.

The room fell silent.

Balais nodded to Kitlyn.

She released her right arm from Beredwyn's and extended her hand into the column up to the wrist.

"Queen Kitlyn Talomir." Balais raised his hand toward her, fingers spread. "You come before Lucen on this day to make a declaration of eternity."

"I, Kitlyn Talomir, state before Lucen and all who are here to witness, that I offer myself in eternal commitment and eternal love to Oona." She hesitated a second. "Baroness Oona of Gwynaben."

Balais leaned around the flaming column to quirk an eyebrow at the congregation. "Truly a monumental occasion. We bear witness today to a royal marriage based on *love*."

Another murmur of chuckling emanated from the crowd.

He raised his other arm outstretched toward Oona.

Still holding Kitlyn's hand, she extended her free left hand into the shifting white flames. "I, Oona, no family name, state before Lucen and all here to witness... I love Kitlyn with everything inside me, for eternity. I could no sooner live without her than without air to breathe or water to drink."

A lump swelled in Kitlyn's throat. She stared at their hands, nearly touching within the flames, their other hands clasped tightly between them. Such silence fell over the cathedral that Evie's soft humming filled the room. In seconds, they would withdraw their hands from the fire. Lucen would show the truth of their love by allowing them to hold a small bit of flame. If either hand came out empty, it would reveal a lie. Kitlyn had no doubt of Oona's—or her own—feelings, but couldn't help worry some external force might cause trouble.

"Let Lucen declare their hearts," said Balais.

Kitlyn and Oona turned to face each other, still with one hand extended in the column. Oona's eyes sparkled with adoration and anticipation. They withdrew their hands at the same time, both enshrouded in brilliant white flames. When they raised their burning hands over their heads, a deafening cheer rose up from the crowd—along with a few shocked gasps. Grinning at each other, they brought their glowing hands together between them, gazing into the white-blue fire. A tingle spread over Kitlyn from head to toe, exhilaration at such a tangible show of Lucen's approval. She burst into silent tears of joy.

In accordance with custom, they raised their fiery hands and pressed them to each other's chests, the magical flame seeping into their hearts—or at least appearing to.

Balais lowered his arms and the column of fire dissipated. "By Lucen's light, I hereby declare you duly wed in the eyes of the gods, and of the kingdom. Queen Kitlyn Talomir, and Lady Oona Talomir, Queen's Consort, Baroness of Gwynaben."

Kitlyn shrank a little inside at the lower title, though Oona didn't show any sign of caring whatsoever.

"You may kiss the bride," said Balais.

"Which one are you speakin' to?" called a random man in the crowd.

A few people chuckled.

"Both of them!" shouted Evie.

Oona's face went scarlet.

Kitlyn's cheeks burned.

For how long had they both been terrified of being caught? Kitlyn thought of the moment after they'd left the orphanage when she'd nearly kissed her right in front of the guardsmen, out in the street where anyone could see. How could she possibly kiss Oona in front of a massive crowd?

Oona lifted Kitlyn's veil.

The room, the crowd, the priests, everything dissolved from her awareness—except for Oona.

Her hands faintly shaking, Kitlyn reached up and lifted the veil away from Oona's face. Her heart pounded in her ears, her palms practically dripped with sweat. The already tight corset became a vicelike crushing force that refused to let any air into her chest.

"Are we really about to do this?" whispered Oona, smiling.

"I think we are." Kitlyn grinned nervously.

She leaned forward—and lost her balance on the damnable heels.

Oona caught her, spinning into an embrace and a kiss that looked far more elegant than Kitlyn felt. She whipped her hand up to catch her crown before it could fall off and bounce, clanging down the stone steps. Oona pressed her lips into Kitlyn's, but didn't kiss her as much as tried not to laugh. A vague sense of cheering entered her awareness despite being petrified at any minute they'd be dragged away from each other and screamed at for being abominations.

Crown repositioned and balance recovered, Kitlyn kissed Oona for real.

Balais patting them lightly on the shoulders broke the spell a moment later.

Kitlyn wobbled upright with help from Oona and Beredwyn.

"Go now, and lead Lucernia with Lucen's blessing."

Within a second of them turning together to face the crowd, the rear doors slammed open—revealing Fauhurst.

The former advisor had the disheveled appearance of a street vagrant, still in the same robes he'd been wearing when the girls had returned from Evermoor and Kitlyn had nearly torn down the castle. He pointed at them and screamed an incoherent drunken diatribe.

"I'd been wondering where that one got off to," said Beredwyn with a raised eyebrow.

"Aye. A right mess." Guard Captain Lorne gestured in Fauhurst's direction.

Furious, Kitlyn drew back her hand, which erupted in an aura of green light.

Three soldiers near the entrance rushed at Fauhurst, but he whirled away and ran off.

Oona blinked at her. "Don't!"

"What?" Kitlyn relaxed her magic and lowered her arm. "I was merely going to knock him out."

"Do not waste another moment of thought on that man." Oona took her hand again. "We have more important things to worry about."

Kitlyn sighed.

"No. Running the kingdom can wait. I was more thinking of those… *things* my mother so feared we had already done."

Again, Kitlyn's cheeks ran with heat. "Oh…"

"Alas…" Oona stared down, faking sadness while swaying side to side. "We have hours of socializing and merriment ahead of us before we can escape together."

"Oh, the horror." Kitlyn wobbled. "The instant we are out of this cathedral, I will rid myself of these awful things strapped to my feet."

Oona took her arm, supporting her as they eased themselves down the stairs to the aisle. "You will be fine with a little practice. Certainly walking in formal shoes is not as difficult as fulfilling a foretelling."

"No, it is *more* so."

Oona laughed.

Warmth spread over Kitlyn's chest at the beautiful sound. "I love your laugh."

"Well…" Oona tapped a finger to her lips. "With all that mess behind us now, I dare say you shall be hearing much more of it."

Kitlyn grinned.

Arm in arm—Kitlyn clinging to Oona to stay upright—they hurried down the aisle toward the cathedral exit under a pelting of flower petals.

7

MATTERS OF ROYALTY

OONA

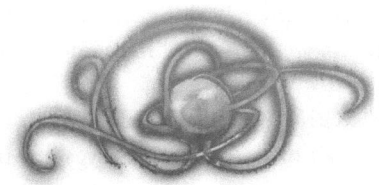

*L*ate that night after hours of festivities, Oona walked with Kitlyn down the curving royal hall. Her love appeared noticeably shorter. She'd ditched her heels and hose within moments of arriving at the grand hall. As she predicted, no one noticed her going barefoot under the massive wedding gown. Servants had spent the preceding week moving the majority of their things into the master bedroom, and a few hours earlier during the wedding reception arranging the rest of it.

Oona turned her head, staring at the door to her old bedroom on the way past it. It felt strange not to go in there, or to think of that as not being her room anymore. Of course, as much of a sanctuary as it had been at times, it had often felt like a prison—and it did remind her of the night an assassin got in. She heaved a mental sigh and glanced away. Her life had been full of leaving things behind as of late. Her old room, childhood, the security of thinking she had a father to take care of her… but also, she'd left behind her worry that she would have to kill thousands of people, marry Prince Lanwick, the war in general, and even the bratty streak she didn't realize she'd had until she no longer did.

"Feels like we're doing something wrong," whispered Kitlyn.

Oona gasped.

"No, not being alone together... or *that.*" Kitlyn grinned. "I mean going into this room."

"Oh. Yes. I don't think I've ever been in here before." She swallowed. "Well, except for that one night when we searched for him."

Kitlyn braced a hand on the door and pushed.

"Umm. Your highness," said Oona in a joking tone. "These doors go outward."

"Ugh. I'm so tired." She grasped an ornate ring and pulled one of the thick double doors open, the hinges emitting a low *creak.* "I barely slept last night... or the several nights before that."

"Nor did I."

"You don't look at all ready to pass out." Kitlyn blinked at her.

Oona followed her into the room and tugged the door shut. The sight of large brackets on the inside for a heavy bar reminded her the room had been built to protect against assassins or invading soldiers. It didn't reassure her as much as make her again feel like a target. "I've had a few years' practice at staying awake half the night. It's much more pleasant to lose sleep to anticipation rather than dread."

"Yes." Kitlyn trudged over and stood beside the bed. "Where are Meredith and Piper?"

"It's our wedding night," said Oona.

"So?" asked Kitlyn.

"Oh, wow... you *are* exhausted." Oona grinned, walking up behind her.

"Wait, we're married?"

Oona blinked in shock until Kitlyn started laughing. She gazed around at the huge room, feeling a bit too much like a child about to be scolded for invading her father's chambers. Of course, the man had gone to Tenebrea, and the room did technically belong to them now. Some of the décor had changed, a few paintings that had been in Oona's room brightened it a bit. The former king had been somber since the loss of his wife, and had servants remove most of the decoration.

"Help me out of this bothersome thing then, will you?" asked Kitlyn.

"Yes, your highness." Oona fake curtseyed.

Kitlyn sigh-laughed.

Oona undid the lacing at the back, and piece-by-piece, peeled her out from the incredibly elaborate wedding gown, setting each section on the nearby table. Most likely, the gowns would wind up on mannequins in a case somewhere. She wondered if someday, as an older woman, she might find herself gazing upon it while wondering how she'd ever fit in it. Then again, Margaret remained quite thin despite being older.

"So you've really never been in here?" Oona tugged the last bit of outer dress off over Kitlyn's head. "You must've been when you were a wee thing."

Kitlyn shrugged. "I suppose. I've no idea if my mother tended to me herself or left me in the care of nannies. Everything anyone's ever said about her hasn't been terribly nice."

"My turn." Oona placed the gown on the table.

She clutched the bedpost for stability while Kitlyn undid the laces. The process felt so much smoother, since she had done it many times before for 'Princess Oona.' Once the bulk of her dress landed on a divan, Oona stepped out of her high heels and spent a moment sitting on the edge of the bed rubbing her calves.

Kitlyn stared at her, cheeks gradually increasing in redness.

"It's not like we haven't seen each other undressed before." Oona shoved her underpinnings down, kicking them away, leaving only her smallclothes on below the waist.

"Things are different now," said Kitlyn.

"Things have been different for a few years, haven't they?"

Kitlyn nodded. "Yes, but that's not what I mean… I mean we *can* do things now and no one will lose their minds."

"Oh, some will." Oona smirked. "But it's no longer improper. We are well and duly wed." She winked. "And, dare I say we're *expected* to do certain things tonight."

Kitlyn gingerly removed her underpinnings and slip. Oona pulled off her slip. They stared at each other in only a bra and smallclothes for a long moment.

"This is real, isn't it?" asked Kitlyn.

"Yes. My heart is about to leap from my chest." Oona smiled, and curled her finger around her bra. "Shall I?"

"Allow me…" Kitlyn leaned in and kissed her.

A brush of cold air swam over Oona's chest as her bra came away. She shuddered in anticipation, then reached up and removed Kitlyn's. It had been more than a while since she'd seen the entirety of Kitlyn, since princesses did not attend to their handmaidens in the bath. They hadn't shared a tub since soon before *those* feelings stirred within her.

Kitlyn glanced off to the side, biting her lower lip as Oona ran her hands over her sides, snagging the band of her smallclothes and pulling them down. After, Oona stood and let Kitlyn do the same, shivering with excitement.

They regarded each other, bare as the day they'd been born. Oona's heart swelled with love — and total cluelessness as to where to go next.

Kitlyn kept glancing away.

"What's wrong? Why aren't you looking at me?" Oona caressed Kitlyn's cheek.

"It's not that." She met her stare, still blushing. "A thought has plagued me since this afternoon I simply cannot dislodge. It devours me."

"What is it?"

"What Balais said earlier made me wonder if it is wise to concentrate so much power in a single person. The mere notion of kings and queens leaves too much opportunity for evil. My father proved how much damage giving so much power to one person can cause." She looked down at Oona's body and blinked a few times, distracted.

"Can we perhaps talk of this in the morning?" Oona smiled. "That is an interesting worry, but this is *our* night." She gingerly set a hand on Kitlyn's hip, the skin surprisingly warm to the touch.

Kitlyn gasped. "Your hands are cold." She grasped Oona's hip, sending warmth shooting up and down. "*You* are cold."

"Oh, heavens. I seem to have misplaced all my clothing."

Kitlyn laughed.

Oona sat on the edge of the bed and pulled at Kitlyn, who fell seated beside her.

"I dislike our rigid social structure as well. Is it true that the servants in Ondar are treated as equals? What if we abolished classes?"

Oona sighed and glanced down at her pale legs. "You shouldn't try to change too much too fast or people will not like it."

"Yes, I know, but that doesn't mean I can't vent about it."

"Can you vent about it in the morning?" asked Oona.

"I'm sorry." Kitlyn put an arm around her. "I'm stalling because I'm nervous."

"I know." Oona smiled. "It's rather obvious."

"I've been dreaming of this moment for so long... and now that it's here, I don't understand why I'm frightened."

Oona scooted back onto the bed, pulling Kitlyn to lay beside her. "Are you afraid of this or afraid that you'll wake up?"

"Wake up. I've never been this happy before in my entire life... except maybe that day when we first met and played in the field. It still feels like we're getting away with something being alone together."

"So..." Oona reached over and caressed Kitlyn's cheek. "Let us do something we can get away with."

8

ARMISTICE

KITLYN

*A*utumnal trees drifted by on both sides of the road, accompanied by the clamor of multiple horses and the rattle of armor. Kitlyn still glowed from the events of her wedding night despite it being nearly a week ago. Neither she nor Oona had much of any idea how to go about consummating a marriage, but they both gave it a rather spirited try… and repeated said spirited try every night since—except for twice when Evie had been too frightened by the vastness of Oona's former room to sleep alone.

Sleeping entwined with the woman she loved surpassed any sense of security offered by a locked door, guards, a castle, or even a sword by the bedside. For the first time in many years, Oona enjoyed a deep rest, not having to worry about war, assassins, or her dearest love rejecting her.

The coach bounced over a rough patch of road. This journey to Ivendar, the capital city of Evermoor, had been expected… though she had hoped it would've been her father undertaking the task. However, after what he had done, Aodh Talomir walking into Ivendar would not have ended well. Kitlyn disliked the truth of it, but the reality of his death being the best possible outcome for both kingdoms couldn't be denied.

Meredith and Piper sat in the rear-facing seat opposite them. The younger girl had mixed feelings about going, to which Oona had offered her the choice to remain at the castle. Piper feared she may get in trouble if anyone in Evermoor recognized her since she had outed herself as a spy and chosen to abandon her mission of assassination. On Kitlyn's assurance that she would ensure her protection, Piper decided to come along.

Oona fidgeted.

"Hmm?" Kitlyn glanced over at her.

"Oh, just thinking about our last trip to Evermoor."

"These accommodations are far nicer." Kitlyn leaned close and muttered, "I'd rather be bound hand and foot in a wagon than killed on the spot. Given how much they hated 'the heir' based on lies, we should consider ourselves lucky Ralen had a true sense of decency."

"Still. They rather treated us cruelly. Making us use a bucket indeed. Not even untying our legs." Oona's face reddened in anger. "I hope I do not see any of those men."

"If what Ralen said has any truth, I doubt *anyone* will see those men." She sighed. "Well, the one wasn't too bad. The man I made sleep."

"I'd just as soon forget that wagon ride entirely." Kitlyn frowned at the window. Hopefully, Ralen *did* kill the man who grabbed her breast. Or perhaps Omun had already done that at the keep. He had left quite a few bodies in his wake. More deaths that should never have happened but for her father's greed.

The previous night spent at a roadside inn had been pleasant despite the surprising number of curious people who wanted to meet her. Most acted as though she'd had no connection at all to the former king and she'd swooped in to save Evermoor. She found it reassuring, especially when traveling so far into a nation that had been calling for her death since the day of her birth, that they had all revised their opinion of her so drastically. Of course, looking at Evermoor, the effect of what she had done couldn't be any more obvious.

All the trees, flowers, and shrubs appeared vibrant and lush. The land itself gave off a tangible sense of life. Even Piper couldn't help but stare in awe at the change in her former homeland. Kitlyn imagined farmers' crops had rebounded as well to a point given how late in the season they had returned the Heart. According to the waitress at the inn last night, some people who lived far from the Alderswood where the land had turned grey also showed signs of withering. With the Heart returned, their entire kingdom brimmed with life.

From the moment they had crossed the Churning Deep yesterday, energy stirred within Kitlyn's chest as if in response to the Alderswood acknowledging her presence here. On top of the glow from all the things she'd done with Oona, the sense of welcome from the great tree lifted her spirits in defiance of the dread she harbored for this meeting with the Evermoor king.

Would he talk down to her or praise her for returning the heart? The man had sent assassins to kill her as an infant and a young child. He'd ordered the assassin who murdered the previous queen. He'd sent the assassin, Ian, who'd nearly forced Oona to drink noxious poison—a story her wife couldn't get through a retelling of without sobbing. She still had the occasional nightmare of watching that man convulse so forcefully his back broke.

Kitlyn narrowed her eyes, entertaining an uncharacteristic moment of viciousness and taking satisfaction in such a painful death. Truly the gods paid him back for his cruelty in the most appropriate way possible.

"Who is to die now?" asked Oona. "You've that look in your eyes again."

"Thinking of meeting King Volduin, which made me think of assassins, which made me think of that man who gave you poison."

Oona cringed. "He is... gone. I wonder if there is any truth to what Ralen said."

"About that order of assassins?"

"Yes. Their idea of where we go after our life ends differs from Tenebrea's realm."

Kitlyn nodded. "I remember. The evil go to the Banefallow, the good to The Glimmering Vale. And those who are neither particularly good nor particularly evil roam the world as spirits until they figure out where they belong."

"If that is true," said Oona, "then that man may be haunting the land still. I fear he may desire revenge. Ralen said those assassins perform some dark magic that spares them from the Banefallow no matter how vile their deeds."

"You should not worry, my love." Kitlyn squeezed her hand. "For what better weapon could there be against dark spirits than Lucen's light."

Oona smiled.

After several hours of travel across placid countryside, the coach slowed. Merchant wagons flanked both sides of the road with men and women selling everything from late season fruit to baubles, clothes, and even a selection of cheapish weapons. Kitlyn caught a passing glance at a table of swords, about a third of which appeared Lucernian in origin, all likely scavenged from dead soldiers. She almost missed having a blade at her hip, but her present attire—a dark green gown and flat-soled shoes—didn't afford her the option. However, as a queen visiting a foreign nation, the odds of her needing a blade of her own didn't seem too high. And in the event of unforeseen circumstance, she had her magic. A five-hundred-pound stone spire jutting up from the ground more than made up for a lack of a longsword.

Piper kept her head down, her pale, delicate face hidden behind a curtain of dark chestnut brown hair. Oona's grip on Kitlyn's hand hadn't loosed at all. She clearly felt a bit like a mouse on her way into a house of cats. However, she had much more practice at royal things and managed to keep an outward poise in spite of her fear.

Soon, the merchant carts gave way to small shops with walls resembling trees grown in spirals and whorls rather than cut planks. Some of them even had leaves still sprouting.

"Are those shops alive?" whispered Oona.

"Good chance of that," said Piper in a timid voice. "The shapers raise them from the earth. Most people here try to avoid harming trees. Cut wood is taken only from already-dead ones."

Kitlyn clenched her jaw. *They dare not hurt a tree but would murder me in my bed as a child?* Her sudden rush of anger leaked out her nose on a sigh. *Anyone would take extreme steps when facing the extermination of an entire kingdom.*

Men's shouts arose outside, greetings called back and forth from the Evermoor soldiers that had joined their escort and the Ivendar guards. Curious citizens trotted over, trying to peek into the coach. Whenever someone caught her eye, Kitlyn returned a smile and a wave.

They'd arrived at the capital city late in the afternoon. Based on the weakening autumnal sun, she guessed it perhaps an hour before dinner. Something Beredwyn had once said came back to her mind. Ivendar and Cimril sat far enough apart that time wound up being slightly different in the two cities. The way the sun passed overhead put the Evermoor capital roughly two hours ahead of Cimril. Not that she really noticed the change during their trip, but it struck her as odd to think about how it would be presently sunnier back home.

Like a curious child, Kitlyn leaned closer to the window, ogling the city. Telltale whirls or patterns in the walls of many buildings suggested they had been more grown than constructed. Despite that, they had a remarkably similar appearance to structures from Lucernia, except for ones where deliberate gaps between the thick roots served as windows. Those resembled the sorts of dwellings she'd read about the elves living in.

Trumpets blared, announcing their arrival at the castle. The King of Evermoor, Lanas Volduin, had constructed a surprisingly normal looking keep of stone, though the lack of visible bricks revealed it as far from being mundane. Kitlyn smiled to herself, thinking of how her magic could liquefy stone, allowing it to be shaped to her desire before re-hardening.

It would've taken an army of stoneshapers to make an entire castle.

The coach came to a stop, and attendants opened the doors on the right side. Oona, being on that side, exited first. Kitlyn followed. Meredith and Piper stepped out after them, though the younger girl took Oona's hand in both of hers, staring down at her shoes as if she'd done something wrong.

She said she's from Lamneth. If I recall, that is far to the south. No one here should know her.

A man with long, black hair, handsome slate-grey eyes, and a warrior's chin emerged from a group of soldiers by the gate. His rich, violet tunic, black leggings, and fine boots suggested nobility or at least wealth. He walked up to them as casually as if he already knew them.

"Princess Talomir." He nodded at Kitlyn, then pivoted toward Oona, hesitating for a few seconds at the sight of a delicate crown on her head as well. "Oona."

The instant she heard his voice, she recognized Prince Ralen. Kitlyn raised a subtle hand at her entourage, stalling anyone from correcting him as to her title. "Oh… Prince Ralen. I didn't recognize you in such fine clothing instead of your armor." She returned a nod of greeting.

"Well, it's not so much armor as a shell I sometimes produce. Though, I occasionally feel the need to shed it and grow a new one." He kept a serious expression for a few seconds before flashing a grin.

Oona giggled. "It is good to see you well, and the Alderswood back to health."

Everyone in earshot let out a small cheer.

"Indeed." Ralen smiled. "Come. My father is quite keen on meeting you."

"Does that mean you have reached an accord with him?" asked Oona. "Last I remember, he had been rather cross with you."

Ralen nodded. "It appears his connection to the Alderswood went far deeper than any of us realized. With the tree's slow death, he had grown ill of temper, mad with fear, and suspecting betrayal and deceit from every direction."

"He is healthy now then?" asked Kitlyn.

"Yes, quite." Ralen gestured at the doors. "There is no need for us to stand around outside."

Kitlyn looked past him at the castle, only two stories tall but much wider than her home. Everywhere she looked, highly detailed statuettes of animals adorned the walls of the interior, along with elf-like beings, faun, and other fey creatures. She had no doubt stoneshapers had crafted this place.

Ralen led them down a short corridor that took them through a twelve-foot thick wall around the main keep to an interior courtyard. The keep itself took up more room than two city blocks in Cimril. The people living and working here didn't seem much different from the citizens of Lucernia, other than having a browner tint to their skin and an affinity for much simpler, looser clothing. With the exception of the southeastern areas around the thicker moors—where Piper came from —the people of Evermoor had a somewhat darker complexion than the average Lucernian. Thick fog and frequent rain in the moors made paleness common in those who'd lived for generations there. This, of course, explained why she had been tapped as an assassin even as a twelve-year-old. She didn't appear obviously from Evermoor.

Everyone who noticed them offered smiles and friendly greetings. Oona responded in kind, though occasionally glanced over at Kitlyn with confusion in her eyes. A pair of halberdiers at the keep entrance snapped to attention as Ralen approached. Kitlyn followed the prince down a series of long, straight corridors with green runners carpeting the middle third of an otherwise polished stone floor. The random statuettes continued throughout, though the place had little decoration otherwise. No paintings or tapestries hung anywhere in sight.

Kitlyn looked around at everything, feeling a bit in over her head. Her father and King Volduin had been dear friends twenty years ago. She wondered how often he might have walked these same corridors, or how many times these walls had heard his name spoken in curse since then.

"I am told"—Ralen glanced over at her—"that around the time I restored the Heart to the great tree, my father collapsed and fell into a deep slumber. He awoke before I returned here, and the change in him was nothing short of dramatic."

"It is good to hear he is well," said Kitlyn, perhaps a little too formally.

Ralen offered a look of apology. "I am sure he regrets what he did."

"He believed he acted to save the lives of everyone in his kingdom, and his mental state had declined." Oona offered a placating smile. "I cannot hold against him things he did that would not have happened if not for Aodh's actions. We are fortunate that it was you who found us, though I am sure Lucen played a hand in it. Had not I been fool enough to attempt to flee…"

He smiled. "Perhaps. We are all fortunate. Had you not, Ondar would have been dragged into this conflict, the war would have escalated, and there would have been little left of Lucernia—and nothing left of Evermoor by the time it ended."

Kitlyn still wanted to drop a stone on someone's foot for how they'd treated Oona in captivity, but if all of that *had* been Lucen's will… better her wife suffer a brief humiliation than thousands die. At first, she doubted Ralen's suggestion that Lucernia would have been destroyed, but the more she thought about it, the more possible it seemed. The closer Evermoor came to death, the more frenzied its people would fight. Rumor said Ondari soldiers wielded terrible weapons to augment their wizards, and had the power to raze entire cities to flat ground.

Despite the truth or exaggeration of such stories, Ondar entering the war would have been a disaster.

"Yes. We are all fortunate," said Kitlyn. "Except for everyone who now walks with Tenebrea for that man's foolishness."

He offered a somber nod, then pushed open a door that led to a large courtyard with clear sky above. Castle wall surrounded it on all sides, though the 'room' covered a vast amount of space. Archways led to branching corridors on the left and right. Straight ahead, perhaps fifty yards away, a giant tree formed a throne dais. Thick, wavy roots bent in such a way as to create a throne flanked on either side by a pair of smaller seats.

The throne held a shirtless, muscular man with rich brown skin, tight black pants, and long, flowing raven hair. He appeared to be somewhere in his thirties, and reclined slightly to the left, his chin propped up on two knuckles. His right hand draped off the armrest. In fact, his entire presence struck Kitlyn more like a pirate king reclining at the back of an alehouse rather than the ruler of an entire nation.

Both Piper and Meredith emitted sighs of desire upon seeing him. Even Kitlyn had to admit he cut a striking figure, though she had little interest in him beyond settling the matter between their kingdoms.

However, the figures in the four other seats shocked a gasp out of Oona and made Kitlyn blink in disbelief.

Four women sat two on either side, each wearing only a diaphanous white skirt and an elaborate necklace of wood fragments and leaves. Three had flowers woven into their hair, one wore wooden bracelets on both arms. All four of them showed as much skin above the waist as their king, decorated with painted-on patterns in dark brown or white lines. Kitlyn stared mostly out of shock, though couldn't help but admire their beauty. Their age eluded her, as they seemed simultaneously old enough to be her mother yet young. She couldn't see their ears due to long hair, and half suspected them to be fey of some kind.

The woman on the far right, King Lanas' left, resembled Ralen and also had jet-black hair. *Is that his mother or his sister?* All four of them stared at Kitlyn with an intensity that put her on edge, though their gazes held no malice. A warm core of energy swirled around inside her as if in response to whatever they thought.

By the time Ralen led the way over to the throne, Kitlyn decided to explain the women's confounding nature as having the bodies of twenty-year-olds but the poise and eyes of people twice that age. They had to be using some manner of magic to stay young. Perhaps that had been what inspired her father's tales of demons. Did he crave that for himself? Immortality?

"Father..." Ralen stopped and gestured at them. "May I introduce Princess Kitlyn Talomir and Oona."

King Lanas momentarily appeared displeased, likely the name 'Talomir' making him think of her father.

Ralen turned to face the girls. "Lady Kitlyn, Lady Oona, may I introduce my father, King Lanas Volduin."

"King Volduin." Kitlyn offered a respectful bow.

Oona mirrored the bow. "It is a pleasure to meet you as well, King Volduin."

"These are my father's spiritcallers and companions." Ralen gestured at the woman on the far left, a blonde. "Aina."

Aina nodded in greeting.

"Beside her is Gerya," said Ralen.

The brown-haired woman somewhere between eighteen and thirty-five offered a pleasant smile.

Ralen indicated the nearer woman on King Lanas' left side. "Elder Naena, the matriarch of the spiritcallers."

Naena did appear somewhat older than the other three, but it showed more in her posture than on her face. She smiled at Kitlyn, then Oona before leaning to whisper something at the black-haired woman beside her.

"Oh, quite so," said the last woman.

"And this is my mother, Lady Ilan," said Ralen.

Ilan stood and padded down the roots to the ground. She passed close by Ralen, pausing to offer a brief embrace, then approached Kitlyn. The painted lines on her chest formed a hawk-like shape at the base of her neck, the tail extending down between her breasts. "The Alderswood is grateful for what you have done. Its energy flows strong within you."

"I am sorry for how it came to be that I have this... power." Kitlyn looked up into the woman's eyes, trying not to notice her incredibly bare chest. Up close, her amulet appeared to be a tiny sculpture of a dozen dancing fey creatures woven among vines.

Ilan rested a hand on Kitlyn's shoulder in a decidedly motherly fashion. "Do not feel regret, child. The powers of the Alderswood cannot be stolen, only given. The great tree trusted you before you were born, and I am overjoyed to see that trust was well placed."

Oona stood stiffly beside her, trying not to look at anything. Her cheeks had the cutest amount of pink. Piper and Meredith continued ogling King Lanas. Even among the laborers at the castle, no man she'd ever seen had such prominent—or perfect—muscles.

"It brings me great joy to have helped restore the Alderswood." Kitlyn smiled.

Ilan turned away, pausing briefly to give Oona a warm smile, then approached the dais. "Lanas, must we attend to all this formality? It is purely for their benefit is not? Though they may be royalty, these girls..." She eyed Oona. "Well, perhaps one of them could do without it."

The other spiritcallers stood. King Lanas rose to his feet and walked down the roots, the remaining three women following. All four whispered to him once he reached the ground, then trailed off into a grove of trees at the left distant corner of the enclosed courtyard.

"Very well." King Lanas walked up to Kitlyn. "As I am sure you are aware, things are not the same here as you may be used to in Lucernia."

Kitlyn found herself eye-to-sculpted-pectoral with him. *Is this why they made those damnable tilted shoes?* She peered up at him, feeling like she'd shrunk back to being twelve. "Thank you for having audience with us, though I would have preferred we met under better circumstances."

"Please, join me." King Lanas gestured at a huge outdoor table that appeared to be a single slice from an enormous tree nearly twenty feet in diameter, and walked over to take a seat in a chair made of woven roots.

Kitlyn followed, with Oona, Piper, and Meredith close behind. The Lucernian soldiers that had made the journey with them, the coach driver, and a handful of attendants would likely be eating and resting in guest quarters.

Once everyone took a seat, King Lanas glanced at Kitlyn while rubbing a finger back and forth over his chin. "You have come in response to my letter to officiate the end of hostilities and re-open trade. I have a simple question before we begin. Why has Aodh sent his child in his stead?"

Kitlyn met his gaze across the table. "Aodh Talomir is dead."

Lanas froze, one eyebrow up.

The spiritcallers, even from some forty feet away, all stopped talking and glanced in her direction. For a moment, only the soft whisper of wind in the unusually green leaves around them broke the stillness.

"Dead..." said Lanas.

"Yes." Kitlyn steeled herself, managing to speak without much emotion, as if discussing historical events from some other kingdom. "For his deceit and betrayal of Lucen, the temple planned to strip him of his title as high priest and excommunicate him. Lucen himself had abandoned him. His gift to bear light and witness truth no longer heeded his call. Rather than suffer that humiliation, he sent himself to Tenebrea."

Lanas shifted his jaw side to side. "At one time, he had been a good friend. It pains me to see how far he had fallen, but it shows the sort of man he was not to be able to face me again."

Prince Ralen glanced at Oona, enlightenment dawning in his eyes. "Oh, forgive me... You are no longer *Princess* Kitlyn."

She smiled at him. "Please forgive me for neglecting to send a wedding invitation… everything went by in a rush."

"A wedding?" asked Lanas, both eyebrows up. "So I am speaking with the Queen of Lucernia?"

"Queens, I'd wager," said Ralen, grinning.

Oona opened her mouth, closed it, hesitated a second more, then said, "I am technically the Queen Consort."

"At the moment," muttered Kitlyn.

"Allow me to express my condolences on the loss of your father." Ralen bowed again.

"You needn't suffer the pretense," said Oona in a gentle tone. "He was not the man I thought I knew."

"He was not a man I knew at all." Kitlyn looked down at her lap, fidgeting at her gloves.

Ralen pursed his lips in thought, then relaxed. "I can feel sympathy for a daughter while simultaneously finding no great sense of sorrow in her father's passing. Truly, it surprises me to hear the two of you speak of his death as though you welcome it."

"I neither welcome nor regret what had to happen." Kitlyn gazed off at the castle grounds, alive with trees. "I can only mourn the time we will not have, but this man squandered the time we were given. What he did to me pales in comparison with the suffering he has caused to Evermoor and to our own citizenry. I cannot even consider my personal feelings in light of that."

"Your feelings matter, too, your majesty," said Ralen.

Ilan broke away from the spiritcallers and approached the table to stand beside Lanas. "It is as they say. Aodh wanders the Banefallow."

What? How… he's not from Evermoor, nor did he die here. How could he possibly have gone there? Thinking of that boy, Kem, talking about the place—where souls constantly fled from ravening wolves only to be caught, devoured, and reawaken to do it over and over again—made her shudder.

Oona blinked.

"Very well." Lanas smiled up at Ilan.

They exchanged a smoldering, long stare obvious enough that Oona squirmed and blushed.

Ralen either didn't notice the way his parents looked at each other, or it didn't bother him.

Once Ilan walked off to rejoin the other spiritcallers, King Lanas drummed his fingers on the giant table. "I do recognize that you personally had nothing to do with this war other than bringing about its end, yet there remains the matter of the war stemming from an act of Lucernian aggression."

"I understand that and do not dispute it. My father stole from you something terribly vital to the existence of this entire land."

"It would only be appropriate for Lucernia to offer reparations."

Kitlyn nodded once. "I have come prepared to discuss such offers, yes." She thought back on hours of discussions with Beredwyn, Advisor Lanon, and High Priest Balais regarding what would constitute fair sums. If the king demanded significantly more, she would request he write things down and return home to confer with them.

The next hour or so drowned in an increasingly tense back-and-forth of requests, demands, and more than a few off-the-hip zingers from both sides. Whenever Kitlyn started to grow heated, Oona would politely cut in and try to soothe both of them. Piper shrank in on herself, continuing to hide her face behind her hair. Meredith—after about forty minutes—finally ceased staring at Lanas' bare chest.

A handful of men and women freely approached offering water and snacks. Kitlyn couldn't think of them as servants since they behaved more like the staff at a tavern.

After another back and forth quibbling the finer points of gold coins per casualty, Lanas' pervasive reinforcement of everything being Lucernia's fault finally tweaked a sensitive nerve.

"Don't forget you sent assassins after me for sixteen years because of a bunch of old men addled out of their minds on dreamstem. Who tries to have an *infant* assassinated?"

"Someone who believed that one death would save tens of thousands of lives," said Lanas, irritatingly calm.

"She could have destroyed Evermoor, and didn't. She confronted the Timeless Watchers." Prince Ralen gestured at her, smiling.

Kitlyn spun her head toward him so fast her crown nearly flew off. "I did not *confront* them. I conversed with them. And no, I most certainly could not have destroyed Evermoor."

"Kit..." Oona gave her the 'please calm down' stare.

She took a long breath. "While I may have possessed the kind of magic necessary to destroy the land from the Alderswood grove, it is absolutely beyond me to do something so cruel."

"Father," said Ralen. "You sought revenge on Aodh. Well-deserved revenge in fact. However, he is dead. Lucernia has two young queens who are not only guiltless for the war, but directly brought about its end and the restoration of the Alderswood. Their kingdom has had its faith in their Lord of Light shaken. As capable a leader as Queen Talomir is, she is still young. Younger even than I, and has the task of holding a fractured kingdom together."

"Perhaps you should take pity on the girl for her father's crimes." Lady Naena appeared behind Lanas as if out of nowhere, her flowing voice washing over the table with a near magical clarity and volume. An unusual sense of calmness settled over everyone in the wake of her words. "The blade is drenched. I see little need to twist it."

"Very well." Lanas bowed his head. "I conditionally agree to your terms, though let us officiate it in writing after a night of food and rest. For now, we shall no longer burden our minds with negotiations or dark thoughts."

Kitlyn eased back into her seat. "That is most kind of you, King Lanas."

He flashed a fey smile. "I am once again myself. Come, let us eat, drink, and savor the wind and sky." King Lanas faced a group of castle staff, and clapped twice.

They sprang into motion, hurrying off into the hallway nearby.

"Make yourself as comfortable as you like." Lanas smiled and briefly bowed his head. "I shall return in a moment." With that, he strolled over to where the spiritcallers lounged among the grove.

Oona looked over at her. "Now what?"

"You're asking me?" Kitlyn took her hand. "You're the one with practice at being a royal."

"Perhaps, though I have never once visited Evermoor. The traditions here are"—she glanced toward the spiritcallers and blushed again —"unusual. If we go to Ondar, I… wouldn't really remember much but how people in the north spoke strange and I spent the entire time sulking."

Ralen chuckled. "The simplest advice I am able to offer you would be to forget those crowns upon your heads and consider yourselves among friends."

Friends… I've spent my entire life thinking of Evermoor's citizens as demonic. There have been too many lies. Too much deceit. It is far past time for change and I do so hate this pageantry. Kitlyn looked around at the delicate, almost elven architecture, then smiled at him. "All right. Friends."

9

ANOTHER WORLD

OONA

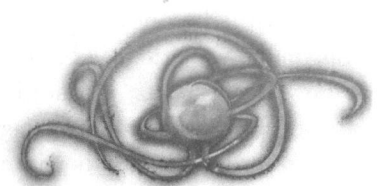

onfusion lasted only a short while before a stream of people entered carrying casks of ale, ewers of wine, bowls of breads, and several long tables. Oona remained in her seat at the huge 'slice of tree' table, watching the workers set up the trappings of a feast. She couldn't quite settle on how to feel about King Volduin after his sudden change from wanting her dead so badly he'd been willing to declare his son a traitor, to the reasonably friendly man presently conversing with four shirtless women.

She would have been studying him, trying to read his intentions, but decided not to look in that direction. He hadn't struck her as deceitful at all during the tedious negotiations. His pressing for increasing advantage did, to Ralen's point, feel as if he sought to somehow punish Aodh rather than seek justified reparations.

Piper continued to keep her head down while Meredith gazed about with curiosity at the frenzy of activity. King Volduin walked off down a side hallway, leaving the spiritcallers to continue talking among themselves. He returned after a few minutes, leading the group of Lucernian soldiers and coachmen into the courtyard, a jovial smile on his face.

Oona leaned toward Ralen. "It is difficult to see that man as the same one who wanted me dead and ordered his men to arrest you. I... could never imagine our former king going off to fetch visitors himself."

"I've been told that before the war, he was quite a merry sort of person." Ralen saluted her with a wine goblet. "Mother says he is much like his old self now."

"Are those women his wives?" asked Kitlyn in a near whisper.

"That would be the simplest way to describe their relationship to someone from Lucernia." Ralen took a long sip.

"Why does he have four?" asked Oona.

Ralen chuckled. "Because they choose to be with him, and he with them. Aina and Gerya are rather fond of each other as well."

That's not exactly what I asked, but… it does seem to be the simplest answer. She decided to change the subject and got into an idle conversation with Ralen about his childhood here. To hear him talk, he'd grown up much the way she imagined a woodsman's son might—running about most of the day in the woods, untamed, going wherever whim took him. Upon entering his teen years, his father taught him the art of the sword, tracking, riding, and various worldly skills as well as what he learned from his mother regarding the magical aspects of Evermoor. Ralen mentioned rather in passing that his father was a bladeborn, which made Oona smile. The prince still tried to deny he had the gift, though after having watched him fight, she felt certain he did.

King Lanas and the spiritcallers joined them at the large table while the rest of the Lucernian entourage took seats nearby at the long, rectangular tables. Oona tried not to blush *too* hard with four topless women across from her. Somehow, Kitlyn already appeared unfazed by their lack of modesty. Meredith kept sneaking glances at the shirtless king.

Castle workers brought out huge bowls of vegetables prepared in small bundles, whole roast chickens, hams, drumsticks, trays of small things that appeared to be golden brown bread loaves the size of fists, and plates of cheese.

Pleasant conversation continued over a copious dinner, as though they had not been previously discussing matters of war-torn kingdoms with the man who had been an enemy for twenty years. That thought again made Oona think about how oddly young he and his 'wives' all appeared to be. It made sense that if they had some connection to the magic within the Alderswood keeping their bodies youthful, they would have been affected more strongly by the absence of the Heart. The king also had perhaps the biggest muscles she'd ever seen as well as towering height.

He could've ended the war himself if he'd walked over the Arch of the Ancients.

Much of the food, including the salad, had been prepared in such a way as to be amenable to hand eating. It seemed the people of Evermoor didn't have much love for forks or knives. Kitlyn and Piper dove right in, unconcerned with using their bare hands to eat. Oona started off hesitant, but it didn't take long for her hunger to overpower decorum especially when surrounded by dozens of people all eating that way. The small 'breads' turned out to be a kind of baked dumpling with a meat stuffing that reminded her of stew with strong but pleasant spices. Meredith hesitated the longest before picking up food without a fork.

Once the sun finally set, glowing orbs of yellow light appeared at random around the courtyard and drifted in lazy paths like living—or magical—lanterns carrying themselves around. They made her little blue one seem tiny by comparison, but didn't glow anywhere near as brightly. However, well more than twenty of them glided around, providing plenty of light.

The king lost himself on a tangent after a few cups of wine and rambled at length about how he and Aodh had once wandered off into the Ebonwolf Shire in search of a dryad. He took great humor in his friend not believing such creatures existed.

"And when we finally spotted one, he turned scarlet in the face." King Volduin laughed, gleefully describing Aodh's discomfort at them encountering a wood nymph.

Oona's cheeks grew warmer and warmer as the Evermoor king described her former not-quite-father's progressively greater embarrassment as the small woman with glowing green eyes and nothing but leaves and vines to wear approached them. He proceeded to poke fun at Aodh's strange notion of 'purity' relating to an innocent being that would shed tears over the death of an ant somehow being impure for not having clothes.

Gerya, one of the spiritcallers, nudged him and whisper-scolded him for making Oona uncomfortable. Being caught blushing and fidgeting only embarrassed her more, which made Aina and Ilan look away to avoid laughing. Lucen's gift allowed her to understand they regarded her as adorable and didn't wish to make her uncomfortable.

Eventually, musicians and dancers drifted out of the shadows and proceeded to act out a dramatic production. Oona watched the dancers' performance with half a hand over her eyes, as the ones portraying elves had garments similar to those of the spiritcallers: gauzy skirts made from multiple layers of leaf-shaped panels and nothing on above the waist.

The story told of elves entrusting the care of a magical seed to a human who had been keenly in tune with nature. She soon figured this story likely entailed the planting of Alderswood and perhaps how the nation of Evermoor came to be. She *almost* thought of it as their 'creation myth' as the former king would've referred to it, but after witnessing Kitlyn's magic, that didn't feel right. It made her wonder what relationship Lucen, Navissa, Orien, and Tenebrea had with other kingdoms. Perhaps gods like them simply chose an area of land to consider their domain. Or, maybe, they focused primarily on the people instead of geography. It's not as though Lucen would abandon her the instant she crossed the border. She pondered if Ondar's reverence for the Steelfather might be more than simple reverence for a skilled blacksmith.

Once the theater play ended, the courtyard became an unusually casual gathering of people standing or sitting around sharing drinks and talking. King Volduin excused himself from the table, encouraging Kitlyn and Oona to wander about and be social. He and the spiritcallers drifted around, falling into easy conversations with everyone from the people refilling drinks to guardsmen, to Evermoor commoners who had simply walked in.

More and more people who appeared to be townsfolk from Ivendar arrived, as though the king's castle had become a local tavern where anyone could come and go as they pleased. Oona couldn't quite reconcile such a concept, and emitted a startled gasp when Kitlyn took her hand.

"Shall we make our way around? That *is* what we are expected to do at social events? I'm still not entirely sure how to be a royal."

Oona grinned. "This is hardly a royal function... or the court. Though I suppose we ought not to be rude."

Upon seeing Piper looking frightened and sad, Oona leaned close. "What's wrong?"

The girl indicated her empty plate. "I haven't had this sort of food in a long time. It reminded me of my parents. And I still fear someone may recognize me."

"Come, then. Stay with us and no one shall bother you." Oona took her hand.

The three of them wandered into the courtyard. She let Kitlyn lead as the official queen. Despite having been at the coronation, it still seemed like everything had happened to someone else. She couldn't think of Kitlyn as a queen, nor herself as a queen's wife. Kitlyn still felt like Kitlyn, albeit in nicer clothing. Somewhere between trying to hide under a blanket from an assassin and strolling back in the gates of Castle Cimril to demand the Heart, Oona had ceased being a child.

Going from twelve to sixteen had been a blur of fear and relative captivity. She so dreaded the foretelling that she hadn't much felt at all like a child—despite having acted like one. Of course, she could allow herself some small measure of sorrow at what had been taken from her without dwelling endlessly on it. Many people suffered as a result of the war, most more than her, but that didn't lessen the pain and terror she had felt most every night.

Nothing for it but to move on, learn, and grow from it. She squeezed Kitlyn's hand. *I would endure it a hundred times again to have her beside me.*

Peasants, merchants, nobles, and castle workers all drifted by to talk with Kitlyn and Oona. Though, she found it somewhat difficult to tell the moneyed from the normal people except for a handful of men and women in obviously finer clothing that consisted of airy robe-like garments that made her think of writings she'd read of elves. Though no one here appeared anything more than human. Quite a few, like Piper, had delicate features and slender bodies, but not the least bit of pointedness in their ears.

Perhaps the fey spirit comes from the tree instead of an ancestor?

"By Carros!" said a man. "It's you."

Oona whirled to her left. A man of average height with broad shoulders and silvery hair hurried up to Kitlyn, his expression a mixture of surprise and amusement. At his rapid approach, Piper pressed herself into Oona's side, half hiding from him.

"Hello," replied Kitlyn.

"You're radiant." The man offered a polite bow. "Quite a bit different from the last time I saw ya. Queen, wot?"

Oona glanced between them, eyebrow raised.

"Yes. It is me. And yes, apparently, I've wound up with this crown on my head. Not exactly the sort of thing I had ever planned on."

"Aye. Awful business, the lot of it. My condolences on your father, such as they are." The man nodded at her.

Kitlyn's eyes hardened ever so slightly. "Thank you. I understand your feelings toward him and do not fault you for them. In fact, some of them, I share."

"Never would have imagined who ya were." He scratched his head, chuckling. "Neither you bein' from Lucernia or bein' the one we all thought'd end us all. I admire the courage you had settin' foot in Evermoor."

We didn't have much choice in that. Oona rubbed a hand up and down Piper's back, distracting herself from making sour faces by comforting the girl.

"I hadn't exactly expected to. *Going* to Evermoor wasn't my choice, but I refused to leave without Oona. And, I'd only recently learned I was the heir… and hadn't quite convinced myself of it as truth when we met."

"You know this man?" asked Oona.

"Forgive me." He bowed. "Nalmas Ourin. Lady Kitlyn mended a broken statue at my inn."

"Oh!" Oona relaxed, remembering the story her love shared in a fire-lit sitting room a night or two after their return to the castle. At the time Kitlyn ate chicken in that inn, she would've been in Ralen's dungeon unsure what had happened to her. A twinge of pain encircled her wrists for a fleeting instant. She closed her eyes and thanked Lucen for keeping her safe while roaming a land full of people who wanted her dead.

"Well met, Nalmas Ourin." Oona almost curtseyed but stopped herself, thinking a queen consort probably ought not to curtsey to an innkeeper.

"I hope she is still intact." Kitlyn smiled.

"Aye." Nalmas grinned. "And I'm happy to see you are in good health as well. The peasant act had me fooled."

"Ehh." She sighed. "It wasn't really an act at the time. I grew up thinking myself an orphan and servant with no station."

"Her own father wouldn't even speak to her," added Piper. "They treated her *so* cruelly… yet they thought w—the people of Evermoor to be savages."

Nalmas shook his head. "Much ill came of that war. Glad it's over, and we've you two to thank for it. Not that I expect you'll ever find yer way ta Dorwick again, but if ye do, I'd be glad to prove ya a proper meal."

"If the chance arises, I'd enjoy that." Kitlyn smiled.

Nalmas bowed at them both and excused himself to wander among the partygoers.

"I find it most... fascinating that ordinary citizens simply walk into the king's court and freely approach the royals." Oona stood on her toes to peer over people at Ralen chatting with a number of... possibly merchants.

"Things are different here," said Kitlyn.

Oona glanced at an approaching figure, which turned out to be Gerya, one of the spiritcallers, and hastily looked away. "Evidently."

Kitlyn giggled.

"How is it you are not mortified at watching them traipse about so?" whispered Oona.

She shrugged. "It is how they are. I think Lucernia worries too much about a person's outside and too little about the inside."

"Oh, shall we fling off our dresses then?" asked Oona in a whisper, blushing harder.

Piper snickered while Meredith nearly fainted.

"I think that would be a grand idea," said Kitlyn.

Oona's jaw hung open.

Piper stared at her with an expression of 'you're not serious,' but also a hint of amusement.

Kitlyn winked. "But not right this moment."

Meredith fanned herself.

For the next hour or so, they mingled with dozens of people who all wished to see them in person and thank them for saving Evermoor. A few even apologized for wishing ill on her due to the misinterpretation of the foretelling.

Eventually, Ralen reemerged from the crowd and walked up to them. "Ahh, there you are. My mother tells me the two of you are quite tired and eager to retire for the night."

Oona blinked and glanced at Kitlyn. She didn't appear *that* tired, though Oona couldn't deny wanting to crawl into bed. Between riding in a coach for most of the day, the negotiation process, and the sudden, unexpected party late into the night, she might not even have the energy to do much more than sleep once they arrived in a bedchamber.

"How?" asked Kitlyn.

Ralen chuckled. "My mother knows things... She also knew you would not be a threat to us. Though, I confess to perhaps not fully believing her. Some of what she claims to know does sound rather outlandish at times."

"In this case, your mother is correct. We have had a long ride today." Kitlyn stifled a yawn. "As grateful as I am for the hospitality of this banquet, it is a battle keeping my eyes open."

Oona nodded.

"Come then." Ralen waved his left arm toward a hallway with a beckoning gesture, then headed off.

Oona walked at Kitlyn's side behind him. Piper and Meredith followed close. Ralen led them past a series of turns to a hallway with five large, ornate doors that appeared to be made of thick roots grown into a solid slab of wood. All depicted dryad-like creatures, slender elf-like people only half the height of a man.

"This is our finest guest room." Ralen opened the door and walked into a large chamber with a fireplace and a great green rug that resembled moss. Their trunk had already been brought inside and left at the foot end of the enormous bed. He headed over to a small stone shelf between the bed and fireplace where a fist-sized blue glass orb sat in a thin metal holder. "If you require any sort of assistance, tap this crystal."

"Thank you." Kitlyn yawned.

Prince Ralen indicated a small door to the left of the entrance they'd come through. "That is a connecting passage to an adjoining room your handmaidens may use."

Oona smiled.

"May Carros watch over your rest," said Ralen, before excusing himself and pulling the door shut behind him.

Oona stood there like a dressmaker's dummy while Piper undid her lacing. Kitlyn squirmed and struggled, taking a more animated role in her liberation from the gown she'd spent the entire day in. Once the handmaidens had helped them change into nightdresses, they retired to the smaller attached bedroom.

Neither Kitlyn nor Oona moved for a few minutes, standing in the middle of the frigid room, looking at each other.

"Your toes are numb, aren't they?"

"Yes." Oona yawned.

Kitlyn looked down at her feet. "Mine aren't."

"I'm rather jealous of how you can tolerate such cold stone," said Oona.

"I'm rather jealous of your beautiful blonde hair."

"I'm rather jealous of your striking emerald eyes."

"I'm rather jealous of your perfect face."

Oona's cheeks tinged with a little warmth. "Your nose is cuter than mine."

"I disagree."

So far, every night since they'd been wed, *things* had happened. Oona grinned at the thought, but could barely summon the energy to walk the few paces to the bed despite her toes feeling frozen to the stone floor.

Kitlyn looked over at her, her expression clearly saying 'snuggle.'

Oona nodded, sharing the feeling.

They slithered in under a thick comforter and cuddled together. Though the mattress had a few lumps unlike any bed she'd slept in before, it practically swallowed her. Between the depth of it, the thickness of the bedclothes above her, and having Kitlyn's arms around her, she likely wouldn't have even tried to get out of bed at that moment even if the castle caught fire.

Oona basked in the warmth, still unsure how to cope with not having a dreadful worry to keep her awake at night. She barely considered it strange to feel so content and safe before her thoughts spiraled into a dream of elves.

THE OTHER SIDE

KITLYN

The next morning, after a breakfast of fragrant sweetbreads and jellies, Kitlyn and Oona accompanied Prince Ralen on a tour of Ivendar. They stopped at the Stoneshapers' Guild, where several elders took interest in her gift, marveling at the amount of power she held. Kitlyn had hoped to avoid mentioning Omun, but evidently they had received word of him already.

Forty-foot-tall stone giants didn't exactly do subtle well.

Upon learning that Kitlyn had essentially called out to the stone in a moment of complete terror and had not performed a deliberate and complex ritual to summon him, the elders all paled. Evidently, they believed that such a feat of magic required great preparation and many hours spent communing with the earth. Kitlyn suggested that she *had* spent many hours communing with the earth, though not all at once. Whenever she had summoned rocks to amuse Pim, or manipulated walls to take a shortcut across the castle grounds or moat, she had always felt in touch with something greater. She hadn't realized what until the stone spoke to her while she'd been confined in a cell beneath Castle Cimril.

This revelation alarmed them somewhat as it appeared to prove she did have the power necessary to have destroyed Evermoor. The more they spoke of her magic, the more she tried to change the subject, feeling guilty that Oona stood there so dutifully smiling, worrying she may have felt overshadowed at all the people fawning over her.

As soon as they left the guild, Kitlyn whispered apologies.

Oona simply hugged her and giggled. "You looked *so* uncomfortable."

"I was," muttered Kitlyn.

Ralen chuckled. "The stoneshapers are an interesting lot. They rather pride themselves on their power, and struggle to accept what you have accomplished without any formal training."

"Nalmas seemed to think a stoneshaper would charge more to repair that statue than it would be worth to replace it," said Kitlyn.

"Perhaps a mild exaggeration... though they do ask a fairly high rate for their services, unless they are necessary."

"Is there some other way to mend a cracked statue?" asked Oona.

Ralen glanced back with a smile. "I meant that in the sense of bridges or fortifications as opposed to decorative statues. In service of Evermoor or its people, they do not take fees."

"Ahh." Kitlyn smiled, feeling a bit more respect for them.

The tour brought them briefly by the firecaller's hall, then the rootcallers' grove. She wondered how many of them had created bridges at the Churning Deep to allow raiding parties across during the war. Though, she had come to understand those 'raiding parties' had been attempting to locate the Eldritch Heart and had not, in fact, been sent in to randomly attack villages as everyone in Lucernia claimed.

From there, they visited the king's garrison and reviewed whatever troops happened to be out and about at the time, along with a contagiously happy older general far better suited to be in charge of an orphanage than a military force. He also appeared to have suffered several strong blows to the head at some point in the past as he continually mistook Kitlyn and Oona for some young cousins of Ralen or nobles' daughters he'd been tasked with entertaining. Ralen reminded him no less than fourteen times that he spoke with the Queen of Lucernia and her wife, but the man continued to exist in his own reality.

After lunch, they returned to the enormous tree-slab table to finish the reparation negotiations with King Volduin. Fortunately, the spiritcallers had decided to wear robes that despite being airy and close to see-through, covered them enough that Oona didn't spend the entire time with pink cheeks.

It seemed that his wives had soothed his temper toward Aodh Talomir, and he accepted terms close to the ones Beredwyn had suggested as a starting point. Having expected another contentious session, Kitlyn exhaled with relief and nearly flopped over the table as all the tension left her body.

Once the treaty had been signed by all, Kitlyn and Oona spent the afternoon wandering the gardens together enjoying a little privacy amid the overabundance of nature. After dinner, more people came into the castle courtyard for another long night of conversation and casual drinking.

That night, they used the bed for a little more than sleeping.

Two days later, Kitlyn climbed back into the coach, eager to return home to Castle Cimril.

The reparation negotiations had taken far less time than she had expected. In truth, she'd gone into Evermoor with more than a little dread, half expecting the king to treat her either like the ruler of a conquered nation or a child. At least a little part of her worried she might have been traveling to her demise. Though, in hindsight, that struck her as foolish. She had, after all, sided with Evermoor against her own father and prevented the ruination of their land.

Her thoughts returned to the stoneshapers gasping about her 'untamed' power. She dwelled on that comment until the coach neared a fork in the road, with a sign pointing at the rightward offshoot labeled 'Ilde Brae.'

Kitlyn stood and stuck her head out the window. "Driver, please stop for a moment."

"Aye, your highness."

The coach slowed.

"What are you doing?" Oona blinked, her expression a mix of curiosity and worry.

Kitlyn peered back into the coach, grinning. "Keeping a promise."

Lieutenant Gann, the highest ranking soldier among the escort, rode up beside the coach and glanced in the window. "Highness? You requested a stop?"

"I did. I wish to take a detour on the way back home. We should be safe enough if your men would prefer to return home sooner."

"Nonsense, your highness." Lieutenant Gann sat taller in his saddle. "Nothing would make us happier than to see you safely back to the castle, no matter the time it takes."

"Very well. I shall not be long. Please send word back to the castle that our trip will extend by several days so they do not become alarmed."

Lieutenant Gann nodded at her, then whistled. A boy a year or so younger than Kitlyn rode up on a light horse with no barding.

While the lieutenant relayed the message to the fast rider, Kitlyn stretched farther out of the coach window and looked up at the driver to the right. "Make way to the village of Ilde Brae, up the road to the right. When we are there, I shall point the way to go beyond."

"As you wish, highness."

The boy took off riding down the road to the left while the coach, the soldiers, and the wagon of supplies headed north.

"What *are* we doing?" Oona tugged on her arm.

Kitlyn jumped back into the seat beside her. "We're already here. I think you should meet Kethaba."

Oona blinked at her, biting her lip.

"I know. I know." Kitlyn patted her on the knee. "It's far more rustic than you're used to. But trust me. You'll love it."

"All right." Oona leaned against her. "I trust you."

UPON REACHING ILDE BRAE, KITLYN CLIMBED UP TO SIT BESIDE THE driver and pointed the way into the woods, further northwest. By early evening, they arrived at the cluster of small homes where Kethaba lived. It remained unclear as to whether it counted as a separate smaller village or part of the town.

She guided the coach to a small clearing within a minute's walk of the village center and directed the lieutenant to have his men set up camp here. That done, she jumped down, waited for Oona, and walked off into the trees, leading her by the hand. Lieutenant Gann hurriedly sent two soldiers along with them. Kitlyn sighed to herself, but didn't protest.

Oona emitted soft noises of irritation as they navigated the woods. "We are not dressed for this."

"I was hoping to remedy that soon." Kitlyn smiled up at a passing bird. "I did bring along some simple dresses."

"Is *this* why you packed those things? I was wondering."

"Indeed."

She emerged from the trees onto a footpath that led to an open dirt clearing around a well in sight of Kethaba's house. The shouts of playing children echoed from the distance, likely near the river.

Kitlyn approached the door, finding it odd this place felt so much like a second home despite her brief stay, and knocked.

A moment or two later, the door opened to reveal Kethaba—looking so much like a storybook witch that Oona failed to fully muffle an *eep* of surprise. Both soldiers also leaned back, near to jumping. Piper smiled at the old woman while Meredith offered a nod of greeting.

"Child..." Wrinkles around Kethaba's eyes deepened with a grand smile. "What a wonderful surprise."

She stepped out and hugged Kitlyn before regarding Oona with a warm glance. "This must be the one you had been so eager to find."

"Yes. This is Oona."

"I sense change in you," said Kethaba.

"That's one way to put it. My father has passed on. I've become queen."

"Pff, that's not what I mean." Kethaba tapped a hard, gnarled finger on Kitlyn's crown twice. "Any fool with eyes could've seen that. I think you left here a frightened girl and have returned a bit closer to a woman."

Oona blushed.

Kethaba cackled. "That is not what I meant either, girl. Though I can feel the love between you." She squished them together in a hug, the fragrance of clove and spices in her shawl bringing tears to Kitlyn's eyes. "There is strength in her that she had only begun to search for the last time we spoke. Come inside."

Soon, they all sat around Kethaba's modest table having tea and small sweetbreads. Piper looked completely at ease, as if once more in surroundings she found natural. Meredith eyed the room and its décor with a note of wariness, but didn't hesitate at taking a seat. Both soldiers sat so stiffly and pale that Kitlyn figured they expected the old one to throw them in her oven at any moment. She found it amusing, though Oona's nervousness bothered her. She scooted her chair closer and held her love's hand while telling Kethaba about everything that happened after she'd left down the river in her root boat.

Piper went wide-eyed listening to the story as if she'd completely forgotten about being a handmaiden. Meredith also, despite being a year into her twenties, leaned forward in her seat and gasped repeatedly during the tale of Kitlyn's swordfight with the soldiers at Ralen's keep.

At the mention of Omun, Kethaba beamed like a proud grandmother whose grandchild had accomplished something amazing. Kitlyn switched topics and told Oona of waking up in 'that bed right over there' with not a stitch of clothing on. Her description of being unsure if she'd been captured or rescued got Kethaba chuckling.

Alin, Kethaba's seven-year-old grandson, walked in yawning. He stopped short, staring in confusion at there being more than his grandmother in the room. Upon recognizing Kitlyn, he ran over and leapt into a hug.

"Well, hello to you as well," chirped Kitlyn.

He sat back in her lap grinning. "Thank you for stoppin' the war. I'm glad people aren't fighting anymore. I'm not upset with you 'cause my parents had ta go to the Glimmering Vale."

Oona covered her mouth and gasped. Redness appeared around her eyes in seconds. "Oh, no... I'm so sorry."

Kethaba refilled Oona's tea. "Why do Lucernians insist on apologizing for things beyond their control? You are no more at fault for this war than Alin would be were I to stick one of those strapping young lads with this table knife."

Both soldiers twitched.

"Aye. I understand that in a logical sense, but I feel as if I... we could have stopped it sooner had we only known the truth. Even years ago." Oona sighed at her lap. "Even as a child, I could have insisted he return the Heart."

"Somehow, I doubt that..." Kitlyn frowned. "I had to threaten to bring down the entire castle before he relented. I do not believe that guilt or wide, pleading eyes would have swayed that man from that particular course."

Oona plucked Alin from Kitlyn's lap and hugged him. "I am speechless at the deceit. You are adorable. To think of the lies he spread of Evermoor and her people. It is an affront to Lucen."

"You're pretty," said Alin.

Kitlyn laughed at the silly face Oona made at the boy in response.

"I do hope you are at least planning to spend the night." Kethaba sipped her tea. "It is much too late in the day for travel."

"Of course." Kitlyn smiled. "Though I do not intend to be a burden.

I've a small entourage along this time, but they shall take their meals in Ilde Brae."

"Nonsense." Kethaba waved dismissively. "I've a big cauldron. Plenty of room for soldiers."

The men fidgeted, eyeing it.

"But I cannot impose upon your provisions for twenty-four men." Kitlyn glanced at them. "She means cooking *for* soldiers. Not cooking soldiers."

Kethaba wagged her eyebrows at them, then glanced around the room. "Perhaps they will need to sleep in their tents as I lack the space for so many, but feeding them is not an issue." She winked. "Now, you two look woefully uncomfortable. Why don't you relax and let me start on supper."

Kethaba didn't wait for an answer, instead hurrying over to the enormous cauldron and nearby pantry.

Oona looked at Kitlyn.

Kitlyn shrugged, then stood. "May as well."

She sent the two soldiers away to bring word to the nearby camp the rest of her entourage set up that food would be provided soon. After they left, she started to head outside to retrieve the simple dresses she'd brought along but Piper insisted on doing that for her. When the girl returned with them, Kitlyn went into the alcove with the beds and waved Meredith over to help her out of the gown she had on.

Oona gasped and rushed over. "What are you doing?"

"What does it look like I am doing?"

"But… this house is one large room."

Kitlyn smiled. "Your powers of observation are surpassed only by your beauty. Kethaba is like family."

Piper crept up behind Oona, reaching for her dress' lacing.

"But." Oona stood stiffly.

"Highness?" asked Meredith.

"I wish to be comfortable. Consider Kethaba to be my grandmother."

Meredith nodded, and proceeded to help her change.

With no small amount of blushing, Oona relented and also swapped gowns. Soon, Kitlyn wore only a simple dress, and drew gasps from both Oona and Meredith when she hung her crown on a wall peg.

"What?" asked Kitlyn. "I've been wearing it all day and it is somewhat heavy."

Piper giggled.

"But, you're the queen," said Oona in a half whisper. "And that's a crown. And that's a simple wooden peg."

"Indeed. And I am on holiday at the moment. Also, we are not *in* Lucernia nor anywhere I care to brag about my station."

"The crown isn't bragging..." Oona glanced at it. "Is it?"

"I suppose it's how you look at it." Kitlyn stretched, savoring the freedom from the tight gown and all the associated mess she had to wear under it. "Remember when we ran off from the lake?"

Oona smiled down at her plain blue dress, raising and lowering her toes. "It *is* comfortable. But we were not responsible for an entire kingdom at the time."

"Were we not?" Kitlyn winked, gesturing around. "Even if it was one we don't rule."

A sigh of resignation came from Oona. She removed her crown and hung it on the same peg with Kitlyn's. The simple 'travel crowns' didn't really weigh all that much, but she'd grown tired of the weight of metal upon her head.

Kitlyn returned to the table and sat. Piper darted over to Kethaba, offering to help cook. Kethaba appeared to be throwing as much glowing green magic into the cauldron as food. Neither changing in the middle of a one room house nor such 'bright' kitchen practices appeared to faze the girl.

I wonder if she truly misses being here. Kitlyn pondered asking Piper if she would like to stay here with Kethaba. Not that she wanted to be rid of the girl, but she appeared happier than she had in a long while.

A little more than an hour later, the great cauldron held a wonderfully aromatic vegetable soup. The entire entourage paraded through the house, each taking a bowl bigger than their helms as well as a small loaf of bread apiece. Kitlyn blinked in astonishment, wondering where the old one had kept so much bread. She suspected more magic had occurred, but hadn't noticed when it happened.

Kethaba sat at the table with Kitlyn, Oona, Meredith, Piper, and Alin—who had a smaller bowl.

While she ate, Kitlyn's mind roamed back to the stoneshapers and their comments on training. She also thought back to her last time here when Kethaba mentioned she didn't have the time needed to properly teach her. With the threat of war at an end, and both kingdoms relatively stable, she intended to bring up that question in the morning.

A glance across the table at Piper reminded her of something the Tenebrea priestess had said.

"Kethaba?" asked Kitlyn.

"Yes, child?"

"Something has been bothering me."

The old woman gave her a look like she'd announced the sky as blue. "I imagine given all that has happened there are many things bothering you. Which of them bothers you more than the rest?"

"A priestess mentioned that my father had gone to the Banefallow…"

Piper shivered. Alin dropped his spoon into his bowl.

Kethaba rubbed her chin. "And you wish to know how a Lucernian managed to find himself there."

"Yes." Kitlyn nodded. "He is not from Evermoor, nor did he die here."

"Hmm." The elder pondered for the duration of a few mouthfuls of soup. "Well… either the Alderswood took him, something tricked him while he strode the Wanderer's Path, or your Lucen thought he belonged there."

She fidgeted. *I am not sure he is* my *Lucen…* While she had nothing against the gods, she felt more drawn to Evermoor and the Alderswood.

"Why would Lucen send him to a place described in the spirituality of an entirely different pantheon?" Oona paused with a spoonful of soup an inch from her mouth. "Does that mean his affront was so great he was exiled even in death?"

"Better than the Pit," whispered Meredith.

Piper shot her a 'not really' stare.

"If indeed Lucen had a hand in it, perhaps he felt that the most appropriate fate." Kethaba shook her head with a sigh. "The *whys* of some things are not meant for us to think about."

The 'lost orphan' look in Oona's eyes made Kitlyn take her hand.

"Your gods are powerful, child," said Kethaba, "but they do not have total dominion over everything. Nor would they seek to. I suspect they are far too wise."

Oona glanced at her. "What would wisdom have to do with that?"

Kethaba gestured with her full soup spoon at Kitlyn. "Does she attempt to rule without the counsel of advisors?"

"I'm only sixteen," said Kitlyn. "I wouldn't even begin to think I knew enough to make every decision on my own."

"How unlike your father you are." Kethaba smiled. "A fortunate difference."

"Oh." Oona cringed. "There are some who would lose their breaths at the suggestion Lucen, Navissa, Orien, and Tenebrea are *equals* with other beings of power and not their betters..."

"And there are some who would lose their breath at us." Kitlyn took Oona's hand in both of hers, kissing her fingers.

Kethaba clucked her tongue. "There are people in your kingdom who would react more strongly to a wealthy individual wearing too common a garment in public than watching two men kill each other."

Kitlyn's eyebrows went up as she sighed. "We *did* get quite a few stares when we returned from Evermoor."

"I do think a few people actually fainted." Oona grinned.

"You may as well ask, child." Kethaba chuckled. "I can see a question hiding behind your teeth, afraid to come out."

"Before, you said we didn't have the time for you to teach me properly."

"Ahh. Yes. In the morning." Kethaba stood and ambled over to an empty spot of wall by the window. "Alin will share blankets with me tonight. Your helpers can sleep here." She held her arms out, both hands wreathed in dark green light.

A mass of roots grew up from the dirt floor, twisting into an approximation of a bed. Meredith gasped in awe. Piper appeared less shocked, more impressed. Once it ceased growing, the elder gathered blankets from one of the freestanding cabinets and arranged them on the springy roots.

One soldier returned with the empty bowls, which Meredith and Piper hurried off to wash without being asked. Kethaba made casual conversation with Oona and Kitlyn for a while after dinner, then bade them sleep once it became dark as if shooing children off for the night.

They shared the bed on the right, the same one Kitlyn had been in when she first awoke here. Oona prodded at the thick hide suspended between four wooden posts, covered in lush animal furs. She winced a little, but didn't hesitate too long before climbing in. Kitlyn curled up with her under the blanket of stitched pelts. Kethaba and Alin shared the other bed.

For a moment, the soft whispery voice of Piper assuring Meredith it was perfectly normal for families in Evermoor to occasionally share beds broke the silence. Soft creaking of roots followed as the older girl climbed in.

While she adored having Oona so close—the suspended hide dipped in the middle, pressing them together—she had zero inclination to be romantic while Kethaba and Alin lay five feet away... not that she had the opportunity.

Oona fell asleep almost as soon as they settled in.

WHEN IN EVERMOOR

OONA

Oona wandered around outside Kethaba's hut the next morning, adoring the sunlight glinting among the branches and the cool brush of grass at her bare feet. Despite it being autumn, the day brought an unusual amount of warmth. Though well short of summer, the temperature allowed her to be comfortable in a relatively light dress without shoes. A wave of rustling swept over the leaves above, driven by a brief gust in the wind. She took in a deep breath, laced with the scent of fallen leaves, and daydreamed of the fast-approaching winter, when Lady Navissa grew in power with the lengthening night.

She looked forward to the beauty of sparkling snow out on the meadow and the enchanting sight of Cimril under a layer of frost. This year's Moon Festival would likely be an event she'd remember for the rest of her life. To honor the goddess Navissa, families exchanged gifts on the longest night of the year. After dinner, they ventured out into their city, town, or village to give another gift to someone they chose at random on their way to the city center, where everyone gathered for the priestesses to lead a ceremony. When that finished, the celebration began.

For as long as Oona had been alive, the Moon Festival had been a melancholy reminder of all the men and women away from home fighting the war. Seeing the faces of the orphans sitting at the edge of the city square with no family left always made her cry. Perhaps the ceremony this year would still have a degree of somberness for the ones who would never come home again... still, it would be the first time in twenty years anyone in Lucernia had hope during the Moon Festival.

Kitlyn emerged from Kethaba's home and hurried over. "Excuse me, have you seen Queen Oona about? I seem to have misplaced my wife."

Oona turned toward her, one eyebrow up, arms folded, and smirked.

"Oh! There you are!" Kitlyn faked a gasp of surprise. "I almost didn't recognize you without a crown on."

"If you're trying to be funny..." Oona pounced, tickling her. "You're doing it."

Kitlyn laughed, trying to simultaneously dodge and retaliate. After a moment, they stalemated, each holding the other's hands at bay.

"This is... nice. Though I do feel like the advisors would scold us if they saw us running about like peasants."

The smile on Kitlyn's face fell flat.

"No!" Oona hugged her. "I didn't mean it that way. I mean they'd yell at us and get all out of sorts over us in such plain attire, no shoes even. I mean, can you imagine the horror? A queen without shoes? I didn't mean there's anything wrong with peasants."

"I know." Kitlyn rested her head against Oona's shoulder. "Few things are as pure as an honest day's work, yet you saw how everyone treated me before they knew who I was. Why do our citizens place such emphasis on station?"

She looked down, tracing her toes back and forth over the grass. "Beredwyn said that people who own a great deal of things look at those who have less than them, and feel as though it means the gods have given them favor while denying the other person. Even your father could scarcely look the commoners in the eye. I've never felt that way despite the false station I had."

"Obviously." Kitlyn smiled. "You associated with the likes of me, and you visited the orphans all the time because you wanted to visit them, not—like my father—because you wanted to be seen visiting them."

"Ooh!" She fumed, fists balled. "I was so stupid! How could I not have seen that! The king would utterly ignore the lower tier of maidservants... someone of your supposed station he should've pretended didn't even exist. Yet... I am so blind."

"I think we both were fairly blind." Kitlyn leaned in and kissed her. "And you had so much on your mind."

"Yes... I almost don't know what to do with myself that I've nothing to fret about at night anymore."

A pack of about a dozen children zoomed by, all laughing.

Oona spun, inheriting their glee, and watched them scramble down a dirt path toward a wide, slow-moving river at the edge of the village. When they reached the grass near the bank, an explosion of animal hide dresses, pants, and tunics went flying. She gasped, pointing.

"Hmm?" Kitlyn looked over at the kids jumping into the water. "Oh, the current's slow. They'll be fine."

"No, not the river... they're not wearing anything... *outside.*"

"How else should one go swimming?" asked Kitlyn. "In a full gown? Perhaps armor?"

Oona blinked, both confused at her love's utter lack of reaction to such a shocking display of impropriety as well as being embarrassed at herself for swimming with Kitlyn while they'd been around Evie's age, though she'd kept her smallclothes on. "Umm... But they're outside."

"We're not in Lucernia at the moment. People here are much closer to the natural world. It's not a concern of theirs. Remember how I told you when they saved me from drowning, Kethaba expected me to get out of bed and sit at the table to eat without anything on?"

Oona blushed at the thought and blushed harder for picturing it in her mind.

An impish smile crossed Kitlyn's lips. She grasped Oona by the hand and started walking.

"Where are you going?" She eyed the river. "You're not..."

"No, but only because I know you would be too mortified."

"But you're the queen..."

"So are you." Kitlyn raspberried her.

"Queens don't do that either."

Kitlyn laughed. "We are on holiday."

Oona kept quiet, allowing Kitlyn to lead her a few minutes' walk into the forest around the village. Soon, the burble of trickling water reached her ears... bringing back the blush. *She is not serious. She can't be seriously thinking what I think she's thinking.*

"Almost there." Kitlyn glanced back with a wink before squeezing between a pair of close trees.

Oona had to let go of her hand to manage the gap. Her foot sank into a plush carpet of thick emerald green moss surrounding a deep pond nestled in the shadow of a tall, rocky cliff with a face broken into jutting wafers of stone, like stacks of books askew. Water collected in a pond about twenty feet across and fairly deep before flowing off to the right in a small creek. Dense trees mottled with pale greenish lichen provided a natural wall but less than perfect privacy.

"I know you've not been swimming in a long time," said Kitlyn. "Aside from your swan bathtub. But, you don't need to be scared. I'll hold you the whole time."

Oona turned toward her. "You *are* serious?"

"Of course." Kitlyn winked. "When in Evermoor…"

She pulled her dress off over her head. Her rich black hair cascaded free from the fabric falling around her shoulders. Oona's heart raced at the sight. She stared down, caught off guard by the shock of it… then remembered they'd married, and gradually lifted her gaze up over Kitlyn's beautiful legs to her stomach, up past her chest, and locked stares with her.

"It's all right if you don't want to." Kitlyn took her hand. "I've thought so many times about jumping in the lake at our garden, but someone would definitely catch us there."

Oona fidgeted. She rather wanted to do it, but worried it might offend Lucen, or the entire population of Lucernia. *Is this wrong?* "Umm."

"No one here would think twice about us having a moment together in a secluded grove." Kitlyn took her hand.

"You haven't any smallclothes under your dress," stammered Oona, trying to buy more time for Lucen to give her an answer.

"Oh, I must've forgotten them," said Kitlyn, sounding sincere.

"How do you *forget* them?" Oona tilted her head.

"Shoes weren't the only things the other servants stole from my room. I haven't actually *had* smallclothes for about two years. Just the tunics and breeches."

Oona frowned. *No signs. No word. Love is pure.* She closed her eyes, basking in how much she loved Kitlyn. "All right. Since we're in Evermoor, we may as well do as the people here do."

Hands trembling, Oona eased her dress off and clutched it. Standing there in only her bra and smallclothes made her fear at any second an army of gasping, fainting townspeople would appear out of nowhere. After a moment, and no one mocking her, she dropped the dress beside Kitlyn's.

Grinning, Kitlyn stepped into the water. "Ooh. It's a little chilly. But not too bad."

Oona shot a pleading stare up at the sky. *Please tell me if it is wrong to be outside like this?* She waited, listening to the soft rush of wind in the branches. The laughter of swimming children came from the distance for a brief moment, then faded. Oona took it as a nod of approval from Lucen. She also didn't want to hurt Kitlyn's feelings, and her wife did seem rather excited to do this.

Certain her face matched an ivenberry for red, she undid her bra and pushed her smallclothes down. The breeze blowing across the entirety of her without fabric in the way almost scared her straight back into her clothes, but Kitlyn's inviting smile from the water gave her just enough courage to hurry in. Despite the chill, the faster she plunged neck deep, the more covered she would feel. She stepped over slimy moss, slipped and went under, then resurfaced neck deep, dog paddling, her toes an inch or two away from the bottom.

Overwhelmed with embarrassment, Oona broke into nervous giggles, her teeth chattering.

Kitlyn glided over to embrace her, also giggling. They shared a moment of pure innocence, laughing and splashing at each other like children. After a while, the impropriety of it in Oona's mind gave way to the thrill of doing something that would make the average Lucernian gasp. Of course, the castle halls had been filled with stories of the rather salacious doings of nobles for centuries.

Yes, but their scandals all occurred behind closed doors. Not out in the forest. Oona blinked. *Wait... no. Lady Harrington supposedly brought a suitor into her garden at night.* She bit her lip. Clearly, King Volduin's spiritcallers had an interesting relationship with clothing. Maybe no one in Evermoor *would* care about a royal in such a compromising position.

Once the nervous giggling finally stopped, Oona brushed a hand over Kitlyn's cheek. "My heart is about to burst from my chest. I'm as excited as I am terrified. It doesn't matter. I love you so much."

"Oona, there is nothing I wouldn't do for you. My oldest and dearest memories are all with you. I love you with all my heart." She glided closer, pushing Oona with her until they sat on a stone shelf at the edge of the pond near the tall cliff face. A cascading waterfall spilled over the jutting rocky slabs, pouring into the pond in multiple separate streams around them, creating a curtain of shimmering light and mist.

Kitlyn plucked a tiny white flower from the wall and tucked it behind Oona's ear.

Rich green leaves, dark grey stone, the burble of water lapping at the rocks, the squish of moss at her bare skin and the warmth of Kitlyn pressed against her... Oona ceased caring if anyone found them and wished this moment would never end.

She threaded her arms around Kitlyn's slippery body, and kissed her.

12

THE GIFT OF ALDERSWOOD

KITLYN

The entire time they ate lunch, Kitlyn kept grinning across the table at Oona.

Neither Piper nor Meredith suspected what they had snuck off to do, though Kethaba wore a knowing smile. Oona's cheeks remained bright red, though she no longer seemed embarrassed as much as still basked in the afterglow of the hour or so they'd spent 'swimming.'

After the meal, Kitlyn pulled Piper aside, bringing her into the bed alcove for a quiet place to talk.

"Is something the matter, highness?" Piper clasped her hands in front of herself, seeming worried.

"No." Kitlyn smiled. "I couldn't help but notice how happy you seem here, and wanted you to know that if you should desire to stay here, I would not object. And, no, I'm not trying to be rid of you. I've grown rather fond of your friendship."

"I understand." Piper smiled. "And it's nice to see things I remember, but there's nothing left in Evermoor for me. Being here also makes me think of my parents. For every smile you see, there's two moments of sadness. Though, I *do* miss jumping in the lake whenever the whim strikes. But I am no small girl anymore."

Kitlyn nodded, relieved. "I'm glad you prefer to stay with us. But I needed you to know you are not required to."

"You are too kind to be a Lucernian royal." Piper bit her lower lip. "I hope they do not see that as weakness."

"Well, if the people no longer want me, I could be just as happy here with Oona living in a hut."

"You'd give up your crown?" Piper blinked.

"I would not impose myself upon a people who did not want me as their matriarch. Something my father never understood is that being king or queen is a responsibility, not an entitlement."

Piper looked around, pretending to check for eavesdroppers, then whispered, "Perhaps you really *are* from Evermoor."

Kitlyn laughed—as did Piper.

"How long will we be staying here?"

"Another day perhaps at most. It depends on what Kethaba has to tell me."

Piper nodded.

Kitlyn went outside to meet the old one, who stood in the shade of an enormous, gnarled tree by the river-facing side of her house.

"All right, child. Let us have a look at you then." Kethaba rubbed a finger back and forth across her chin, her right eye wide, left narrowed. "Hmm. You have reached deep inside yourself more than I had expected you to be able to so soon."

"That's something like what the stoneshapers said. I wound up in a rather frightening position, dangling on a vine over a room full of Nimse."

"Indeed." Kethaba lowered her arm, smiling. "Experiences like that can do wonders for one's training. You have come to know that your magic draws on the power of the Alderswood. The great tree is the focal point where our magical energy crosses into our world."

"Yes. The tree... sometimes it feels as though it talks to me." She tilted her head. "But not with words. Is... King Volduin older than he appears? Ralen said that he had changed, almost mad, with the Heart missing."

"It has been a while since I traveled to Ivendar, so I do not know what he looks like now." Kethaba's eyes sparkled as she no doubt pictured him. "However, you are correct. The king's life essence is intricately woven into the great tree. It is the same with all spiritcallers. Now, let me see you open that gate."

Kitlyn widened her stance and concentrated on her magic, envisioning the way she had poured energy out when creating a maelstrom of flying stones in Castle Cimril. Only, she didn't beckon any stones, merely pushed and pulled at the mystical forces. Thin serpents of brilliant green fire coiled around her arms, darting back and forth across her chest.

"Your power comes from the tree, drawn up from the earth. Your contact with it strengthens you."

"Is that why I feel strange whenever I have shoes on?" She tossed one of the energy streams back and forth between her hands.

Kethaba nodded. "Your power comes from the earth. Shoes or boots do not block it, though they do weaken it. Though, bracing your hand on a tree or earthen wall would have a similar effect. However"—she tugged her skirt up enough to show off her bare feet—"this is far easier."

Kitlyn grinned. "Is it also why I don't really feel cold? Oona's toes go numb right away."

"Yes. We can draw upon the natural energies, attuning ourselves to the elements." She spent a few minutes demonstrating how to focus on earth magic to provide warmth or shed heat.

"Oh. I didn't realize it was so simple. I think I have been doing that already." She explained about the castle servants stealing her shoes all the time, and never bothering to make a big deal of it... nor feeling chilly in the castle during winter despite the thin tunic and breeches she'd worn at the time.

"Our magic is not the same as your priests who study for years and years to learn how to light a small candle." Kethaba chuckled. "It is as natural as walking."

For the next two-ish hours, Kethaba stood beside her, showing her how to fully open her connection to the Alderswood and to the Stone. While the old one could also call upon fire or air if need be, Kitlyn's attempts to reach for flames or create even a small breeze met with little success.

"Your connection to the Stone is remarkably strong," said Kethaba. "It may be that you will never speak to the fire or the wind."

Alderswood gave me what I needed. She thought of calling Omun, and smiled. *I can hardly complain about not being able to light a fireplace with the snap of my fingers.* "I'm grateful to have what I have been given." Kitlyn glanced at a ten-foot-tall stone obelisk she'd raised from the ground, and willed it to return from whence it had erupted. A faint tremor shook the earth until it disappeared from sight.

"Your rootcaller abilities could use some practice." Kethaba flashed a faint smile. "Let us work on that for a while."

Kitlyn followed her to the riverbank and spent the next several hours summoning and bending roots and vines. With the elder's guidance—and no distracting need to worry about Oona's safety—she felt out a subtle difference in the magic. Where touching the Stone raged within her body like a thundering river, the vine magic brushed her skin with the delicate caress of meadow grass. Shaping stone gave her the sense of commanding a primal force that moved however she directed it, while root magic almost felt like she whispered to something alive and asked it to come closer, curling around her hand.

As the sun began to show signs of setting, Kitlyn sat back on her heels and admired the nearly life-sized 'statue' of Oona she had grown. It almost even resembled her.

"A talented learner such as yourself will do well by your people." Kethaba patted her back.

Kitlyn picked at a bit of leaf forming the statue's gown. "I don't think I'm ready to be queen, but the gods seem to. I've not told anyone else this, but..." She looked up, meeting the elder's gaze. "Aside from Oona and Beredwyn, I don't have any family. It's difficult to explain but you feel like—"

"I am." Kethaba smiled. "Did you forget what I said last time? By leading you back from the Wanderer's Path, I have become your family."

Is that why I feel so much like she's my grandmother? Or maybe it's the energy from the Heart that my mother drank... Kethaba must be connected to the Alderswood like King Volduin. I bet she's older than she appears... and she appears rather old. "I'm afraid of being queen. Too young. Too common. Too full of magic from some place other than the gods. Too... abnormal."

Kethaba put an arm around her. "Well, your father ascended to the throne as a boy and look where that got him." She suppressed a cackle. "However, you may be young yet, but you are much stronger of spirit. I won't tell you that you face an easy path. Being a leader is not for the faint of heart."

"What if the people don't trust me? Or what if they hate me for loving Oona? Tenebrea herself *appeared* and smiled at us, and yet some still look at us like we're evil."

"You already know the wants of gods can be overlooked when the wants of men are different. Lucernians are nothing if not rigid. You could sooner bend the side of a mountain than some of them."

Kitlyn flashed a crooked smile.

"Well, I suppose *you* could bend the side of a mountain... given enough time." Kethaba chuckled. "Magic aside. You are a strong, dedicated, and brave young woman. I have met very few people so full of empathy and love as you."

"Oona's much sweeter," said Kitlyn. "I am quicker to anger."

"That's your father talking." Kethaba winked. "Yes, some decisions you will have to make in years to come will be difficult. Follow your heart"—she tapped Kitlyn twice over the heart with one finger, setting off a ripple of warmth and rings of green light—"and you will do well for your people."

Kitlyn hugged her, feeling as though she had a mother to comfort her for the first time in her life. She shed a few tears of happiness, then sat back on her heels again, wiping her face. "Thank you."

"Dare I suggest that after what you went through to put a stop to that war, most everything else you shall face will be minor... except arguing with merchants over taxes. You'll likely prefer to fight another twenty-year war than suffer that discussion."

"Is it wrong of me that I sometimes wish to forget about being a queen or having to lead people or even being an adult? I don't mean run away, just take a day or two and escape."

"Not at all. Your father's biggest flaw was that he never allowed himself any time to simply *be*." She winked. "Even an old bat like me knows that sometimes... you just need to fling your clothes off and jump in the river."

Kitlyn laughed.

The old one held up a finger. "While it is often figurative, take that literally as well. The whisper of nature and the world around you is often the most insightful teacher."

She nodded.

"Come then." Kethaba stood with a grunt. "I imagine everyone is becoming rather hungry."

Kitlyn followed her back to the hut, feeling a bit like an ordinary young girl in some tiny village no one cared about sharing a day with her grandmother. For at least the next few hours, her crown, and all the burdens that came with it, would hang on that peg.

13

OF GODS AND DECEIT

OONA

Oona found herself alone in Kethaba's home, trying to understand how she'd gone from pampered princess to staring at her toes leaving marks in the dirt floor of a hut somewhere in Evermoor. She didn't so much mind her common dress, bare feet, or the lack of luxury around her as much as it befuddled her that she didn't mind it. Kitlyn had gone off to learn magic from the old woman and Piper wanted to show Meredith around. Fifteen minutes of silence sitting in someone else's house alone managed to convince Oona to explore the village as well.

Not since she'd foolishly run off into the woods had she spent so long wearing such a simple garment. Except for being noticeably paler than most everyone here, no one would have the slightest idea they looked at the Queen Consort of Lucernia. People back home would never believe she'd spent two days wandering a rustic village like any other peasant girl. She grinned to herself, thinking her present attire and surroundings came close to what her life might have been like had King Talomir not taken her from her home.

"Well, not exactly," she whispered to no one in particular. "I'd be much more used to rather arduous work. Feeding chickens, milking cows, harvesting crops…"

Of course, had she not been whisked off to Castle Cimril, she never would have met Kitlyn, so she didn't have any real regrets. In fact, when she thought about her mother, Ruby, and that woman's reaction to her daughter being in love with another girl, she felt rather lucky to have escaped. A momentary waking nightmare of Ruby catching her kissing another girl out in the barn and losing her mind nearly made her cry.

I wonder if word of our wedding has reached her, wherever she's scurried off to. Does that woman miss Evie at all? After several weeks looking after her little sister, she'd grown sorely attached, and dreaded the thought Ruby may change her mind and come back for her.

She navigated a cluster of roaming chickens and made her way into the heart of the village. Kethaba's hut stood at the outskirts. The rest of it, perhaps thirty small roundish acorn-shaped homes much like the old woman's, dotted the woods. About a third of them clustered together at a 'village square' around a larger hall.

The people mostly welcomed her with smiles, though a few regarded her with suspicion or something else. She sensed they had lost family during the war, so accepted their chilly stares. It didn't take too long for her to attract a crowd of local children, curious about a newcomer with such long blonde hair and a little army of soldiers all her own. They ranged in age from five or so up to eleven, all in basic garments of flax or animal hide. That some of the girls wore only skirts and most of the boys had long wild hair reminded her she no longer trod upon Lucernian soil.

This, of course, made her think of the spiritcallers.

Things are so very different here. It's almost… freeing. They don't care that I'm wearing a drab thing and no crown. Everyone here all seems so happy…

The children peppered her with questions about Lucernia and also wanted to hear how she 'healed the tree.' Oona plopped down in the grass and sat with them, whiling away an hour or two telling stories. One small boy thought people from Lucernia were made from metal. She explained plate armor and how some important soldiers covered themselves with it for protection.

A young black-haired girl of around nine scratched at a smudge of dirt on her chest. "The old king was mean to want to kill everyone in Evermoor. Even us kids."

Oona's heart nearly broke. "He… well, I don't think he *wanted* everyone to die as much as thought he could make himself powerful, and didn't care what happened."

"That's even worse." The girl looked down. "Not to care."

"Did you kill him?" asked a boy a year or so older than the girl.

Light brown, nearly blond, hair hung in an unruly tangle over half his face.

"No. He... When people do things that are really bad, the gods—and the spirits of Evermoor as well—make sure they answer for it." Oona let out a slow sigh.

"Why did they say you wanted ta hurt us all?" A smaller boy, perhaps six, tilted his head at her.

"Because they were confused." Oona patted him on the head. "Everyone was angry and scared, and they deserved to be. After the seers came up with a foretelling, peoples' emotions made them all take it in the worst possible way."

"What?" The black-haired girl stopped fidgeting with a wooden amulet and made eye contact.

Oona thought for a moment. "Let's imagine there is a girl and a boy who know each other. A seer says that someday this girl will make the boy cry. How do you think she would do this?"

"Kick 'im in the berries," yelled a boy.

"Tell him she hates him," said another brown-haired girl.

The black-haired girl let the amulet drop against her chest. "Go away and live somewhere else so he can't see her anymore."

"Punch him in the nose," said a redhead boy about seven.

"Well." Oona smiled around at the kids. "You could all be correct."

"How?" The black-haired girl blinked. "We said different things."

"Exactly. There are many ways to make boys cry. What if the boy really liked her? If she stops talking to him or goes away or even dies... he would be sad. If he hates her, merely following him around and pestering him might make him cry. Of course, if she hit him, he'd probably cry, too. There's too many ways she could make him cry, and for every one of them, what the foretelling said would still be true."

About two-thirds of the kids got an 'oh, I get it' look in their eyes, including the black-haired girl.

"So, when the old men huffed up a bunch of dreamstem and said the king's heir would end the war... people who were angry and frightened let that convince them we would do something horrible."

Oona spent a little while telling them about how she had lain awake in bed so many nights dreading the foretelling because she couldn't bear the thought of destroying an entire kingdom despite all the lies she had been told of the people here. Soon, the kids asked her for a happier story. Not having brought any books along, she did her best to remember one. She wound up half remembering, half making up a tale about a talking cat and his friend the talking mouse trying to protect some chickens from a crafty fox.

The occasional rumble of moving stone or crackle of shifting roots came from off to the west, likely from Kitlyn practicing her magic. Eventually, the children thanked her for the story and ran off to their homes in search of a mid-day meal.

Feeling a little peckish herself, Oona stood and made her way back toward Kethaba's hut. At a glint of metal in the distant trees, she changed course and visited the encampment where the soldiers, coachmen, and staff had set up tents. While none complained, she had a strong feeling they all had an eagerness to return to Cimril. She found the village pleasant, peaceful, and a welcome respite from the demands of royalty, though also looked forward to going home. A few soldiers regarded her with shocked expressions, no doubt at her being dressed like a rustic villager.

Satisfied her people appeared in good health and spirit, she cut through the woods in a straight line for the old woman's dwelling. Upon reaching a quiet spot in the trees between the camp and Kethaba's home, Oona paused to look around. Voices drifted in from here and there along with the occasional laugh of a child.

Other than being a bit on the primitive side, the people here were nothing at all like the savages described in the stories she'd been told her entire life. Certainly, the average person from Lucernia would be horrified at people, especially women, walking around half dressed. It would be easy to misconstrue their simple lack of preoccupation with propriety for something dark like cavorting with demons. Many Lucen priests assumed an association between sexual desire or sexuality in general with demons. And of course, they equated too-revealing dress as something sexual, hence demonic. She frowned.

Those spiritcallers weren't at all doing anything inappropriate, merely not covering their breasts. Then again, the citizens in the large city of Ivendar rather reminded her of people in Lucernia: fine attire, houses, wagons. The villagers out here in the forest had a much more casual attitude about clothing. *No one is used to it back home. Forbidden fruits are always more tempting than the basket of apples set out on the table for all to see.*

Oona blushed at the thought of forbidden fruit. She wondered if ever the day would come when she and Kitlyn could enjoy each other's bodies without feeling as though someone would kick in the door at any second and scold them for doing something wrong. *Is that normal? If Lucen had made me different and I fancied a boy, would I feel the same way?* She pondered that for a while and came to the conclusion that she would. Never before in her life had anyone ever spoken with her about carnal pleasures. The subject simply was *not* discussed in Lucernia. At least, not in any place a proper lady would be. Some citizens married at sixteen, though not all. Almost everyone who intended to marry wound up wed by at least nineteen. Lucernians in their twenties without a bride or groom often drew ridicule. Of course, with all the dead from the war, the priests would be encouraging everyone to have babies. She found amusement in the thought that men who'd spent their lives equating sex with evil would be advising people to have more of it.

However, the average citizen probably never heard much talk of 'bedroom activities' at all until they found themselves staring confusedly at their new spouse on their wedding night. Of course, they also didn't have an entire castle worth of people watching their every move either. Fair bet commoners her age knew a lot more about that topic than she did.

Three small boys ran by in the forest on their way to the river. Their joyous laughter lifted Oona's spirits and made her grin... then brought an overwhelming crash of guilt.

She lowered herself to kneel and bowed her head.

"Lord Lucen, please forgive me for believing the lies about the people of Evermoor. Thank you for revealing the truth." She paused in case an answer might come, though only the wind rustling the trees replied. "Lady Tenebrea, I am eternally grateful for your show of acceptance. You are the reason our kingdom hasn't torn itself apart. Please grant me the poise and strength to withstand what the future may bring. I wish only to do what is best for our people, whether or not I bear the weight of this accursed crown or live a simple life with Kitlyn."

A disconcerting thought came out of nowhere and set her hands shaking. She hadn't considered it at all given the chaos of late, but at thinking of the crown as cursed, she recalled the words of her tutors going over the royalty of Lucernia. King Talomir had ascended to the throne at the age of eleven after his parents, Queen Glema and King Eoim died together when a snapped wheel sent their coach plummeting off the Arch of the Ancients, leaving then-eleven-year-old Aodh as king. He had spent the remainder of his childhood at the temple of Lucen.

Before Eoim and Glema, King Iastor and Queen Moeth had ruled.

Iastor had fallen ill and died soon after the birth of Eoim, leaving Moeth on the throne with three small children. She'd lasted only six years before an unexplained illness claimed her life in the night. Their eldest son, Branok, who'd been seventeen, fell from a horse and broke his neck within a week of ascending to the throne. The daughter, Avalina, refused the crown, allowing Eoim—Aodh's father—to become king.

Of the past royals, only Avalina had lived beyond forty years of age, surviving well into her eighties as a mostly-forgotten noble before Tenebrea took her peacefully in her sleep.

Oona shivered with dread at the thought Kitlyn might come to harm purely for being the ruler of Lucernia. Could inexplicably bad fortune of that magnitude have come from their displeasing Lucen? Surely, he would only have permitted such a series of catastrophes for a good reason. Perhaps the others had craved power too much, like her not-father.

Forgetting her desire for food, Oona prayed for a while, beseeching Lucen to watch over Kitlyn and echoing her love's statement that she didn't really *want* to be queen so much as agreed to because the people needed her. Whatever Lucen wished, she would do if that meant abdicating the throne or keeping it… as long as they would be together.

"… and if Kitlyn is to leave this world, please allow us to remain together even in the next one."

When Oona looked up and opened her eyes, she found herself kneeling in a stone-floored chamber amid old, dusty bookshelves awash with cobwebs. A vaulted ceiling overhead had the look of purposeful construction rather than a cave, though solid stone and no windows suggested her surroundings existed underground.

Only the cool softness of dirt at her knees—still forested ground—prevented her from panicking. She hadn't been transported elsewhere, but rather experienced a vision of sorts. Trusting Lucen, she calmed herself and looked around.

The scratching of soft footsteps came from beyond the labyrinthine bookshelves. Oona tried to stand so she could walk closer, but her body wouldn't move. Still, the urge to do so caused her view to glide forward like a flying faerie. Dust so thick it had congealed into a substance like pale grey felt shrouded books, some as thick as her leg. Spiders the size of hens' eggs lay in wait for whatever unfortunate insect stumbled by.

Oona peered around the massive bookshelf at an aisle between many others. A figure in a black hooded cloak stood six shelves away with its back turned. By size and overall shape, she assumed a man. By his somewhat hunched-forward posture, she guessed an *old* man.

Does Lucen reveal the past? Is this a former king of Lucernia? Wide eyed and hoping Lucen might be showing her the reason for the seeming curse that affected the royals of her kingdom, she floated along behind him, trying to get a view of his face.

No matter how hard she wanted to 'fly' faster, her vision kept a steady pace behind the figure. He shambled past rows of bookcases to a door at the end of the vast library. Another windowless hall bereft of torches or any source of light led on for some minutes before he reached out for the knob of an ancient wooden door covered in scratches and gouges from numerous claws or swords.

A skeletal hand, still with fragments of flesh and sinew attached, gripped the handle. Oona tried to gasp, but couldn't make a sound. The man glanced back over his shoulder as if worried about being followed. Beneath the voluminous hood lurked a face of dried bone coated in the same dust that shrouded the books. Pools of sinister pale yellow light gathered in his otherwise empty eye sockets. Traces of muscle and darkish rotting body still clung to the neck. Though the creature didn't look directly at her, the shock of its visage rattled her so much that she jumped away—straight out of the vision.

Flat on her back, Oona stared up at the branches breaking the sky up into thousands of blue spots between leaves. Her mind swam with fear so strong she could barely remember how to breathe.

By Lucen, what was *that!?*

"Highness?" yelled a man.

Three of the soldiers ran over, hurriedly grasping her arms and pulling her up to her feet.

"Are you all right?" asked one.

Another looked around. "Were you attacked? We heard you scream."

"No, no..." She smiled at them, still shivering from the dreadful creature she had seen. "I believe Lucen granted me a vision, but I don't know the meaning of it yet. I saw something most horrific."

The men exchanged worried glances.

"May it please Lucen nothing ill befalls the queen." The middle soldier made a hand sign of reverence to the gods.

Oona hesitantly shook her head. "I do not yet understand the full purpose of what I have seen, though it didn't fill me with immediate concern for her safety… no more than I usually have."

"Very good, highness." The man on the left emitted a sharp exhale of relief.

Though, whatever it is… I fear it is *a threat to Lucernia.* She eyed the soldiers. *No sense alarming them with vagaries.* "Thank you for your concern. I am all right. Merely going to fetch a bit of lunch."

The soldiers returned to the camp, leaving her to stare at the trees for a moment more.

"Thank you Lord Lucen for your insight. May I have the wisdom to understand it in time."

14

STATUS

KITLYN

The warmth of a hundred or so bodies filled the Royal Court of Lucernia with a persistent soft din.

Kitlyn sat on the throne, trying her hardest not to let her boredom and discontent show on her face. Fortunately, her elaborate white-and-gold gown concealed that her feet didn't quite reach the floor. Her one little scrap of rebellion—skipping shoes and hose—had thus far gone unnoticed by everyone except Meredith, who couldn't look at her without snickering.

If I must suffer forty pounds of gown, at least it can do something productive.

The nine days since they'd returned from Evermoor had been mostly consumed with the endless tedium of internal politics. Presently, most nobles and courtiers of note occupied the wings of the throne room behind two rows of columns, all standing in the wash of multicolored light cascading in the stained glass windows lining both sides of the hall. The central aisle that led from the main doors straight to the throne dais remained clear as per protocol. Somewhere amid the bustle of political affairs, unwed young nobles and the well-to-do conducted courtship rituals... some seeking a spouse, others chasing the friendship of more powerful individuals.

Endless discussions of minor policies would likely continue for some months in the wake of the former king's death. It seemed everyone from the dukes and earls to the small boys polishing shoes in the city square for one tin crown per foot feared what may change under a new ruler. Kitlyn let her head back against the padded throne and counted dust motes cavorting in the air. When that became too tedious, she tried to see if she could exhale hard enough that her corset ceased feeling tight.

She couldn't.

Absentmindedly, she traced a finger around the embroidery on her gown. The advisors had dispersed among the room, speaking to anyone with concerns.

She glanced to her left at Oona, who somehow managed to sleep while sitting upright and not appearing to be asleep, rather having a moment of intense contemplation. That made her think of the troubling vision she'd mentioned of a walking dead man roaming some vast underground library. None of the advisors offered much help, as Oona's description of the figure or the location failed to resonate with them. They didn't question she had seen it, though suggested the vision may have been of the distant future.

So, for now, Kitlyn and Oona had set it aside... though she did send scouts to investigate all known underground locations within Lucernia.

High Priest Balais had accepted appointment as an advisor as well as a man by the name of Naldun, a commoner from a farming village near the city of Imric. A few years into his fifties, the man had a liberal amount of grey in his otherwise black hair and a weathered but strong look to his features. According to Beredwyn, he had a reputation for being both humble and wise. Most of the nobles had been alarmed by his appointment as an advisor citing his low station and near total lack of wealth.

At Oona's suggestion, they had added another new advisor, Lady Alonna, whose primary role entailed representing the other three temples and bringing their concerns and opinions to the royal court. In her father's reign, only the Temple of Lucen had any true sway in matters of state. With their high priest serving as an advisor, they still held quite a bit of influence, though she wished to grant followers of the other three gods the same courtesy.

She'd expected the wealthy to view her selecting Naldun, an ordinary citizen, as a signal she intended to be hostile to the titled gentry. Many whispered and fretted 'in secret' about her 'common' upbringing creating a lasting resentment toward those with high station. Of course, the only secret involved in the fretting related to exactly who or how many complained.

In the same speech where she announced a decree that no future king or queen may simultaneously hold a rank within the temple of any god, she'd also stated that any resentment she may yet harbor toward anyone for her 'common' life was directed only at those who believed their station served as an excuse to treat others with less status or wealth as inferior beings. She claimed that if her father had not been deaf to the concerns of the least wealthy citizens, he may well have had a change of heart many years earlier and ended the war himself. Some of the courtiers bristled at her associating their snobbishness with the war lasting for such a long time, but the tactic proved effective at forestalling complaints.

Previous kings or queens had all been named High Priest of Lucen by virtue of their holding the crown. That she'd tasked the temple's elders to *choose* their high priest, and by extension declaring such a choice should come from Lucen himself, had won her much favor with the temple. She wondered if Lucen would have granted magic to anyone named high priest simply for bearing the title. The Talomir line had all supposedly been quite strong in magic, perhaps the reason they'd taken the throne in the first place. She stared down at her hands, wondering what—if any—form her magic might have taken had not Queen Solara, her mother, drank from the Eldritch Heart while pregnant with her. *The stonecallers said I was unusually strong. Perhaps the magic I would have had combined with what the Heart gave me? Or maybe the Heart knew I would need to be strong to return it home.*

Kitlyn replayed the speech in her head, trying to remember the mixture of expressions on the people listening. She had caught a few quiet grumbles from people still unhappy with her choice of wife instead of taking a man to be king, though she couldn't *quite* tell if they clung to old prejudices about two girls in love or merely thought a woman didn't belong ruling a kingdom. Beredwyn had his spies out and about, listening for dissent. Thus far, the people had been overjoyed at an end to the war. Except for a few elders who had the most trouble changing their thoughts, the citizenry appeared pleased with her and Oona.

Also, according to Beredwyn's spies, Ruby had relocated to Pirolen, a village in the far north beyond Orien's Glade... about as far from Cimril City as one could get without leaving Lucernia. It seemed she'd made her choice, abandoning her daughters for want of money. Kitlyn suspected Oona still held a little bit of hope the woman might someday change her heart and reconcile, since she had never known a mother's love.

Kitlyn secretly traced her foot back and forth across the carpeting in front of the throne. No one could detect the motion under her huge dress, nor could they notice she'd gone barefoot. The sensation of fabric upon her toes became a screaming rebellion against the burdensome pageantry and ridiculous focus on station and propriety that plagued Lucernia.

The advisors continued mingling with the courtiers. She glanced over at Beredwyn, arguing with four merchants. As soon as she looked at them, their conversation clarified out from the chaos... something about their demanding a repeal of an 'unfair' tax King Talomir had levied on them. Beredwyn's cool and calm deflection of their insistent requests made her think the merchants expected a young female monarch would be easy to manipulate.

In truth, Kitlyn did worry about Oona for that exact reason. Her hope to be accepted—not necessarily liked—for loving a woman constantly made her second guess saying no to people. She didn't want to give them *another* reason to suggest she may be unfit for the crown. It seemed doubtful any of them would protest the monarch being too young if she'd been a boy. Of course, she'd come in at the bare minimum age to personally take power. Fifteen or younger, a regent—most likely Beredwyn—would have technically ruled the kingdom until she'd come of age.

On the left side of the room fairly close to the throne dais, Lady Alonna chatted with three priests, one each from the temples of Navissa, Tenebrea, and Orien. They all appeared in good spirits, which made Kitlyn smile. The other new advisor, Naldun, had gathered a group of middle-class citizens in the far right corner nearest the doors out. He looked a bit like a philosopher lecturing a class of students. Though she couldn't hear them at all given the distance and the noise in the room, she figured they spoke of the damage the war caused their farms and families.

Oona suggested offering a modest reduction in tax to families who adopted war orphans. However, she insisted on personally meeting all prospective parents to ensure that none would mistreat the child and only wanted to take one in for financial reasons.

For the next several years, Kitlyn stared vacantly at the swirling dust, counted stitches in her gown, or daydreamed of the time she shared with Oona in the pond... or at least, it felt like years. She fixated on a disoriented moth or butterfly fluttering in endless circles at the top of a tall window on the left while trying to fly through the stained glass. Time all but sat still. She stared at her fingers until she felt certain she could perceive her nails growing longer.

A distant *clonk* finally broke the monotony as the outer doors opened. The noise woke Oona, who turned her head to stifle a yawn.

A twentyish blond man in brown leather armor strolled down the aisle, headed for the throne. Beredwyn emerged from the crowd and arrived at the dais simultaneously with him.

"Your highness..." The scout dropped to a knee.

"What news?" asked Kitlyn.

The man stood and gave a curt bow of greeting to Beredwyn before handing over an envelope. "Highness, there are reports that a man by the name of Fauhurst is attempting to stir discontent among the citizens."

"Oh?" Beredwyn raised an eyebrow.

Advisor Lanon hurried over as well. The ever-nervous thirty-something man hadn't enjoyed a restful sleep since Advisor Yelem had been revealed as an Evermoor spy. With the end of the war, he at least managed to cease trembling all the time.

Kitlyn grumbled in her head. As tempting as it had been to exact some sort of revenge on Fauhurst for all the misery he had caused her, the man had not broken any laws. Whatever she did to him would have felt petty.

"Yes, my lord." The scout nodded to Beredwyn, then glanced at Kitlyn for a moment, seeming unsure who to address. "We have word that he is attempting to foment discord mostly among the lesser nobility as well as officers within the military. He is recruiting those who, despite the clear blessing of Lucen and his daughter, cannot accept umm... certain personal matters of the queen."

"It is all right...?" Kitlyn twirled her hand about.

"Breen, highness." The scout bowed again.

"Very well, Scout Breen. It is all right for you to speak the plain truth. These men object that I love another woman."

Breen looked down. "Yes, highness. They disregard the signs given us by Lucen and his daughter."

"Scout," said Oona, "can you not say Tenebrea?"

At the mention of the name, members of the court close enough to the dais to hear it all hushed and looked over. The priestess of Tenebrea next to Alonna smiled.

The scout opened his mouth, shut it, pondered a moment, then took a deep breath. "Yes, highness. I was merely attempting to be respectful. They disregard the signs given us by Lucen and Tenebrea."

"Speaking her name no more invites her to escort you to the netherworld than speaking mine would make you suddenly desire the company of men." Oona smoothed a hand over her gown.

A few nervous chuckles came from the court.

"Of course, highness." Breen bowed again. "I am pleased to report that his numbers are quite small."

"Perhaps"—Lanon pivoted toward her, his eyebrows up—"since Tenebrea appeared with her blessing and the other gods said nothing, they are afraid?"

Kitlyn emitted a silent sigh. "I do not require everyone to approve of us, only mind their own business. If they feel our love is unnatural, they are certainly free not to love as we do."

"That man..." Oona scowled. "He must hate us so to commit treason."

"He doesn't hate us, my love. He hates me. The man likely still cannot think of me as anything more than a lowborn orphan. No doubt, he does not consider our reign legitimate. His supposed distaste for our union is merely a fancy dress upon his inability to accept I was never a commoner."

"You mean *your* reign?" asked Oona.

Kitlyn took her hand. "I know what I said."

Oona smiled, though appeared embarrassed.

Beredwyn beamed with pride. Advisor Lanon looked away, uneasy. He had once confided in private that he found their love 'unsettling,' though he didn't mean any hostility by it.

"What exactly is Fauhurst doing?" Kitlyn reached toward Breen.

The scout handed over the envelope.

Kitlyn opened it and read accounts of dates and times where Fauhurst or his agents had met with landowners, merchants, and soldiers of officer rank.

"Our belief is that he attempts to gather the support of enough nobles to challenge the crown. Though at this time, he does not quite have enough with him to displace one groundskeeper," said Breen.

Beredwyn chuckled, as did Lanon.

"Sedition is a delicate matter." Oona frowned.

"Treason is not delicate." Kitlyn waved the papers at her.

"His reason is not political, it is personal." Oona clenched her hands into fists. "Had you wed Lanwick instead of me, he would not be attempting to overthrow you. Acting against him might be exactly what he wants you to do. He could take that to the old traditionalists and attempt to twist it into us 'forcing our abnormal ways' on the nation."

"It is well known that he had a particular vendetta against her from the first moment he began as an advisor." Beredwyn flared his eyebrows. "That you have an exceptional love is a convenient excuse for him. I dare say most citizens would be more apt to believe he is unable to move past the public mockery your true lineage made of him. Had she wed Lanwick or some other man, he no doubt would have devised some codswallop about her not truly being Aodh's heir."

Kitlyn nodded. "Regardless of his motivation, he is attempting to stir insurrection. No ruler would sit idly by and fail to react, for to do so would invite more challenge."

Oona bit her lip. "He knows this."

"I shall not make him the prison martyr he likely hopes to become. The man tormented me for years purely because he thought my status too low to be near the princess. Since he is so obsessed with status..." She glanced at Breen who stood with an overly conspicuous expression. "Is there something more?"

"No, highness."

Kitlyn smiled. "Very well. Thank you for your message. May Lucen guide you."

"And you as well, highness." Breen bowed, turned on his heel, and hurried back down the long strip carpet to the doors, seeming eager to be out of there.

"As I was saying." Kitlyn tapped her fingers on the armrest of the throne. "I shall not yet order him to the dungeons. As of this moment, Fauhurst will forfeit his land and holdings, including all wealth and possessions less clothing, any holy texts he may own, and six gold radians. Given his relatively young age, that should provide modest meals for the remainder of his life. Since the man is so obsessed with status, the most appropriate punishment is for him to have none."

Beredwyn nodded, seeming neither pleased nor opposed to the decree.

Oona squeezed her hand.

"And"—Kitlyn held up one finger—"his estate is to become a sanctuary for war widows, orphans, and any soldier too injured to live alone until there are none left who need it. The Temple of Lucen is overburdened."

"I love it." Oona beamed. "The temple is so crowded."

"A wise option." Lanon waved over one of the court scribes, and had the man draft the writ of proclamation to send to the magistrates.

Kitlyn closed her eyes. *I am where the people need me to be. Forgive me for loathing this tedium.*

15

UNREST

OONA

*O*nce again, the continuous murmur of the courtiers threatened to drag Oona to sleep. It probably would have if not for worrying about Fauhurst. While the man had been petty and cruel, she wouldn't consider him unintelligent… or at least not of subpar intelligence. The man surely couldn't have expected to circulate among the gentry in search of others willing to unseat the queen without being noticed. She worried that any form of retribution would be exactly playing into his hands. And, with her recent thoughts on the potential truth of there being a curse on the Talomir family line, Fauhurst's insurrection may well bring about Kitlyn's death.

Though *not* reacting to sedition sent an equally unwelcome message, perhaps a more dangerous one. Fauhurst most assuredly would try to claim Kitlyn attacked him to silence anyone for daring to object to their marriage. Her father had imprisoned several people who had claimed he didn't speak for Lucen. He'd also imprisoned a few prominent nobles for attempting to speak out against the temple. Kitlyn's first official act as queen had been releasing those prisoners. It had shocked Oona to find four Lucen priests among them. She wept openly upon seeing them and realizing King Talomir had done such a thing. Much to her surprise, none of the priests had been bitter. All claimed Lucen had given them visions of their release at this moment.

As peaceful as the kingdom appeared, she couldn't help but worry that too much lurked beneath the surface to allow things to remain quiet for long:

Lucernia had a queen who questioned the validity of monarchy.

The citizenry spent centuries shunning people who loved those of their own gender.

With the cause of the twenty-year-plus war now known, the citizens might want a new family to hold the crown.

Some nobles, despite Aodh Talomir starting the war, thought reparations undeserved.

Many soldiers had become bitter at being lied to about why they fought.

Many citizens questioned how Lucen could permit such deception for so long.

And on top of everything else, Fauhurst wanted to start a rebellion.

She doesn't really even want to be queen. I'm sure she would be happier in a tiny village. She looked over at the throne. Kitlyn, still fuming, noticed her staring and glanced back, anger gone to a smile in an instant. Oona grinned. *She is happy being with me.*

"I fear I may be threatening the very stability of our nation," whispered Kitlyn.

Oona blinked. "What?"

Kitlyn pointed down. When Oona looked, she lifted her gown enough to reveal a bare foot, then dropped it. Oona's jaw hung open at the impropriety of it. She may as well have perched upon the throne nude. To the courtiers, it would've caused the same amount of shock and hand waving. A gasp started to come out of her, but at the devilish glee in Kitlyn's eyes, it turned into a giggle.

Oona caught herself before she laughed openly on the throne dais by clamping a hand over mouth, but still wound up making a noise similar to someone drop-kicking a pigeon—loud enough that it echoed over the chamber, bringing silence to the court.

Everyone stared at her. Increased scrutiny only made Kitlyn's immodesty funnier. That no one could even tell what she'd done further increased the awkwardness. The more she tried not to let herself laugh, the more she had to. She couldn't remove her hand from her mouth or she'd cause a scandal that would destroy their short reign.

"It's all right," said Kitlyn. "She likely saw a large flying insect or something."

Oona bowed her head, hiding her face in her hands while trying to laugh in silence.

"Are you all right, highness?" asked Advisor Lanon.

"She is merely overcome with joy at our nation enjoying peace." Kitlyn paused. "We have been at war for so long we may *lack the underpinnings* of how to function without it. It is times like this where people will truly bare their soles."

Lanon bowed. "You are wise beyond your years, highness."

Oona gasped again and had to bite her arm not to erupt in giggles while firing a 'stop it!' glare at Kitlyn. None of this would've been at all funny if not for the complete wrongness of a sitting monarch (or her consort) laughing on the throne.

Fortunately, the advisors and the court lost interest in Oona having made such an odd noise.

It took her a few minutes to walk back from the edge of bursting into laughter, though she couldn't help but grin. She leaned close and whispered, "You would shock them less by wearing nothing at all."

Kitlyn made an appraising face, then nodded. "About the same I think. Though, I dare say they'd prefer me seated here in nothing than my servant's rags."

Oona gasped. "You wouldn't dare."

"No." Kitlyn leaned back in the throne. "Can you imagine their faces if I did that? No one would be able to speak for at least an hour."

"Stop it," whispered Oona. "They already think of us as children. If we sit here giggling the whole time, they'll be right."

"Since when did we require kings and queens remain dour all the time?" asked Kitlyn, at a normal tone. "I say we are now in happy times. The war is over and we have much to celebrate. We *are* young, but is it a bad thing to be filled with life?"

Mixed stares met them from the court, but over the course of a few minutes, they changed mostly to smiles.

"My father was too severe. Always angry, was he not?" asked Kitlyn. "Because he constantly feared his deception would come to light."

"Are we to expect you will never deceive us?" asked Lord Parrington, Duke of Tandren.

"I shall not knowingly deceive anyone." Kitlyn nodded to him.

"Your father swore on Lucen he spoke truth." Parrington glanced around him before looking back at her. "I suppose at least you do not invoke Lucen in that claim."

"No. While I would not wish to offend him either, I could not bear to break my wife's heart. She took Oona's hand. "She would know."

"Yet," said Parrington with an air of haughtiness, "*Princess* Oona did not sense the deceit within Aodh?"

Kitlyn bit her lip, at a loss to explain that.

"Lord Parrington..." Oona glanced at Balais, then back to the duke. "A little known truth in our nation is that *all* magic does not, in fact, come from the gods."

The room fell silent. Balais appeared worried, annoyed, and confused in equal measure.

"I believe most magical abilities among our people are gifts from the gods, but there are some who possess an inborn talent. Aodh Talomir was one such man. For his treachery, Lucen stripped him of whatever abilities he had granted, but he retained enough natural talent to construct an arcane shield that befuddled the gift Lucen gave me. As you have so often pointed out, good Lord Parrington, I am but a child of sixteen. I have not had decades to study and hone my gift. Yet now you imply as an even younger girl than I am now, I had been somehow remiss in lacking sufficient mastery to see through the deceptions of a former high priest?"

A mix of murmuring and soft chuckling swept over the room.

"We believe," said High Priest Balais, "that the gods may allow some to be born with a certain level of magical ability as a test. The faithful are rewarded with greater knowledge and power. However, Lady Oona is correct. Whatever innate talent a person may have is often not rescinded upon a breach of loyalty."

The duke appeared satisfied with the answer and nodded. "Forgive me, highness."

Gradually, the din returned as advisors, nobles, merchants, and commoners resumed discussing matters.

"I look forward to the day's end," muttered Kitlyn.

Oona leaned close and whispered, "Are you honestly wearing nothing under that gown?"

"No." Kitlyn grinned. "I only omitted the hose and shoes. All the other useless fluffery is there."

"You flirt with scandal." Oona smiled.

"It is a matter of security." Kitlyn held her head high. "Touching the stone beneath my feet allows me to draw greater power."

"You are still expecting assassins?" whispered Oona, the sudden grip of old fear back in full force.

Kitlyn looked around at the assembled court. "Not from Evermoor. If someone does attempt to sneak up behind me, I would rather much like to feel them coming. Shoes are like blindfolds."

"Are you sure you merely don't hate the feel of them?" asked Oona.

"That, too." She winked.

Oona blinked, then covered her mouth to giggle.

"What now?" Kitlyn looked over at her, raising an eyebrow.

"Perhaps Lucen inspired the servants to keep taking your shoes so you would have your powers at their strongest?"

Kitlyn smoothed her hands down the front of her gown. "Perhaps. I was certainly on my hands and knees enough, scrubbing, for it not to have much mattered."

"Ooh." Oona scowled. "You're making me angry all over again at the way they treated you."

Clonk.

Again the doors flew open, startling the room to silence.

A burly orange-haired man with ruddy cheeks and common brown robes rushed in, trailed by a slim brown-haired young woman in studded leather armor. Both wore amulets bearing the symbol of Orien: a hand upturned with sun rays above it.

None of the soldiers moved to intercept them, instead offering reverential bows as they passed.

The two priests rushed up to the throne dais. Before they arrived, Kitlyn stood and glided down the four steps to the floor to meet them at eye level… or at least eye-to-chest level with the man. Oona followed. A few of the nobles emitted shocked gasps at the queen not only standing for a visitor but stepping down from the dais, but then again, these two appeared to be priests. King Talomir had never done so, but he had been a priest himself which he believed coupled with his title as king had elevated him above any need to show deference to anyone.

"Lifebearers," said Kitlyn. "You seem troubled. What can I do for you?"

"Highness." The man offered a shallow bow. "We've rushed here as fast as we were able to from Crows' Corner. There's been an attack. Nine are dead."

The room fell quiet.

"An attack?" asked Kitlyn. "From who?"

"*What*, highness." The thin priestess shook her head. The girl couldn't have been much (if any) older than her. "Demons, we think. We're not entirely sure, but no one saw the fiends, only found the bodies the next morning."

"They came in the night," said the big priest.

"Lucen protect us," whispered Oona. "No one saw anything of the fiends?"

"Not that told us, highness." The woman faced her. "We tended to a number of survivors, but they claimed not to have seen anything, as if the darkness itself attacked them with tooth and claw."

Murmuring started in the court. Oona caught a few whispers of people questioning Lucen's protection. The doctrine stated that Lucen once drove the demons from his kingdom and prevented their return. Most of the whispers blamed Aodh's betrayal for this lapse, but one or two suggested it could be due to his daughter being impure.

Caught between wanting to cry and scream in anger, Oona's voice hitched in her throat. Before she could clear it, a man pointed out that if Lucen had objected to them being in love, Tenebrea would not have manifested, and the wedding ritual would not have let them hold flames. An argument started among the men about why Tenebrea would manifest to condone two girls in love but Lucen wouldn't show up to slap Aodh into the Pit for such a malignant lie.

Guilty of wondering that same thing, Oona kept quiet, but felt grateful that someone defended her and Kitlyn.

"So, we do not know for sure there are demons about. It could be bears or some manner of animal?" asked Kitlyn.

The big priest heaved a breath, raising a hand to beg a moment.

Kitlyn glanced to the left where three maids sat on seats by the wall. "Will someone fetch some water for the priests?"

One of the maids jumped up and hurried off.

"We do not know for a fact that demons are involved." The young priestess offered a grateful smile in response to the request for water. "It only appears that way due to how they appeared in the night and vanished with no trace. We could not locate any tracks in or out of Crows' Corner."

"Perhaps winged demons?" Advisor Lanon glided closer.

Kitlyn shifted her jaw side to side. "Not everything that is neither human nor animal is a demon. Our kingdom is tamed from the wild but magical beasts still run rampant in more distant lands. It is not beyond imagination that one may have roamed here."

The maid returned with a ewer and two large wooden mugs. Both priests gratefully accepted the water.

"Send twenty soldiers and some trackers to investigate." Kitlyn nodded to Advisor Lanon.

"Right away, highness." He hurried off.

While Kitlyn welcomed the priests to spend the night in the castle resting and eating, they politely declined and would take refuge at the Temple of Orien. Kitlyn appeared to expect that answer as the priests had expected the offer from her.

Oona returned to her seat and wondered if that vision of the robed skeleton might somehow be related. Worry started again. If a demonic attack had truly occurred on Lucernian soil, it would represent the first such attack in centuries. The history books claimed Lucen had banished all demonic entities from the kingdom more than a thousand years ago… but of course, history books offered no guarantee of truth, only what those in power wanted the population to believe.

Where did that come from? Oona blinked at herself. *Oh, do I doubt everything now that I have seen the depths of my fath—that man's crimes?* She looked up at the rustle of Kitlyn's gown as she settled back into the throne. *The day at court cannot end fast enough. I wish to be alone with her and confide my fears.*

A boy of about twelve in a plain brown tunic, breeches, and boots rushed in the door. His outfit reminded her of the messenger who had accompanied them on the journey to Evermoor, so Oona figured he worked for the military as a courier—either an orphan or the son of a soldier.

He slowed from a sprint to a tentative walk about halfway down the aisle, looking around. Upon spotting one of the tall advisor's hats, he stopped short, staring at it with hesitant urgency.

"It is all right, boy." Kitlyn beckoned him with a wave. "Do not be afraid."

The boy swallowed hard, but walked up to the dais and knelt. "Your highness. I have a message from Wick Hollow. Some unknown creature has attacked them in the night two days prior. Three are dead."

"Anyone of political significance?" asked Beredwyn.

The boy shrugged. "I do not know, sir. The lieutenant didn't give me any names or mention anything about that. I think they were simple villagers."

"Where is Wick Hollow compared to Crows' Corner?" asked Kitlyn.

An attendant ran over a few minutes later having fetched a map. Crows' Corner only stood a short distance into Lucernia from the Churning Deep. Wick Hollow sat due east from the town of Moonbrook and due south from Eastmarch, located at an intersection in the roads connecting the towns. About five miles separated the two villages.

"So…" Kitlyn paused a few seconds in thought. "They are both reasonably close to each other, near the Churning Deep, and fairly isolated from large cities."

"Do you think it's Evermoor?" asked Balais, his tone suggesting he didn't.

"No." Kitlyn shook her head. "I have heard that some among the military feel lost without the war and do not know what to do with themselves in a time of peace. While I think it unlikely one of them would create the appearance of continued aggression, I am not so quick to dismiss the idea. However, the priests spoke of bite and claw wounds. The most likely explanation is some manner of bear or beast prowling that region. Both villages are within a day's travel of each other. Send another group of soldiers and a tracker to Wick Hollow as well. Have both sets of troops encamp there to protect the villages until further notice."

"Very good." Beredwyn nodded.

Kitlyn sat back and rubbed the bridge of her nose. Her frustration and pain for those who had been hurt shone clear as Lucen's light to Oona. She took her love's hand and squeezed. Kitlyn glanced over at her with a grateful smile.

"By Lucen, I hope the next crisis that runs through that door does not involve people being killed," whispered Kitlyn.

UPON RETIRING TO THEIR BEDCHAMBER THAT NIGHT, OONA BROUGHT up her worry that the throne of Lucernia might be cursed. She reiterated the long list of unfortunate circumstances that befell whoever wore the crown.

Meredith assisted Kitlyn out of her dress. She'd worn most of the underpinnings, only skipping the hose to allow her feet to remain bare and in contact with the ground.

"Well, I should thank you for giving me something new to have nightmares about." Kitlyn put on a playfully angry scowl. "Curses now…"

"I'm sorry. These thoughts have plagued me since we left Evermoor." Oona clung to the bedpost to steady herself while Piper undid her back lacings. "I don't want anything to happen to you."

"I would prefer nothing happened to me, too. Do you think it may be mere coincidence?"

"Could be," muttered Meredith, while tugging Kitlyn's slip off over her head.

"I did not find anything in the library about any curse on your line." The instant the corset released Oona's chest, she drew a great breath. "Oh, I wish we could outlaw these damnable things."

"We can," said Kitlyn, now bare from the waist up.

"Oh, I'm merely complaining to complain. The very fabric of our society would unravel if we interfered with fashion. The nobles need their expensive finery after all." Oona fanned herself.

Piper undid the fasteners holding up Oona's crinoline. "You don't need to outlaw them. Merely cease wearing them. The nobles usually mimic whatever those with more status do."

Kitlyn shoved the rest of her underclothes off to the floor without waiting for Meredith and stood there wearing only her crown. "I've learned to pick my battles. It would be my luck that something so trivial would turn the noble houses against me." She grabbed her nightdress right away, a sign that she felt too tired to do much more than cuddle and sleep tonight.

"It may well be a coincidence." Meredith gathered Kitlyn's undergarments from the floor one by one. "From what I've heard of the past royals, they've all been a rather certain sort of person."

"What does that mean?" asked Kitlyn.

Meredith looked around for eavesdroppers and lowered her voice. "Right proud of themselves. Vain. Loved having power and reminding everyone else that they had power. Though, my grandmother said the one woman, umm… Avelina was almost as sweet as Oona."

"She refused the crown." Oona stood still while Piper undid her bra, then basked in the cool air over her chest. *Oh, that dress was dreadful. Perhaps those spiritcallers have the right idea.*

"Oh." Kitlyn yawned, and plucked the crown off her head, staring sleepily at Oona. "I'd give up the throne if I had to for you."

"The kingdom is more important than me."

Kitlyn paced over, standing right next to her. "In a way, I can appreciate the truth to that, but I don't really care if it's foolish or selfish. If I ever found myself in a position to have to choose between you or being queen, I wouldn't even have to think about it."

Oona's heart melted. She pulled Kitlyn into an embrace despite having only her smallclothes on and two handmaidens watching. Of course, neither of them batted an eye at a simple hug, and Kitlyn wore a nightdress.

"Perhaps Lucen punished the Talomir line for their arrogance," said Meredith in a low voice. "And the one thing Aodh did right was sparing you that."

Oona bristled at the notion the cruelty Kitlyn suffered from the castle staff could be thought of in any way as a good thing, but couldn't quite bring herself to snap at Meredith. Truth be told, as much as she wanted to believe Kitlyn's true self would have been the same no matter what, had the king raised her like a princess, she may well have been another person entirely.

Piper offered Oona her nightdress, giggling when Oona decided to mimic Kitlyn and shove her smallclothes off before putting it on.

"I suppose." Kitlyn sat on the edge of the bed and yawned. "Let us hope the troubles in the east are a simple matter of an errant bear."

"By Lucen's will," muttered Meredith.

Piper flashed a cheesy smile. "Carros willing."

Kitlyn laughed and crawled into bed. "I'll accept help from any deity willing to give it."

"Thank you, Piper." Oona hugged her. "Sleep well."

"Good night, Meredith," muttered Kitlyn, already close to unconscious.

Oona scrambled into bed, clinging to Kitlyn. She closed her eyes and prayed to Lucen, asking that he shielded her wife from whatever curse might cast a shadow over the Talomir line.

THREE DAYS PASSED WITH NO WORD COMING BACK FROM EITHER group of soldiers.

Fortunately, no word came of additional attacks either.

Still tired from the morning training session with Guard Lorne, Oona reclined in the grass by the big tree in the castle gardens, occasionally rubbing her arm, sore from swinging a wooden blade. Much the same way she hadn't cared what anyone thought of her wearing breeches during their sword lessons, she didn't care what anyone thought of the queen consort flat on her back in the grass.

Of course, the pair of them in pants—plus Kitlyn shoeless—had elicited quite a few raised eyebrows and hushed whispers, as did her love's habit of wearing plain dresses whenever the day didn't call for meeting with anyone in an official capacity. They'd come to view the gasping and hand waving as humorous, given all that had happened in the land over the past twenty years and people still found the time to be shocked at the queen in a 'merely expensive' dress as opposed to one even the goddess Navissa couldn't put on without help.

She imagined the nose-in-the-sky crowd gossiped endlessly about the 'commoner queen' and so forth. It no doubt frustrated them that Kitlyn didn't care at all what anyone thought of her. *How un-Lucernian of her*. Oona grinned and glanced to her left.

Kitlyn lay nearby in the grass as well, wearing a nice-but-simple crushed blue velvet dress. Her mouth hung open in the midst of a midday nap, a beetle as big as a man's thumb struggling to climb her cheek.

For an instant, Oona nearly let out a yelp at the sight of it, but bit it back to a soft whine of unease. Screaming would throw the castle staff into a panic. Not to mention, that particular type of beetle posed no threat at all and she'd grown too old to shriek at simple bugs. After having men try to poison her and take her head off with swords, a garden beetle hardly deserved a reaction at all.

She clenched her jaw, leaned close, and gently plucked it off Kitlyn's cheek before setting it in the grass.

Kitlyn's eyes opened. Since Oona had obligingly half draped herself over her, she leaned up for a quick kiss. "What time is it? I think I fell asleep."

"You did. I'm not sure… two hours after lunch I think?"

Evie appeared on the arched walkway they had so often made Kitlyn sweep, and dashed across the grass into the garden, carrying a big cloth sack. When she arrived beside Oona, she dropped the bundle, revealing a mess of cloth dolls.

"How were your lessons?" asked Oona.

"Okay." Evie picked up two dolls. "Today was all reading and writing. Why do I have to learn that?"

Oona sat up and fussed at her little sister's hair. "How else will you be able to read storybooks?"

Evie grinned. "That sounds fun."

They talked for a while about lessons, which led into Oona and Kitlyn scaring Evie a bit with their tales of Miss Harper, the mean governess who'd watched over them when they'd been her age. Naturally, the paddling story came up.

Evie gasped and grabbed her rear end. "What'd ya do that ya got paddled?"

"Oh, we did a lot that should've gotten us paddled, but that time I think we'd rearranged the books in the library," said Kitlyn.

The child stared at Oona in shock. "*You* misbehaved?"

"Hard to picture, isn't it?" Kitlyn threw an arm around Oona.

"We didn't do anything *bad*." Oona rolled her eyes. "Just playful."

Talking about lessons reminded her of history, which again made her dread that something would happen to Kitlyn. King Talomir had been thirty-seven years old, and took the throne at eleven. He'd lasted a good while before he died, but that didn't guarantee anything. One heir had broken his neck within a week.

Annabelle, the new governess, strode into view on the grass outside the garden appearing flustered. Straight dark-brown hair hung to her waist, framing a delicate porcelain face set with pale slate-blue eyes. Midway through her twenties, she retained enough youth to not object to entertaining the girl and playing with her—far unlike the dour Miss Harper who had watched Oona and Kitlyn as children. Had either of them approached her to play, the woman likely would've thrown the dolls in the fireplace.

Evie, used to running around the village of Llanoen, still hadn't acclimated to the expectation that she shouldn't simply dart off and go wherever she wanted at a whim. Or at least, the governess responsible for her care thought so. Evie, not so much. The woman plopped down in the grass beside the child, and huffed. Though, with the queen right there, she didn't scold her. Oona couldn't help but feel awkward in her presence, still feeling like a child by comparison yet having authority over her.

Unlike what Queen Solana likely would have done with Kitlyn had she not been murdered, Oona had no intention to leave her little sister entirely in the care of the governess and pretend she didn't exist otherwise. Annabelle did play a vital role, as Oona's station frequently demanded her attention away to conversations and places unsuitable for a seven-year-old. However, at times like this when she could spend time with the girl, she did so.

Somewhat less than an hour after escaping into the world of a little girl and her dolls, the rapid tromp of approaching footsteps made Oona instinctively brace for Fauhurst's verbal assault, but remembered after a few seconds he no longer prowled the castle and even if he did, she could have sent him on his way. She looked up.

Advisor Lanon hurried into the garden and rushed over to them. "Highness, there is an emissary from Evermoor here insisting on seeing you. She won't speak to any of us regarding the reason for her visit other than to say it is official and there are potential problems between the kingdoms."

Kitlyn sprang upright. "We have not sent anyone across the Churning Deep, have we?"

"No." Advisor Lanon shook his head, catching his over-tall hat to keep it from falling off.

"All right." Kitlyn reached down to help Oona up. "The emissary is presently in the throne room?"

"Yes," said Lanon.

Kitlyn started walking, pulling Oona along.

"Uhh, highness?" asked Advisor Lanon, trotting along beside them.

"Yes?"

"Are you planning to take audience with her like that?" He kneaded his hands.

Kitlyn stopped. "Like what?"

"Well, you're..." He gestured at her and Oona's bare feet. "And..." He gestured at their plain dresses. "And..." He indicated their lack of crowns.

"The emissary from Evermoor will not bat an eyelash at how we are dressed." Kitlyn sighed. "However, we should fetch the crowns at least since this is an official matter. I shall not make the poor woman wait while we labor with pointless fluffery."

Lanon turned pale, but only nodded.

Oona raced after Kitlyn, feeling a bit like a kid again as the clap of their feet echoed in the stone-floored hallways. They rushed past several maids and guards who all stopped and stared at them, most likely alarmed more at their running rather than their simple dresses.

Once in their bedchamber, Oona helped Kitlyn seat her crown properly, then stood dutifully while Kitlyn returned the favor. With the literal burden of leadership upon her head, Kitlyn fast-walked instead of running down to the throne room, entering via a rear passage intended for the royals and close attendants.

The woman standing on the strip of carpet in front of the dais didn't look terribly happy. She wore a mixture of chain mail and leather armor over a green tunic, the panels of her skirt and shoulder guards styled to resemble long leaves with engraved vine patterns. A slender longsword hung on her belt and she held a large de-strung bow like a walking staff. Dark red hair hung down to the middle of her back with numerous small braids decorating the otherwise loose mane. Rich blue eyes held a stare of accusation, which softened somewhat the instant she spotted the two of them.

Kitlyn walked straight up to her, ignoring the throne.

Oona followed, standing half a step behind her. Upon noticing that, Kitlyn backed up so they wound up beside each other.

"Queen Talomir," said the woman in a cautious tone. "I am Raesa, an emissary of King Lanas Volduin on an official matter of state."

"Welcome to Lucernia, Raesa of Evermoor." Kitlyn nodded in greeting. "I hope you had a pleasant journey."

"My journey was more pleasant than the reason for it. I apologize if my manner seems brusque. My entire life has been spent thinking of your people a certain way."

Kitlyn nodded. "I understand. Our kingdoms knew four years of war before I drew my first breath. This new world we are in is a great—and welcome—change for both of us. What urgency has brought you here? Shall we discuss matters over dinner or would the minor delay be worrisome?"

A few servants and courtiers took note of Kitlyn and Oona's overly plain attire and stared.

"I would not object to discussing the matter over a table. Perhaps I have been hasty in my judgement. There have been a series of raids on our villages nearest the Churning Deep, and some within Evermoor fear that your soldiers have not realized the war is over."

"Attacks? I have ordered no such thing."

Raesa shook her head slightly. "Considering what I have heard of your deeds, I would not expect such. We think it may be a rogue element within your military or perhaps an isolated group."

"By Lucen," whispered Oona. "What do you know of these attacks? Did anyone see our soldiers?"

"No. The attacks occurred at night. A number of villagers caught outside were killed. We were unable to track where the enemy came from or went, though I did find claw marks on several doors and huts. The oddness of them led me to suspect someone is attempting to fool us into thinking an animal is responsible for the attacks."

Kitlyn rubbed the bridge of her nose. "There have been similar attacks at two villages in Lucernia. I have sent soldiers to each one as a defense, but have not yet received any report back from them."

Raesa blinked in surprise. "That news is both a relief and a concern. King Volduin will be delighted to know the aggression is not from Lucernia."

"Upon your return, kindly inform him that I will see these attacks stopped. Personally if need be."

"I shall." Raesa smiled.

Kitlyn waved one of the throne room maids over. "Please inform the kitchen staff that we will be having a guest during our evening meal."

Oona studied the woman. *She looks like a tracker, yet she could not find where these creatures came from or went to?* A pall of lightheadedness came over her. The periphery of the room blurred and spun. Oona grabbed Kitlyn's left arm, clinging to stop herself from falling over. A sick feeling swirled around the pit of her stomach. Fleeting images of darting shadows swarming around the streets of Cimril flickered in her mind, along with screams of the dead and dying. The brief, but horrifying sights faded, leaving behind a strong sense that she could potentially prevent such tragedy.

"Oona?" Kitlyn pivoted toward her, holding on. "Are you all right?"

"We should go," muttered Oona, still waiting for the room to stop wobbling back and forth. "I... saw people dying. *Things* running around Cimril. It's... the soldiers can't do anything. We have to go."

Kitlyn grasped her cheeks, holding her head steady. "What do you mean? What did you see?"

"I think Lucen is telling me we are needed to help more directly." She stared into Kitlyn's rich emerald-green eyes. Her wooziness abated and she found her footing again. "I'm okay. Just... another vision."

A silence fell over the court.

"King Talomir never had visions," whispered a distant man.

"Did you forget the high priest of the God of Truth spent twenty years lying to us all?" rasped a woman. "Why *would* he receive actual visions?"

"Oh. Yes. Fair point," whispered the first man.

"A-are you seriously suggesting you and the queen leave in person because of a handful of killings?" Advisor Lanon paled. "I understand that you are eager to help, but you are the queen and, umm, well, queen..." He scratched his head under his hat. "Perhaps you are young, but it is unwise to try and do everything yourselves."

Raesa regarded Oona with a note of increased respect.

"In most cases, Advisor Lanon." Kitlyn stared into Oona's eyes. "I would agree with you. However... I have rarely seen her this frightened before."

"Many more people will die if we don't go. I can't explain why I feel this is true." Oona bowed her head. "It must be Lucen guiding me."

16

CROWS' CORNER

KITLYN

*E*missary Raesa joined them for dinner, which became a pleasant hour or so of conversation. Kitlyn initially asked her about what she found at the village where the attack occurred. The woman did happen to be a trained tracker, but still hadn't noticed any signs of an invading force.

"If you are not in any great rush to return home, I would be honored to have you join us tomorrow. I intend to travel out to the village of Crows' Corner and see for myself what happened there," said Kitlyn.

Raesa pondered the idea for a short while, then nodded. "I would be most curious to compare what I can find there with what I observed at Wolf Glen."

"No tracks at all?" asked Oona, a hint of nervousness in her voice. "In my vision, I saw darting shadows. Just black blurs, and many of them. We could be facing an enemy that is magical or spectral."

"There are no users of magic in Evermoor who wield anything like that. The only 'black' energy I can think of belongs to followers of Navissa." Raesa picked up her goblet of water. "And they do not randomly attack small villages."

"Most certainly not," said Kitlyn.

"Not that I am at all suggesting such a thing possible, but their magic would have left dark burns and frost on whatever it touched." Oona delicately sliced up her portion of turkey.

Kitlyn smiled, finding it cute the way she tried to make all the pieces of meat the same size.

The remainder of conversation over dinner dwelled on the return of the Heart to the Alderswood. Raesa admitted to almost fainting when she'd heard that Kitlyn had set foot in the grove where the sacred tree grew, since the Order of the Sundering claimed the heir would do exactly that—and destroy the entirety of Evermoor.

By the time they finished the meal, talk had segued to funny stories about some mischievous wolf cubs Raesa had tended a year or so earlier that had them all laughing. They agreed to set out early the next morning for Crows' Corner, and Kitlyn requested a castle steward show Raesa to one of the guest rooms.

Kitlyn sent word to gather the advisors and headed straight from the dining hall to the throne room. Beredwyn, Lanon, Balais, Alonna, and Naldun all arrived within fifteen minutes. She figured the advisors tired for none appeared to notice or care about her simple dress or lack of shoes.

"I appreciate you all arriving on such short notice. I needed to make you aware of my plans for the morning." Kitlyn explained her intention to travel personally, with Oona and the Evermoor emissary, to Crows' Corner. "I do not expect to be away from the castle for too long, but I will once again need to leave the small decisions to you."

Advisor Lanon made an odd face and craned his neck as if listening to a whisper at his ear.

Kitlyn glanced at him. "Do you hear something?"

He smiled. "No, I was merely enjoying the absence of a particular nuisance saying 'that is highly irregular.'"

His passable impression of Fauhurst's tone got a laugh from Beredwyn. Kitlyn didn't much enjoy being reminded of him, though considering the man mocked him, she forced a smile.

"To his, somewhat humorous, point," said Balais, "why do you feel the need to attend to this in person rather than rely on the vast resources at your command?"

Oona stepped forward. "I have had a vision of death and pain in what I believe to be Cimril. Shadowy figures flying around setting upon everyone with their fangs and claws. I fear Lucen wishes us to go ourselves and has given warning of a great loss of life if we do not."

"My father would have ignored such an inclination, not wishing to burden himself with such a task, especially when only simple farmers have suffered… if even he had sufficient faith to receive such word from Lucen," said Kitlyn. "I trust her."

"One who does not heed the word of Lucen is likely no longer to hear it." Balais faced Oona and offered a short nod.

Lady Alonna raised both eyebrows at his quick acceptance of Oona's statement, then bowed at her.

"What manner of beast may move as Oona has seen while not leaving any tracks? Wraiths? Shadows? Something of that sort?" asked Kitlyn. "Have any of you knowledge of such things?"

"There have been wraiths." Beredwyn pulled at his beard in thought. "Though they would not have caused bite and claw wounds. Nor are they usually seen in groups."

"They are quite dangerous, but solitary." Alonna shivered in dread. "I can think of several forms of demon that could appear that way, though no creature from the Pit has been able to set foot or hoof in Lucernia for an age."

Kitlyn paced. "We assume that my father's transgression has not so angered Lucen that this protection broke."

"I do not sense that to be true," said Balais. "The affront of one man, no matter how powerful, would not turn Lucen's wrath against the whole of his people."

"But many turning their backs on his teachings for what Aodh did might." Advisor Lanon folded his arms. "We must demonstrate to the people that his crimes will never be repeated."

Beredwyn gestured at her, beaming. "Our queen's decree that no king or queen shall come from any priesthood, yet shall always be advised by them is a good first step."

"Distribution of power." Kitlyn folded her arms. "Too much of it concentrated in one person creates temptation that can lead to great suffering. If a monarch ceases to act in the best interests of their subjects, they should not be in a position to malign the name of Lucen to obtain blind acceptance of their words and deeds."

Advisor Naldun offered a rare smile.

"Very well. We shall make haste for Crows' Corner at first light. And, I think I shall retire early."

Oona nodded. "Yes. We will need our rest."

The murmuring advisors drifted off in different directions to their rooms—or in Balais' case, heading for the connecting passage that led to the temple.

Kitlyn hated seeing Oona so rattled. The vision had left her wide-eyed, pale, and trembling faintly. She didn't seem frightened as much as horrified by whatever she had seen. "We will make this right, whatever it is." She pulled her into an embrace.

Oona's shaking stilled and her grip tightened. "I don't think I will sleep much tonight."

"We must. Both of us will need our strength." Kitlyn swayed side to side while holding her. "I'll keep you safe."

"Hah." Oona poked her in the side. "I'm not a frightened child. I'm worried about what may happen to our people."

Kitlyn walked with her to the door. "As am I. We will have all day tomorrow for worry."

THE SUN HUNG LOW IN THE SKY, THE BOTTOM EDGE BARELY touching the meadow grass in the west and making the waters of the distant Lake Orien glow like a pool of liquid flame. Kitlyn, much to the disapproval of the majority of her advisors, had left her crown safe in the castle. While she didn't expect to be attacked, it struck her as unwise to wear a metal ring on her head in the midst of a fight—or have it go rolling away the moment she tumbled or fell over.

She had taken inspiration from Emissary Raesa and hastily arranged for a set of light armor, mostly leather with a bit of chain mail in patches for extra protection. Past kings had ridden into battle wearing armor, but the sight of her and Oona in breeches instead of gowns had set off a flurry of whispering and gawking. Women had fought in the military for as long as she could recall, so there hadn't been any shortage of ready-made armor in her size sitting around in Cimril.

While hers lacked the leafy motif of the emissary's, it offered quite a bit more protection than a flimsy cloth tunic and loose breeches. Kitlyn narrowed her eyes, thinking about the man who yanked her pants down in the middle of a swordfight to trip her up. That couldn't happen with her present attire.

Oona's squirmy discomfort at the armor so reminded her of a cat forced to wear clothes that she'd spent most of the day stifling snickers. While she didn't complain about her pants riding up or how strange she thought it to mount a saddle like a boy, her body language did all the grousing for her. If anything should happen that required them to ride faster than walking, it would be Kitlyn who turned into the awkward one. Princess Oona had taken riding lessons from age ten or so up. Every so often, she'd whined the stable master into allowing Kitlyn to participate, but by no means had that occurred with any regularity. Controlling a horse at high speed scared her as much as walking a tightrope between two of Castle Cimril's towers.

Once again, a group of twenty soldiers, two messengers, and a handful of attendants had accompanied them. Kitlyn had opted to ride instead of taking a coach for greater speed. Oona's horse, Cloud, a pure white stallion with a long snowy mane, seemed ecstatic to be out of the castle stables. Kitlyn had taken an unassigned dark chestnut warhorse named Apples from the military stables. His former rider had died a year ago during the war. Kitlyn thought the animal lacked the disposition for a warhorse, being too friendly and docile.

The pleasant day made the ride reasonably quick, the time passed with easy conversation. Raesa mostly asked about Lucernia, commenting on the relative lack of forest. Evermoor lacked meadows or open fields, being almost entirely covered in dense woodlands or swampy moors toward the southeast.

They arrived at Crows' Corner with perhaps an hour and a half of daylight left, having made haste throughout the day. Several dozen dark brown buildings of austere design emerged from the rolling meadow up ahead, coming into view as Kitlyn crested a shallow hill. A rickety wooden sign beside the road with two arrows stuck in it bore the town's name. The occasional bizarre root gnarl stuck up in the grass off to the right. Kitlyn puzzled over them for a moment until she realized they'd come from Evermoor rootcallers, likely during a battle here.

Raesa didn't react to the signs of war, her attention fixated straight ahead.

Soldiers, likely some of those she had sent to reinforce the town, gathered at the south end by the road to meet the approaching group. Kitlyn rode up to them and managed a not-too-clumsy dismount, jumping to the ground beside Apples. She patted him and waved over one of the attendants.

"We have been traveling fast all day. Please see to the horses. I wish to use what little daylight we have left."

"Yes, highness," said the man before taking the reins.

Oona slid from her saddle as gracefully as a faerie gliding down from a branch. She spent a little longer talking to Cloud and rubbing his face and mane affectionately.

"What news?" asked Kitlyn, approaching the oldest looking soldier. "And you are?"

Some of the men eyed Raesa with thinly-veiled hostility, likely recognizing the design of her armor as being from Evermoor.

"Edgar, highness. 'Tis been quiet. No further attacks, though the locals are spooked. There is talk of demons about."

That pulled Oona's attention away from Cloud. She walked over, craning her neck to gaze around as if searching but not finding something.

Kitlyn surveyed the spread of buildings. The center of town had a modest attempt at cobblestone streets and some more well-constructed buildings, but a loose scattering of homes and farmhouses in the surrounding meadow comprised at least half the town. "Where did the attacks occur?"

"One moment." Edgar sent another man off to 'summon the three,' then turned back to her. "The dead were all in the southeast, except for one found inside his house. A few who survived the attacks had been near enough to shelter to get inside. They claimed the spirits refused to enter."

Oona whispered, "I do not sense anything unnatural here."

"Shall we encourage the people to cease speaking of demons?" Edgar's pleading smile looked more like a grimace.

Kitlyn held up a hand. "Not until we know for sure."

The younger soldier returned with three more men in chain mail armor that appeared noticeably less well kept than the others. The black-haired man appeared to be in his early twenties, behind him a taller man with dark brown hair who approached thirty. The last soldier had the look of youth about him, perhaps not quite twenty yet.

Edgar gestured at them. "This be Jesh, Marus, and Paul. They are the permanent guard."

"Only three?" asked Oona.

"Used to be forty," said Marus. "We lost about half to fighting, and the others not born here went home once the war ended. Crows' Corner's not got much worth takin', so we don't need too many acting as the law. 'Bout half the town's got blades close at hand if need be, but they have better things ta do all day than walk around makin' sure no one picks pockets."

"What can you tell me of the attacks?" asked Kitlyn.

Jesh and Paul gave her odd looks, but kept quiet.

"We lost nine men, includin' Fann and Willam." Marus glanced to the east.

"Those two men had some significance politically?" Kitlyn looked in the same direction, but noticed only meadow.

"No. Just the town drunks." Marus chuckled. "Seems anyone out and about at night had a bad time of it. Only one poor sot, Anders, went to Tenebrea while inside."

Oona fidgeted at her belt, shifting her armored pants. "Perhaps he was the attack's true target and the others may have been a diversion? Who was Anders?"

"Just a farmer." Paul, the youngest, scratched at his unkempt hay-blond hair. "Kept to himself. Lived alone. Wasn't much for bein' around others."

"Did he have any troubles with anyone?" asked Oona.

"Two, yeah." Jesh nodded. "He got a little rough with a couple of young boys for messing around in his field and ruining some crops. The boys' fathers gave him a good ol' punch up for it, but I don't think they'd have gone so far as to summon something from the Pit to take him."

"Can we see the sites of the attacks?" asked Raesa.

"Wot's she doin' 'ere?" Jesh eyed her.

"Similar attacks are occurring in Evermoor." Kitlyn gave him a 'back off' stare. "She is a diplomatic emissary."

The soldiers all seemed to relax at the same time, except for the three locals who continued to sneak suspicious glances at Raesa.

"Aye, this way." Marus waved her to follow as he walked off.

Kitlyn assumed the almost-thirty man the one in charge of the other two, nodded, and followed him.

They spent the next half hour or so touring areas of open meadow within the town's boundaries. Some still had patches of dried blood in the grass that suggested grievous wounds. Wherever signs of violence existed, Raesa squatted and studied the ground. Kitlyn also crouched and pressed her hand to the dirt since she'd worn boots. Upon opening her thoughts up to the Earth, she tried to feel the memory of the stone as she had when tracking Oona across Evermoor.

A brief sense of multiple small beings running around came and went. She sighed and relaxed her magic, having no interest in reading the route taken by a bunch of town children at play. At the fourth attack site, Raesa honed in on a small patch of dirt where the meadow grass had failed to cover.

"Oh, darn," muttered Raesa, sounding disappointed.

"What is it?" Kitlyn walked over. "A track?"

"Yes, but probably just one of the locals. Looks like a young boy." She traced the outline of a bare footprint, the front quarter lost to the grass at the edge of the dirt patch. "His toes came down on the grass where most of the weight landed. I'd say this is a ten-to-twelve year old quite used to being barefoot."

"How can you tell that from a track?" Oona raised her eyebrows.

"You've not observed how she walks?" Raesa nodded toward Kitlyn, smiling. "People used to shoes land on their heels with each stride. Otherwise, people put most of their weight on the front of the foot."

"Hmm. I've sensed children walking around at every place where someone was killed." Kitlyn crouched to examine the track. "But I imagine there have been kids roaming the town for quite a long time. The Stone has little sense of time. I could be feeling the steps of people who've already grown old and died."

"You're not suggesting a pack of little boys did this?" asked Jesh.

"No," muttered Oona. "She said the footprints are likely much older than what happened here."

"What did the bite marks look like?" Kitlyn continued staring at the footprint. She tried to push the grass out of the way to look where the toes should be, but the ground offered no more clues.

"Horrible," said Marus. "Like a butcher carving out hunks of meat the size of melons."

"With a dull saw," added Jesh.

The men shuddered.

"A large bear, I think." Paul gestured at the meadow. "Grass is tall enough to hide a decent sized one. Could lay out there waitin' for the dark."

"A bear with wings." Raesa glanced sideways at him. "There are no tracks from animals here."

Kitlyn stood up, clapping dirt from her hands. "Where is Anders' house?"

"Over that ways, north a bit." Jesh raised his arm in a gesture somewhere between waving and pointing, then walked in that direction.

Kitlyn followed, Oona trailing close. Emissary Raesa lagged a few paces behind them at a much slower gait, still studying the ground. A handful of soldiers appeared quite fascinated with her—especially whenever she stooped to examine something.

The woman either didn't notice them staring at her rear end or didn't care. Kitlyn clenched her jaw. She'd take it up with a lieutenant later, not wanting to make a scene on the off chance Raesa hadn't noticed the boorish conduct of her soldiers. Since they only stared in silence, it could wait, though she kept an eye on them.

A few minutes later, Jesh hopped a low wooden fence onto a plot of farmland. Kitlyn vaulted it without hesitation while Oona ducked between the uppermost and middle rails. Raesa almost had long enough legs to merely step over it, though she, too, jumped. Jesh headed straight across a field of mostly-harvested wheat to a large-framed single story house made of plain wood, dark near to the point of black.

"Strange bit of business, this." Jesh cringed. "We found him in the chair by the hearth. No sign of a fight, though plenty o' blood went everywhere. You, uhh, may not want to look inside. Hasn't been cleaned up as yet."

"Blood does not weaken my nerve," said Kitlyn, a twitch in her jaw. Looking at a patch of it on the floor couldn't possibly bother her as much as staring into the eyes of a man she'd impaled on a longsword.

Some of the soldiers chuckled. The tone of it implied they thought her 'cute' for trying to act tough.

Ignoring the wordless insult, Kitlyn approached the house and examined the walls while Raesa checked the ground. While walking around the outside, Kitlyn noted numerous scratches in the wood that appeared fresh, free of dirt or grime like the dark brown muck collected in the gaps between boards. The pattern of scuffs going up to the roof, some even traversing the wall sideways, confirmed what she'd started to suspect from the combination of child-sized footprints, enormous bite wounds, and Oona's description of dark shadows racing through Cimril.

Nimse. She closed her eyes, thinking of those accursed creatures, and pressed her hand to the ground. In seconds, her skin crawled with a sensation like mice racing back and forth all over her in every direction. The feeling made her think back to the cave-dwelling creatures scurrying around the walls of Underholm in defiance of gravity. *What are they doing out here?*

She rounded the rear corner of the house, navigating a collection of farm equipment, and made her way down the other wall, where Raesa stood staring upward.

The tall redhead glanced over at her. "Something climbed to the roof here. There's a small attic window with no glass. No bear could've fit through that, but look." She pointed. "A smear of blood on the roof."

"Nimse," said Kitlyn. "The blood must've been on its hands when it climbed out."

Raesa blinked. "Are you certain? I've heard of them, but only as a myth."

"I'm quite certain they exist as I came *too* close to them not long ago."

Oona moved around to the side of the house. "What is it?"

The soldiers followed her, everyone eyeing the house.

"Oy. There's blood on the roof." Paul pointed at it. "How'd we miss that before?"

"Not looking up, perhaps?" asked one of the soldiers from her escort.

Some of the men chuckled, while the three local soldiers grumbled, somewhat embarrassed.

"The scratches all over the house." Kitlyn pointed. "They were searching for a way in. I'd not be surprised if more dwellings here had similar markings. See that everyone secures all windows and doors at night until we determine why they are attacking."

"Demons," said a fiftyish man in armor as disheveled as the three locals', shaking his head. He nodded at Kitlyn. "It's got to be demons. What'd we expect? Lucen has turned his back on us because the queen loves a woman. 'Tis only going to get worse."

Most of the soldiers turned as white as ghosts, except for Jesh, Marus, Paul, and the one who'd made the comment.

Oona's dark blue eyes simmered with anger.

"Uhh, Harold," whispered a soldier from the group who had arrived days before. "You are speaking to the queen."

Jesh, Marus, and Paul blinked and stared at her. In seconds, the color ran from their cheeks as well. Paul took a half step away from Harold.

The older man's eyes fluttered. He seemed about to faint. Most of the soldiers glanced anywhere but at Harold or Kitlyn. Raesa folded her arms with an 'oh, this should be good' sort of expression.

Oona, her voice surprisingly calm, said, "This is not the work of demons. It —"

"These are not demons." Kitlyn rested a hand on Oona's shoulder to apologize for cutting in while glaring at Harold. "The creatures who did this are known as Nimse. They dwell in Underholm, vast in number, and are able to scale walls and ceilings. Though they stand not much taller than a man's stomach, their heads are as big as melons with enormous mouths full of triangular teeth."

"Nimse…" Raesa resumed looking around at the dirt.

Oona stepped up on Harold, holding her right hand up, cradling her pet light ball. Its shimmering blue radiance made some of the men squint. "While you are free to have your opinions about who I love, do not use Lucen as an excuse for the bleakness in your own heart. If Lucen objected, he would take his gift back from me as he did from the former king."

Kitlyn tugged at her shoulder.

"I shall never understand your society." Raesa leaned on her bow like a staff. "Why are your people so preoccupied with such trivial things as the quality of one's clothing matching their social status or who complete strangers choose to give their heart to?"

"Forgive me, highness." Harold bowed his head. "I did not… no crown… armor…"

"Yes, yes." Kitlyn sighed. "I'm well aware I look like a common soldier at the moment. Shall I traipse about in the mud and fields wearing a gown that barely allows me to move? Would you expect a *king* to tour the countryside dressed in his finest?"

Everyone kept quiet.

Raesa stood. "The tracks I assumed to belong to young boys are likely Nimse. It seems these creatures are raiding both kingdoms. Wolf Glen is rather near Underholm, and had similar tracks."

"I did not come here to impress anyone." Kitlyn approached the house and ran her fingers down a particularly long groove likely from a Nimse claw. "We're here to put a stop to these attacks."

The moment she ceased staring at Harold, the man nearly fainted.

Oona stepped inside the house, her light ball floating around above her head. "Little is disturbed in here. It appears to have attacked the man and… Kit."

She hurried in, her gaze following Oona's pointing finger to a bizarre series of bloody prints on the wall leading to a hole at the top of a rickety staircase.

"How did your people fail to notice that?" asked Oona.

Marus, Jesh, and Paul entered, along with a few of the soldiers who'd come to reinforce the town.

"Beggin' your pardon, highness." Marus gestured at the wall. "'Tis dark wood. Without that light of yours, we didn't see it."

Kitlyn folded her arms. "I don't think this man died for any particular reason other than they found a way inside. The only intrigue here is why the Nimse are attacking at all, not why they chose this man." She turned to the most senior of the soldiers. "Be on alert after dark. If they return, they will do so at night. They are small and fast, but their strength comes from numbers. One at a time, they should prove no match for any of your men."

"Yes, highness." The man snapped to attention.

"Tomorrow in the day, we shall attempt to find their trail. It would be foolish to pursue them in the dark." Kitlyn glanced at Oona. "Shall we seek lodging for the night, then?"

"Yes. That sounds lovely. We've been riding all day."

After one last look around at the large stain of dried blood, Kitlyn bade one of the soldiers to lead them to the town's best inn.

It turned out to be the town's *only* inn.

A ROYAL MESS

OONA

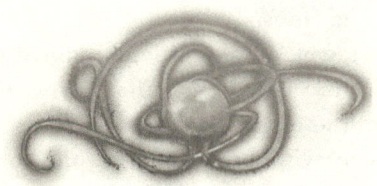

*N*either lying awake for a while after Kitlyn fell asleep, nor dreams provided any answers or eased Oona's mind.

Over dinner, she'd asked Kitlyn to talk more about what she had seen of the Nimse in Underholm. Hearing how they flowed up walls and over ledges matched what she had seen in the brief vision of shadowy figures racing across buildings in Cimril. The feeling she'd experienced during the vision—absolute certainty that many lives depended on her —kept her awake trying to figure out what might make the Nimse invade.

They've attacked Evermoor as well, so it may not be anything Lucernia did.

Despite resting at a countryside inn as opposed to their bedchamber in the castle, Kitlyn had talked her into going without a nightdress. They hadn't done anything more fun than cuddle, though the warm comfort of being close to her love had made sleep possible. The potential invasion from Nimse paled in comparison to the dread she'd once felt over wiping out a whole kingdom, but still proved sufficient to keep romantic thoughts away.

ONCE MORE IN HER RIDING OUTFIT, A LIGHT TUNIC UNDER LEATHER armor, Oona wandered Crows' Corner, still fidgeting at the weight of a longsword on her belt and the foreign sensation of pants. Despite the cured leather being much less flexible than fabric, its design offered more freedom of motion than most of her gowns, and it would laugh off thorns or other brambles in the wild.

Kitlyn wanted to search for a trail and hopefully track the Nimse back to wherever they'd come from. They both assumed that meant Underholm. Though it did have doors facing the Lucernian side, neither of them had ever been there. Based on Kitlyn's description of the cave-in that blocked her attempt to flee Evermoor via the old underground city, she half expected to find ruins.

Emissary Raesa as well as four soldiers joined them on the way to the eastern part of Crows' Corner. The townspeople swarmed over them, having realized the queen had come to their humble little slice of land. All greeted them with broad smiles, offering thanks for finally ending the war. The crowd thickened to the point where the small group found themselves stuck in town, unable to head off in search of tracks.

Kitlyn smiled and tried to make her way eastward. People attempting to avoid being rude by coming too close edged away, allowing her a slow creep to the right that gradually plowed a path among them... at least until one man held his ground, somewhat red in the cheeks, breathing fast, and apparently fighting his emotions.

"Why did it take so damn long to end?" rasped the man. "My sister and brother both died to them savages, not even a year ago."

Kitlyn reached out and took his hand. "I am truly sorry for your loss. But, please, the people from Evermoor are not savages. They are not so different from us."

"Forgive me," said Oona. "I spent so many days trying to figure out what I needed to do. I wanted more than anything to end the war, but I couldn't accept what some seers claimed, that I would destroy them all."

"The burden wasn't yours, princess." The man fought sniffles while staring at Kitlyn.

"I didn't even know I was the king's daughter." Kitlyn looked up into his eyes. "I only learned the truth a few days before confronting him about what he did."

Several voices rose from the crowd, defending Kitlyn as not being responsible for the former king's deeds.

The man bowed his head. "I'm sorry, highness. It's hard to understand why such things happen. They're right. It is not your fault." He backed out of her way.

Eventually, the townspeople parted enough to allow them to continue onward. A few commented at the queen wearing 'common scout' armor, but several said they found it reassuring they had a monarch who didn't consider herself so far above the people they never left the castle.

Oona kept smiling back at the villagers, both elated and surprised at the overwhelming show of acceptance and gratitude. Then again, anyone who disapproved of them would likely have remained at a distance. Being this close to the Churning Deep, Crows' Corner had experienced a great many incursions from Evermoor during the war and likely many dead.

While Raesa discussed with Kitlyn her opinion that too much time had passed for there to be much chance of finding any useful tracks, Oona kept looking around at the people, heartsick that they had been made to suffer so much over the king's lust for power. She wound up locking stares with a young boy watching them from behind the corner of a house. He appeared about Evie's age with sandy blond hair and a deep tan.

She smiled at him, but he shied back, hiding more. "Kit, go on for a bit. I'll catch up."

"What?" asked Kitlyn, turning toward her.

"I've the strongest urge to talk to that boy over there."

Kitlyn stopped walking and peered toward the child. "All right. Why don't we both go? Another few minutes won't affect the tracks, which are probably gone by now anyway."

The instant both Kitlyn *and* Oona looked at him, the boy darted out from behind the corner and crawled under the small porch attached to that house. Worry welled up in Oona, driving her up to a jog. Her bouncing longsword swatted her in the leg a few times before she remembered to brace a hand on it.

Upon reaching the house, she squatted by the opening at the porch side and peered into a tiny space where the boy had curled up amid weeds. "Hello." She put on her most reassuring smile. "Why are you frightened?"

Fearful hazel eyes regarded her for a long few seconds before his lips moved, but he didn't say anything loud enough to hear.

"I'm Oona. What's your name?"

"Ral," whispered the boy.

She smiled. "Hello, Ral. Why are you under there? I know small boys and dirt are good friends, but it's filthy."

"I saw demons," whispered the boy.

"Oh." Oona exaggerated a slow nod. "Well, then, I have good news for you." She flared her eyes with eagerness and summoned her light orb in both hands. The two brighter 'eye spots' tilted inward as if it grinned at him. "There are no demons here. They're afraid of Lucen's light."

"Ooo." Ral gawked at the glowing blue orb.

Raesa crouched by the porch, looking at the ground. "His feet are too small. He wouldn't have made the prints we found by the attacks."

"Why don't you come out of there," said Oona still using her soothing voice.

"I don't want them to bite me like Tarl. The demon bit his whole arm off."

Oona let the orb float up to the side and reached both arms toward him. "I won't let anyone bite you."

He tentatively crawled closer until she could reach him. Oona grasped him under the arms and pulled him out, cradling him in a hug. Ral trembled for a little while, but eventually, her rocking him and patting his back calmed him enough to relax.

Oof. Oona struggled upright, still holding him. The boy weighed a bit more than Evie. Then again, her sister would make an elf feel thick, and she figured Ral for a little older.

"Hi." Ral waved at Kitlyn.

"Hello." She smiled.

"Is this your house?" asked Oona.

"Aye. Live here with me mum an' sis. Me pa went away."

Kitlyn and Oona sighed at the same time.

"I'm sorry about your father," said Oona.

Ral sniffled. "He dis-peared. Mum finks 'e lost out there. But is 'kay. Kell 'n I know 'e's gotta be wif Ten-brea."

Oona squeezed him again, then set him on his feet, at a loss for anything to say.

He looked up at her. "You gonna get rid o' the demons?"

Kitlyn crouched to eye level with him. "The creatures you saw aren't demons. They're alive."

"Oh. I saw them bite Tarl, but I ran 'way 'cause Mama don' want me fightin' nothin' 'til I'm 'least fifteen. I'm only eight."

"Did you see where they went?" asked Raesa.

He glanced up at her, tilted his head, then nodded. "Yeah."

"Ral..." Oona squeezed his shoulders. "Would you be brave enough to show us where?"

"I don't wanna be eated." He ground his toe into the dirt.

She threw an arm around his back, turning him to look at Kitlyn, Raesa, and the almost forty soldiers that had collected behind them. "How about if they all come with us?"

The boy's eyes bulged in awe at the soldiers. "Okay. You sure I won' get in trouble?"

A dark-haired woman in her mid-thirties peered at them from the door, likely his mother. Her guarded expression suggested her as one of the people Oona assumed had not been terribly thrilled about their presence here. Her imagination filled in the woman yelling something about her wanting to take her son as well as her husband away from her, but to her surprise, the woman nodded.

"You'll only ask him to show you the place?" asked the mother.

"Yes." Oona gave the woman an expression of sympathy and apology. "I'm so sorry for your loss."

Kitlyn beckoned her closer. "Why don't you accompany us? Once he shows us the spot, you can bring him straight back here."

"It's daytime," said one of the soldiers. "Those fiends won't be anywhere near."

The woman debated for a few seconds before stepping out of the house. A girl of around twelve with mouse-brown hair appeared in the doorway, a worried glint in her eyes. The woman told the girl to mind the house for a few minutes, then came down the stairs and took Ral by the hand. Oona's floating ball of light appeared to soothe her.

After giving it a long stare, she patted Ral on the head. "Go on and show the princess what she asked you to."

Oona bit her lip, not quite sure if the woman wasn't sure what to call the wife of the queen or hadn't yet learned of the king's death. She exchanged a glance with Kitlyn, and decided not to pester a grieving widow about titles.

"Here." Ral pointed off to the northeast, then dashed away.

The eight-year-old led them east past the edge of town into a field. He eventually stopped by a crude shin-high wall made of gathered stones arranged in a passable attempt at a square. A taller tower, about shoulder high to him, stood in the middle.

"This is our fort." Ral looked up at her. "My friends and I built it to fight goblins."

Some of the soldiers chuckled, some had 'get on with it' expressions, and one told Ral they'd built quite an impressive fortification.

The boy grinned. "We was in here watchin' for goblins. Mama started callin' me home fer dinner. But we saw somethin' movin." He pointed at a swath of sparse woods east of town. "Olin and Tom ran home, but I didn't."

"Brave of you," said a soldier.

Ral glanced up at Oona. "I's not brave. I's too scared ta move. Tarl was out inna field collectin' 'is sheep. Coupl'a them things came out the woods right there." He pointed at the trees. "Then a whole lot of 'em. Tarl screamed. They eated alla sheep and then bit him."

His mother scooped him up and hugged him so hard he gurgled. Evidently, she hadn't known how close he'd come to being a Nimse's dinner.

Oona closed her eyes and thanked the gods for protecting him.

"Thank you, Ral." Raesa patted him on the head. "We might find some tracks leading back to where these fiends came from."

"Yes." Kitlyn nodded to the mother. "Thank you. Please stay safe in your home."

Oona bit her lip watching the mother and son hurry off. The soldiers, Raesa, and Kitlyn strayed off toward the field where that child had witnessed the Nimse attack a man.

We must stop this, and soon.

18

BY LUCEN'S LIGHT

KITLYN

Kitlyn walked among the soldiers, following Raesa toward the woods.

"Highness?" asked a man.

She stopped and glanced back over her shoulder. "Yes?"

"How many should accompany you into the forest or stand watch over Crows' Corner?" asked the same soldier.

Despite the scare they'd given her in Underholm, the Nimse didn't seem as though they would be as much of a threat above ground. The prospect of smaller numbers, no walls to leap at her from, plus a longsword and more trust in her magic brought perhaps too much confidence.

Kitlyn looked over the soldiers, mostly men with about six women among them. "I'm not expecting to encounter them during daylight. Five should be sufficient."

He nodded and appeared to randomly select five soldiers, one woman included, to go with her.

Oona, Raesa, and the five soldiers—Burin, Aleah, Fortin, Lem, and Darrow—followed her across the wide field of grass between Crows' Corner and the woods. Kitlyn stooped to press a hand to the ground, asking the Stone to lead her the same way the Nimse had gone.

A gentle patter of footsteps ran up her back along with a faint pull ahead and to the right. Kitlyn walked among thin birch trees for a few minutes. Oona and the soldiers crunched through the underbrush behind her, though Raesa moved without any detectable noise. She glanced back over her shoulder at everyone, faintly shook her head, and resumed examining the ground.

We couldn't sneak up on Omun.

No one direction felt any more appealing than another. Kitlyn looked around again, then pulled her boots off before bundling them and hanging them on her belt.

"What are you doing?" asked Oona.

The soldiers also appeared to share her confusion, though none voiced it.

"Feeling the earth, the memory in the Stone. This is less annoying than stopping every five minutes to touch the ground."

"So it's true…" Raesa raised both eyebrows. "You are attuned to the Alderswood."

"Yes." Kitlyn opened herself to the energy in the ground.

In seconds, the cool autumn air no longer bothered her bare feet. Soon after, the echo of small footsteps manifested as a feeling ahead of her. Though she couldn't see anything with her eyes, she somehow knew where the Nimse had trod. Also, the weight of Oona, Raesa, and the soldiers entered her awareness. The sense didn't permit her to recognize someone's identity, but being able to detect the presence and general size/weight of someone standing at a given distance and direction away from her added to her confidence.

No Nimse could sneak up on her unless it jumped among the trees.

"They went this way." Kitlyn pointed where the trails led. "There are at least seven, though I'm sure multiple Nimse followed each path. There could be dozens of them."

Raesa offered a respectful nod, then advanced to where Kitlyn pointed. She soon located marks on trees and a bitten-in-half small boar. "They didn't come here to feed, or they would not have left so much meat behind."

"They're smart?" asked Aleah.

"You would not know it to look at them, but I believe so." Oona peered up at the trees as if searching for something.

Kitlyn followed the memory trail in the earth, subconsciously stepping where the Nimse had. They walked for the better part of an hour until the distant roar of the Churning Deep emerged from the silence up ahead.

"Do you think they came up the canyon wall?" asked Oona.

"Maybe." Kitlyn closed her eyes and tried to reach ahead with her magic, expecting a telltale bend in the trails at the canyon, where they angled straight down. Such a climb would be a triviality to the Nimse, as she'd seen them scoot like spiders across smooth stone walls within Underholm. The natural rock of the Churning Deep with its crags and small ledges had to be many times easier for them to traverse. Much to her surprise, the trails converged at a single point not far ahead before diverting downward in a winding path that reminded her of a giant root. "They didn't scale the canyon. I think they... burrowed."

She advanced toward the tunnel-like wound in the earth that floated in the darkness upon the backs of her eyelids. Every few steps, she opened her eyes to avoid running into trees. The soldiers formed a single-file line behind Raesa, who strode along behind Oona.

"Be ready," said Raesa in a near whisper before pausing to string her bow. "There may be danger ahead."

"But it's not dark." Oona nervously gripped her sword.

"Listen." Raesa gestured at the trees.

Everyone stopped moving.

Kitlyn considered the forest for a moment before saying, "It is completely silent. That means something but I'm not sure what."

"You're right." Raesa smiled. "There should be at least the chirps of birds or the rustle of small animals. Something is here that does not belong, and the animals are avoiding the area. However, the disturbance could be merely a person."

"Still, best to be ready." Kitlyn eyed the soldiers, who drew their blades in response.

"Shouldn't you put your boots back on?" whispered Darrow, an incredibly tall man with broad shoulders but a relatively lanky frame.

"Her magic is stronger without them." Oona half drew her sword, thought better of it, and put it away.

Raesa chuckled. "You know how the savages are, running about the forest with nary a scrap of clothing."

Two of the soldiers gasped in shock, as though she had called the Queen of Lucernia a savage.

"There is a bit of truth in every exaggerated story." Raesa grinned at them. "The stoneshapers draw power from the earth. Spiritcallers take energy from the wind upon their bodies."

That's why... Kitlyn thought back to King Volduin and his wives all bare from the waist up. Could he be a spiritcaller as well as a bladeborn? *Like I draw power from the earth.*

"Do the firecallers douse themselves in lamp oil?" Lem chuckled.

Kitlyn smiled, as did Oona.

"Not usually, but some do carry lamps." Raesa loaded an arrow but didn't draw it.

Hand on her longsword, Kitlyn crept ahead, stepping between roots and around low-lying shrubs. A few paces later, a pile of disturbed ground became apparent to her eyes where her magical sight revealed the twisting passage plunging into the earth and continuing too far down for her to perceive the end.

She approached, circling around a hole roughly two feet wide, ringed by a dirt mound like an enormous version of an anthill. The soldiers followed, splitting up to search the area. Raesa examined nearby trees and crouched to hunt for tracks. Oona hung back, wary.

Kitlyn felt the weight of someone walking up behind her, along with the soft rattle of chain mail. She cast a brief glance back at Darrow, and relaxed. The tall man leaned forward to peer into the hole. Something down in the tunnel moved. Several somethings, racing toward the opening as fast as a person could run.

"Look out!" shouted Kitlyn while hurling herself into a tackle.

Alas, she hit him like a kid jumping onto a tree, barely moving him a half a step. Rather than knocking him flat, she wound up hanging on him. A Nimse burst out from the hole, its spherical head split nearly in half by an enormous gaping mouth filled with triangular razor teeth, which it sank into Darrow's shoulder. All four of its clawed hands raked at his armor while it grunted and growled in a disturbing high-pitched voice.

A second one came flying at Kitlyn's face, but an arrow flew in from the left, spearing it in the head. The dead Nimse crashed like a limp rubber doll into her, its round black tongue lolling from between its teeth.

Darrow screamed in pain, backpedaling as more Nimse spilled up out of the hole. The one attached to him flailed for a better grip, raking its claws over Kitlyn's chest but failing to slice her armor. The *swoosh-thump* of a second arrow from Raesa somewhere behind her announced another dead Nimse. Kitlyn briefly considered trying to pry the thing off the man's shoulder, but didn't want to put her fingers anywhere near its mouth.

She let go and dropped to her feet. Her hands glowed with green light as she called a pair of thick roots to shoot up from the earth and wrap around the Nimse's head. Somewhere off to the right, a brilliant blue flash accompanied the pained wails of tiny inhuman voices. Soldiers roared battle cries.

Darrow seized the creature on him by the wrists of its upper two arms, though it kept raking at him with its second pair as well as its legs, the same length as its arms. A gurgling noise came from it in response to the magical roots prying its mouth open. Lem, about fourteen yards away to the left, emitted a freakishly loud howl that muted to gurgling.

Kitlyn spun, gasping at the sight of a Nimse tearing his throat out. She made a shoving gesture with one hand; a pointed spire of rock slammed up from the ground, launching the creature higher than the treetops. It landed some thirty feet away with a sickening *crunch.* Lem grabbed his throat and fell over.

Snarling, Darrow pried the Nimse from his shoulder and hurled it to the ground. The magical roots pinned its ball-shaped head to the earth, holding it down while he recovered his sword from the mulch nearby and ran the creature through.

Aleah, Burin, and Fortin stood back to back, holding off a group of ten or so Nimse. Kitlyn started to turn her attention to the crowd, but caught sight of another five surrounding Oona—and two more rushing out of the hole toward her.

What's going on? They're not supposed to come out in the day!

She leapt back, heading around Darrow toward Oona. He obligingly attempted to block the Nimse going for Kitlyn. One leapt for his face—but he punched it dead-on in the front of its spherical head and sent it flying. The other one ran over, snarling, and chomped him on the thigh.

Oona called a brilliant column of white-blue light around herself. All five Nimse going for her screamed and cowered away, covering their eyes, tiny raisin-sized spots in the middle of their round faces where nostrils should be. They looked more like they'd gotten a whiff of something foul.

The Nimse Darrow punched landed on its back a few feet away, bounced over onto its front, snarled, and scrambled right back at the man. Kitlyn reached a hand toward the ground. A potato-sized rock shrouded in glowing emerald light burst up from the soil, hung in midair for a second, then zoomed at the one biting Darrow's leg. It smashed into the creature's chest with a dull *thump*, flipping it onto its back, bloody teeth bared to the sky. The Nimse clawed at its side where the rock had undoubtedly broken several ribs. Darrow stepped into a swing that beheaded the one rushing at him.

Raesa fired arrows rapidly into the group surrounding the three soldiers, who appeared so busy defending from attacks they couldn't find a chance to strike back. The blazing column of blue light Oona summoned drove the Nimse back from her. Kitlyn took a step closer, thinking only of protecting her love, but her tactical mind got in the way of her heart. Oona didn't appear to be in immediate danger, unlike the soldiers. She clenched her jaw and focused on the ground by the frenetic blur of blades and teeth. Serpents of emerald light emerged from the dirt by her feet, coiling up her legs, crisscrossed over her chest, and shot down her arms, gathering in her hands.

Jagged stone spires erupted from the earth near the soldiers, throwing the small Nimse into the air, knocking them away two and three at a time. The ones menacing Oona shrieked in response to a brighter flash and scrambled back into the tunnel. Relieved that her love appeared safe, Kitlyn drew her longsword and headed for the remaining group, leaping over the hole to save a few seconds.

Oona sent her little light ball zooming into the fray, its glow a brilliant white instead of the usual soft blue. The Nimse shrieked in agony and ran for the hole. Kitlyn raised her blade to cut one down, but somewhere between its terrified demeanor and childlike size, she couldn't bring herself to slay it. It ran past her and dove headfirst into the tunnel. Aleah cut down one of the fleeing Nimse.

In seconds, only one remained—the one with half its ribs smashed that still lay on the ground where it had fallen. Kitlyn approached it, pointing the tip of her blade at its tiny throat. The diminutive creature would've stood about three and a half feet tall if upright, its head a near-perfect sphere with two tiny eye dots where a human's nostrils should be. Skin of dark charcoal grey let it blend into the stony surroundings of Underholm, though out here, it could only hide at night. Wicked little claws on its hands and feet possessed magical sharpness, as they'd cut a few chain links on her chest and easily scratched stone.

However, this one appeared to lack any strength to fight on.

"Why are you attacking us?" asked Kitlyn. "Can you understand me?"

It kept looking at her, breathing in heavy rasps that made its chest swell and collapse over prominent ribs. Unfortunately, the mostly featureless surface of its 'face' couldn't convey any sense of mood. Deep wrinkles crisscrossed its thick, grey skin, but it lacked eyebrows or true lips, its mouth opening little more than a wide slit.

"Lem!" shouted one of the soldiers, running over to the man who'd had his neck ripped out.

Kitlyn clenched her grip on the longsword, furious at herself that a man had died. *I should've brought twenty, not five.*

A delicate hand grasped her wrist.

She looked to her right at Oona, who shook her head.

"It's defenseless."

"A man is dead." Kitlyn gestured at Darrow. "Another has deep wounds."

Oona kept pushing her sword arm down. "This one is already defeated."

Kitlyn glanced at the helpless Nimse on the ground at her feet. She thought back to the first one of those creatures she'd seen—and killed. It had hurled itself at her with manic ferocity and didn't stop trying to bite her until she'd rammed a dagger into its chest. Still, she had felt guilty for doing it, more guilt in fact than she'd experienced at killing the soldiers who had held Oona prisoner.

Bears do what bears do because they are bears. People can choose to kill or not. These creatures perhaps cannot help their nature. "All right." Kitlyn lowered her blade and pointed at the hole. "Go."

The Nimse emitted a pitiful noise.

Oona started to crouch over it, but Kitlyn pulled her back.

"Don't… It could hurt you."

"It's all right. I think it knows I mean it no harm." Oona waited for Kitlyn to let go of her shoulder, then crouched.

"You're not going to kill it?" asked Aleah. "One of those fiends killed Lem."

"During the war, did you make a habit of murdering Evermoor's wounded after they surrendered?" Oona slid her hands under the creature.

It gurgled in response.

"Of course not." Aleah eyed Raesa. "But they are people. These creatures are… umm… not people."

"It is still wrong to kill the defenseless." Oona eased the wounded Nimse into the tunnel.

Once headfirst in the opening, it clawed at the earth with its left arm and leg, dragging itself down out of sight with the help of gravity.

Darrow helped Oona up and nodded at her. His acceptance of her act of mercy appeared to placate the others who gathered Lem up to carry him.

"I will be a few minutes," said Kitlyn. "I'm going to seal this tunnel."

"Highness." Fortin shook his head, making his bushy beard wobble. "We cannot leave you alone out here."

"The Nimse are gone for now," said Oona. "And I do not think they will be a threat anymore."

Kitlyn glanced at her. "While I adore your optimism, I think it will take more than one skirmish to make them stop their attacks."

"I mean we are safe from them." Oona indicated her hovering orb, which bounced in midair as if pleased with itself. "They flee from Lucen's light."

"Demons?" asked Darrow.

Oona looked up at him. "No. Demons would have caught fire or disintegrated. These creatures live in complete darkness. The light blinds them, and I think they find it painful. While I do not enjoy causing them pain, better that than killing these creatures."

"I shall stay with them," said Raesa.

"Highness…" Darrow stepped closer. "You shouldn't be without guards."

"Go. You need the attention of an Orien priest. Return to Crows' Corner. Have your wounds tended as best they can here, then make your way to the temple at Eastmarch." Kitlyn looked over at the dead man. "We shall bring Lem with us back to Cimril."

The soldiers appeared to accept Oona's confidence that her light would provide an acceptable shield against more Nimse. They lifted Lem and carried him off into the woods. Raesa wandered around, recovering her arrows from fallen Nimse, and a few from the ground.

Kitlyn stood at the edge of the tunnel, holding her arms out, palms down. She projected her magic into the earth, drawing stones of various size from the surrounding area and sending them tumbling into the dark. All the while she filled in the tunnel, she contemplated whether digging it had been difficult for the Nimse or if they could merely tunnel up again nearby. Covering the hole may well be pointless, but at least she would stop a child or villager from falling in.

A while later, the pour of rocks built up into view. She doubted she had filled the entire depth of the tunnel, most likely, a curving bend somewhere had clogged. Still, she'd created a plug more than thirty feet deep. After liquefying the top stones and re-solidifying them into a single, solid mass, she stopped concentrating on her magic and the glowing green aura around her arms went out.

Exhausted, Kitlyn swooned to her knees and sat back on her heels. "They won't be coming back up this way."

"Are you all right?" Oona hurried over.

"Yes. Just need a moment to catch my breath." She looked up into her love's beautiful blue eyes, her head framed in sunlit branches of green, brown, and gold. "It's my fault."

"What?" Oona crouched.

"Lem. I didn't think the Nimse could be a threat in the day. Only asked for five soldiers. I should've brought twenty."

"None of us thought the Nimse would be a threat in the day." Oona brushed a hand over Kitlyn's hair.

"I've never seen these creatures before." Raesa poked a dead one with her boot. "They have such tiny eyes. But if they live in the dark, they probably rely more on hearing or even feeling vibrations. Forgive me for saying so, as it is not my place to counsel a queen, but I would not place the blame for that man's death at your feet. These creatures are too much of an unknown. Until today, I had believed them a myth."

"You have my thanks, Raesa. And no, I do not mind hearing the counsel of those with wisdom to share. While I may be queen, I have not forgotten I am also young."

Raesa raised both eyebrows.

"I'm not calling you old." Kitlyn smiled. "Only myself lacking in experience. You have probably spent more time out of Evermoor than I have out of our castle."

"I find that difficult to believe. It's only been about five days," said Raesa.

Oona smiled. "Well, we have been out of the castle more than she's been away from Evermoor... but only by about another week or so."

Raesa opened her mouth to say something, but took on a somber expression and kept quiet.

"The assassins aren't your fault." Kitlyn pushed herself up to stand. "I blame only my father."

"But, sending people to murder you as a child is a bit extreme, even for a kingdom facing total destruction." Raesa wiped a bit of Nimse blood from her armor. "As much as I may have felt hatred toward Lucernians in the past, I would never have taken the life of a child."

"Even the one foretold to bring about your doom?" asked Kitlyn.

"Only fools put total faith in prophecies." Raesa glanced off in the direction of Crows' Corner.

Oona rolled her eyes. "I wish more people thought as you do. I *hate* foretellings."

"Let us return to town and think on what next to do." Kitlyn glanced at the boots hanging off her belt, shrugged, and headed toward town.

19

LIFEBLOOD

OONA

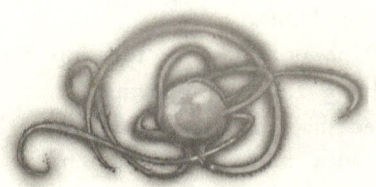

*T*he oddest sense that the Nimse had intelligence beyond what their appearance suggested prickled at Oona's thoughts. Being surrounded by them had reminded her of the highwaymen who'd attempted to rob her, so she had shrouded herself in a wall of searing light. The instant its glow fell on them, they went from menacing, devouring fiends to frightened little creatures.

Perhaps Kitlyn is right and I am too nice. The Nimse would not have hesitated in tearing me to pieces.

More so than those five, the injured one she had helped dwelled on her mind. Somehow, despite having no real way to make facial expressions, it had given off a sense of gratitude when she eased it into the tunnel. Kitlyn's enchanted stone had hurt it to the point she questioned if it would survive. Certainly, those creatures didn't visit temples of Orien, nor would bandages offer much help to a crushing injury.

I am thinking in terms of people. Those Nimse may be quite a bit tougher than us. Oh, I wish I could understand why they are attacking us. For how long have they existed beneath the earth without anyone even knowing about them? Could someone have done something? Perhaps they think we attacked them?

These thoughts plagued Oona as she walked beside Kitlyn across the forest, sometimes glancing down at her wife's bare feet, alternatively cringing at the idea of being outside without shoes and grinning at the innocence of it. Of course, Oona adored walking barefoot in the grass, but a curated garden in the castle was quite a bit different from being *outside*. Much the same way as she had gotten over her fear of being naked around Kitlyn in private but wouldn't dare show even bare shoulders in public.

Raesa stopped short, raising her bow. "Someone's—"

Kitlyn spun toward Oona and shoved her hard with both hands, tossing her off her feet. She careened over sideways, brushing a man who grabbed at empty air, and landed on her back, staring at another man seizing Kitlyn from behind.

"No!" shouted Oona, not bothering to sit up. She thrust her arm out, a bolt of blue light flying from her fingertips.

The beam clipped the man in the side of the head simultaneously burning and hitting with the force of a punch. He stumbled to the left away from Kitlyn, who whirled after him, screaming in pain and anger.

With a growl, the man who'd been creeping up behind Oona rushed at her, a dagger in his right hand. She summoned a blast of magic light in his face, which blinded him for a few seconds, enough time for her to scramble upright and pull her longsword out of its scabbard.

Raesa loosed an arrow into the trees up ahead. A man fell from the branches, but before she could fire again, another man charged out of the weeds mere feet away from her. She dropped the bow and spun under his sword stroke, gracefully drawing her blade into a slash across his chest that scored his leather armor. He backpedaled, attacking again, but she parried, their blades crossing with a loud *clang*.

Oona raised her sword and stared at the man for three seconds until Kitlyn's roaring distracted her to peer past him. She weaved between two men also in leather armor, ducking and swinging, blocking as many strikes with her weapon as she dodged.

Before Oona could toss another bolt of light, the man shook off the blindness and sprang at her, thrusting his dagger at her stomach. She shoved her butt backward while two-handing her longsword into a crossing high slash. The dagger tip scraped the armor over her stomach, clicking on the chain mail reinforcement, but he abandoned his attack to dive away from her sword.

"Hah!" shouted one fighting Kitlyn. "Won't be long now, whelp. Merry greetings from Fauhurst."

Oona cringed at the continuous ringing of swords behind her. A wet *crunch* came from Raesa's direction along with a man's gurgling.

Furious and worried for Kitlyn, Oona called another flare. The instant she raised her hand, the man appeared to expect it and turned his face away. Closing his eyes may have spared his vision, but his face still blistered. She didn't hesitate, lunging at him with a desperate upswing.

He pivoted to defend. Alas, his dagger lacked the reach to catch her blade before it cut into his side, stalling several inches up into his ribcage. Stunned, the man stopped moving and gawked at her. Oona took a step back, wrenching the sword out with a hard yank that threw her into a spin. She whirled with the momentum and brought her weapon around into another swipe that opened the front of his throat. Blood welled out of the slash, rolling down the front of his chest. He slumped to his knees and fell over sideways.

Oona turned toward Kitlyn, who stood between two dead men. A *clank* came from the right. Raesa finished off another man with a thrust to the chest, then braced her boot on his pectoral and gave a kicking shove, which knocked him away. Her slender blade, thinner and lighter than a Lucernian longsword but about the same length, gleamed red.

Kitlyn leaned most of her weight on one leg, her sword all but hanging from the fingers of her right hand. She looked tired more than hurt, though something seemed woefully wrong.

"Kit!" shouted Oona, running over.

"That wasn't..." Kitlyn swayed. "Too hard. These men barely know how to fight." She fell to her knees. "I'm..." She looked up at Oona and smiled. "You're okay."

Kitlyn's eyes rolled up into her head and she fell over, blood gushing from the left side of her neck, all over her left arm and chest.

"No!" Oona screamed, dropping her sword to jump on Kitlyn and clamp both hands over the slash. It appeared to be the work of a dagger from behind. *She'd been bleeding the whole time she fought those men.* Tears streamed down her cheeks. "Kitlyn!"

Kitlyn lay sprawled in the dirt, arms askew, eyes unfocused, barely breathing.

Oona squeezed her hands tighter. "Lord Lucen, please help her." She gasped and sniffled. "No. Please, no.... Kitlyn! Tenebrea, I beg of you, please don't take her from me yet... or take us both."

Leaves and twigs crunched behind her from someone approaching, too heavy to be Raesa. Oona couldn't find the will to care if another assassin prepared to stab her. If she let go of Kitlyn's throat, her love *would* die. If she ignored the man, she would die, then Kitlyn would die, too.

Nothing mattered.

"Please," sobbed Oona, already suspecting the wound mortal, and them too far from anywhere they could obtain help. Despite it being a near certainty Kitlyn would die in seconds, her heart refused to accept the truth of it.

Blue light welled up out of her hands, warming them, bathing the forest in harsh shadows. Oona briefly questioned her magic manifesting without her attempting to do anything more than stop Kitlyn from dying. Lucen's gift of light could see lies, know a person's intentions, burn the wicked, and chase shadows from the darkest caves... but her magic could do little for a wound so deadly.

The blue glow intensified with her grief—and turned golden, yellow-orange like the sun.

Oona kept pressure on the wound, wanting more than anything for Kitlyn to survive.

Her strangely golden light shrank down beneath her hands, settling in a comforting, tingly warmth. Oona gawked in shock at the bizarre effect, her heart racing, tears still pouring from her eyes. A moment passed before she noticed blood no longer dribbled out between her fingers and a strong sense of tiredness had come over her.

She tentatively lifted one finger. Then half her right hand, and nearly fainted at the sight of a thin red line across Kitlyn's neck that looked like a week-old healing wound. "By Orien..."

"My sister seems to like you," said a strong, male voice from above, as though a man stood less than a half-step behind her. "And she's not quite ready for you two yet."

An overwhelming presence washed over Oona, energy unlike anything she had ever felt. Her tears dried themselves in the wake of a warm, reassuring confidence enveloping her. Somehow, she *knew* Kitlyn would be okay. She bowed her head until it touched her wrists, her hands still clamped around Kitlyn's neck. "O-Orien? I-I..." She couldn't find the words to express her gratitude, and simply tried to radiate it as pure emotional energy.

The presence faded.

After a moment, Oona lifted her head and peered back at open ground. Raesa stood a few yards away with an expression of stunned awe.

"Ow..." Kitlyn sat up and held her neck. She pulled her hand away and looked at it. "Guess I wasn't as fast as I thought."

Oona stared dumbstruck. *She shoved me... Her boots are off. She had to feel them coming... and she shoved me with a guy about to grab her, too.*

"What was that light?" Raesa gestured at empty ground.

"Light?" Kitlyn peered up at her.

Raesa stepped closer. "A column of golden light appeared there, so bright I couldn't see you."

Orien spoke to me. She blinked and stared at her bloody hands. *He saved Kitlyn.*

"Oona? Are you okay?" Kitlyn pressed her hand to Oona's cheek.

"You're alive. You pushed me and just let that man slice your throat!"

Kitlyn's dark green eyes flickered with anger. "I didn't notice them at first because they weren't moving. When they did, they were too close already and... I couldn't let them hurt you."

Grief, anger, panic, and love crashed together in an explosion of emotions that left Oona unable to talk. She lunged at Kitlyn, clamping on in a desperate hug. For the first time in her life, she *hated* someone enough to consider initiating a swordfight... not that she expected Fauhurst knew how to fight with a blade.

She didn't much care about that point.

20

PURE HEART

KITLYN

*H*azy forest wobbled back and forth in Kitlyn's vision.

The man had started to slit her throat, but she'd spun away before he could cut across the front. Judging by the amount of blood on her arm and chest, she'd been gushing the whole time she fought those two cowards. Yet… her neck felt intact. She hadn't even realized the severity of her wound until she started to black out. By the time she understood she'd been mortally wounded, she'd become too out of it to even say goodbye to Oona.

But, here she sat, alive.

"How am I… not dead?" Kitlyn clung tight to her wife, as if letting go would kill them both.

"Orien," whispered Oona, bowing her head. "I think he… appeared here."

Kitlyn blinked in astonishment and gazed up at the canopy of autumnal leaves overhead, backlit in the late morning glow of a clear sky. *Certainly Orien has better things to do than attend in person to the likes of me.*

"My magic." Oona raised her hands as if cupping water. "I tried to stop the bleeding, but my magic started making light. I begged the gods to help you. It went from blue to golden… like an Orien priest."

Again, she pressed a hand to the side of her neck, finding it tacky with drying blood and only mildly sore. No worse than had a housecat raked her with a claw. "Some priests have the favor of more than one god."

"I'm no priestess."

Kitlyn grasped Oona's hands together, squeezing them. "You are more faithful than at least half of them."

Oona laughed.

"And so kind and loving and caring and sweet." Kitlyn sniffled. "Orien must have sensed how much you want to help others."

Oona sniffled and brushed her fingers over the healed wound. Her touch sent a charged tingle down the left side of Kitlyn's body. "You need to practice with Lorne a little more."

"Wouldn't have helped… the coward ambushed me."

"You fought the whole time, bleeding," whispered Oona.

"Yeah," said Kitlyn in a sighing whisper while looking at the dead men. "That's probably why I fell over at the end."

"Don't do that to me again," half-shouted Oona. "Protect yourself first."

Kitlyn wiped at blood on her left arm. "I saw them coming. You didn't. He would've killed you. I had a chance to move, you were defenseless."

"Don't lie." Oona dragged her into another hug, shivering. "You expected to die."

Kitlyn's heart turned into a ten pound stone. "I would do the same thing again, without hesitation. I could never let you be hurt."

"But you're the queen."

"People seem to think so." Kitlyn chuckled. "But you are the other half of my soul. The gods put us together for a reason."

"We should hurry back to Crows' Corner." Raesa jogged over to them. "In case there are others. I hear horses not too far from here, so I believe this ambush was hastily arranged. These men have not been here that long."

"Yes. To Crows' Corner," said Kitlyn, still resting her head against Oona's shoulder. "I need a moment. Too dizzy to stand."

"Fauhurst," muttered Oona.

"What about him?"

"Did you not hear what that man said to you?"

Kitlyn cringed. "Not really. I wasn't paying attention to anything but where swords came from."

"That man said that Fauhurst sent them to kill us."

"He's turning into a real pain in the neck," muttered Kitlyn.

Oona grabbed two fistfuls of her leather breastplate and shook her back and forth. "Not funny!"

Kitlyn tolerated the throttling. "Sorry. I have to find something to laugh at or I will kill him."

"I can't believe I'm about to say this, but I think that is probably a good idea." Oona sighed. "Or at least, put him in prison."

"Yes." Kitlyn took a few deep breaths. "I suppose we now have *two* important problems. What has driven the Nimse to form raiding groups?"

Raesa approached and handed Kitlyn a bit of paper. "It appears that someone at the castle sent word to this Fauhurst that we would be here."

She unfolded it to reveal handwriting: *Crows' Corner. Both abominations.*

"Probably Fauhurst." She handed the paper to Oona.

Soft blue light flickered in her hand as she waved it over the paper. "I feel his guilt upon it."

It had to be us tearing through Underholm. We caused a lot of damage. "Omun."

"What?" Oona blinked. "I'm not sure that is wise. He would rip apart half the city to find Fauhurst."

"No." Kitlyn chuckled. "I'm not going to ask him to find that worthless man, though I'm not above daydreaming about Omun throwing Fauhurst at the wall. I mean it had to have been us breaking a path across Underholm. Maybe he caused a cave-in or an old tunnel to open that gave them access to the surface they didn't have before? Perhaps they are simply angry at the disturbance, like a hornets' nest hit with a rock."

Oona stood and pulled Kitlyn upright. "We should return to town."

Raesa nodded and led the way toward Crows' Corner. Kitlyn, arm around Oona's shoulders for support, kept up as best she could, still weak and dizzy.

"Something else might be bothering them," said Oona out of the blue a few minutes into the walk. "If Omun stomping around down there did it, why did they wait weeks to start attacking humans? And… why are they coming out in the daytime? They clearly hate light."

"I suspect they would likely have remained hiding in that tunnel had not the tall man peered right in at them." Raesa glanced back at them for a few seconds before looking forward again. "If it is too much for you to walk, please say something."

"Thank you. I think I'm all right. Well, not all right, but at least able to make it to Crows' Corner." Kitlyn stared down to watch where she planted her feet. One root or rock and she'd be on the ground. "It is odd that they waited so long. Maybe it took them a while to find a broken passage that led to the surface?"

"The Nimse are going into Evermoor as well." Oona slowed her stride a little. "More than our people are in danger."

"King Volduin will know what to do," said Raesa. "I am sure he will send word once he determines the best course of action."

While she didn't think the woman meant to imply her a child, the statement left Kitlyn feeling like one. Then again, Lanas Volduin had been on the throne for a long time. *I should consider the wisdom of my elders regardless of the source. This threat affects us equally. There is little reason to distrust him.*

Wooziness made it difficult to think about much in great detail beyond how much she loved Oona. After such a close call, she wanted only to crawl under some heavy blankets and hold onto her for a few days. Considering it would probably be at least that long before she ceased feeling dizzy and weak, that amounted to a *great* idea.

"We should make haste for Cimril," said Kitlyn. "I believe I need bed rest."

"You are in no shape to ride. And yes, you do. Plus food and water."

She smiled at Oona. "You even sound like a priestess of Orien."

21

LESSONS AND CURSES

OONA

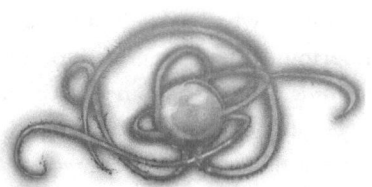

Four days later, Oona scurried around the library at Castle Cimril, a load of books clutched in her arms.

She'd spent most of the first day back in the temple of Orien consulting with their high priest and meditating on her gratitude for the god answering her plea, still lapsing into tears every time she described Kitlyn's wound. The priests interrupted her after a few hours of prayer and reflection on the second day, bringing her to a small room where a woman clutched a bleeding hand. At the urging of the priests, Oona had asked Orien to mend the small cut, and he had listened.

Witnessing the truth that he had indeed bestowed his gift upon her froze the words in her throat. Calling on Lucen's light magic had always been second nature to her, though she did gain skill and proficiency under Aodh's instruction. She believed that she had been born with some innate talent, but her loyalty to Lucen had made it stronger. However, the more she thought of the former king's teaching, the more she wondered how much had been real.

Still, with some instruction at the Orien temple, she gained a modicum of confidence in being able to call upon him in times of need. Due to her being the queen consort, the priests did not ask her to join the temple, as almost always happened in cases of gods-given magic. Of course, people who demonstrated *any* magic often wound up compelled into a temple since most Lucernians did not believe such gifts happened in any way other than at the gods' behest.

Kitlyn planned to change that, but likely not for a little while yet. At least not until the citizenry became used to their new rulers and it no longer felt as though they might not accept two queens. Those with magic feared they would be taken from their families, often upon displaying the first signs of talent as children. They would be forced into whatever priesthood most aligned with their gift. Changing that dreadful law sounded like the right and pure thing to do. Oona thought followers of the gods—especially priests and priestesses—should be there because they had such love for their chosen deity they *wanted* to be. Compelling them to be priests was as wrong as forcing people to marry and calling it love.

With a huff at the thought, she dropped her load of books on a table and sat, searching for any information about Underholm. A few of the older tomes had brief sections that told of a long-ago civilization known as the Na'vir. In one book, illustrations resembled small humans. A man in an elegant yellow robe and red hat labeled 'Na'vir' stood next to a much larger man in commoner's clothes, labeled 'human.' The top of the Na'vir's head came up to about an inch past the human's belt buckle. Other than size, the drawing made them look quite human.

Several books later, she found a written description of the Na'vir that claimed them 'stumpy' and ill tempered, overly vain in regard to their beards and with four muscular arms. Oona went back to the first book with the drawing. The man in the yellow robe did not appear to have four arms. A third book described the Na'vir as having features of 'Anthari mixed with Man.' It went on to detail pointed ears and the delicate facial features of the Anthari, but copious facial hair and more pronounced muscles similar to humans.

"Nothing about the Nimse." Oona sighed. "The old men who wrote these books can't even agree on the number of arms involved."

Three young maids entered, red-headed Rowan, Mary with long brown hair, and Laura, a contagiously happy flaxen-haired girl. Only Rowan looked at Oona with a smile, the other two seeming afraid of her. Without a word, the twelve-year-olds set to their task of dusting. Oona returned Rowan's grin. She'd been the one who brought food to Kitlyn while she'd been locked in the dungeon, and found her stolen shoes.

Oona spent a little while more poring over books in search for any mention of the Nimse, but found nothing. *No wonder Raesa thought them a myth.* Oona bit her lip, momentarily wondering if they even had books in Evermoor, then cringed at herself for the condescending thought. *Of course they do. Ivendar is as civilized as Cimril—only with more trees.* A blur of bright blonde glided by at the corner of her eye. She looked up at Laura, dusting a nearby shelf.

"Girls?" asked Oona.

All three froze and turned to face her. Again, only Rowan didn't appear worried. Usually, a noble or royal speaking directly to them typically meant they'd done something wrong or would soon be given additional work.

"It's all right. I am merely curious. I recall you telling me that none of you are able to read."

"Yes, highness," chimed all three at once.

Oona tapped a finger to her chin. "Well, since you are living within the castle and you are almost always the ones tasked with cleaning this room... I think it only fitting that you shall have reading lessons." She smiled. "If, of course, you want them."

They glanced at each other in disbelief.

"Wouldn't we be going beyond our station?" asked Mary.

"For learning how to read?" Oona rolled her eyes. "Of course not. And if anyone thinks so, I shall explain to them myself how that is not true."

The maids bounced on their toes.

"Oh, that would be wonderful." Rowan clung to her duster as though she hugged a doll. "I have always wondered what is in all of these books."

Laura nodded rapidly enough to throw her hair around in a fray. "Aye, highness. It would be so generous of you to allow us to learn."

Mary smiled.

"Then it is settled. I will instruct the tutor to include you three in reading lessons, and inform Elsbeth that it is my wish you attend. Also, one night a week, I shall work with you myself, in here."

They made noises of delight, bouncing.

At a rattle from the doorknob, they zoomed back to their places and resumed dusting, though all three continued grinning.

The door wobbled. A tiny grunt came from the other side and it wobbled again. Oona tilted her head in confusion. Another, louder grunt preceded the door swinging inward, revealing Evie in a frilly pink and white dress. She scowled at the heavy door, then darted over to Oona.

"Will you read me a story?"

Oona pulled her sister up into her lap, grinning at her adorable pink slippers. "Of course. But I need to finish some reading first."

"Okay." Evie leaned forward to look over the books spread out on the table. "What do they say?"

"These books tell of a place far away underground where another whole civilization lived a long, long time ago. But, they closed up their giant doors and disappeared. No one really knows what happened or why they went into hiding."

Evie mouthed 'wow' without saying anything. She peered back at her. "What's a cibilabation?"

Oona repeated 'civilization,' pronouncing it slow enough for Evie to get after a few repetitions. "It's a whole people. Like all of Lucernia is a civilization."

"Oh. Why did they make it underground?"

"That is a good question. None of these books have the answer." She tapped a finger to the tip of her sister's nose, grinning. "I guess they simply like it down there."

"I hope they aren't afraid of the dark." Evie offered a sheepish smile. "Like me."

Oona patted her on the head. "You don't need to be afraid of the dark. The dark can't hurt you."

Evie blinked.

"It's what's hiding in the dark that'll *bite* you." Oona playfully dug her fingers into the girl's sides, making a 'rawr' noise.

Evie let out a short scream that dissolved into giggling. The sudden worry that the evident curse upon the throne of Lucernia may affect her sister caused Oona to hug her tight. *Lucen, please watch over her. Let her keep her innocence until she's grown.* That Kitlyn had nearly died only days ago set her trembling in fear. She couldn't bear the thought of Evie walking into some room of the castle and finding either Kitlyn or her dead.

"I'm cold, too," said Evie. "Why did the old… ci va la za shin hide?"

"Good!" Oona grinned. "You said that perfectly."

The girl beamed.

"I'm not sure. This one book"—Oona pointed at a tome larger than the girl—"mentioned something about a curse, but didn't really explain what it did or why it happened."

Evie shivered. "A curse like those words Mama sometimes says real loud at the chickens?"

"No." Oona chuckled.

"I said one once when I dropped the milk." She paled. "Mama hit me."

Oona rocked her. "I'm sorry, Evie. Mama doesn't know how to be a mama. And, no, this isn't the same kind. This is a *magical* curse."

"Oh." Evie nodded. "Like the ones Mama uses that make the neighbors blush and gasp."

Despite her mind stuck on thoughts of Ruby beating on her little sister, Oona somehow found the ability to chuckle at that. "I mean bad magic. A curse like someone evil doing magic."

"How can evil people do magic? The gods aren't evil and they won't give evil people magic."

Oona took a deep breath. "People make mistakes. And you know sometimes how I can say something that's a little bit too complicated for you to understand without me saying it again or in a different way?"

"Yeah."

"Well, it's the same with the gods and people. They're so much wiser than us, sometimes what we think they say isn't really what they said. Like magic. Not *all* magic comes from our gods. Some comes from spirits or nature itself."

The three maids gasped and stared at her.

"Some even comes from deep inside a person. The gods absolutely give people who they find deserving great magic, but other kinds of magic exist, too."

"Okay." Evie smiled.

Oona glanced over at the shocked maids. "What's wrong?"

"You just spoke against Lucen," said Laura.

"I didn't." Oona smiled. "I spoke against lies the former king told. Well, the king before him. You know the people of Evermoor have magic, and they do not follow our gods. And you also know that the stories of them having demons everywhere were lies. Also, you remember how the former king did small bits of magic even after he'd been lying for so long? He'd lost the gift that Lucen gave him, but he still had the little he'd been born with."

The girls nodded, then took on 'oh… okay' expressions.

After having de-scandalized the young maids, Oona picked Evie up and carried her from the long table to a more comfortable cushioned chair in the corner. On sudden inspiration, she whisked off to fetch the book *Grengwylf.* Evie sat patiently waiting for her return with a look of mild confusion. Oona showed her the richly illustrated cover with bright green forest surrounding a small boy on his bed. Evie oohed at it, smiling.

"I loved this story when I was your age, even if it did scare me a little."

Evie blinked up at her, seeming both curious and worried. "Okay."

Oona plopped down, pulled her little sister into her lap, and read to her, loud enough for the maids to hear as well.

22

FLUFFERY AND PRACTICALITY

KITLYN

*S*unlight glowed in multicolored patches on the empty floor of the throne room at Castle Cimril, tinted to dozens of hues by the giant two-story stained glass windows running down both walls. Kitlyn sat in her throne, left hand pressed against the side of her neck. It had been six days since they arrived back at the castle, and though her strength had mostly returned, she couldn't stop thinking about how close she had come to breaking Oona's heart.

Better her alive and heartbroken than dead.

Of course, the more she dwelled on that idea, the more she suspected Oona might send herself to Tenebrea were Kitlyn to die. She had already almost done so once, albeit at the point of a sword, to protect her.

So, to distract herself from such somber thoughts, Kitlyn decided to focus on her anger at Fauhurst. For once, he managed to accomplish something beneficial… improving her mood. Thus far, his whereabouts remained unknown. The advisors and generals had all been shocked to learn of such a brazen attempt on her life.

Their third day back, while Kitlyn rested in bed, Oona had stormed around the castle with Guard Captain Lorne and several soldiers, questioning everyone regarding the mysterious note. Word rapidly swept over the castle that the queen consort intended to ferret out the spy with Lucen's gift, yet no one disappeared or ran away. Everyone they spoke to truthfully denied providing information about their trip. However, quite a few reported disturbing things going on in the castle. Doors open that shouldn't be, moved furniture, footsteps while no one was there. Many thought the ghost of a restless King Aodh prowled the halls.

Where Fauhurst had managed to find the money to hire assassins defied explanation as much as how he knew of their trip. Surely, the man must have had hidden money away as the six gold radians she'd ordered he be left with couldn't have been enough to hire those men. At least, not while leaving him anything. Either he had stashed coins somewhere or had help from the nobility. Kitlyn sent several priests and priestesses of Lucen out with military escorts to interrogate all the nobles that Beredwyn's spies had discovered to be in contact with him. It reassured her that none of them had aided him, but that also made her worry he possibly received money from outside Lucernia. Of course, the most likely explanation other than sympathetic nobility is that he'd either stolen it or made arrangements with organized thieves, the sort of people who wouldn't care what money would be used for and tended to charge interest in blood.

With the guards actively hunting for Fauhurst, and his estate confiscated, she hoped it wouldn't take long for him to be found. And... if he should happen to choose the same escape from humiliation that her father had, she wouldn't be terribly bothered by it.

Oona presently sat in the queen's throne to her left, clinging to Kitlyn's arm. As the day didn't call for public court and only the advisors stood before them, both had worn more comfortable dresses of matching forest green velvet with soft shoes.

The advisors, standing in a row at the base of the throne dais, continued discussing the best way to handle Fauhurst. In light of Kitlyn's continued hesitance to officially sentence the man to death, mostly because she didn't want to project the sense she retaliated for their long-standing animosity, they considered arranging it so he didn't survive his meeting with the soldiers who went to arrest him.

"The man is a coward." Beredwyn stroked his long, wavy beard. "He would not raise a weapon at the guard. We cannot force those soldiers to become executioners."

"I must object to the deceit of it," said Balais.

"Even a cornered rat bites." Advisor Lanon brushed lint from his sleeve. "The man is clearly desperate to have sent assassins. He has nothing left to lose, and by rights, he would be executed for his crimes anyway."

"Prison would be a far harsher fate for him." Alonna, hands clasped in front of her robes, spoke with her head bowed. "We should allow fate to occur as it is wont to do. He may decide that he prefers the end of a guardsman's sword to a cell."

A faint shiver slid down Kitlyn's back at the memory of her brief time in the dungeons. The thought of being locked alone in a small room like that for years struck her as too cruel, even for someone like Fauhurst. Kitlyn lowered her hand from the side of her neck, and Oona grasped it.

"It would please me more to see him in prison and alive, however… I will need to make some changes." With the release of those her father had imprisoned unjustly, the castle dungeons held only six prisoners. One had been caught attempting to steal from the royal vaults, the other five were supposedly assassins who'd attempted to kill Oona throughout the years. The city's ordinary criminals went to a larger above-ground jail in the northwestern portion of Cimril City, the dungeon reserved for the harshest punishments of those who acted against the crown directly. "The current prisoners… assassins? Are they from Evermoor?"

Oona blinked. "King Volduin never mentioned them."

"Four are." Beredwyn nodded once. "One of them almost succeeded many years ago, though you likely do not remember."

Kitlyn and Oona both stared at him.

"He'd disguised himself as a groundskeeper and scooped Oona up on the pretense of allowing her to ride a pony. If I recall, she'd been about five at the time."

Kitlyn squeezed Oona's hand. She *did* remember that, mostly for being hurt that the man ignored 'the peasant child' and only the princess would get to ride a pony. Oona wailed in protest, demanding Kitlyn be allowed to go with her, but the man carried her off nonetheless.

"It is somewhat familiar." Oona's eyebrows scrunched in thought. "Did I not have a bit of a tantrum that he refused to bring Kit?"

"Exactly the reason his plan failed." Beredwyn smiled.

Kitlyn scowled at nothing in particular. Those men had come here to kill her, but due to a war her father started and under a false interpretation of an old man's ramblings. After consideration, she decided that they had a choice to murder a child or not, and deserved to remain incarcerated. Though, she still intended to use her magic to rearrange the dungeons. Keeping prisoners isolated defied the gods with its cruelty.

She spent a few minutes explaining her intention to arrange the cells into spaces big enough for four prisoners together. Oona brightened at the idea, and the advisors—especially Balais and Alonna—appeared to agree.

"That decided..." Kitlyn leaned back and gazed again at the stained glass. "There remains the matter of the Nimse."

"I do not think it wise to send our forces into Underholm." Lanon clasped his hands, each disappearing into the opposite sleeve. "They would be at too great a disadvantage within the depths."

Beredwyn pondered a moment. "On open ground, they are relatively weak. However, our soldiers would have no way to defend against those creatures dropping on them from above."

"I am not convinced it is necessary to invade them at all," said Oona.

Advisor Lanon looked around at everyone. "Perhaps we can establish a blockade at the doors, shut them in?"

"They are not using the door." Kitlyn made a drilling motion with one finger. "They tunneled out of the ground at Crows' Corner. Though, I do not know how readily or rapidly they can dig." *Perhaps that is why it took them weeks to attack us?* She thought back to Omun stomping through Underholm and the Nimse swarming after them along the walls. The small creatures had been furious with her for touching those glowing purple rocks. Could they *still* be upset about that? But if so, why would they randomly attack people in Evermoor as well? *Do they lack the reason to recognize which land I came from so they attack both? Strike a hornets' nest, and the little demons aren't too particular about who they sting.*

Emissary Raesa would have made it to Ivendar by now, though no word had yet reached Lucernia regarding what King Volduin wished to do regarding the Nimse threat. Their villages had less sturdy homes than those on this side of the Churning Deep. Angry Nimse could shred thatch roofs with ease. Something needed to be done *soon.*

The advisors muttered amongst themselves, debating various ideas to cope with a nearly invisible enemy that could appear anywhere without warning.

"Have we not been doing exactly that for the past twenty years?" asked Beredwyn with a hint of a smile. "Evermoor's raiding parties crossed the Deep wherever and whenever they cared to courtesy of their rootcallers."

"This is true, but Evermoor's forces at least trod *upon* the ground, not under it." Advisor Alonna fidgeted at her medallion of Navissa. "These Nimse can appear with far less warning. Perhaps the Night Goddess can offer her protection since they fear the light."

Lanon rambled about distributing small numbers of soldiers to all towns and villages near Underholm to conduct a night watch. The other advisors clustered in and they began murmuring in conference a bit too low to follow along with.

Oona leaned close, brushing her fingers at the side of Kitlyn's neck while whispering, "The wound is nearly invisible."

"You are a gifted healer." Kitlyn drew her love's pale hand up and kissed it.

"I'm hardly a healer. I've only just begun to learn how."

"And yet you mended a mortal wound. You are gifted."

"If in the sense of receiving a gift from Orien, then you are correct."

"So humble," whispered Kitlyn.

Oona blushed.

"Perhaps it is wrong of me to divert so much of my thinking toward another land, but the Nimse will cause many deaths in Evermoor. Thatch huts and windows without glass."

"It is not wrong of you at all to fear for the lives of the innocent." Oona's lip quivered. "We must act."

"Do you still have the same feeling?" whispered Kitlyn. "Did Lucen wish us only to be at Crows' Corner?"

"I…" Oona closed her eyes.

The advisors continued their discussion, considering sending soldiers to every village or town within reasonable distance of Underholm.

A moment later, Oona shuddered and her eyes snapped open. "I still see the shadows racing across Cimril. I fear we are still entwined with this."

Kitlyn nodded. "I will go to Underholm."

All five advisors stopped talking simultaneously and stared at her. Beredwyn wore a look of worry, Lanon shock. High Priest Balais lifted both brows in an expression of surprised respect. Alonna gave off an air of caution.

"So soon after you were attacked?" asked Lanon.

"The Nimse are not going to wait for us to find Fauhurst or his sympathizers," said Kitlyn.

Oona sat tall. "I am sure Lucen wishes us to have a more direct hand in this."

"The former king always said 'Lucen wants' certain things." Lanon cringed ever so slightly. "He claimed to know the desires of the God of Purity, yet clearly did not."

"Dear Lanon,"—Balais pivoted to face him—"you will note her highness said she believes Lucen wishes her to be involved, not that he wishes her to be involved."

"Are they not the same thing?" asked Lanon.

"The difference is small." Advisor Nalden smiled. "But meaningful. She speaks for her own feelings rather than claims to know the mind of a god."

Balais nodded to him. "And does not demand others obey without question."

"I understand there is danger." Kitlyn stood. "However, I feel the risk to my personal safety is small compared to the risk facing our people. We have little reason to suspect Fauhurst will move against me so soon, especially with our soldiers searching every inch of Cimril for him."

"This is perhaps a bit rushed," said Beredwyn, attempting to sound consoling. "I am concerned for your safety."

A phantom pain nipped at Kitlyn's neck. She resisted the urge to cringe and descended the stairs off the dais. "I am not insisting that I travel alone, and you are all aware of Oona receiving Orien's favor. I have the utmost confidence in that she truly has received Lucen's counsel."

"Of course you are not going alone." Oona leapt to her feet and ran down the four steps.

Kitlyn smiled. "I would prefer you stay safe."

Her blonde eyebrows flattened.

"However, what I prefer and what is best for all are not the same." Kitlyn almost leaned close and kissed her, but decided against it. Even in front of only the advisors, a public display of affection would not be received well. *Even a king and queen would not dare to show...* She blinked, glanced at Oona, and pulled her into a kiss.

The advisors gasped.

Oona *mmphed!* into her mouth, but didn't protest. After, she stared in surprised delight, no small amount of blush on her cheeks.

Uneasy throat clearings came from the advisors, except Alonna, who smiled.

"To the Pit with purposeless dourness!" Kitlyn whirled to face the advisors, the fire of inspiration in her eyes. "Lucernia is hurting from an awful war. Let our love fill the castle with joy that spreads over the land. It is time to heal. Why must royals and the nobility pretend they are incapable of happiness?"

Beredwyn's eyes sparkled with a single tear. "This castle is in dire need of happiness."

"Now then..." Kitlyn gathered her hands in front of herself, her trumpet-like sleeves draped down to her knees. "Ready our horses and prepare an escort. There is no need for the coach or the royal pavilion." She internally rolled her eyes at the smaller version of her grand bed, rugs, shelves, and an enormous tent. "I will sleep like the soldiers."

"But..." Advisor Lanon raised a hand.

"What need have I of fluffery in a matter such as this?" asked Kitlyn. "It is an unnecessary burden."

"Some fluffery *is* nice," whispered Oona. "Like our bed."

"Yes." Kitlyn turned toward her. "But there is no need to make anyone haul it around in the woods. We are not going out there to be seen. We're going to deal with a problem."

"Oh, I agree." Oona grinned. "Merely stating that fluffery is not entirely bad when appropriate."

Kitlyn looked over the advisors, nodded before any could offer further protest, and walked briskly toward the throne room's rear exit. "We shall depart within the hour."

23

THE WHIMS OF GODS

OONA

During the time Oona and Kitlyn changed into their traveling clothes, another messenger arrived with news of additional Nimse sightings in Wick Hollow last night. According to the report, three soldiers had been wounded, though would likely survive. Fortunately, the precaution of demanding all citizens remain indoors after sunset had prevented any injuries or deaths outside the military, except for a few unfortunate chickens and one highly surprised cow.

Oona didn't feel quite as awkward this time in the saddle as she had the first, but still would've preferred a nice dress to the leather armor. However, even the most comfortable dress in her wardrobe didn't suit overland travel without a coach. Again, Kitlyn wanted them to leave their crowns safe in the castle, claiming the heavy metal rings would only get in the way should they wind up in battle. Oona had teasingly suggested some people may not believe her the queen.

What girl my age in Lucernia can summon stone from the ground? asked Kitlyn in her memory.

Remembering the expression on her love's face accompanying the question made Oona laugh. For the first hour or so of their journey east along the road from Cimril, they had discussed the nature of royalty, specifically how one person could command so much power over so many. While Aodh had been somewhat competent with a blade, he had lost the bulk of his magic and any of the seasoned castle guards could have bested him with ease. Why had so many people blindly obeyed him when he had no capacity whatsoever to *make* them? It would've been one thing if he held the trust and love of his people and they respected his wisdom, but that man ruled by fear—proxy fear of Lucen instead of himself—but fear all the same.

Oona cringed at Kitlyn saying she believed her father ought to have been deposed a long time ago. Worse, she proceeded to flirt around the idle notion of replacing the monarchy with something akin to a council of elders. Distributing power, she reasoned, would make it more difficult for one person to abuse the trust placed in them. Oona countered by saying that without the prestige and power of being a king or queen, a 'councilor' would be more vulnerable to influence by bribes or personal whims.

Her argument appeared to quench any sincere desire on Kitlyn's part to abandon monarchy, at least for now. Perhaps when they grew old—*if* they grew old—she would try to dissolve it then, making her the last queen. That would, of course, obviate the issue of their not having an heir. Perhaps it had come time for the Talomir bloodline to part ways with the throne; after all, they had held it for five generations already. Kitlyn eventually suggested *adding* a council instead of replacing the monarchy with it, creating a power split.

Oona felt more open to that idea than utter removal of a king or queen, though cautioned her not to speak in public of such things yet. She feared too much change too fast would cause unrest. People still coped with twenty years of Aodh's lies, the end of the war, a new monarch—and a woman at that—not to mention their queen taking a *wife*.

They reached the crossroads near the Arch of the Ancients by early evening, though Kitlyn insisted they press onward rather than lose three hours of daylight by stopping at the garrison there. Darkness fell approximately a quarter of the way north to Wick Hollow.

Lieutenant Hain, the highest-ranking soldier among the thirty that escorted them, ordered her troops to set up camp off the side of the road. Upon stopping, Oona dismounted Cloud and proceeded to remove his harness and saddle before feeding, watering, and brushing him. Kitlyn tended to Apples in a similar manner, the larger ex-warhorse having a disposition that reminded Oona of a sedate puppy.

When Kitlyn broke out a few apples, Cloud stared at her with huge, black eyes. She tossed one to Oona, who happily offered it to the horse.

Eventually they, the horses, and the soldiers settled in to camp. Within the hour, the smell of roasting chicken and wood smoke overpowered the subtle fragrance of meadow grass.

Oona and Kitlyn stood on line and collected plates from the cook rather than waiting for anyone to bring them food, which earned odd looks from some of the soldiers. Kitlyn walked over to a spot of ground and took a seat. The soldiers gathered in groups here and there to eat, some making small fires to chase away the autumn chill. They initially kept quiet and appeared uncomfortable at having the queen in earshot, though at Kitlyn tearing into her chicken in much the same way she must've eaten at the servants' table in the kitchen, the soldiers relaxed and a din of conversation filled in the silence. A few slips suggested they tried to avoid coarse language or crude humor while near the royals, but otherwise appeared in high spirits.

With the promise of good weather, the soldiers set up bedrolls in the open and established a watch rotation. Oona, studying them, managed to arrange her sleeping area without too much frustration, and felt proud of herself for accomplishing such a simple task... never once having even changed the sheets on a bed before. She didn't much relish sleeping fully dressed except for boots, or upon such a crude bed, though it still surpassed her 'guest room' in Ralen's dungeon. Also, Kitlyn's sneaky wisdom made sense. In armor, without crowns, under a blanket, they blended in among the soldiers. An assassin would have trouble differentiating them. In truth, the only awful part had been the total lack of a garderobe, having to relieve herself directly on the field—a task that reinforced leather breeches made woefully cumbersome. Fortunately, Kitlyn created a barrier of vines for privacy.

Oona reclined under a thin blanket beside Kitlyn, who had a separate sleeping mat. Nothing more than hand holding would happen that night. She gazed up at the endless stars overhead, surprised by how relaxing the open air and gentle breeze could be. The occasional wisp of campfire smoke drifted by across a sea of dark blue swirled into black.

"That group there looks like a deer." Kitlyn pointed upward.

Oona squinted. "I don't see it."

"The two bright stars are the tips of the antlers," whispered Kitlyn.

They spent a little while hunting for shapes in the stars, enjoying the brief escape from their worries. Distant soldiers around the camp discussed the trip to Underholm, never having been near it before. Few appeared to know anything about it or the Nimse, or the Na'vir who once lived there.

"I feel old," muttered a man a distance off to the left. "Still remember Kitlyn being a wee thing, runnin' about the castle. Used ta be so happy."

Oona squeezed her hand, smiling at the voice: Garon, a soldier who'd been around the castle as long as she could remember.

"I still can't believe how the king treated her," said another man from the same direction. "Do you think it's true she didn't even know who she was?"

"Of course she didn't, Karlin." The woman sitting with them mumbled as if chewing food for a few seconds. "That girl wouldn't have tolerated half of what she did if she knew the truth."

"Look at 'er," said Garon, a note of affection in his voice, "beddin' down with the likes of us. Hard to think of that little girl as a queen."

"She doesn't act much like it." Karlin muted a laugh, then slurped a drink.

The other two coughed.

"Easy," whispered the woman. "Mind your tongue."

Oona glanced over at Karlin, a thirtyish man in chain mail with pitted cheeks and a thin mustache. He sat in a circle around a small fire with Garon and a younger woman, perhaps thirty feet from where Kitlyn and she lay in the grass.

"I didn't mean that in a bad way, Lanis." Karlin wiped some chicken grease from his lip before pointing a half-eaten drumstick at the woman soldier. "It's just unusual to see a royal not constantly remindin' everyone they're better than us."

"I'm not," whispered Kitlyn. "Only the gods are better than us."

"They know you don't feel that way." Oona reached over and clasped her hand. "And they probably think we're asleep."

A younger soldier wandered up to the group by the fire, speaking in a hushed tone. "I can't believe everyone's just tolerating... you know."

Oona scowled.

"The gods didn't challenge it." Lanis, the female soldier, lifted a bit of chicken to her mouth, but hesitated before biting it. "I hear Tenebrea even showed herself."

"Aye, but the gods didn't do much about King Aodh causing a war that raged for twenty years either." The young soldier stared off at the dark sky. "Maybe the gods don't care what we do as much as the priests try to tell us they do."

Oona started to sit up, but Kitlyn pulled her back.

"It's not worth it. We can't force people like him to approve of how we feel for each other. Only ask them not to attack us. If we confront everyone who speaks ill of us, it will make us seem petty."

Oona grumbled, rolling on her side to face Kitlyn.

"Look here, Donal." Garon wagged a fork at him. "If you aren't willin' ta die ta protect your queen, go on back ta yer farm."

"Aye." Karlin took another bite of his drumstick.

"This queen beds down with her soldiers." Lanis gestured toward them. "Aodh would *never* have even pitched his grand tent close to us. I don't care who she marries."

"It's unnatural," muttered Donal.

"Unnatural would be weddin' a bloody sheep"—Garon looked him up and down—"like yer mother must 'ave."

Kitlyn clamped a hand over her mouth to hold back laughter. Oona gawked, stunned both that someone defended them and by the crass remark.

"Who says it's unnatural?" Lanis sat tall and held her arms out to the sides. "People? The gods have said no such thing."

"You carried a blade to defend a man who defied Lucen, lied to us for decades, and started the war that took half the boys ya grew up with." Karlin hurled his bare chicken bone into the field and picked up another drumstick. "And yer goin' on about her only on account o' who she loves? By Tenebrea's tits, that makes no sense."

Oona gasped—as did the soldiers. No worse a profanity existed within Lucernia.

Donal flopped to sit, rambling about his parents always saying such relationships came from the work of demons. A long, circuitous conversation followed mostly about how Aodh's transgression of deceit was an *actual* affront to the gods. Karlin said he didn't personally like the idea of the queen marrying a girl, then added his reason: it meant he didn't have a chance to be her suitor.

This, of course, set off the others teasing him for having a face that could make an oxen scream and run the other way. He laughed with them, also adding a few jokes about his unfortunate appearance. Eventually, Donal slipped away in silence.

Somewhat suspicious that he might be loyal to Fauhurst, Oona watched him. When he neared the edge of the camp and kept going, she rolled onto all fours, grabbed her sword, and hurried after him, not wasting time to put her boots back on.

Donal stopped about fifty yards from the campsite and knelt in the meadow. Oona crept to a halt far enough away that he hadn't seen her. He bowed his head and began praying to Lucen for guidance. Oona listened for a moment until she discarded her notion he might be a traitor. Right as she shifted her weight to crawl back to bed, she froze at what the young man whispered.

"Lucen, please give me a sign. Were my parents wrong? Is it wrong for me to feel as I do for Tavin?"

She stared at the young soldier, perhaps a year or two older than her. A bluish tint to the strong moonlight made his reddish-brown hair seem dark. Her initial contempt for him melted away to pity and reawakened her fears at how her life might have gone had the king not taken her from Ruby. If Llanoen had been her home, and she didn't have Kitlyn or any place else to go, she likely wouldn't have been able to stand up to her. Might she have been forced to marry a boy to avoid her mother's retribution? Could her mother have warped her thoughts to the point she made herself hate others like her to preserve her mother's love? Could she even call a parent doing that *love*?

"Donal," said Oona.

The young man jumped and spun around, one hand on his sword.

"Calm down. It's only me." She pushed up from her crouch to stand.

Donal coughed and fell back, seated. "H-highness... I-I'm..."

"Shh." She walked over and sat on the grass next to him. "After what you said, when you slipped away from camp, I suspected you might be with Fauhurst. So I followed you."

His cheeks reddened. "You heard..."

"I did, and I wanted to tell you something."

"But... you're the queen consort. I'm just a soldier, and only a footman at that."

Oona rested her elbow on her knee and stared down at her foot, skin so pale it practically glowed in the moonlight. "I don't think a difference in status makes people any better than each other. Certainly by now, you know that I was born in Llanoen, the daughter of common farmers. By birth, you and I have the same station."

He managed a feeble nod.

"The woman who gave birth to me has similar views as your parents. I met her by chance. At first, she seemed happy to be able to reunite with me after the former king swore her to secrecy. But upon realizing I was in love with Kitlyn, she completely changed. I went from daughter to abomination."

"I'm sorry," said Donal, his voice heavy.

She looked up, making eye contact. An emerald darter—a harmless four-winged shiny insect—landed on her hand and crept over her knuckles. "I heard what you said about your parents. If Aodh hadn't taken me away from my mother, I would have been treated much the same way. Probably worse. Ruby is quick to drive home her opinions with her fists." Oona talked for a while about Evie, who still hadn't quite stopped flinching whenever an adult made sudden motions near her. "If I'd been left to grow up under her roof in Llanoen, and she ever caught me kissing another girl, I shudder to think what would have happened. The woman used to strike my sister for making small errors or not understanding things fast enough. She may well have killed me for that."

"Tavin and I grew up in River's Rest. We started off as friends, but I always felt we had something more." His voice caught in his throat. "I... we haven't been able to be together. I can't choose between my parents' love and his."

Oona reached out to put a hand on his arm, startling the emerald darter to wing. "You've already made two choices... one outside, one inside."

"He's always sad. I fear he might forget me. But, he doesn't understand how my parents are. His mother and father know about him and... don't mind." Donal's lip quivered. "By Lucen, I admit to being jealous of him for that. His parents love him. Mine love who I pretend to be."

"I still cannot fathom what made our people believe Lucen's purity would in any way condemn real love. It's been that way since long before either of us were born. But simply because something has become tradition does not make it true, or right."

"If I am open with Tavin, he will be overjoyed. We could be so happy together." Donal looked around, then shrank in on himself. "Lucen forgive me but we have... known each other, and we are not married."

Oona blushed. *Perhaps if two people truly love each other, the gods won't care so much that they show it before some mortal-made ceremony. If not for our station, I'm sure Kit and I would've... experimented before marriage, too.* She suppressed the urge to frown at being under such constant scrutiny her entire life. "Only with him?"

Donal nodded. "Yes. I would never betray him."

"My mother chose her love of money over any love she had for her child... twice."

"Twice?"

"My sister..." Oona flicked at a blade of grass by her toes. "I had to get her away from that wretched woman. But what I mean is, if your parents love the appearance of being 'normal' more than their son, I say you should be rid of them. But, I also admit that I had only just met my mother before deciding to allow her to remain apart from my life. Yours raised you, so the decision cannot be as easy."

He nodded.

"If they try to blame Lucen for their views, tell me and *I* will explain the truth to them."

Donal gawked at her. "Highness... you can't be serious. *You* would travel all the way to River's Rest for me? One soldier who"—he cringed—"you likely overheard saying unkind things about you?"

"Now that I understand why you said those things, yes. I will not allow anyone to use Lucen's name to cause others pain."

"Oona?" asked Kitlyn. "Where did you go?"

She twisted back to peer over her shoulder and waved, making a tiny blue light at her fingertips.

Kitlyn jogged over. "You scared me. What are you doing out here?"

"Just talking." Oona smiled at Donal. "Listen to your heart."

"That light." He shifted his stare from her hand to her eyes. "I begged of Lucen a sign, and... perhaps you are that sign."

"I feel I've missed something significant." Kitlyn's eyebrows flattened.

"Highness." Donal sprang to his feet and bowed at her. "I should return to my duties watching over the camp."

"Of course." Oona stood and took Kitlyn's hand. "Let us return to bed."

Donal trotted off across the field.

"What *were* you doing so far off? You gave me a fright."

"Lucen needed me here." She leaned against Kitlyn and explained the conversation she had with the young soldier as they walked back to their sleeping mats.

24

MERCY IN DARKNESS

KITLYN

*A*round noon the following day, Kitlyn brought her horse to a stop near two tall obelisks of pale grey stone wrapped in vines and covered in cracks that stood on either side of a long-untended road descending into an artificial canyon. Some ancient workforce had carved a ramp downward into the earth over about half a mile. Boulders of various sizes, abandoned wagons long since collapsed into loose boards and metal slats, weeds, and even animal bones littered the once-highway.

The Lucernian side of Underholm suited the kingdom's staid philosophy, a straight passage cut into rock without frill or fanfare, quite unlike the beautiful moonstone path on the Evermoor side winding lazily down to the giant goblin-faced doors. While the grass strewn with glowing gemlike stones reminded Kitlyn of a scene from a storybook, the bleakness in front of her made it quite apparent no one had traveled this road for centuries.

She vaguely recalled Kethaba saying something about the Na'vir vanishing about a thousand years ago, though Oona had been unable to find any official records about trade with them. Such trade must have occurred at some point given such a grand opening, so it bothered her that no information whatsoever remained anywhere. The royal library only even mentioned Na'vir in four books, all as a minor addendum to other information.

There ought to have been at least one book solely dedicated to an entire civilization. The library has six on the Anthari and no one has seen an elf on this continent since before the Na'vir died out.

Kitlyn narrowed her eyes as a sudden sickening suspicion swirled in her stomach.

"What's wrong?" asked Oona. "That look on your face... You're either about to deposit your breakfast on the grass or order someone executed."

She relaxed her glower. "I was merely thinking about how the library has so little information on the Na'vir. It's almost as if someone deliberately tried to erase them from history."

"I did find a few books, but they didn't have much information."

"Yes, but all of them only mentioned the Na'vir in passing. Someone trying to remove any reference to them and being hasty about it could have missed those."

"Oh." Oona blinked, glanced at the distant huge doors, then looked back at her. "Why would anyone want to alter history?"

"To conceal a crime or control people's opinions," said Kitlyn.

"That sounds a little farfetched, no? What sort of crime could be so bad that a former king or queen allowed it to be concealed?"

Kitlyn patted Apples' mane. "A war perhaps. Maybe Lucernia wiped out the Na'vir."

"Surely not. There would have been *some* record of such an atrocity, even in folklore."

"From a thousand years ago?" Kitlyn blinked. "We don't even have records of who the king was that far back."

"Well, if a war had occurred, they would speak of it as a victory, would they not?" Oona shot an uneasy glance down the road.

"Only if the war had been justified... though you may be right. It would have been easy to claim they cavorted with demons as my father did with Evermoor."

"The curse," whispered Oona. "Could this be it? An unjust war? The dying breath of a Na'vir seeking revenge?"

"My family has not been in power for a thousand years... but the curse may not be on us so much as the throne." Kitlyn fidgeted. She hadn't given much weight to Oona's worry about curses, despite the rather compelling streak of bad luck experienced by her most recent ancestors. That the only one to survive to old age had abdicated the throne to live a reclusive life as a noble only served to make the idea of a curse seem more likely. Again, she rubbed the spot where her neck had been sliced open. *I am fortunate Tenebrea and Orien favor us.*

"What orders, highness?" asked Lieutenant Hain, riding up on Kitlyn's left.

She glanced over at the woman, almost thirty, blonde like Oona but nowhere near as 'delicate-pretty.' Hain had a strong jaw and an athletic frame from her spending the last twelve or so years fighting in the war. A tiny scar marked her left eyebrow.

"I am still considering." Kitlyn clutched the reins tighter, gripped by a sudden bit of nervousness. *Perhaps I should beckon Omun.* She pondered, but dropped the idea. *No… we're not going in to exterminate the Nimse. And I cannot simply bother the stone ancient with every little problem I have.* "What weighs upon my mind at the moment is marching thirty men into the dark. Those creatures can swim over the walls."

"What is it you hope to accomplish in there?" Lieutenant Hain eyed the road ahead. "Those creatures do not seem given to receive a diplomatic visit. Our force is too small to accomplish much, despite how simple they are to slay."

"Simple out in the open. In the dark with three running at you and six more falling from above, it is not so simple," said Kitlyn in a toneless voice.

Oona swallowed hard. "You went in there *alone* last time?"

"Yes." Kitlyn thought back to that boy Kem who'd been too frightened to go inside. Perhaps he had known about the Nimse, though more likely, he succumbed to folklore about ghosts. And well, he had admitted to being a bit of a coward. "I had not known the Nimse existed then." She glanced at Oona. "Though even if I had, I would have chanced it."

Oona teared up and took her hand. "We both flirted with death. Damn that war. But…" She took a deep breath and chased away her melancholy. "We now know they shy away from Lucen's light. I am certain I can keep them back from us, though I do not expect all of these soldiers will fit close enough to be protected."

"Something has caused the Nimse to dig to the surface and attack both Lucernia and Evermoor. I am inclined to think that their aggression may be simply their nature and they attack only because a way has opened for them to escape Underholm. Omun left a path of destruction in his wake, though I do not think he meant to—he is simply large. I intend to search for the cause of their agitation, or if it is only exposed dirt, I will seal it with stone and contain the threat."

"That feels right." Oona squeezed her hand. "This aggression is something they cannot help, not the act of a hostile civilization trying to make war."

"No more than a pack of wolves could declare war on a human village," said Lieutenant Hain. "How many soldiers are to accompany you inside?"

Kitlyn thought of the dead man, Lem, and the tall man, Darrow, who'd been wounded. Saying 'five' again, a reasonable number Oona could most likely shield felt too much like selecting soldiers for slaughter. All thirty plus Lieutenant Hain would be too much for the light to protect. Those too far ahead or behind would be picked off. Ten might test the limits of the Nimse's distaste for light.

"I went in there last time with no idea what awaited me and much less understanding of my magic. I cannot ask your men to risk their lives when I am capable of protecting myself."

Lieutenant Hain opened and closed her mouth.

"Last time, you needed Omun to get out of there alive," said Oona a little louder than a whisper.

Kitlyn winced. "True, though I may have done something to anger the Nimse. They have these sacred glowing stones. I thought them a handy light source, so I took some. With your light, we won't need to disturb the shrines."

"You assume the creatures will not remember you," said Lieutenant Hain.

"They might." Oona eyed the ramp. "I am certain they are smarter than they appear."

"Very well then." Kitlyn nudged Apples into motion, guiding him around the boulders, six-foot weeds, and wrecked wagons.

Smooth stone walls rose on both sides, marred with cracks and tufts of green. Once the top edges reached more than a story above their heads, the formerly-plain rock bore crumbling bas-reliefs of scholarly people in robes. A handful depicted a four-armed man wearing a combination skirt-and-pants garment, plus sandals. His bare chest revealed defined but sinewy musculature. He raised his upper pair of arms over his head, holding a glowing crystal and a scroll. The second pair, he extended out to either side, one hand gripping a book, the other a chisel. An expression as if staring off into the distance, deep in thought as well as the symbolic nature of his pose made Kitlyn think the image depicted a deity rather than an individual.

"That's strange." Oona guided Cloud around the smashed remains of a wagon behind her. "The books I read couldn't seem to decide if the Na'vir had four or two arms. Most of the images in these carvings look like humans, except that one. And all the ones with four arms appear to be the same man. Could that be one of their gods?"

"I was thinking that, too."

Kitlyn stopped her horse about ten feet from the massive, but plain, stone doors, and managed a shaky dismount that only caused a handful of soldiers to chuckle under their breath. Oona again descended from Cloud's saddle as if lofted by invisible wings.

"Are you absolutely certain you do not wish *any* soldiers to accompany you?" asked Lieutenant Hain. "It seems quite reckless."

"I..." Kitlyn glanced back at the men and women assembled behind her. While she didn't want to be responsible for more soldiers dying, it didn't seem possible to be queen and avoid that. Almost any order she issued had the chance of resulting in her military being injured. She took some comfort in that she would be in as much danger as any of them, not asking them to risk their lives while safe back in Castle Cimril. How many men and women had her father sent off to their deaths while perched on soft cushions eating luxurious meals? "All right. Please ask for five volunteers. Any more than that and the light may not be enough to shield them."

Lieutenant Hain repeated the call for five volunteers. Donal stepped forward first, as did about half of the rest. The young man hurried over to Kitlyn and Oona. The lieutenant picked four others: a large-framed man with dark brown hair, and three women all of whom appeared quite early in their twenties. Kitlyn didn't recognize any of them, but Lucernia had thousands of soldiers.

"Thank you for your bravery," said Kitlyn. "May I have the pleasure of your names?"

The tall man bowed. "I am Lonn, highness."

"Marta," said a woman with auburn hair, the youngest of the lot who might not have even been twenty yet.

A thin woman with her black hair cut short bowed to them. "Gwynn."

The last, a statuesque blonde, introduced herself as Janna.

Kitlyn thought the woman resembled the forgemaidens from Ondar, powerful warriors who aided their Steelfather, mostly by crafting weapons and helping the souls of those who fell in battle find their way to the Great Hall.

"You know what this means," said Oona in a somewhat whimsical tone.

"What?" asked Kitlyn.

She eyed Donal. "Last night, he spoke of his love for another that he has been thus far unable to be with. He will likely perish in Underholm."

Donal gawked. "A-are you speaking in jest or as an agent of Lucen?"

"Sometimes fate dislikes being teased." Kitlyn patted Donal on the shoulder, pained at the idea he may die under such circumstances. "I will not turn away your bravery, but if you wish to make right with your love before volunteering for dangerous expeditions, I would not hold that against you."

"Thank you for your kind words, but I will not waver." Donal stood tall, despite being nearly a head shorter than Lonn. "Lucen heard my call and answered. It is the least I can do."

"All right," said Oona. "But please be careful."

Kitlyn faced the entrance of Underholm and stepped out of her boots onto a dusting of grit that covered the broken stone path. She sent her magic into the earth, calling out to the great stone doors. Brilliant green energy swirled around her body. Seconds later, a matching glow shone from around the seams. The earth shook with a heavy *thud* that spooked Cloud. Apples' ears twitched, though he didn't flinch.

With a grating scrape, the forty-foot tall goblin-faced door on the right eased outward. Kitlyn pulled at it until she'd created enough of a gap to fit past. A hollow windy howl yawned from the impenetrable darkness inside, as though even the light of day feared to venture past the threshold. Kitlyn released her concentration on magic, and the green energy sank back into the ground.

After stuffing her boots into the saddlebag, she walked up to the opening and peered inside. *Yeah, that's as dark as I remembered it.* Her ability to 'see' via the stone wouldn't help anyone else.

Oona's small blue light orb floated over Kitlyn's head and entered the tunnel, revealing a massive corridor forty feet square littered with stone chunks, the occasional rusting weapon, and more broken wagon parts.

"This is quite a bit nicer when I can see." Kitlyn stepped into the vast tunnel, looking around. Thick pale grey dust coated the floor, making it feel as though she walked on a mattress.

Roots had broken through the ceiling in places, the likely cause of stone fragments on the ground, though none of the openings appeared large enough for a Nimse to squeeze into. The soldiers entered behind Oona.

"Wow…" Gwynn barely had to turn sideways to fit past the narrow gap in the doors. "How far beneath the earth does this go?"

"Far enough to cross under the Churning Deep into Evermoor," said Kitlyn. "Except, I remember there being a cave-in. I should be able to get us past it except for one problem."

"What? A cave-in?" Oona gazed up at her glowing blue orb.

"I tried to return to Cimril to request help, but the ceiling had collapsed. Nimse tunnels riddled the dirt like a nest. Let us hope your light keeps them at bay." She looked at the soldiers. "Of course, if you need to defend yourselves, by all means, do so. However, do not kill any Nimse that isn't presenting an immediate threat."

The soldiers nodded.

Kitlyn led the way down the passage, stepping around rocks and debris. Oona's light sent long shadows creeping over the walls from square columns every hundred feet or so. Every breath carried the flavor of wet stone and the thickness of cold humidity. Near the base of the dark grey walls, a band of gold pattern, simple design of woven lines about two feet tall, ran the apparent length of the tunnel.

"This place is massive." Janna let out a soft whistle of awe.

"Never imagined anything like it." Lonn paused to trace his fingers over the gold decoration.

Donal stared at the ceiling. "Hard to believe an entire nation existed underground… or built a tunnel so massive."

"All these wagons." Oona gestured at a pile of smashed wood with a bit of recognizable wheel sticking out of it. "This passage looks like a highway. It must have once carried a robust trade."

Kitlyn spotted a pale pink glow emanating from a small cubby ahead on the left. An image of the first Nimse she'd ever seen, leaping at her from the dark, brought her right back to her last time down here.

"Don't touch those stones." Kitlyn pointed at the glow. "Better we don't go anywhere near that shelf."

Murmurs of agreement came from the soldiers.

They walked a while more in silence.

Kitlyn's nervousness increased. Eventually, the silence grew intolerable. "So, this is what I was doing while you were Ralen's guest."

Oona cringed. "I'm not sure which of us had it worse. I might've preferred a pack of Nimse to those wretches who tried to slice my dress off."

"You may rethink that if we are unfortunate enough to see a swarm like what chased me into Omun's chamber. It was as though the walls came alive with teeth."

"I think I would prefer a quick death to what those men wished to do to me."

Kitlyn shivered. "I'm not so sure the Nimse would've offered a quick death… and I think if I were given the choice of those two fates, I would prefer to remain alive."

Oona glanced at her with a 'how could you say that?' expression.

"It's a bit difficult to hunt down and kill Nimse after they've eaten you. Once out of that cell, I would not have rested until I'd tracked those wretched men to wherever they hid and sent them to Tenebrea."

"Yes, but even if you killed them, there's still the memory of what they did."

"I…" Kitlyn sighed. "Perhaps we should stop talking of such things. I am on edge enough down here."

"Yes. I agree."

Soft whispers and scratching noises came from up ahead.

"They're watching us," said Kitlyn.

"I don't see anything." Donal grabbed his sword but didn't draw it.

Kitlyn opened her thoughts to the Stone. Hundreds of small feet and hands gripped here and there, staying just beyond the radiance of Oona's light. "They are close, but calm. Either the light is keeping them at bay or they saw us bypass that shrine."

Marta jumped and whirled to look back at a soft scrape. "Perhaps both?"

A clatter of falling small stones came from ahead. Moments later, the cave-in Kitlyn remembered—or at least the opposite face of it—emerged from the darkness.

"Is this the damage your giant caused?" asked Lonn.

"No. It was here already. Maybe Lucen did it. If this passage had been clear, I never would have found Omun." She put her hands on her hips, studying the complete blockage. Dirt had fallen in from above along with many giant slabs of rock that had once been ceiling. "If this had been clear, I'd have walked straight out into Lucernia, gone back to the castle hoping to get help for Oona... and probably been locked away. Either in a cell or a bedroom."

"Speaking of things I'd rather not talk about..." Oona rubbed her wrist.

A Nimse leaned out from one of the holes in the giant dirt wall, lips peeled back enough to emit a tentative snarl.

"That's different." Kitlyn braced for it to rush at her. "Last time, they came after me pretty much right away."

"Perhaps they are afraid of six people?" asked Donal. "Or the light?"

Kitlyn couldn't tell if the Nimse remained oddly calm because she hadn't disturbed a shrine. Maybe it feared Oona's light, didn't want to attack seven people, or some act of the gods held it back. Regardless of its motivation, she didn't want to waste time on a pointless question.

She opened herself to the sense of the Stone. As she had pictured the tunnels behind the dungeon she'd escaped from, a sense of her surroundings manifested in her awareness. The cave-in continued for about sixty feet, riddled with tunnels like a termite nest, though no chambers existed, suggesting they'd burrowed only to be able to go back and forth past the collapse. *If I can tear Castle Cimril apart at the seams, I can clear this.* "Can you understand me?"

The Nimse tilted its ball-shaped head, still snarling. Both bean-shaped nostril eyes might've been focused on her. Hard to tell as they lacked pupils, being solid black. It continued to lean out and duck back, emitting low growls like a frightened dog hiding in a burrow.

Kitlyn looked at Oona. "Be ready with the light. This may disturb them."

"What may disturb them?"

"I'm going to clear this corridor."

The soldiers gave her various looks of incredulity.

Oona nodded.

"If you can understand me, you should leave that tunnel," said Kitlyn.

She closed her eyes and held her hands out in front of her, palms down. As Kethaba had taught her, she reached inside herself to the 'core' of her magic, sending warm tingly waves of power throughout her body. The stone beneath her feet warmed. A faint rumbling started in the ground in response to her wrapping her consciousness around the massive blockage of dirt and stone.

Like molding clay, she commanded the great hunks of rock to melt and slide out of the way of the earth, which she pushed upward. Startled Nimse screams pierced the roar of upheaval. Soldiers ran close on either side of her, but Kitlyn didn't break her concentration or open her eyes. Letting go of the effort too abruptly might trigger an even worse collapse and kill all of them.

"Go back," yelled Oona. Armor rattled. A second later, "No, I'm talking to *them*."

"Oh, right," said Marta.

Warmth intensified from the right, no doubt from Oona making her orb brighter.

In Kitlyn's mind, the image of a liquid mass of dirt flowed up the side walls, pouring into the opening above from whence it had fallen. As the last of the doughy mass settled into place, she guided the liquid stone back to the ceiling, shaped it flat, and melded it with the parts that had not collapsed. She sealed hundreds of cracks and fused the walls of Underholm solid once more.

Bewildered high-pitched chirps echoed in the distance.

"By Lucen," whispered Lonn. "I've never seen anything like that. Not even the high priest has such power."

Kitlyn gradually relaxed her magic until she trusted the ceiling to hold, then let go entirely and opened her eyes. "I am sure the high priests have as much or more than I do. Mine is merely different."

"From Evermoor." Donal took his hand off his weapon. "She is using stoneshaper magic."

His tone didn't imply insult, so Kitlyn nodded at him. No trace of any Nimse remained visible in the wide open corridor, except for the faint scratching of small bodies running away. Some traces of dirt remained, a sixty-foot wide swath of damp brown ahead of them instead of the pale grey dust everywhere else.

"That was… incredible." Oona gazed around at the ceiling, her eyes wide. She made her light ball glide upward for a better look at the perfectly flat stone. "It would've taken workers many months to clear such a collapse if at all."

Kitlyn resumed walking. "I now know where I am. It truly is a straight line between Lucernia and Evermoor. The central chamber had enormous passages leading north and south. Their city may stretch for miles underground. This highway cuts across it."

A short while later, the passage leading to the chamber where she had discovered Omun came up on the left. Seeing it made her shiver at the memory of the wall swarming with Nimse. She crept down the side corridor, curious to survey the damage or look for ways the Nimse could've escaped to the surface. She remembered the ceiling had allowed some sunlight in. The cracks remained as they'd been before, still packed with thick roots. It didn't look as though any Nimse had used it as an exit, so she saw no need to mend the stone.

Oona advanced to the end of the ledge, peering down the four-story-deep room. "That must be where Omun slept."

"Be careful." Kitlyn took her hand and looked down as well. An Omun-shaped hole remained in the wall and floor where his lower body had been buried. The Nimse that had fallen to its death no longer lay there. "The pool at the bottom is only a few inches deep. One of them fell and died, but it's gone. Do they care for their dead?"

"Something bothers me about the Nimse," whispered Oona.

Donal moved closer to her. "Other than their enormous teeth and vicious little claws?"

Oona managed a feeble smile at his whimsical tone, but nodded. "Yes. Something else."

"They are not quite animals." Kitlyn headed back to the main passage.

The group walked in relative silence for a few hours, the constant whispering and scratching of Nimse coming from beyond the reach of Oona's light. The soldiers kept close behind them, all on edge and spooked at the constant sense of being surrounded.

Eventually, the light fell upon another pair of enormous doors, hanging ajar. Kitlyn slipped past the gap into the massive chamber that looked like the main street of a city in miniature. Most of the façades in the walls only came up to her face, roughly two stories' worth of construction in the span of ten feet.

Gwynn whistled. "This is the city of the Na'vir. It's much more elaborate than I imagined."

"Such ruin." Donal advanced in a gradual, rotating spin, looking around at everything. "What caused this?"

Oona shook her head. "I only wish I knew the answer to that."

"You should put your hair up, highness." Marta started to swipe her fingers at it, but hesitated. "It's nearly past your seat and will get in the way during a fight."

"I'm hoping we do not have to fight." Oona fidgeted. "If I am crossing swords with someone… or some*thing*, circumstances have already gone quite awry."

Kitlyn looked back and forth over the huge chamber while walking forward. Every time her foot hit the ground, she lofted a cloud of swirling grey dust. On the far side, the opposite doors to the ones they entered lay bashed down, the result of Omun carrying her back out to Evermoor. A line of destruction cut across the square where he had trampled benches, statues, and columns.

"There…" She pointed, and moved up to a fast walk, approaching the smashed door.

A sizeable hunk of ceiling had fallen along with the doorjamb, exposing earth. Though the ground had a healthy collection of small dirt piles, it appeared the Nimse had cleaned most of it up. A large recently-dug tunnel led nearly straight up from the spot of exposed earth.

"This is where they traveled to the surface." Kitlyn gestured up at the opening.

"Excellent." Marta nodded. "Will it be enough to repair that and be on our way?"

Kitlyn widened her stance and slid her feet back and forth to get past the dust to solid stone. "I do not know, but I shall try."

Omun had left enough rubble in the city square that she had no shortage of material with which to repair the ceiling. She raised spires of stone from the ground to push the gargantuan door upright. However, lacking the ability for her magic to affect the hinge plates, or any ladders for someone to reach them by hand, she propped the door against the wall and proceeded to liquefy rubbled stone and move it to the damaged area. Before long, she had mended the ceiling and wall.

"Navissa's nethers!" rasped Lonn. "Here they come!"

Kitlyn whirled around. The city center had exploded to life with Nimse. The four-story-tall chamber with eight stories of walkways and building faces turned black under a wave of thousands of diminutive bodies. The creatures crawled sideways upon the walls, darted across the ceiling, and swam down to the floor, rushing toward them like a liquid mass of teeth.

Lonn grabbed Kitlyn by the arm and whisked her into the corner by the doorjamb. Within a second of her catching herself on the wall, Janna shoved Oona in beside her, mushing her against the stone. All five soldiers formed a human barrier between them and the onrushing legion.

Kitlyn gawked at the size of the horde. Even bringing all thirty soldiers wouldn't have mattered.

Damn. I should have asked Omun to come with us. I could call for him, but he would never make it in time to matter. She summoned a large rock, shrouded in green magic light, readying to hurl it into the crowd. The soldiers drew their weapons. Twelve feet of open floor separated them from the charging Nimse.

Ten.

Six.

Kitlyn launched the stone at one, smashing its ball-shaped head open like a rotten melon. Its companions swarmed around the dead one like it didn't exist.

Teeth and swords clashed in a clamor of clanking and screeching.

Oona thrust both her arms upward, and her orb bloomed from dark blue to pure white, blinding in its intensity.

The mass of Nimse screeched in unison and recoiled, stopping like water against an invisible barrier.

Kitlyn raised rock spires in front of the soldiers, trying to create a defensive wall. One clipped a Nimse, knocking it over backward. Janna kicked the first one to get close to her in the face, flinging it away. Another leapt in teeth first, but she raised her sword to block. The creature dove back howling, black blood pouring from its mouth. Gwynn slashed one on the arm, then suffered a bite to her thigh before pounding that one in the head with the handle of her blade. It collapsed to the ground and curled up. Marta swung her sword back and forth in an effort to keep Nimse at a distance.

"Wait!" shouted Oona. "Don't kill them."

Donal looked up at her in bewildered alarm after killing his second one.

"What?" Kitlyn whirled to stare at her. "Are you serious?"

Donal whispered apologies to Tavin for not being able to see him again.

"They're hesitating. Praise Lucen!" said Gwynn.

Oona took a step closer to the soldiers. Wisps of azure energy swirled up her arms, adding to the orb, brightening it. Hundreds of Nimse raised their arms to shield their tiny eyes, all recoiling. A few whimpered in fear. Seconds later, the nearest ones screamed in panic and raced away into the mass, seeking cover of darkness.

"Please," said Oona. "Don't hurt them. I... have a feeling. I think I understand why *we* were sent here. We are not meant to destroy them."

25

THE COURT OF NAZADUR

OONA

Keeping her light high and bright, Oona squeezed between two soldiers, advancing on the wall of Nimse.

They continued shrinking back from her, wailing in pain and turning their heads away—until their secondary eyes a little behind where human ears should be caught the light. They screamed again before darting into the crowd.

While hiding behind the soldiers with her back against the wall, staring at the vast army of small murder-mouthed horrors, a sudden inspiration she could only credit to Lucen changed her terror to pity.

The touch of Lucen urged her toward mercy, not conquest.

"He sent us here to help them," said Oona. "That's why I felt like we had to come ourselves. If you had sent only soldiers, perhaps with other priests of Lucen, they would have thought nothing of slaying the Nimse... and likely would've been overwhelmed. *Look* at all of them." The sheer amount of Nimse presently staring at her frightened her at the implications of how that battle might have gone. And after wiping out the likely small force, they would have spilled out and fulfilled her vision, crawling all over Cimril.

Kitlyn drew a sharp breath. "You are the kindest, most gentle soul to walk upon Lucernia. Only you could possibly feel compassion for these creatures."

Oona glanced back at her. "You do not?"

"I didn't mean it that way. Though my first meeting with them wasn't exactly on wonderful terms. Attempting to bite my head off is not what I would call a pleasant greeting."

"They cannot help themselves." Oona turned and rested a hand on Gwynn's thigh. "Something compels them." *By Orien's mercy, may your wound be cleansed.* Sun-orange light welled up around her hand, seeping into the young woman's leg.

Gwynn made a face like she'd stepped barefoot in slime. A moment later, she stared in reverent awe. "Highness... you're a healer as well?"

Kitlyn rubbed the left side of her neck.

"Orien has bestowed his gift to me, yes. It is somewhat recent. I'm only still learning." Oona bowed her head and offered a quick prayer of thanks to him.

"Not to challenge you, highness." Janna kept her shield high, trying to position herself between Oona and Nimse. "But how do you know?"

"I am sure of it, but I know not why."

Donal muttered a brief prayer to Lucen.

"Stay close and do not stray from the light." Oona moved the orb to a point directly above her head and advanced at the mass of Nimse, following the inexplicable pull urging her deeper into Underholm.

The brilliant light parted the sea of snarling creatures, changing growls to simpering whines of pain. As each front row scrambled away from the searing light, the next moved in, preparing to attack, but recoiled once the glow fell upon them at close range.

Oona veered to the left, following the path of the subterranean city street.

"You're going south," said Kitlyn. "Why are you going that way? It's deeper into their city... let us head for the exit."

"You know it is south?" Lonn pointed his sword in that direction.

"Yes. The Stone tells me where I am."

Oona smiled. "I feel we must go this way. Trust in Lucen."

"Oh, I do." Kitlyn looked around. "I trust him. It's the Nimse I have little trust in."

The street narrowed from the great open square, reminding her of a large thoroughfare in the heart of Cimril, only with stone overhead instead of sky. Ruined shops and dwellings lined both sides, painstakingly carved from solid stone. Oona suspected something akin to stoneshaper magic had a hand in it due to the exactness of lines. The soldiers huddled close, keeping their blades pointed outward at the aggressive Nimse hovering just beyond the circle of light. Every so often, one swiped a claw at the air.

Oona stared at the Nimse in front of them walking backward as fast as she advanced. The creatures focused on her appeared less hostile than the others, almost as if they could somehow sense she didn't wish to harm them. An inexplicable notion that they all suffered some sort of intense pain—other than what her light caused—increased her pity for them as well as her urge to help.

"Perhaps Orien rather than Lucen led me to this path," whispered Oona. "It matters not, I understand and will do as you ask."

The fist-sized light ball drooped, its eye spots making it appear tired. Before the light could falter too much, Oona bolstered it with another prod of desire.

"Please don't let that light fail… or we will all wind up in lots of rather small pieces." Kitlyn gave her arm a squeeze.

The soldiers emitted uneasy noises.

"Worry not." Oona reached up to brush her hand over the orb. "He's tired. Not used to being this bright for this long."

"He?" asked Kitlyn.

"Don't you see his little eyes?" Oona smiled.

"Is he really alive or is it something you did… like a puppet?" Kitlyn tilted her head.

"I'm not really sure, but I like to think about him that way. He's cute." Oona again 'pet' the light ball. It wobbled in response.

Lucen leads me here for a reason, and it is not slaughter.

She followed the odd urge pulling her forward past dozens of abandoned shops, dwellings, decorative archways, and statues depicting fairly human-like figures, mostly in robes. Here and there, another four-armed man occupied a position of prominence, also holding the crystal, scroll, book, and chisel.

"There's gems all over the floor in there." Marta pointed off to the left with her sword.

"Touch nothing," muttered Janna.

"I'd have to wade past three hundred of those things to get there anyway." Marta laughed. "No chance of that."

Oona continued advancing into the dark. The street widened again, becoming another large open square where stairwells at four corners led down to a pit that may once have been a fountain or pool surrounded by terraces and benches. Nimse spilled over the railing at the top, clinging to the walls inside, trying to follow without coming too close to the painful light.

She peered over the edge when she neared, picturing small people relaxing or talking, perhaps even swimming in the now-dried up pool. Scratching claws came from everywhere, echoing in the stillness. Oona jumped at a sudden scrape from directly above her. Nimse clung to the ceiling four stories overhead, all peering down at her. They shifted around as if debating their chances of survival if they let go and dropped.

Fearing they'd dive on her at any second added speed to her step.

A courtyard abutted the end of the giant fountain/pool area, bordered on two sides by solid walls that stretched forty feet up to the ceiling without so much as a ledge or tiny window. Thousands of glittering points emerged from the darkness at the back end of the alcove. A sense of menace radiated from it, though the urge pulling Oona onward didn't wane.

She slowed again, advancing at a tentative pace. Walking into a dead end with so many Nimse behind them didn't seem like the wisest idea she'd ever come up with, perhaps even more foolish than running away in the night to escape a political marriage and all the pressures of being the princess she wasn't.

Her light fell upon an intricately carved façade trimmed in silver and gold at the innermost end of the courtyard. Flashing glimmer danced among thousands of gemstones embedded in support columns, the frames of windows, and around two large onyx doors. A woven gold line pattern similar to the one in the great tunnel decorated the black stone in bands near the ceiling and floor.

"Wow." Kitlyn walked up to a column and ran her hand over the gemstones. "This wall is worth more than Lord Parrington's entire estate."

The soldiers laughed nervously.

"This must've been their palace." Oona approached the double onyx doors, the top of which stood even with her nose. The light orb circled around behind her to stay out of her eyes.

"Yes. It does look important." Kitlyn edged past her and pushed at the doors, which opened with surprising ease.

Oona ducked the low top of the doorframe and stepped into a grand hall. Whitish marble tiles stretched out across a space at least equal to the throne room in Cimril. Round columns of polished black stone glimmered with an uncountable number of tiny flecks. Long banners of rotted yellow, gold, and black fabric hung in tatters along the ceiling. The slightest breath of air upon them would likely cause them to disintegrate.

"Wow. It's so beautiful." Kitlyn crept forward.

More Nimse emerged from the shadows on either side of the columns, still hesitant to walk into the light. They growled and hissed with greater urgency, as if trying to scare the intruders away from whatever lay deeper in the chamber.

Oona raised her light over her head again, calling a little more magic to brighten it. The Nimse recoiled as a singular mass, responding with a collective wail. She set her jaw in determination and strode down the aisle between the columns as if visiting a foreign ruler. *Please don't be that walking skeleton I saw in my vision.*

The aura of her light spread into the deeper shadows, revealing a throne of carved onyx with a row of Nimse standing close in front of it. Upon the throne sat a wretched figure neither person nor Nimse, though with a much more human face. The torn remains of a once-grand gown clung to an emaciated frame with a generally female shape. Ink black skin awash with wrinkles covered a body no larger than one of the youngest castle maids. Despite having the stature of a child, her bosom appeared quite adult. Long, white-grey hair spilled down over her shoulders like a tangle of spider silk as long as her shins.

All eight or so Nimse standing in front of her cringed at the approaching light. They screamed and wailed in pain, but refused to move from their spots. The Nimse Queen raised one small arm to shield sunken gem-like eyes of gleaming amethyst. She hissed, her eerily human-like lips parting to reveal tiny, pointed teeth.

Oona stopped and urged her light to back up a little.

"Dim that wretched light," shouted the Nimse Queen, in a raspy but shrill tone.

"I shall do as you ask, but only after you command your subjects to back away," said Oona.

The queen pointed a talon of a fingernail at her. "You are fools for venturing into the Court of Nazadur! Surface-dwellers are not welcome here." She grasped the armrests of her throne, leaning forward, snarling like a feral creature. Wispy white eyebrows rose in gleeful anticipation. "For what has been done to us, you shall know suffering."

26

THE QUEEN WHO ONCE WAS

KITLYN

*K*itlyn stepped in front of Oona, glaring at the diminutive woman.

The row of 'guards' continued to squirm and wail under the glare of the light orb. Hissing, the queen snapped her teeth at Kitlyn. Hundreds of Nimse surrounding them mimicked the gesture with a cascading rattle like stone chips clapping together.

"What has happened here?" Kitlyn narrowed her eyes the moment realization dawned. "You were Na'vir once, weren't you?"

The queen snarled, then roared, "Speak not that word!"

"We do not understand what has befallen you," said Oona. "We have come to help."

"You have come to be eaten," rasped the Nimse Queen, raking her claw-like fingers at the air. "Feast!"

The Nimse at the edges of the light grew agitated, tentatively stepping closer but cringing away after mere seconds. All five soldiers pivoted outward, forming a defensive circle with Kitlyn and Oona.

Donal leaned close and whispered, "They don't look happy."

"They don't look anything," replied Janna. "They've got no faces… like someone drew eye dots on a pumpkin."

"Pumpkins aren't that round." Marta chuckled nervously.

"Please." Oona took a half step toward the throne. "I want to help."

The queen cackled, leaning forward again. "And I want to eat you."

Annoyed, Kitlyn raised her arms to the sides, glaring at the wretched creature on the throne. "If that is your only answer, I shall collapse the entire Underholm." She pushed magic into the earth.

At her command, the ground shook. Dust fell from the ceiling. Small statues off at the sides of the room fell over. The limitless mass of Nimse all screamed in terror at once.

The queen's eyes flared wide in response to the emerald light swirling around Kitlyn. She leaned back in her throne, grabbing two fistfuls of her hair. "No. Please do not. Do not slay all of us."

Kitlyn ceased rattling the walls, happy her ruse worked. "We have come to talk, not fight. Give us your word that your subjects will not attack us, and we shall lessen the light that causes you pain."

"Talk?" muttered Gwynn. "They can talk?"

"Yes," snapped the queen. "My people can talk, but not in your language."

The queen looked around at the walls and ceiling. Once the last of the rumbling subsided, she sat up straighter, arms limp in her lap, and nodded to Kitlyn. "Please do not destroy our home any further. For at least as long as you visit us at this moment, my people will cause you no harm." She stood upon the seat of the throne and called out a few sentences in an incomprehensible language, then sat once more.

Kitlyn blinked, unable to tell where individual words ended or began.

"You have our thanks." Oona glanced up. The light orb dimmed from the blinding white radiance to its normal blue. Like a giant jelly raindrop, it plopped down to rest on her shoulder as if tired.

The Nimse guarding the throne ceased squirming and whimpering, though remained in place. However, none of the creatures in the room snarled anymore, all standing in eerie silence.

"We know little of you or your people." Kitlyn took a step closer to the throne. "Please tell us what happened. Are the Nimse and the Na'vir the same?"

The queen bowed her head, emitting a sad sigh. She shifted her gaze up, still with a hungry gleam in her eyes, but looked down again. "An age ago, many times a human's lifespan, a surface-dweller came here to the Court of Nazadur. At the time, my people traded openly with both the humans in the west and the Anthari in the east."

"Anthari?" asked Oona. "They lived in Evermoor?"

"Yes. They distanced themselves from humans some time ago,

migrating across gateways into another realm. Some Anthari still exist in this realm, but far to the north, and far to the east across a vast ocean." The Nimse Queen shifted her attention back to Kitlyn. "A surface dweller came from Lucernia in search of forbidden knowledge. Your people would say he wished to draw upon the powers of demons."

Oona gasped. "But Lucen drove all demons from our land eons ago. They cannot tread upon the blessed land."

The queen chuckled. "Is that what they teach children now?" She shook her head, sighing. "Perhaps demons are uncommon, but there is no magic on your ground holding them back. Your priests have been quite efficient at concealing the ancient ways, hunting down those who traffic with demons, purging them."

"Is... that bad?" asked Kitlyn.

"Likely not." The queen scratched at her chin, claw-like fingernails scraping like blades on hardened leather. "Demons are rather dangerous."

"Forgive the indelicateness of the question, but did the Na'vir deal with demons?" asked Oona.

"In minor ways, occasionally." The queen traced a fingernail around the armrest of her throne, etching a faint line into it. "However, you must understand my people were driven only by the desire for knowledge and understanding. To us, learning and thinking are the highest virtues... which is why our fate is so cruel." She scowled at the side, snarling. "To be reduced to near-mindless animal creatures. It is the greatest torture."

Oona clung to Kitlyn's side, her voice heavy with sorrow. "That's... I'm sorry."

"Some of my people called minor demons into existence, fusing them into items such as lamps or other things as a power source. We understood them to be quite dangerous, so none risked attempting to harness power from anything greater than the most minor of entities. However, as we crave knowledge, we researched and understood *how* to bind more powerful ones."

"By Lucen," whispered Oona.

The queen raised a hand. "Knowing the process to do something is not the same as doing it. I'm sure you're quite aware of how to take that sword of yours and stick it through the girl standing next to you, but you would not do so."

"Never," said Oona, her voice hard yet wavering with sadness at the thought.

"Did someone lose control of a demon?" Kitlyn gazed around at the ruin.

"No. Our people were known over great distances for our vast libraries. The surface dweller came here seeking knowledge of powerful demons. I refused to grant him what he sought. He pretended to leave with little protest, though he would soon bestow a curse on me and my people. Many died when the first ones turned into the beings you know as Nimse. Those slow to succumb to the dark magic fell victim to the teeth of their brethren. Eventually, only these pitiful creatures remained."

"Y-you're a thousand years old?" Oona blinked.

"Something to that effect, yes." The queen scraped her claw-like nails at the throne arms, the noise shooting tingles down Kitlyn's back.

She squirmed, trying to ignore it. "Is that lifespan normal for a Na'vir?"

"We consider ourselves elderly after about eight hundred years. I was 297 the day the curse took effect. I should be gone by now, but the darkness won't release me. Perhaps I shall forever exist part way between who I once was and a monstrous creature that desires warm flesh."

Oona urged her light orb into the air again off her shoulder, and stepped forward, leaving it hovering behind her. She gingerly reached out a hand and cradled the side of a Nimse guard's head. The creature appeared to sense her grief for it and simply stood there without growling or much moving at all. "We will break this curse. Will you stop your attacks on the surface?"

"That happened over a thousand years ago. The man who did this is already dead. Where would we even start?" Kitlyn glanced at her.

"Come, child," said the Nimse Queen, before muttering in the indecipherable other language.

The guards in front of the throne moved aside, clearing a path.

Kitlyn eyed the space, hesitating.

"I am surprised surface dwellers would help us after our last dealing with one. But, if you will help, you have my word we shall not harm you."

"We…" Oona gave her a meaningful stare.

Kitlyn forced her nervousness aside. "We will do whatever is within our power to assist you."

Oona beamed.

"Then, come." The Nimse Queen raised both hands to her like a beckoning grandmother.

Kitlyn steeled herself and stepped two paces forward. Still standing atop the dais, the queen wound up nearly the same height as her. The small, old creature grasped her face in two cold, leathery hands. Fingernails like the tips of daggers prickled at the skin by her ears, but didn't cause pain. The elder leaned close as if to kiss her, a stink like a days-dead deer rotting in the woods emanating from her mouth. Her faintly-glowing amethyst eyes widened, and she exhaled a sudden, sharp breath that appeared from her lips as wispy glowing tendrils. A foul-scented breath burst into Kitlyn's mouth.

Her surroundings changed in an instant. As if seated on the throne, Kitlyn gazed out over the same room lit like daylight with no apparent source of illumination. The banners overhead appeared intact, and the blurry forms of tiny human-like beings packed the court. A man in his later twenties with long black hair and beard walked toward her, the crowd of blurry, small people filling in behind him. An elaborate mantle of dark fabric topped a robe of crimson. Numerous pouches and small cases hung from his belt. The most unsettling quality came from his stare, as though he would think nothing of killing her should the whim take him.

Instead of speaking when he stopped in front of her, he aged rapidly into an old man, then appeared to die on his feet before her eyes. His skin dried and turned grey, darkened, then fell away revealing bones and rotten flesh beneath. Despite his obvious lack of life, he glowered contemptuously and stormed off, a long black cloak fluttering behind him.

The sight of a rotting body added to the taste of carrion in her mouth from the Nimse Queen's breath and made her gag. She stumbled away from the throne into Oona's arms, choking for air. "That's... that's horrible..."

"What did you do?" Oona leaned forward, defensive.

"I showed her the surface dweller." The queen gestured at her. "Much easier than speaking."

Kitlyn flailed her arms, coughing, and grabbed onto Oona's side.

"I'm fine. Just… disoriented. I do hope when you have visions they are not as overwhelming."

Oona brushed at her hair, fussing over her like a worried mother. "It varies. Though I've only had two."

"He does not live, yet he remains." The queen picked at her hair. "He has stolen my crown."

"The man who did this is a walking skeleton," muttered Kitlyn, describing what she saw.

Oona looked back and forth between her and the queen a few times before shaking Kitlyn. "I saw the same thing! Lucen gave me a vision of this creature. We have to put it to rest."

"Where is he?" asked Kitlyn.

"Voldreth the sorcerer dwells among titans, beneath the elder frost in the halls of stolen memories, a plague to the father of steel." The queen lowered herself back into her throne.

Kitlyn blinked. *Titans? Actual titans? No, she must mean the Titan Peaks. The Steelfather? He's on the Ondari side of the mountains.* "I think I understand. North, in the mountains."

"Titan Peaks," said Oona.

"It's a long way north." Kitlyn scratched her head.

"We're already out of the castle."

"True."

Oona patted the guard Nimse again and stepped back. "And I want to help them."

"You want to help everyone." Kitlyn grinned. "But this will be more involved than bringing some coins to the temple."

"I confess you are right about that. The Na'vir suffered a demon's curse. Lucen has led us here for a reason."

Kitlyn sighed, nodding. "You convinced me already."

"Oh." Oona clasped her hands and smiled.

"You made up my mind right around the time you said 'wait, don't kill them.'" Kitlyn winked at her before turning to face the Nimse Queen. "We will find this sorcerer. Will you agree to cease your attacks on the surface?"

The queen leaned back, her ancient gown rustling. "I am hesitant to trust the word of surface dwellers, so I will not swear an oath as yet. However, I will grant a short armistice to allow you a chance to keep your word." She tapped a fingernail a few times on the stone. "You will have ten years."

Kitlyn opened her mouth to protest, but realized she hadn't heard 'ten days.' *Short armistice? Ten years is short?* "All right."

"We had better make haste." Oona gave Kitlyn the side eye, trying too hard to sound serious.

"Indeed."

The queen shot upright in her throne and shouted in the Na'vir language. In response, the vast gathering of Nimse flooding the room receded, streaming out the door and up the walls to window holes as well as jagged tunnels near the ceiling that must have been made after the curse.

An entire civilization of scholars reduced to near-mindless savages. Truly that is the work of a demon.

"Until we meet again." Oona curtseyed at the Nimse Queen.

"We will return." Kitlyn bowed her head.

The queen chuckled. "Of course you intend to… but in order to return, you must survive meeting Voldreth. May you fare better than I."

Oona's face faded even paler—a true feat.

HEIGHTS

OONA

*O*ona stared at their bed, her armor laid about on the floor of the royal bedroom around her bare feet. The sweaty tunic she'd worn under it clung to her, making the room feel even colder. Several days of riding and camping in the same clothes left her feeling too filthy to touch anything.

"Are you all right?" Kitlyn, who'd not spent the past few minutes staring at the bed, padded around to stand beside her, wearing only sweat.

"My thoughts are going in all directions." Oona plucked at the wet fabric. Overcome with disgust, she peeled the tunic off and dropped it, then cringed. She felt too filthy to even touch Kitlyn. "I am sure we must go alone."

"Alone?" Kitlyn stepped closer, pulling Oona's hair off her face and tucking it behind her ears. "Go where alone?"

"To the north. 'Tis a vague but strong feeling. Death will follow if we travel with soldiers."

"All right."

Oona blinked. "You aren't protesting?"

Piper poked her head out from a heavy burgundy curtain filling an archway on the right side of the room. "Highness, the bath is ready."

"Thank you." Oona spun to grin at her, and took Kitlyn by the hand. "Come. It is chilly in here."

The girl disappeared back behind the curtain.

"No, I'm not protesting. I roamed all over two kingdoms by myself for over a week. I think we can handle a journey together."

Oona hurried over to a relatively small chamber filled with shelves of scented oils and soaps. The collection of bath accoutrements had more than quintupled since the room belonged to Aodh. Piper, in a short white slip, barefoot, stood beside the tub, ready to assist with their bath, grinning from ear to ear in anticipation of the magic she expected would occur soon. Oona smiled at her, wondering how much longer the fourteen-year-old would retain her childish delight at the light show. Then again, old people still found the displays the Lucen priests created in the skies for holidays fascinating, so perhaps she never would outgrow it.

Hands outstretched to the tub, Oona focused on her magic. The bathwater glowed blue in response, a pool of liquid light. After a moment, steam rose in clouds. Satisfied the bath had become warm enough, she hurried in, gasping in delight at escaping the autumn chill. The soothing, heated water felt as though it physically scraped away the sticky grime of the road.

Kitlyn climbed in and eased herself to sit beside her.

For the next wonderful forty-or-so minutes, they bathed. Piper assisted with washing their hair and backs, and wound up almost as wet as them. Once they stood to dry off, Meredith entered with fresh towels. Soon, they donned simple dresses and sat on two nearby cushioned benches while their handmaidens combed and tended to their hair.

Oona's stomach growled. They'd returned not long after noon and it approached time for the evening meal. Restlessness plagued her, a sense that they shouldn't remain idle too long. Though she felt more than a little trepidation at confronting an undead sorcerer who had existed for a thousand years, she trusted Lucen wouldn't lead her down this path if she couldn't do what he asked.

Still, her hands shook. Though her vision of the undead sorcerer had been brief, it horrified her and sent her mind awhirl with all manner of wild assumptions of what he could do.

Evie raced in, cheering that they had returned, and proceeded to bounce up and down on Oona's bench seat while asking about their trip. Her little sister's joy chased away the dread of what awaited them, and for a while, she thought only of family.

AFTER A WONDERFUL MEAL, THEY RELAXED IN A SITTING ROOM WITH a glowing fireplace. Kitlyn and Oona sank into the cushions of a sofa with Evie nestled between them, and read to her until the girl had trouble staying awake. Oona carried her up to the curved hallway and helped her change into a nightdress. She sat on the edge of her former bed, singing softly to her little sister until the child fell asleep.

Kitlyn hovered close, smiling, silent until they'd stepped out into the hall and closed the door. "It is so good to see her happy. I wonder if this is how it feels to have a daughter."

"I'm not one to ask that." Oona smiled. "Perhaps you could speak to Margaret and see if she concurs."

"I could. Speaking of seeking counsel… let us do just that."

Oona nodded, and followed Kitlyn across the castle to Beredwyn's chambers. He answered the door after a moment, still dressed in his advisor's robes—though without the hat on.

"Ahh, no two better faces could appear at my door to bring an old man a moment of pride." He grinned while resting a hand on each of their shoulders. "I hope nothing troubles you at this hour."

Here in the relative privacy of the advisors' hall, he behaved more akin to the grandfather of two young women than advisor to the queen and her wife. Perhaps because the man had always been kind to Kitlyn, Oona didn't at all mind the casualness. In fact, she found herself drawn to him even more in the absence of her not-father. *He knew who I was all along…* Overcome for a brief moment, she hugged him.

Beredwyn patted her back. "There, there, girl. What's wrong?"

"Oh, nothing is wrong." She stepped back, smiling. "I am merely happy to have you looking out for us. You're the closest I have to a father."

"Something troubles you, however." Beredwyn glanced back and forth between them.

Kitlyn nodded. "The situation with the Nimse is not yet at an end. There is more we must do, and I believe you will not be fond of it."

"Oh, by Lucen." Beredwyn's thick grey eyebrows went up. "This is not a conversation for a doorway. Please…" He backed up and gestured into the room.

Oona entered, heading for a small table with cushioned chairs around it. Kitlyn sat beside her, Beredwyn across from them. Having returned from Underholm directly to their bedchamber, they spent a while telling him of their journey, what they had learned of the Nimse — and what they promised to do.

"That is quite a remarkable tale." Beredwyn stroked his beard with slow, sweeping pulls.

Kitlyn sat forward, head in her hands. "I cannot discern a reason for why most mention of the Na'vir was removed from the library. It suggests something occurred that one of my predecessors had felt great shame over."

"The sorcerer was... or is from Lucernia." Oona fidgeted. "It may be possible that they simply wished to conceal that one who trafficked in demons had ties to the kingdom."

"But to conceal the existence of an entire civilization?" Kitlyn looked over at her. "Why?"

"To speak of the Na'vir would invariably lead to talk of their downfall, and the source of that downfall came from Lucernia." Oona plucked a bit of lint from her dress. "Or I suppose a prior king tried to cleanse the demons from Underholm and failed to do so, thus he wished to conceal the shame of defeat."

Beredwyn exhaled. "It also may simply be the thought that the Na'vir hoarded knowledge of all kinds without regard for what it contained and they wished to prevent anyone from venturing there in search of the forbidden."

Oona bit her lip, staring at him. "Oh. Yes. That also makes sense."

"There is more." Kitlyn broke eye contact with him. "We intend to locate this creature and confront it."

Beredwyn paled. "Kitlyn, you speak of an ancient horror steeped in demonic power. I cannot advise you to confront it directly. Bad enough you risked entering Underholm."

"I also question how it is we are to face such an old and powerful horror." Oona grasped her knees, trying to hide the trembles in her hands. "Such a thing ought to terrify me into hiding under my blankets, but it doesn't. Lucen will protect us."

A pained grimace spread over Beredwyn's lips.

"Do you not trust in him?" asked Oona.

"Oh, it isn't that. You are both so young. To challenge even a living sorcerer seems... dangerous, much less one who defies Tenebrea."

Kitlyn reached toward the floor, liquefying a tiny blot of stone that flew up to weave among her fingers, shrouded in green glow. "How many people our age could topple Castle Cimril?"

He sighed.

"There is something more." Oona glanced aside. "I feel we must go alone."

Beredwyn coughed. "Out of the question. Too risky. Too dangerous."

Kitlyn let the small stone glide back where it came from and smoothed the floor before hardening it. "You care for us like a father—or grandfather—should. Yet, we are no longer little."

He regarded her with sad eyes.

Oona reached over the table and took his hand. "I am certain that if we do not go alone, needless death will occur."

"Do you think that this sorcerer may turn our soldiers against you?" asked Beredwyn.

"I hadn't even thought of that." Oona pressed a hand over her heart, her nerves prickling. "Is something like that even possible?"

"Alas, I know not. Lucernia is quite civilized. Few 'creatures' roam our lands. Not like the northern reaches of Ondar or the woods of Evermoor. Magical beasts of all types roam the untamed lands west of the Dawnspire Mountains or elsewhere on the continent. We have tamed our land."

Oona looked down. "Why does that sound so much like we killed everything?"

"Oh, child," said Beredwyn with a hint of sigh in his voice. "All of that happened long before even I was born. Some creatures still exist here but they are rare. Yet, Lucernia still holds dangers. Bandits for example. And there is still a small chance you may stumble across something inhuman."

Kitlyn scowled at the wall. "We already have. Can you consider what my father did to be the work of a human?"

Beredwyn leaned back as if slapped.

Kitlyn's glare softened. "I am referring to his theft of the Heart, not the life he forced upon me. Thousands died to his futile quest for power. The gods are watching us. After the crimes Lucernia committed against Evermoor, if we can help the Na'vir, we must. And if Oona says we are to venture off alone, I trust her."

"Let us not forget the lesson of The Foretelling." Oona shook her head. "We are all succumbing to fear and jumping to conclusions, assuming we will need to destroy this sorcerer. It may well be possible we discover a means to assist the Na'vir without laying eyes on the fiend at all."

"The queen said he stole her crown. That may be the focus of the curse. If we can find it, perhaps all we need do is sneak in and recover it?" Kitlyn sat tall. "You're right. This could be much simpler than we are assuming it to be."

Oona gazed into nothingness for a moment. Indistinct shapes of men in armor, smiling bearded faces, a woman raising a mug in toast, came and went. "I am not afraid. We should set out in the morning."

"You've only just returned." Beredwyn grasped the edge of the table. "However, I should place my trust in Lucen. Though, after Aodh, I worry that our people may question those who claim to act in his name."

"There is a difference quite obvious to me." Kitlyn took Oona's hand. "She says Lucen guides *her* to do this, not that he wants others to heed her words. My father constantly spoke of how Lucen demanded people fear and hate Evermoor, but he spoke of his own desires. Oona is not asking or demanding anyone else act."

Beredwyn gazed at the table for an awkward long moment. "That is an interesting observation. But what if Lucen does command the people?"

"Then he would speak to them individually." Oona smiled.

"I still object to the idea that the two of you should venture out without protection."

"No entourage of armed soldiers followed me across Evermoor." Kitlyn folded her arms.

"At the time, no one knew who you were." Beredwyn tapped the table. "Now you are the queen."

"And now the war is over. There are no assassins… except maybe for the ones Fauhurst may send."

"Exactly." Beredwyn also folded his arms, seeming satisfied.

"Simple." Kitlyn pointed at him. "Tell no one that we have gone nor where we are going for at least two days, if at all. If there *is* still anyone about who would betray us to that wretch of a man, he would need time to set up another ambush. We shall deny him that."

A sense of confident peace settled over Oona without apparent cause. "That is a good plan. I feel it will work. Lucen guides us."

"Very well." Beredwyn leaned over the table and took their hands. "I shall do as you ask, but know that you cause an old man a great amount of worry. However, I shouldn't diminish that I no longer see the spoiled princess nor the quiet-suffering young girl you were not so long ago sitting before me. Both of you have strength beyond anything I could've imagined or hoped for. May the gods protect you."

"They shall." Oona stood, filled with inexplicable confidence. "We should rest now."

"Indeed." Beredwyn yawned. "Though I dare say I shall not be sleeping well this eve."

"You sound like Princess Oona." Kitlyn smiled.

Beredwyn laughed and stood to hug them both.

A SHRILL CHILD'S SCREAM RIPPED OONA FROM A RESTFUL SLEEP. Kitlyn sat up at the same moment, and they both stared at the door of their room. Once the fog in her head cleared enough to recognize the shout as Evie's, Oona leapt out of bed, grabbed her longsword, and ran down the hall to her former bedchamber, Kitlyn running close behind.

By the time she reached the door, the screaming faded to soft sobs and Evie wailing Oona's name.

She barged in to find the girl cowering under the bedding, completely out of sight. "Evie?"

"Oona!" Evie pulled the blanket back enough to peer out.

"What's wrong?" Oona set the blade on a divan she passed on the way to the bed, hopped up to sit on the edge, and pulled her sister into a hug.

Evie clung, and burst into tears again, shaking.

"Shh." Oona rocked her. "Shh… what happened?"

The girl continued trembling for a few minutes. Kitlyn sat nearby and helped hug her.

"I saw a ghost," whispered Evie, pointing toward the tall wardrobe cabinets. "He was standing there watching me."

"Was it my father?" asked Kitlyn.

Evie lifted her face away from Oona's shoulder, eyes red from crying. Despite appearing terrified, her downcast posture suggested she believed she'd done something wrong. "I don't know. I didn't really look at him. I screamed and hid under the blankets."

While Oona held Evie, Kitlyn went over to examine the cabinets and wall between them, yawning the whole time. Eventually, she shrugged.

"Nothing… it takes the Stone a while to build a memory. And there are quite a bit of footsteps here."

"It's where I always used to stand to be dressed." Oona sighed.

"Please don't become maudlin over my not being your proper handmaiden." Kitlyn returned to the bed and kissed Oona on the cheek. "I'm at peace with it."

"Can I sleep with you tonight?" Evie trembled. "I'm scared the ghost will come back. He looked mean."

Oona lifted her and stood. "Of course. Ghosts know better than to mess with me and Kit."

Kitlyn ruffled Evie's hair.

The girl sniffled, managed a weak smile, and rested her head on Oona's shoulder.

She's having a scare because we're leaving again. Or maybe she's heard so many in the castle talking about ghosts of late. Frowning, Oona carried her little sister back to the royal bedroom.

With Kitlyn and Oona on either side of her nestled in warmth, the child went back to sleep.

PERCHED IN A SADDLE ATOP CLOUD, OONA DWELLED UPON THE SAD-eyed stare Evie gave her when they told her they needed to leave the castle again. Despite the girl not protesting or complaining, one brief expression of disappointment weighed more heavily on Oona's heart than Beredwyn's worries for their safety. Of course, they hadn't told Evie anything about an ancient sorcerer, only that they had to help a great number of people.

The Mistral Wood passed on both sides as they followed the road north from Cimril. Even if another group of bandits did lurk so close to the capital, she doubted they'd be active this early in the day. Bandits tended to stay up late with drink. Kitlyn and Oona had departed right after breakfast.

Halorne, the stable master, likely suspected they didn't intend to go out for a relaxing morning ride considering the saddlebags, supplies, and provisions they'd packed. In response to the look he gave them, Kitlyn explained the truth, and bid him keep quiet for at least two days —unless Fauhurst showed up in the dungeon sooner.

A gentle wind rustled the treetops overhead, causing the occasional leaf to fall or drift by in a meandering path like a moth that drank too much ale. Clear blue sky peeked past gaps in the branches. The beautiful day still had enough crispness that her armor didn't feel overly warm. In fact, she'd added a cloak. She glanced with amusement at Kitlyn wearing boots, a sign she didn't expect much trouble—at least not yet. Of course, on horseback, she couldn't exactly touch the ground anyway.

They reached the edge of the woods a little before midday and decided to stop there briefly to eat and rest while discussing how much they *didn't* know about the ancient sorcerer or where exactly he might lair.

"Well, we at least are sure we need to pass into Ondar first." Kitlyn wiped her hands of crumbs and repacked her satchel. "Finding our way to the border is as easy as following the road. Once we're there, we should encounter no shortage of tales among the people warning us where not to go."

Oona stood and attached her provisions bag to her saddle. "Oh, that sounds dreadfully reckless. Ask people where we shouldn't go, then proceed to rush straight there."

"True, though tales like that are meant to frighten village children away from danger."

"Kit." Oona pulled herself back up upon Cloud. "Some would still consider us children, and I do happen to be from a village."

She sighed. "Only the elderly consider us children. It's not as if we're still fifteen."

"Oh, yes." Oona exaggerated a nod. "From child to adult at the stroke of midnight."

"In terms of law, that is true." Kitlyn laughed.

After a few hours traveling along the road northwest from Cimril, they passed a sign indicating a branching road to the right led to the city of Imric. Oona had spent enough time over the past four years staring longingly at maps of the kingdom while confined to the castle to know that they would be making camp in the meadow tonight. The route they followed led to Gwynaben. Oona's official estate sat an hour west of the city in the foothills, though she had not yet visited it. Upon the former king granting her that land and title, a trickle of money began to flow to the property, supporting a small staff to tend the house and grounds.

She spent a while trying to decide if she wanted to holiday there during the winter or wait for the spring. *No, that far north, it would be unwise to go there in the winter. We'd be snowed in.* Regardless of the season, she should at least spend a week or two getting to know the place she owned. She would be unlikely to take up permanent residence what with being the queen consort, unless something dreadful happened.

They chatted about the Na'vir, the wretched queen, Evie's lessons, as well as Oona's desire to have the youngest maids also educated enough to read, and other minutiae. Kitlyn appeared to be avoiding talk of the sorcerer beyond repeating that she much preferred the idea of sneaking in and out.

When darkness fell, they steered their horses into the grass beside the road, unburdened them of saddles and gear, and set up a little camp near a burbling stream. The sky had a hint of overcast, so Kitlyn drew a mass of roots up from the meadow, weaving them together into a dome in case of rain.

"Oh, you are cheating." Oona tickled her. "That's far simpler than figuring out how to assemble a tent."

Giggling, Kitlyn grabbed the poking finger jabbing her in the side. "We didn't even bring a tent!"

"So unprepared we are." Oona folded her arms in mock scolding. "How do you expect to challenge an undead sorcerer when we can't even remember to pack properly?"

Kitlyn stuck out her tongue.

They fell seated together beside the dome, laughing, eventually making a meal of hard cheese and bread. Kitlyn showed no sign of objecting to the basic rations, but Oona had to force herself to eat enough to feel full. She already missed the fine dinners prepared in the castle. Though, more to the point, she wanted *hot* food as a stronger chill came with the darkness.

"It is quiet and peaceful." Kitlyn leaned her head against Oona's shoulder.

"Yes. I don't mind it as much as I thought I would."

"What's that?"

Oona played with Kitlyn's hair. "Being out here. Sleeping in the meadow instead of our enormous bed. The smell of the grass and flowers."

"Serene."

"Yes."

Kitlyn traced a finger under Oona's jaw and gently tugged her chin into a kiss. "I could let myself forget all about our being queens for a while and enjoy the simplicity of it."

"I think I may like that." Oona initiated a second kiss. "It is nice to pretend we have no worries or responsibilities."

"Let us run off to a village and raise chickens in obscurity."

Oona giggled. "I know you speak in jest."

Kitlyn brushed a hand over Oona's chest. "This armor is not made for being romantic."

"It stops a gentle caress as well as a blade."

"'Tis leather with some chain. It doesn't really stop blades. At least not well-aimed ones."

"Then I shall endeavor to duck." Oona tapped a finger to Kitlyn's nose.

"We're doing this, aren't we?"

"Yes."

"Out here alone again."

Oona snuggled closer. "We are, but we're not running away this time."

"Do you yet understand why we needed to travel alone?"

"No, only that people would die if we didn't."

"There is too much death."

Oona yawned. "I agree."

"We can't run away."

"I didn't suggest that in seriousness." Again, Oona tried to tickle her. Alas, leather armor protected rather well against probing fingers.

Kitlyn wriggled, bit her lip, and thrust a finger up into Oona's armpit, bypassing the armor.

"Eep!" squealed Oona, before clutching her arm tight to her side and falling against Kitlyn, laughing. "Without the war hanging over us, life in the castle is quite pleasant... but we should allow ourselves the occasional break."

"Agreed."

A droplet of rain landed on Oona's head. "Oh. The skies are about to render their opinion."

Kitlyn groaned and sat up, pressing her hand into the earth. Green light surrounded her arm and distant roots sprang up from the ground forming a shelter for the horses. Cloud startled at the sudden growth, while Apples gave the new structure a blasé glance. Soon after the root shelter stopped becoming larger, the horses meandered under it.

Oona crawled into the dome and unrolled her sleeping mat. Kitlyn slipped in and grew roots shut over the opening before removing her sword belt, boots, and armor. For comfort, Oona decided to follow suit and they curled up together, wearing light tunics in place of nightgowns. She summoned a tiny orb of blue that gave off more heat than light.

In the coziness of their small shelter, Oona huddled close to Kitlyn, finding the patter of rain on the roots above them comforting. Between the warmth and the soft, regular breathing of her love, she fell asleep in minutes.

BY AFTERNOON THE NEXT DAY, THEY REACHED A RIVER WHICH OONA suspected to be the one that ran southeast to Lake Orien. Fortunately, the road they followed had a bridge. They stopped briefly at a small village on the other side to buy some dried meat, bread, and cheese. None of the townspeople recognized them as anything more than a pair of young travelers. One old woman even called them 'adventurers.'

Around early evening, Oona steered Cloud onto a dirt road leading somewhat to the left that she figured went to Valor Pass, the border between Lucernia and Ondar.

"Are we doing something wrong?" asked Kitlyn.

"How do you mean?" Oona glanced over at her.

"Well. We aren't ordinary people anymore."

Oona chuckled. "I don't think we ever were 'ordinary.'"

"That's not what I mean." Kitlyn playfully swatted at her. "I mean we're the queens of Lucernia."

"You are the queen. I am your wife."

Kitlyn sighed. "As far as I am concerned, we are of the same station."

"I do not object, but it is not me you need to convince of that." Oona reached forward to straighten Cloud's gossamer white mane. "You are referring to us riding into Ondar unannounced?"

"Yes. Are we required to have a great procession of guards and attendants, fancy gowns, and whatnot to enter a different kingdom?"

"It is probably a breach of etiquette, yes. However, we're not making an official visit and while I am not suggesting we lie, we should probably not go out of our way to announce our identities."

"Do you expect trouble?" Kitlyn squinted ahead into the breeze, surveying the increasingly hilly terrain.

"Not from the Ondari nation as a whole. They have been friendly to us for many years. Attracting too much attention and fanfare would slow us down. Not to mention what thieves or brigands might believe they can do with two innocent, defenseless young girls of high station."

Kitlyn let her head loll to the left, staring at Oona from under flat eyebrows. "Defenseless?"

"Your face!" Oona giggled. "I tease. But they would not know that until they attempted to accost us. And I would much rather avoid conflict."

"As would I. We should—"

"Look out!" yelled Oona, her voice echoing.

Kitlyn whirled to face forward and found herself only a few feet from a canyon of pale beige rock. She pulled back on the reins, but didn't really have to. Apples stopped on his own. The soft roar of a moving river came from below. A bridge of heavy wooden planks and thick rope spanned a gap of about thirty feet. It appeared sturdy enough for horses, despite swaying in the wind.

"I don't think this is Valor Pass." Oona let out a nervous laugh and slid from the saddle. She approached the end of the bridge and peered over the side. A modest-sized river ran at the base of the ravine some forty feet down, the walls dotted here and there with little shrubs and beautiful azure flowers. The sight of the drop stirred a queasy feeling in the pit of her stomach and made her light-headed. She bit back her worry, leaned away from the edge, and forced a smile at Kitlyn. "It might not be a bad idea to cross here. We would avoid scrutiny at the border garrison."

"Aren't you afraid of heights? And must we sneak about like a pair of fugitives?"

Oona closed her eyes and shivered, trying not to think about the ravine's depth. "I am... quite unhappy with heights. But I do not want either the garrison commander on our side to insist on sending soldiers with us or the military on the Ondari side to insist we travel directly to Bellsford and have an audience with the king. Especially not in *these* clothes." Oona blushed. "I'd sooner meet King Lanwick with nothing on than dressed like a highway brigand."

"Oh, you most certainly would not." Kitlyn grinned.

"I would at that!" said Oona, almost shouting despite a nervous smile.

"You're being dramatic again. I do not for one instant believe you are more embarrassed at wearing un-fancy armor and *pants* than you would be impersonating a dryad."

Oona let go of her joke long enough to consider it as a real question. "Well, yes, you're right. Perhaps, then, I am not a proper Lucernian noble. Lady Harrington would refuse to wear common clothes even if it meant streaking the city."

Kitlyn laughed, and faced the bridge.

"Would you be more frightened of crossing that dreadful bridge or running like a dryad across Cimril?" Oona flashed an impish smile, picturing that.

"Both frighten me. Though permanently destroying my dignity would not kill me."

"So you'd rather…" Oona raised an eyebrow.

"Only if you joined me." Kitlyn winked and stepped out onto the bridge.

Oona gasped into a giggle. "We would scandalize the kingdom for centuries."

"Precisely why we will *not* be doing that."

A wave of relief swept over her. *She's not serious. And, now that she's gotten me thoroughly terrified of being bare in public, the bridge doesn't seem too bad.* Oona gathered Cloud's reins.

"Wait on the horses. I want to check the bridge first. We probably shouldn't bring both horses over this at the same time."

"Oh." Oona let go of the reins, watching the bridge bob and sway. Her stomach clenched and relaxed in response. Fear rooted her to the ground but love pulled her forward. Once Kitlyn reached about a third of the way across, she rushed out onto the swaying suspension bridge. Her rapid stride made the planks buck up and down like rough seas.

Kitlyn grabbed the main rope on the left, as thick as her forearm.

Despite not looking down, the unstable footing blinded Oona with fear. She sprinted into a collision with Kitlyn, clamping her arms around tight.

"Gah! What are you doing?"

"Umm. I know what you tried to do with talking about going outside naked, but it didn't quite work. I'm still scared. I can't manage this bridge alone."

"We could go back and find the actual pass."

"We could," said Oona.

Apples snorted at the bridge and trotted off. Cloud flicked his ears, looked at the departing warhorse, then followed him.

"Hey!" shouted Oona. "Come back here!"

Neither horse paid her any mind, continuing to trot off out of sight.

The bridge lurched downward.

Oona screamed, peering around Kitlyn (who also screamed) at the far side. One of the main poles supporting the giant ropes had tilted forward, pulling up from the ground. She froze in terrified horror as the smaller base rope unraveled. Two planks slipped free from the right side and dangled by one end.

"I'm sorry. I'm sorry. I'm sorry," whispered Oona.

"Grab the big rope on this side. We can climb it."

Oona, shivering, forced herself to let go of Kitlyn and clung to the massive rope. She couldn't bear to pull herself up on top of it as that felt too much like trying to jump off the side.

A clump of earth in front of the left pole behind them fell out from the cliff face. The rope they both held dipped down.

"It's going to fall!" shouted Oona.

"Hurry. We have time. Walk!"

"I can't." Oona stared at her legs, which refused to move. That of course, let her see between the boards at the river forty feet straight down. "Oh, Lucen. I'm sorry for saying we should use this bridge."

"Ugh!" yelled Kitlyn. "I am a fool."

Oona looked up, confused at why she would feel in any way at fault here. The bridge dipped another few inches, making her scream again.

"The Churning Deep." Kitlyn reached her right arm out toward the far side, extending her left the other way.

"This is not the Churn. It's many times smaller." Oona shivered, refusing to even think about the view from Omun's shoulder while he walked them across the Arch of the Ancients.

"Exactly."

Crackling and creaking arose from both sides. It took a moment for Oona to find the courage to open her eyes. Thick clusters of creeping roots grew out from the cliff wall, threading along the path of the bridge. When they reached her, Oona released her grip on the rope and resumed clinging to Kitlyn who stood unassisted in the middle of the planks, emerald light shrouding both her hands. Wood groaned in protest as the roots pulled tight, lifting the bridge back into place. She coiled more roots around the poles and added several layers to the bridge surface.

In about ten minutes, Kitlyn had essentially replaced the suspension bridge with a rigid one made of dozens of interwoven roots. Solid footing, even a bridge, reassured Oona enough to regain her composure. The bobbing and swaying had been too much.

"The rootcallers! That's what you meant by the Churning Deep."

Kitlyn took Oona's hand, the last vestiges of magical light fading from around her fingers with a waft of strong herbal fragrance. "Are you all right?"

"Heart's beating a bit fast, but yes."

A horse nickered from the right.

Oona and Kitlyn turned to gaze across the bridge at Apples. Cloud meandered up behind him.

"How…" Oona blinked. "Where did they cross? How did they even know…?"

Shaking her head, Kitlyn hurried across the root bridge and patted Apples on the cheek. "You're one smart horse. Took one look at that bridge and thought 'no possible way.'"

Apples bared his gums, perhaps attempting to smile.

"I'd almost swear he understood you," said Oona. "But animals don't talk."

Kitlyn shrugged. "Someone managed to teach Fauhurst how to walk on two legs."

"Hah!" Oona cackled, her voice echoing down the ravine.

"Well… we're in Ondar." Kitlyn climbed back into the saddle. "The Titan Peaks are east from here. I think we're still among the Dawnspire Mountains since we have not seen Valor Pass."

Oona hugged Cloud before mounting. "I agree. We should travel east, and perhaps look for a town where we can find information, food, and lodging."

"You are so wise. No wonder they made you queen." Kitlyn winked.

Oona raspberried her.

THE LOST REGIMENT

KITLYN

*T*he dark shadows of mountains offered an easy way to navigate eastward.

As long as Kitlyn could remember, people in Lucernia quibbled over the distinction between the Dawnspire Mountains and the Titan Peaks being the same. Some argued that Valor Pass made them into two separate ranges despite both following the same contour.

Sometimes, the names of rivers could change from one area to the next even though the water remained part of the same flow. She didn't really care one way or the other if the gods intended the mountains that bordered Lucernia on the east and north to be one or two ranges. Giving it two names only helped people differentiate between north and west. Though both the Dawnspires and the Titan Peaks each spanned several hundred miles of hostile terrain, the ranges being considered separate spared them quite a bit of confusion when talking about location. Perhaps the Nimse Queen had not said ten years due to her vast lifespan making the time seem trivial to her, but instead implied that it may take them that long to find the sorcerer.

She glanced at Oona with pity. She couldn't ask her love to spend so long roaming around the land. Her little sister, a girl who had started to feel somewhat like a daughter to Kitlyn, would be older than they were now after ten years. Selfish as it seemed, separating them for that long felt like a cruelty she couldn't ask on behalf of the Nimse.

I have to hope Oona's vision leads us true. She'd been too insistent to hurry up. Maybe this won't take years.

"The last time I visited Ondar, I was twelve."

Kitlyn chuckled. "I remember. You cried all the way to the coach."

"And all the way to Ondar. And almost every day there." Oona sighed. "I suppose I *was* a spoiled little thing."

"You'd been so forlorn, Aodh cut the trip short and brought you home."

"I find it odd you refer to him by his first name. But yes, I didn't overact. I *was* sad. With all those new sights around me, all I could think about was not having you near."

A bit of warmth crept up into Kitlyn's cheeks. "I think I may have suspected our friendship had become a bit... different even then. Though I had no name for how I felt. I just loved being with you."

"You could be right. I suppose it was a bit unusual for me to pine so much for a simple friend. Even if you were my *only* friend."

Kitlyn rode for a few minutes lost in thought about how miserable some of the castle staff had been to her while Oona had been away. Without the princess there, they'd made her work... and they continued making her work from then on. Upon his return, Aodh had barely taken notice of her sobbing while scrubbing floors or lugging buckets of water around. How many nights had she cried herself to sleep fantasizing that she'd been the child of some troubled noble who'd ride in the gates upon a magnificent black horse and claim her as his daughter. Oh, how she wanted to see the shocked faces of the servants upon realizing she *did* have station. And all the while, she had—only her father never told her.

I'd rather have been a village peasant with a real father.

Sadness crashed into anger.

I could have played the part. It wouldn't have bothered me at all to work if I had known.

Oona's attempt to find a village led them to a small dirt road. Wild growth at the sides and even a few weeds in the middle suggested the path saw little traffic. Ondar's southlands brimmed with thick forests that prevented much of a view into the distance in any direction. Above, an endless canopy of autumnal colors stretched to infinity, an equal amount of reds, browns, and yellows crunching under their horse's hooves.

"This road appears too small to lead anywhere of consequence."

Kitlyn took a deep breath in her nose, adoring the smell of the fall: leaf, sap, and a touch of wet wood upon an invigoratingly cool rush of air.

"It is a road, so it must lead to somewhere. Even if only to a small village, we should be able to at least obtain directions to a larger town."

"Darkness will fall soon." Kitlyn looked up. "The days shorten with the season. Perhaps we should ride for a time after the sun sets."

Oona made a noise of agreement.

Several hours later, the sun waned. The early stages of autumn had not yet stripped the branches entirely, and the remaining canopy made the forest dim much faster. Not long before the light weakened to the point Oona would need to call her orb for them to see at all, a whiff of wood smoke came by on the wind.

"Someone has a fire," whispered Kitlyn.

"Why are you whispering?"

"Umm. Because a fire out here could belong to bandits and I would rather avoid them."

"It could also belong to a woodsman or a small village." Oona smiled.

Kitlyn nodded. "I do not expect the worst of people. But perhaps I am overly cautious."

"If you were overly cautious, you would not have let me talk you into taking this journey alone."

"Fair point, but I can still be overly cautious and trust you."

Oona gazed adoringly at her for a few seconds.

"Who approaches?" asked a man from the dark trees ahead.

Kitlyn looked away from Oona, locking stares with a wiry blond in his mid-twenties—wearing the armor of a Lucernian soldier, though quite worn and battle-damaged. *Did he steal from the dead or is he one of ours?*

"A pair of travelers," said Kitlyn. "Looking for a village or town for the night."

The man glanced between them, clearly not recognizing either of them. "Bit young ta be off on your own, eh?"

"Your arm is injured," said Oona.

"Ehh." He glanced at his left bicep. "Just a nick. How the heck did ya see that in this dimness?"

Oona glided out of her saddle and walked up to the man. "You assume I *saw* it. May I?"

He let his hand slip from the longsword at his hip, evidently not feeling too threatened by a willowy girl a full head shorter than him. "May ya what?"

She placed her hands on his arm. The glow of golden light radiated from under her fingers for a few seconds and faded.

"By Orien," muttered the man. "You're a priestess. Please forgive my suspicious greeting. I'm Frith. Come on ahead. 'Tis safe for ya in our camp."

Kitlyn dismounted, jumping to the ground with a soft *thump*. She decided to leave her boots on for now, since the man didn't strike her as dangerous. Though, she couldn't shake a sense of suspicion at his armor —and his invoking Orien.

Frith walked off in the same direction they had been riding. Minutes later, the road bent to the left but he kept going into the woods. Kitlyn and Oona followed, leading their horses.

Oona peered over at her, eyebrows up, and whispered, "What do you make of this?"

"I'm not sure yet."

Kitlyn paused at the top of the incline, gazing down at a camp arranged in a wide bowl-shaped depression. Six more people, one woman among them, occupied it, all wearing Lucernian armor in various stages of disrepair. A burly, bald man sat upon a fallen log tending to a cauldron over a fire, evidently cooking soup or stew. The youngest, near in age to her, carried cut firewood from a chopping stump to a stack. His armor appeared in the best condition, dirty but with no sign of battle damage. The woman, her shoulder-length dark brown hair wild as a fey creature's, crouched over a dead animal that may have been a goat or sheep, in the process of cleaning it.

"Oy, you lot," said Frith. "Look about. We're visited by a priestess of Orien." He slapped himself on the left arm. "Mended me arm right."

"Sorry," said the young man.

Kitlyn and Oona tilted their heads at the same time.

"Heh. Young Galfred there ain't the best shot with a hunting bow." Frith shook his head.

Oh... Kitlyn's eyes widened. *No wonder we had to travel alone. They're deserters. If we came with soldiers, this would've turned into a battle straight away.* She glanced at Oona.

"Hmm?" asked Oona, finally noticing the pointed look.

"Never mind. I'll explain later."

"Beowyn, how's that soup comin'?" Frith waved at the big bald guy by the fire.

"Couple minutes." The man kept stirring.

A red-haired man in his twenties jogged over, reaching for the horse's reins. "Well met, priestesses. Name's Keal. I can tend ta your horses for ya while ya rest."

"Thank you." Oona smiled. "I'm not a priestess, though I do bear Orien's gift. Are any of you hurt?"

Keal led Cloud and Apples off to the right toward a makeshift pen where the soldiers had tied four-inch thick logs as horizontal fencing to larger still-standing trees. Five other horses milled around inside.

A brown-haired man in his thirties waved from where he lay by a tent. "Aye. Bear."

Oona hurried over to him. Kitlyn followed.

"We are blessed to have you come this way, lifebearer." The wounded man smiled. "I'm Niron."

"I'm not a lifebearer..." Oona paused. "Well, I suppose I am in a sense, but I'm not part of the temple." She rested her hands on his leg.

Niron cringed.

The burly man at the cook pot froze, eyeing Oona. After a moment, he gave a brief shake of the head, dismissing some notion, and went back to his task.

Oona bowed her head. "The grace of Orien comfort you."

The golden-yellow light welled up around her hands and flowed into his leg.

"Thank you, and praise be to Orien." Niron rubbed his thigh, but still winced.

"I have done all I can. The wound will still need time to fully mend." Oona sat back on her heels, apologizing with her expression.

Niron propped himself up on his elbows and managed a slight bow, more of a deep nod. "I understand. It does feel quite a bit better."

"Would've cost him the leg without your aid." Another man near to his thirties emerged from a crude wooden shed nearby. Short, sandy blond hair framed a well-tanned face with a strong jaw and an odd sense of familiarity. "The gods have heard you, Niron."

"Heh. I had begun to wonder if they still listened."

Kitlyn looked up at the oddly familiar man. "Have we met?"

"I don't think so, child. Name's Bertan. You don't look like anyone I know."

She studied him a moment more, unable to place ever seeing him before. Still, something about him seemed too familiar. "I suppose not. Could be you remind me of someone."

"Oy, Beowyn, how's that soup comin'?" shouted Frith.

"Couple minutes," said the big bald man by the fire.

Frith showed them to another cut log which had been smoothed flat on top creating a bench.

Kitlyn lowered herself onto it, looking around at a few tents mixed among wooden shelters. "Have you been camping here long? Is this a woodsman's outpost?"

Everyone looked at each other as if a silent conversation went on somehow between their minds.

"We've made this little bit of woods our home." Frith gestured at the camp. "Tryin' ta do right by those who wander by, keepin' travelers from gettin' lost or eaten by bears or wyverns."

"Wyverns?" Oona's eyes shot all the way open. "There are wyverns here?"

About half the people nodded.

"Aye." The woman wagged her bloody knife at them. "But they don't usually come this far away from the mountains. If ya do see one, your best bet is to hug a tree and stay low."

"Don't scare the poor lass, Isha." Frith waved at her with a gesture like he threw something, then turned back. "I need ta get back out there on watch. If'n ya need anything, don't 'esitate to ask. We're all a friendly lot 'cept maybe Keal."

Keal looked up from the horse enclosure with a big grin while making a rude hand gesture at Frith.

"I'm teasin'." Frith chuckled. "But really, watch out for Galfred. He'll just as soon put an arrow in yer arm as hunt up dinner."

"Sorry," yelled Galfred, still chopping wood.

Frith nodded once more, winked, and jogged back up the hill to where he'd been standing when they first saw him.

Kitlyn and Oona sat on their log in silence for a little while.

"Beowyn, 'ow's that soup comin' along?" asked Isha. "You want any of this goat?"

"Couple minutes." The big man leaned in to sniff. "Put the last of the other goat in it. Don't need more. May as well salt that one."

Isha looked over at them, mostly Oona, squinted, then resumed cutting the dead goat. Bertan and Niron spoke in hushed murmurs, occasionally glancing over at them as well.

Beowyn, close enough to hear them, raised his head. "Don't be daft."

Another short while later, Bertan carried two metal bowls of soup over, offering one each to Kitlyn and Oona. "Mind, they get hot."

"Thank you." Kitlyn took the bowl by the edges and set it on the log to her right.

"It smells good." Oona smiled at him, gasping when she pinched the sides of the bowl and hurriedly set it down on the tree as well. "Thank you."

The others took bowls and sat to eat.

"What was it you wanted to say?" whispered Oona.

Kitlyn leaned close enough to kiss her ear and whispered, "I think they are deserters."

"What?" Oona looked around again then stared at her. "Oh… you may be right."

"This is why you thought we should go alone."

Oona shivered. "That would have been a mess."

The weight of someone watching them made Kitlyn look up. Niron had moved to sit on a fallen log, his hurt leg stretched out straight in front of him. He spooned soup into his mouth, his attention fixated on Oona.

"I think they recognize you," whispered Kitlyn. "But they doubt their eyes because they can't believe it possible you'd be in armor, or out here alone."

"And the princess didn't have Orien's favor." She blew on a spoonful of soup and slurped it.

"Nor would a princess slurp her soup." Kitlyn winked.

"It's hot!"

Kitlyn held her chin high. "You've been spending too much time around that lowborn servant girl. All those manners they tediously taught you over the years, gone."

Oona poked her in the side, snickering.

Once Keal finished eating, he jogged up the hill where Frith had gone. The thinner man returned to camp, taking a bowl of soup and sitting near the cook to eat.

The young soldier walked over and plopped down on Kitlyn's side of the log, giving her the unmistakable 'gosh you're pretty' stare of a dumbstruck seventeen-year-old. He fussed at his hair, jet-black like hers. "Hi. I'm Galfred."

"Hello, Galfred." Kitlyn raised another spoonful of soup, but hesitated, caught off guard by an unexpectedly large hunk of meat. *Not sure I've ever had goat before… it's not too bad.*

"You're kinda beautiful."

"Thank you." Kitlyn elbowed Oona. "But I'm nowhere near as pretty as her."

Oona batted her eyelashes. "Flattery will get you everywhere."

Galfred perked up.

Oona chuckled. "I was talking to her."

"Oh." He smiled at Kitlyn, apparently oblivious. "What are you two girls doing out here in the woods?"

"We're looking for a place called the Hall of Stolen Memories or something like that." Kitlyn drank the last bits of soup right from her bowl. "An undead sorcerer there stole something I have to get back."

"*We* have to get back." Oona made a series of awkward faces, but decided to throw decorum to the wind and upend her bowl as well.

"So ladylike," whispered Kitlyn.

Oona nearly choked, and sputtered into giggles.

"Never heard of anything like that." Galfred scratched his head. "But there's a town not too far from here. Someone there might help, but you probably shouldn't go tangling with any sorcerer, especially one that's already dead." He pointed off to the woods. "There's a little waterfall out that way a bit. If you want to see it, I can show you where it is."

Beowyn chuckled.

Isha walked over and folded her arms. At her approach, Galfred sat stiffly, no longer leaning close to Kitlyn.

The woman stared pointedly at Oona for a long moment. "Mind if I ask what a pair of Lucernian priestesses are doing in Ondar, unescorted?"

"Aww, leave off it," said Beowyn. "There's no way. Just looks like 'er."

Kitlyn peered up at the wild-haired woman. "I will answer your question if you can tell me why such a small group of Lucernian soldiers have camped out in the Ondari wilderness for quite a long time."

Everyone fell quiet.

Isha's expression shifted about halfway between worry and hostility.

"Hey, easy…" Niron struggled up to his feet. "She's still an Orien priestess. Don't dare raise a hand to her."

Kitlyn set the bowl on the tree by Galfred. "You're deserters."

Isha drew her blade and pointed it at Kitlyn. "And you two are probably not leaving this camp."

Galfred leapt to his feet and moved in front of her. "What are you doing?"

"I'm not going to kill them." Isha took a step back. "We'll leave them alive, tied to a tree. By the time they're loose, we will be long gone."

"No." Galfred kept leaning toward her. "That's no way to treat a priestess."

"It isn't." Niron limped over. "But that's no priestess. That's the princess. I'm sure of it. And the only reason she would be out here alone, dressed like that, is if she ran away. Relax yourself, Isha. She is like us, seen the foolishness of it all."

"Foolishness?" asked Kitlyn.

"Yes. What else could you call it?" Niron shifted his weight onto his good leg. "The king constantly spouts off about Lucen this and Lucen that, yet this war is endless. You have to have seen the lies. They call them savages, primitives, animals… but they are no different from us. Training, armor, weapons. And *magic*. The High Priest of Lucen speaks falsehoods as freely as breathes, yet there is no retribution."

"Indeed." Beowyn lumbered over. "But this cannot be who you think it is. Princess Oona is too delicate to leave the castle. The fragile flower wouldn't dare sit on a dead tree in the woods."

Kitlyn didn't much care to have three soldiers looming over her, so she stood. Still, she had to look up to make eye contact with any of them, but at least she didn't feel quite as small as when sitting. "Please bring Keal back to the camp. You all need to hear what I have to say. Surely, you cannot be in that much danger here that a few minutes absent a lookout while everyone is awake will create risk."

Frith hooked his fingers in his mouth and let out a shrill whistle. Keal appeared atop the hill soon after and headed down when everyone beckoned him with waves.

"What's going on?" asked Keal.

The deserters all gathered close. Isha still appeared ready for a fight, but at least put her sword away. It probably helped that both Galfred and Niron stood on either side of her giving her a 'back off' look.

"Little lady here's got somethin' ta say." Bertan gestured at Kitlyn.

I hope he doesn't hurt himself falling over when he realizes he called the queen 'little lady.' A hint of a smile played on her lips. "First, let me say that I agree with you on at least one point. The war between Lucernia and Evermoor *was* based on lies. King Talomir betrayed his friend King Lanas of Evermoor and ripped the Eldritch Heart from the Alderswood tree. They have been attacking us for twenty years trying to recover it before the tree died and took all of them with it. Every man, woman, child, animal, and plant would have withered away."

The deserters emitted a collective gasp.

"That is a bold accusation." Beowyn stared at her. "To speak so ill of the king would be dangerous were you still within Lucernia. Have you any proof of this?"

"King Talomir attempted to steal the power of the Heart. He drank of its sap, but it did not give him what he sought. He bade Queen Solana to drink of the sap, but it did not give her any power either."

"Who is this girl that she speaks so freely with disdain about the king and his dead wife?" whispered Keal.

Kitlyn reached her arms out toward the ground and sent her magic into the earth. Emerald light glowed at her hands, drawing forth a pair of six-foot stone spires behind the tree she'd been sitting on. She raised her hands, making the magic glow brighter. "The Alderswood trusted that I would help set things right. It gave me its power when I was within Queen Solara's womb." She hardened her stare not out of anger but to increase her resemblance to her father. "I am Kitlyn Talomir, daughter of Aodh."

A gentle hand gripped her left arm. "And I am Oona. A simple farm girl who bore Lucen's gift, taken as a decoy for assassins to protect the true heir."

The deserters stared in silent shock.

"W-w-what is… if you…" Galfred blinked at her. "If you're the true princess, why are you here in Ondar? Has Castle Cimril fallen?"

Kitlyn sent the stone back underground and relaxed her magic. "No. My father is dead. The war is over."

"If King Talomir is dead then…" Frith pointed at her. "Were you chased into exile?"

"No." Kitlyn took Oona's hand.

"That would mean you've become…" Keal blinked.

"Queen. Yes. And Oona is my wife."

Galfred emitted a weak moan and passed out. Isha caught him before he fell flat and eased him to the ground.

"The entire war was a lie." Kitlyn looked over the deserters. "I am inclined to understand why you fled to Ondar, though I am not entirely sure if it counts as you having abandoned the people you had sworn to protect."

Niron coughed, pounding a fist into his chest a few times. "I am mostly responsible for this. I was a captain. Being on the front lines, I saw with my own eyes that the Evermoor forces didn't attack innocent people as the king claimed. I suspected they searched for something. The more I saw, the more I couldn't reconcile it with the orders coming out of Cimril. My soldiers were dying for nothing, and Lucen stood idly by."

"Gods' time is not our time." Oona squeezed Kitlyn's hand. "Lucen *did* set things right."

"Did you usurp the throne?" Isha tilted her head at Kitlyn with an expression that suggested she would cheer an affirmative answer.

"No. It is with reluctance I accepted the crown. I did not want power, nor did I truly wish my father to die. The temple was to declare him apostate. Rather than suffer that humiliation, he sent himself to Tenebrea."

Isha snarled at nothing in particular.

"I didn't black out because you married a girl," said Galfred from the ground. "I can't believe I asked the *queen* to go for a walk in the woods."

"His skill at charming the ladies is about as honed as his marksmanship." Frith rubbed his arm.

Oona laughed.

"Speaking of…" Beowyn tilted his head. "I imagine that did not go over well in Cimril."

Kitlyn lowered herself to sit on the felled tree and explained her father's challenge to the gods to show their disapproval in person followed by Tenebrea appearing to bless the two of them. That led into a more detailed explanation of her unexpected journey into Evermoor via abduction, and eventual return of the Eldritch Heart to Prince Ralen.

"That is… quite a tale." Bertan exhaled, raising both eyebrows.

The gesture made him look like a small boy impressed with a bedtime story—and Kitlyn realized why he looked familiar.

"Do you have a son named Ral?"

Bertan bowed his head. "Aye." He paused, then looked up, head tilted. "How do you know that?"

"I met him. He... well, your family believes you are dead. He misses you." Kitlyn put a hand on his arm.

Bertan clenched his jaw, two tears racing each other down his cheeks.

"Go to them." Kitlyn grasped his arm.

"If we are caught... they will execute us." Frith shuddered. "Bert's family already believes he's dead. We may as well all be."

Oona set her hands on her hips. "That isn't right."

"Oh, it is." Isha frowned. "Deserters are executed."

"No, I mean it isn't *right*." Oona looked at Kitlyn. "The whole war was an affront against Lucen. Their refusing to participate in it is no more a crime than us demanding your father return the Heart. In fact, barking at the king and publicly calling him a liar is probably far worse."

Galfred rolled to his feet. "You did?"

Oona indicated Kitlyn with a jabbing thumb. "She nearly tore down the castle. The man was rather stubborn."

Kitlyn suppressed the urge to chuckle and kept a serious face. "There is no reason for any of you to stay here. The war is ended and its pretense was false. You all saw the lie of it and refused to perpetuate the deception and killing." Kitlyn looked from one soldier to the next. "I can't hold it against you for acting in accordance with Lucen's ideals. I realize we're out here in the middle of nowhere with nothing to write on and my crown is back in safe keeping, but I will decree you are all reinstated if you wish, or pardoned."

The former deserters glanced around at each other with tentative smiles.

"What brought you to Crows' Corner?" Bertan cleared his throat in a poor attempt to hide the loss in his voice. "You saw Ral? Is he okay?"

"He's healthy but misses you. I understand you might not wish to return before I've had paperwork drawn up, but I cannot go back to Lucernia until I finish what we came here for. As far as why we were at Crows' Corner..." Kitlyn explained the Nimse attacks and their meeting with the queen.

Most of the deserters shuddered at the description of the underground city filled to teeming with giant razor-toothed mouths.

Niron stepped up to Kitlyn. "Highness, it would be my pleasure to accompany you on this journey. I would not feel right standing idle while you travel unescorted."

"Aye." Galfred bowed.

One by one, the others all nodded.

"I will return to my family." Bertan took a knee. "After I have seen you safely back to Lucernia."

Kitlyn put a hand on Oona's shoulder, thinking of Donal tempting fate. "Don't say it."

"Don't say what?"

"Donal," muttered Kitlyn.

"Oh." Oona opened her mouth, pondered, then closed it. "Yes. I don't think Lucen would lead us here only to allow that to happen."

"Right." Kitlyn clapped. "Do any of you know a place on the Ondari side of the Titan Peaks like what we're looking for?"

"Not rightly." Niron leaned on a tree. "But the town of Imbrec is close. We may find someone there who can help with information."

"Didn't you say we hoped to avoid appearing like an invading army?" Oona raised an eyebrow. "We'd be traveling with seven soldiers obviously in Lucernian armor."

"We've got cloaks and know how to blend in. No point to that out here in the woods." Niron grunted and stood away from the tree.

Kitlyn walked over to a spot of open ground near the lean-tos and tents. "Will you be ready to break camp in the morning? Is your leg up to the task?"

"Aye. Merely sore. Decent enough to ride with, thanks to Orien. Morning it is."

The soldiers stood frozen in enthralled silence as Kitlyn summoned roots into another dome-shaped shelter. She retrieved their bedrolls from the area by the horse enclosure and crawled inside to unfurl them.

Oona scooted halfway in, helping, humming to herself and grinning.

"He guided you to find these soldiers so we could bring them home."

"I believe that, yes." Oona crawled the rest of the way in and lay on her side. "And maybe we needed their help, too."

Kitlyn flopped on her back, then removed her sword belt and boots. "I do not know what surprises me more… that I continue to pursue an ancient undead sorcerer without feeling like we travel to our doom, or that none of the soldiers appeared in the least bit horrified at us."

"Why would they be?"

"At *us*." Kitlyn rolled her head to look at Oona. "You know."

"Oh." She shrugged, still smiling. "You should be more surprised that you're not afraid of the sorcerer. Love shouldn't even compare to an undead horror."

"Alas, that's not the kingdom we live in." Kitlyn took her hand. "But perhaps it is the kingdom Lucernia can become."

"Kit?"

"Yes?"

"Lucernia has two queens on the throne. Why do we still call it a kingdom?"

Kitlyn laughed. "That is a good question. Queendom sounds strange."

"Only because you're so used to hearing *kingdom*."

"Does it bother you to use kingdom?"

Oona remained silent for a few seconds. "No, not really. Just struck me as odd."

"Are you going to stay up all night worrying about what to call Lucernia?"

"No." Oona snuggled close beside her. "I'm going to stay up all night terrified of an undead sorcerer."

IMBREC

OONA

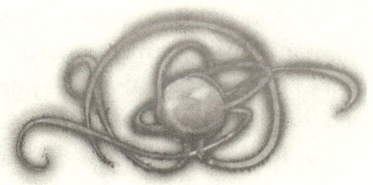

*O*ona yawned. The gentle sway of Cloud's walking gait nearly rocked her to sleep.

Her joke to Kitlyn came partially true. She had difficulty falling asleep, but not exactly due to fearing Voldreth… more the conflict of knowing she should be terrified but found herself believing they had a reasonable chance of survival. Debating between trying to be sneaky or perhaps suggesting Kitlyn ask Omun to come mash the entire place flat kept her thinking late into the night.

He's only a skeleton in a robe. We don't even need Omun. Kit could flatten him with a big rock.

She yawned again and tried to sit up straight so she didn't pass out and fall off the horse. The soldiers had all wrapped themselves in brown or dark blue cloaks with voluminous hoods that made them look more like an esoteric order of woodland mystics than soldiers. As they had only five horses, Beowyn walked while Isha and Galfred, being the two lightest, shared one. He clung to her back while she had the reins—and he still blushed from Isha's hours-ago suggestion that he ask to ride with Kitlyn. Of course, she hadn't been serious.

Oona grinned to herself. *Kit would've agreed just to get him back for flirting with her.*

A few hours past noon, the woodland road led them to a large break in the woods where stone walls surrounded a square city a little over a mile on each side. Four men in blue tunics over full chain mail armor stood guard by the gate. They offered only passing glances at them. She doubted anyone from Ondar would recognize her or Kitlyn, especially without crowns or ridiculous dresses. If anything, someone might question their armor being of Lucernian design, though theirs didn't have as much chain mail reinforcement as the soldiers' did.

Inside, most of the buildings also appeared quite similar to each other, of regular size and mostly square. Some structures taller than one story resembled castle towers. All the streets formed a perfect grid with no hint of meandering alleys or curved paths. None of the citizens wore bright colors, their relatively drab garments designed for function and comfort rather than appearance. With the exception of children, most people she saw hurried back and forth with evident destinations and little time to spare. A handful of merchant types wore somewhat finer clothing of deep green or dark blue, but also moved down the street at purposeful strides, barely sparing anyone a glance.

When people did happen to look at each other, which twice occurred more as an unavoidable circumstance due to near collision—they stopped and got into a friendly conversation. Oona turned her head to continue watching one such chat as they rode past.

Is everyone afraid to make eye contact to avoid an hour-long talk? She chuckled to herself.

Niron, who led their group, turned at a corner. Four cross-streets later, they entered an appropriately square town square. At its center stood a moving fountain statue depicting a well-muscled man in armor with a winged helm, bulging arms, and a long beard. The larger-than-life-sized figure held an unfinished sword across an anvil while his other arm moved up and down with a hammer. Each time the hammer came close to the anvil, spurts of water shot out in all directions, a simulation of sparks flying.

That must be the Steelfather.

She ogled it, marveling at the craftsmanship. Shops on the left offered various items from clothing to jewelry to pocket watches, even weapons. Oona sighed internally at them, as they reminded her how, not too long ago, her greatest desire had been freedom from the castle to go into the city and spend money on random useless things. *How naïve I was.*

Compared to Cimril, this small city at the edge of Ondar looked quite clean and noticeably happier. *They haven't suffered twenty years of war.*

Niron turned right at a blacksmith's shop and continued past several city blocks of plain four-story buildings. Each had a footprint not much larger than a normal city home, but made from stone like castles instead of wood. Steps on the outside led to three doors with the fourth at ground level.

It's four separate houses stacked on top of each other… Not easy to expand the city with such a big wall around it.

Their procession came to a stop at a large inn named The Hammer and the Anvil. Niron eased himself down from his horse and stiff-legged it over to the porch where he handed some coins to a boy of about ten in a neat grey tunic.

"Minnit." The child bowed and dashed inside.

Since the other former deserters all dismounted, Oona did as well. The boy returned soon with two others, one the same age, the other closer to fifteen. The boys proceeded to lead the horses around the back, presumably to a stable. Oona spent a few minutes patting and talking to Cloud until one of the smaller boys approached her. She patted him on the head and handed over the reins. The horse didn't appear to mind the child, so she trusted him and headed inside with the others once the eldest took Apples with him around back.

The soldiers had taken seats around a huge circular table near the back corner of a large room. Dark brown wooden stairs along the right wall led to the second floor, likely lodgings. The scent of ale and roasting meat thickened the air to the point Oona almost felt full from merely breathing. Men and women in tunics of brown, grey, and black sat at tables eating, drinking, or talking. A few snippets of conversation as she hurried to her table suggested Ondari people had great difficulty ending social meetings. No one appeared to want to be the 'rude one' to say they had to go somewhere else.

She kept her head down and took a seat beside Beowyn. His size made her feel tiny, but having him between her and the rest of the room lent a sense of security. Kitlyn sat on her right side. Within a few minutes, a late-thirties woman with light brown hair and perhaps the most elaborate dress she'd yet seen in Ondar approached. The stone-grey garment bared the woman's shoulders, trimmed in white at the top, cuffs, and hem. A white tunic/apron ran down the front. Soft black shoes bereft of decoration covered her feet. Oona thought it compared to the castle maids' dresses, in color, complexity, and overall look.

The woman spoke rapidly in a heavy accent. Oona managed to pick out that she introduced herself as Astrid.

Beowyn responded in a similar rapid cadence sounding almost exactly like the woman. His deep voice created a vibration in the seat of Oona's chair. The woman nodded at him. The others all said short phrases back to her as she looked around the table, Galfred's answer of "mead" the only one she recognized.

Are they speaking another language or is… Prince Lanwick didn't sound at all like this. The words are similar but they pronounce them oddly. She glanced over at another table, catching the word 'Steelfather,' but it sounded more like the man said 'stale feather.'

Oona smiled when the woman looked at her. "House wine."

Astrid nodded before glancing to Kitlyn. "And for you?"

"Wine as well."

"Aye, Miss." Astrid bowed slightly and whisked off to the bar.

Niron cleared his throat. "Once we're done eating, I'll check with the bartender here since my leg… Isha, you check with whatever temple you can find. Galf, head west and check other inns and taverns. Keal, north. Beowyn, south. Bert, east. Frith, you and I will stick here with the ladies."

"Fairly certain the waitress already knows we're from the south." Frith chuckled. "Lady Oona rather gave it away."

She leaned forward. "*Are* they speaking another language?"

The soldiers chuckled.

"This far south, they tend to speak in a blend of Ondari and Lucernian. Go north or west from here and the influence fades. Then it becomes another language." Niron yawned. "People here use words from both, but they accent them differently."

"Yes, so it seems." She pondered people in Evermoor speaking mostly the same language as Lucernian with altered inflections… similar to the difference between nobles and commoners. But if what the Nimse Queen said is true, perhaps the humans in Evermoor had originally migrated east from Lucernia some ages ago when the elves retreated? That would explain the similarity of language.

Astrid returned with a big tray and handed out drinks. "There ya be. We've got a lovely roast ham ready, chicken, venison, nibbler stew, mutton stew, and fish."

Oona ordered fish, Kitlyn took the chicken. The soldiers varied, many opting for the ham. Astrid returned right away with a tray of bread, cheese, and apple slices, which everyone picked at. A while later, the actual food came out, another woman and the two smaller boys that took the horses helping carry.

The fish, descaled but whole with head attached, stared up at Oona from the plate beside a lump of greens. Its buggy eyes and gaping mouth made her imagine the expression someone might make when stubbing their toe, and she burst into giggles.

Kitlyn raised an eyebrow.

"I'm just not used to my food looking at me." Oona turned the plate so it stared in another direction. It smelled appetizing, so she tried her best to ignore it having a face, and dug in.

Eventually, once everyone had more or less finished eating, Astrid walked over. "We've got apple or cherry pie if anyone's interested."

Beowyn grinned. "I'll 'ave the cherry."

Everyone else patted their stomachs and passed.

"Couldn't help but notice you lot are from Lucernia." Astrid let off a sad sigh. "Right awful mess that war. Glad it's over. Sad about the king, though. I hear the new queen's got a decent heart. Hoping she'll keep the peace a while. Been too much war. Damn lucky it ended when it did. We all thought Ondar was going to be dragged into it."

"Yes. Fortunate." Kitlyn raised her wine glass. "And I'm sure their new queen would be grateful to hear you think her heart is good."

"Well." Astrid chuckled. "I wouldn't know the lady from a Lucernian seamstress, but it's what I hear."

"I've heard the new queen is quite even-headed, wise, and rather beautiful, too," said Oona. "Men going by walk into posts for staring at her."

Kitlyn's cheeks reddened.

Galfred, Isha, and Bertan coughed at the same time.

"Ah, the joke's on them then." Astrid slapped her leg. "I hear she's not terrible interested in men. Poor thing. Not really the kingdom one wants to live in if that's where your heart goes. I got a lot of respect for her though. Took a lot of courage to admit it. Heard her own mother disowned her."

"Not quite." Oona fidgeted. "The queen mother died years ago to an assassin. You're thinking of her wife's mum."

"Ahh." Astrid rolled her eyes. "Well, 'poor thing' to that girl, too. Such silly people to get so worked up over that—no offense. So, what brings you lot to Ondar? Wouldn't ya be liking to be there now that the wars over? Must feel like a different kingdom altogether."

"It is starting to." Kitlyn smiled. "We're soon to return once we find what we're looking for."

"What be that if you don't mind the asking?" Astrid leaned on the table. "I hear a lot of things talked about in this place."

A loud, meaty *smack* came from the left side of the room.

Oona jumped and whirled to stare.

"Oof!" yelled a man in a dark green tunic, flat on his back beside an overturned chair. He rambled something too fast to comprehend and sprang to his feet.

The other man at his table also jumped up—and punched him square in the face again, but didn't knock him down. The twice-punched man slugged his dining companion who made no attempt to block or dodge. Oona stared in mute horror as they proceeded to pummel each other back and forth several more times, neither making the slightest effort to avoid blows. None of the other patrons, the bartender, or the wait staff reacted at all. Eventually, the man in grey wobbled over and hit the floor, at which point, they both burst out laughing. The man in green, still on his feet, gestured at the bartender and blurted something while pointing at the man on the floor.

Ondar is strange.

"Idiots," muttered Astrid. "So, what are you lot looking for? Fame, fortune? Chimera hide?"

"None of those, I'm afraid." Kitlyn sighed.

"We're trying to find something a bit less pleasant." Oona picked up her mostly-empty wine glass and swirled the contents. "Have you heard anything about where an undead sorcerer might be? All we've been able to find so far is that he's somewhere in the Titan Peaks."

"In the Hall of Stolen Memories," said Kitlyn, her voice tired.

"Oh. Well, I have heard tales of there being a lich off in the Titan's Peaks." Astrid folded her arms. "Nothing about a Hall of Stolen Memories, but there's a Vale of Forgotten Sorrows. Used to be a town up that way, Wirlen's Gorge or something to that effect. Nothing's left of it other than death and emptiness. You two shouldn't be anywhere near a place like that. Got far too much life left ahead of you, and there's not much to either one of you. Find a man, have a family... find a girl, do whatever... but don't go near a lich."

"Did find a girl." Oona took Kitlyn's hand and held it up.

"Oh. Is that why you're in Ondar?" Astrid looked at them the way she might've stared at a waterlogged orphan kitten in the street.

Before the woman could pick her up and squeeze her, Oona shook her head. "No. We're all right. What's a lich?"

"That's what I hear people call a sorcerer or wizard or sometimes even a priest who dies and forgets to sit still." Astrid chuckled. "Just means has magic, is dead, still walks around."

"How dangerous is this thing?" asked Niron.

"Only bones, right?" Isha tried to drink from her empty goblet, and sighed.

"One moment." Astrid hurried off to the bar, returning soon with a pitcher of ale and a ewer of wine.

"Wait." Oona held up a hand. "I should have water. The last time I drank more than one glass of wine with dinner I did something rather foolish."

"Of course." Astrid smiled and refilled Isha's wine. She again went to the bar to get a pitcher of water and poured it into their glasses once they drained the last bits of wine. "They call the place the Vale of Forgotten Sorrows because anyone who goes there will forget their sorrows right quick."

"Because of the lich?" Oona tilted her head.

"Yes. Word is it can control people just by looking at them. Lock eyes with it, you're its slave. Good as dead." She patted them both on the shoulders. "You're far too young to tangle with the likes of that thing."

People at another table called Astrid.

"Pardon. Let me know if you need anything more." She smiled at everyone and hurried over to the other patrons.

Kitlyn paled. "Sounds like this has become more complicated."

"Yes." Oona bowed her head. "I will need to ask Lucen for guidance. He would not have led us this far if we had no chance of succeeding."

Keal and Frith glanced at her in a way that almost called her nuts.

"Same plan as before." Niron patted the table. "Check temples and tap houses, but don't roam all night."

"Captain." Isha saluted him.

The others chuckled.

"What?" Isha set her fists on her hips. "I wasn't being sarcastic. We're reinstated."

Galfred, Frith, Keal, Beowyn, and Bertan blinked at her, then all turned to Kitlyn at the same time.

"We're trying not to be obvious. It doesn't bother me if you pretend to be civilians." Kitlyn smiled for a moment before her expression went somber. "In light of everything that's happened with what my father did, if any of you wish to resign once we are back home, I would not think less of you for it."

The soldiers exchanged looks. Anger and sadness flashed across Isha's eyes, but everyone shook their heads.

"It would honor me to once again serve the crown and be able to take pride in doing so." Beowyn banged his fist on the table.

The others responded in kind.

"Right then. We have work to do." Niron's face reddened as he forced himself up to stand.

"You should stay off that leg for a few days." Oona hurried around the table and pressed a hand over the tooth marks on his leather-covered thigh. Within seconds of touching it, she sensed that he had no further injuries her magic could repair, though likely experienced a fair amount of pain.

He braced his weight on the table. "I will. Once this matter is attended to."

Kitlyn finished her water and stood. "All right. I'll try to find someone who knows where Wirlen's Gorge is."

"We'll do that." Bertan nodded toward the bartender. "You two should stay here and keep safe."

Oona drew a breath to protest being coddled, but held her tongue. True, he may be implying them too young to do anything on their own. However, more likely, he referred to Kitlyn being the queen and didn't want to risk some random thief ambushing them.

"I am perfectly capable of—"

"Kit." Oona hugged her from behind. "It's fine. Generals don't go out and do scouting missions themselves."

"All right, but I'm at least capable of talking to the bartender in the inn we plan to spend the night at. Niron needs to rest."

The captain bowed his head in resigned acceptance. Once Kitlyn paid for the rooms and started talking to the bartender, Ulf, about rumors and Wirlen's Gorge, Oona took two room keys and helped Niron upstairs. She tried—and failed—to convince him to wait here at the inn until they returned.

Oona checked his leg wound again, but didn't sense any further ability to help. She knew many injured soldiers had taken weeks to recover from battle wounds even at the temple of Orien in Cimril. The priests' magic had made the difference between death and survival, but serious injuries didn't disappear instantly. Though Kitlyn's wound had been mortal, it amounted to only a small slice, deadly because of its location, not for the amount of injury.

She headed across the hall to her room, removed her sword belt, armor, and boots, then sat on the side of the bed, praying to Lucen for guidance.

30

IN THE SHADOW OF TITANS

KITLYN

O ver breakfast the next morning, they discussed what they had learned.

Ulf, the bartender and owner of the Anvil, had told Kitlyn the previous night that traveling to Wirlen's Gorge would only take about four hours by horse. The soldiers had heard all sorts of rumors about the 'lich to the east.' Several innkeepers thought it pure rumor. A few believed it, but had vastly different opinions of its danger. Isha heard from a shopkeeper who thought the ruined town had no supernatural curses at all, but likely served as a base of operations for dangerous thieves who used the stories as a defense tactic.

All the soldiers who had spoken to people who believed the lich real received similar information to what Astrid provided. It seemed that most townspeople feared the undead sorcerer's ability to take over the mind of anyone who looked at it.

"I can help." Oona closed her eyes for a moment. "Last night, I prayed for guidance, and I believe Lucen heard me. I know things I didn't before."

"Such as?" asked Niron.

"The people are mostly correct. Voldreth does have the ability to control us, but it's not simply from looking at him. It is magic he must try to use. I think if we spot him from a distance and he doesn't notice us, we'll be safe. Also, I had a vision or dream that I had gone back to

Cimril and spoke to High Priest Balais. He taught me a way to use Lucen's light to guard a person's mind from impure thoughts."

Galfred blushed and squirmed in his chair. "What sort of impure thoughts?"

Kitlyn looked away so she didn't laugh at him.

"Demonic magic. The influence of darkness taking over." Oona tilted her head at him. "What other sort of impure thoughts would there be?"

Beowyn roared with laughter. Isha's face went red and she succumbed to laughter as well.

Galfred shrank in on himself.

"Oh." Oona shook her head. "*Those* thoughts aren't necessarily always impure."

"How's that?" Galfred swallowed hard. "Not impure?"

"It depends on who you are having those thoughts about. If it's someone you love, someone you're married to, they're not impure."

"So that means general random thoughts about every girl he sees still count as impure?" Bertan clapped Galfred on the back, grinning.

"That counts as being seventeen," muttered Niron.

Oona huffed. "Well, as long as he doesn't act on them, I'm sure Lucen understands being young."

"Right." Kitlyn patted the table. "So you were saying you can protect us from mental enslavement?"

"Yes... but unlike my light which lasts a while on its own, I need to keep thinking about Lucen's protection. Balais told me the magic becomes weaker for everyone I shield."

"How dangerous is this lich other than mind control?" asked Kitlyn.

"All sorts of rumors." Frith rolled his head around, making his neck pop a few times. "Much of it could be nonsense."

"I've fought living skeletons before." Beowyn speared a sausage on his fork and held it up to his mouth. "Fast with a blade but not too strong and pretty brittle. One good wallop and they fall apart." He bit off half the sausage.

Oona surgically sectioned off a piece of her eggs and ate them.

Kitlyn pictured summoning a jabbing rock spire that launched a Nimse like a catapult stone. If this lich turned out to be as brittle as Beowyn claimed, she could deal with it. Then again, if the creature lacked in physical strength and toughness, it would likely protect itself with other means. Sorcerers trafficked in demons, so they may well have to contend with one of those. She looked over at Oona, who appeared quite calm.

May Lucen protect us.

A FEW HOURS BY HORSEBACK TO THE EAST OF IMBREC BROUGHT THEM to the forest's edge.

Woodlands gave way to rolling meadows in the foothills of the Titan's Peaks, which loomed high and close. The mountains vanished into the churning gloom of an overcast sky, taller than the clouds that enshrouded them. Bleakness in the sky made the mild wind feel colder, chilling her in spite of her leather armor and hooded cloak. Contrary to the heavy clouds, the dry air and lack of gusts suggested the day wouldn't bring rain. Kitlyn considered walking instead so she could draw warmth up from the ground.

The ghost of a long-untraveled highway continued into the hilly terrain, its path hinted at from the occasional marker post or suspiciously flat spot in the grass. Weeds the size of small children popped up here and there, including in the middle of the road. Grape-sized insects buzzed about flat-topped flowers as big as dinner plates covered in fuzz similar to dandelion seeds.

Beowyn rode at the lead due to Niron's injured leg, on a new horse they bought before leaving Imbrec. The captain insisted on being second. Frith rode third, with Kitlyn and Oona behind him. Isha and Galfred still shared a steed, riding by Oona's left. Keal and Bertan brought up the end.

A mile or so after leaving the forest, the nearly-absent road went over a hill to the long, sloping downhill of a valley. The mountains blocked off the sky ahead, seeming a barrier tall enough to even hold back gods.

Soon after they entered the valley, the skeletal remains of large animals dotted the landscape. Kitlyn couldn't identify them beyond being approximately the size and shape of cows, though the horns didn't look at all like anything she'd ever seen before.

"Why are there so many bones here?" asked Oona.

All the soldiers echoed, "Wyverns" at the same time.

Kitlyn looked up. "Will they come after us?"

"They'd be more interested in the horses." Isha patted her steed's mane. "People on foot they'd probably leave alone unless ya got too close to their nest."

"Town ahead." Beowyn pointed.

Kitlyn stood higher in the saddle for a better view.

The bottom of the valley held the ruins of a large village, little more than loose stones outlining where buildings had once stood. Only two structures stood taller than knee high rubble, both near the farthest end. On the right, a three-story tower with a pointed roof sported several massive holes charred black at the edges. Somewhat closer on the left, a large square building that resembled a miniature castle keep remained mostly intact.

Niron whistled.

"That tower." Kitlyn pointed. "I think the sorcerer lived here after he fled Lucernia. I wonder if he destroyed this village or if some army came to kill him did."

"An interesting question, but I don't think its answer will help us." Beowyn drew a large sword from a scabbard across his back.

Kitlyn grabbed the handle of her longsword. "Did you see something?"

"No. But this place *feels* wrong." The big man halted his horse in the approximate center of what had once been Wirlen's Gorge.

Oona nudged Cloud closer to Kitlyn and grabbed her hand, eyeing the area with obvious worry. "Demons have been here."

"Are you certain?" asked Galfred.

"Do none of you smell that? The wretched fume of sulfur taints every breath." Oona coughed.

Kitlyn shook her head. "I smell nothing."

"Forgive me, highness. I had beans." Frith fanned at the air behind him.

"By Orien's beard," bellowed Beowyn, "you speak to the queen's consort."

"It's all right." Oona cough-giggled. "At least, it's all right if he's merely joking."

Frith nodded, smiling.

"Well, we are not going to find anything in this village. What we're looking for is most likely up in the mountains." Niron urged his horse onward, sliding past Beowyn.

The big man made a clicking sound and his horse lurched forward.

On edge from the odd energy in the air, Kitlyn kept looking around at the foundations of old buildings. Here and there, a sword, axe, or hammer lay dropped and rusted, many concealed by weeds. When they reached the intact square building, she peered in past broken doors bearing the likeness of the Steelfather at smashed chairs, tables, and a few mugs.

"Is that a tavern or a temple?" Kitlyn glanced back at him.

"Yes." Beowyn stopped his horse, staring left. "Poor sots."

The group collected around him, all looking past the far wall of the temple. Crumbling stacked stones outlined the foundation of another demolished structure. The interior had been dug out and filled with a vast pile of human bones in the most basic attempt at a mass grave.

Kitlyn gasped. "That's horrible. They didn't even try to bury them, just piled the bodies on top of each other."

Oona bit her lip, fixated on the grisly sight.

"These poor people." Isha sighed. "I thought the war was bad, but I've never seen so many dead in one place like this."

"A massacre." Bertan bowed his head.

Kitlyn dismounted Apples and walked over to the edge. Someone dug a shallow pit within the boundary of the ancient wall, about four feet down from ground level. The bodies had been there so long that no trace of dried blood, gore, or any foul smell remained. Dozens of rusty weapons stuck out from the pile, along with a shield or two. She studied the remains, breathing a silent sigh of relief upon not seeing any tiny skeletons.

"These are probably soldiers." Kitlyn decided not to disturb the site and backed up. "We don't know who destroyed this town, but I don't see any small bones... and there are weapons."

Oona wiped tears from her cheeks. "The townspeople might have fled. That sorcerer could've taken over the village and brought men to fight for him."

"Or the civilians and their families were buried proper, not dumped." Niron grimaced.

"Oh..." Oona flinched at the thought.

Kitlyn jogged over to her. "Most invading armies wouldn't have merely slaughtered civilians. I'm fairly certain we didn't invade Ondar. Barbarians might have done this, but they don't kill unarmed women or children." *They take them.*

"That's good." Oona looked up with a weak smile, her eyes red-rimmed.

Frith appeared about to say something, but reconsidered. Kitlyn shot him a grateful stare before climbing back into her saddle.

"The mountains are not too much farther." Beowyn pointed ahead, and urged his horse into motion again.

Open ground continued after the village. Kitlyn glanced left and right at seemingly endless sloping hills stretching away in either direction, wondering if the valley had an uphill end or if it might continue straight into the side of the mountain. A few hundred yards later, a standing wall of grey fog thinned enough to reveal an opening in the side of the mountain itself, a massive crack in black stone that formed a canyon wider than two houses.

A leathery flutter from above made Kitlyn look up at thick, grey fog.

"Think it's in there?" asked Niron.

"It's the only thing here." Beowyn chuckled, starting to put his blade away.

The shadows of two enormous birds dove toward the group. At another leathery flutter, Cloud's eyes bulged from their sockets. He reared, neighing a most horrible sounding wail, and leapt forward. Oona managed to leap off the saddle in a relatively controlled manner, landing in a tumble. The pure white horse took off at a full gallop, heading back the way they came from, toward the ruined village.

"Attack!" shouted Kitlyn. "From above!"

"Dismount!" roared Niron.

With a shrill screech, the left shadow dove faster, emerging from the mist in a glimmering array of blue-violet scales. A dragon-like head tipped the end of a long prehensile neck. Two reverse-jointed legs tucked tight against its belly, each foot bearing wicked talons the size of longswords. Unlike a dragon, it lacked forearms, its wings more like those of a bat. Brilliant violet feathers lined both sides of a narrow, trailing tail connected to a body about twice the size of a warhorse.

Those aren't birds... Kitlyn leapt to the ground. Apples lifted his head at the sky and snorted, unimpressed.

The diving wyvern went for Oona, who'd rolled to a stop face down, extending its feet as if to scoop her up and fly off. Kitlyn yanked her longsword free of its scabbard and ran to her, swinging at the talons with all her strength. Her sword bounced off the gleaming indigo claws with a resounding *clang*. The creature's bulk and speed knocked Kitlyn over onto her back, but she managed to skew the wyvern sideways enough that it grabbed dirt instead of Oona.

"Tenebrea's teacups!" shouted Oona before leaping to her feet.

Screeching, the second wyvern angled after Beowyn's horse.

"Oh, no ya don't," roared the big man. "I just got him."

Beowyn hurled himself into a leap and raked his huge sword at the beast. The blade struck the scaled hide with a dull *thump*, sending the wyvern into a lateral roll and causing it to crash upside down in the meadow about thirty feet away.

Apples turned to keep facing the still-flying wyvern. Evidently angered, the quasi-dragon turned and came racing back at Kitlyn. She widened her stance, raising her blade. Seconds before impact, she spotted its barbed tail coming, and dove to the side. The bone-hard tip passed over her with a loud *whuff* and a shrill cry of irritation from the wyvern. She landed on her chest, pounding the air out of her lungs.

"Formation," yelled Niron.

The soldiers gathered close, all facing out.

"Get inside the ring." Galfred waved at Kitlyn and Oona, beckoning them.

Kitlyn pushed herself up, scowling at the airborne menace. The wyvern that crashed flapped back into the air, climbing high. The other one circled back for another try, skimming low over the meadow straight at her. Kitlyn dug her fingers into the earth, her hands aglow with green magic. At her command, a stone spire erupted straight up out of the grass mere feet in front of the racing wyvern.

The creature barely had time to emit a squawk of alarm before crashing into the pillar with enough force to crack it. A collective groan of sympathetic pain came from the soldiers. The rock spire fell forward like a cut down tree, the wyvern practically hugging it with its wings, and shook the ground upon impact.

Kitlyn raised a tangle of grasping roots from the ground, winding them over the creature's wings, around its body, and pinning its jaws closed. A brilliant blue flash happened off to the right along with a startled wyvern shriek.

The other one crashed in an ungainly heap, tumbling in a heap of flailing limbs and wings several times before jumping upright on its feet, swinging its head back and forth, biting randomly at the air.

"What the devil's wrong with that one?" Isha pointed her sword at it.

"It's blind." Beowyn broke formation, advancing on it.

"The beast still has teeth." Niron limped after him. "Give it distance."

Kitlyn sent more roots up from the ground, tangling and binding the blinded wyvern before dragging it to the ground and cocooning it in place. Both creatures struggled and squirmed, emitting piteous—and painfully loud—shrieks.

"That makes it easy." Beowyn walked up to the blinded one, angling for a beheading strike.

"Be some good coin." Isha nodded. "That leather's worth quite a bit."

Bertan headed for the other wyvern by Kitlyn.

Oona moved in his way. "Please don't."

Kitlyn stood, dusting her hands off. "Don't? Those things almost ate us."

"I know, but..." She cast a pained glance at Beowyn. "It feels wrong to slay something that is helpless. They're no harm to us now."

Beowyn lowered his blade, staring at Oona. "I pity your father. How long will those roots last?"

"My father?" asked Oona.

He chuckled. "That look you gave me. No man with a soul could look into those eyes and deny any reasonable request... even unreasonable."

Oona glanced at Kitlyn. They both seemed to be thinking the same thing... King Talomir had never acquiesced to her request to give 'the servant girl' enough status to be a handmaiden.

"He said 'with a soul,'" muttered Kitlyn.

"You don't mean that. He wasn't *that* bad." Oona pulled her into a hug.

Kitlyn sighed. "Maybe. I'm upset with him. He shouldn't have poisoned himself. I had so much more I had to say to him. He had so much to answer for."

"He is answering for much if he's in the Banefallow," whispered Oona. "That is perhaps even too cruel for him."

Kitlyn gripped Oona tight, trying not to cry at the thought of her father being ripped apart by spirit wolves over and over... and over. As furious as she was with him about the war, she had still lost her father and had been powerless to stop it.

"Highness?" Isha approached and rested a gentle hand on her shoulder. "How long will those roots hold them?"

"Long enough." Kitlyn swallowed, released her grip on Oona, and tried to stand tall and confident despite having tears on her cheeks. "A few hours at least. We should be well out of their sight."

"Bah." Beowyn put his sword away. "Carryin' two hundred pounds of leather would be a right pain in the"—he glanced at the girls —"something."

Apples glanced at the nearer wyvern and tossed his head like a nobleman refusing a cheap wine.

"Cloud!" shouted Oona. "Cloud?"

"There." Keal pointed. "Cowardly thing ain't he? Pretty though."

Oona brushed dirt off her armor. "We don't have wyverns in Lucernia. He's never seen one before."

"He isn't a warhorse." Kitlyn patted Apples' flank.

Bertan laughed. "Neither is Beowyn's."

"Aye. This one's too damn lazy to run." Beowyn ruffled his new horse's mane.

Oona called for Cloud a few more times before the horse cantered over. She hugged him around the neck and spent a few minutes murmuring soothing things. The not-quite-dragons eventually gave up screeching, staring around with wild panic-stricken eyes.

Maybe they'll think better of attacking us again.

She climbed back into the saddle and rode with the group to an opening in the mountainside. Walls of black rock rose straight up to the clouds on both sides of a dirt-floored passage. It hardly looked natural, like the earth had sprouted two mountain 'teeth' right next to each other. The width of the canyon varied, but from here, it didn't seem as though it ever became narrower than about twenty feet.

"Perhaps we should leave the horses." Beowyn looked up at the walls. "It could get a bit tight, and the terrain might become impassable for 'em."

"Captain Niron can't keep up too well," said Isha.

"Yes. You're both right. Well, someone will need to keep watch over the horses. I suppose that is me this time." Niron nodded to Beowyn. "Sergeant."

Kitlyn jumped down from her saddle, crouched, and pulled her boots off.

The soldiers stared at her in confusion.

"Could be rough ground up ahead… and it's cold. 'Course I'm just a grunt, and it's wildly out of my station to even ask the queen why she's doing something even if it does appear strange." Bertan dismounted.

"But I hope you're the type of young monarch that appreciates wisdom from age if not status."

Kitlyn stood, smiling. "I understand, and appreciate anyone who offers their wisdom in sincerity. My magic draws upon the Alderswood and direct contact with the earth makes it stronger."

She stuffed her boots in the saddlebag.

"You sure you don't want to bring them in case of rough ground?" asked Bertan.

"I should be all right. And if we stumble on a field of broken glass, Galfred can carry me."

The boy coughed and turned bright red.

Oona snickered.

Niron remained on his steed and held Cloud's reins. The other horses responded to commands except for Beowyn's, though it seemed inclined to follow the crowd of horses anyway.

A little bit of magic chased the chill from her toes—and everywhere else. The gloomy, blustery day became as comfortable as a perfect spring afternoon. Beowyn took the lead, heading into the black-walled canyon.

After about a hundred paces, they waded into a bank of low-lying fog about knee deep. The peculiar mist unnerved the soldiers, Galfred more than the rest. Kitlyn's connection to the earth allowed her to feel the roots binding the wyverns, revealing them as still secure. She kept the sense of it at the back of her mind, focused more on avoiding putting her foot down on sharp stones, which she sensed with the same magic she'd once used to 'see' her surroundings in the pitch dark of Underholm.

Some minutes later, the wyverns began to thrash against the roots with renewed fervor that verged on panic. Both root bundles tugged harder and harder as if the creatures tried desperately to flee from something that terrified them. Feeling a touch guilty—and not expecting the wyverns to find them in the canyon—she unraveled the roots, releasing them.

The frenetic shrieking cries of wyverns receded off into the sky.

"Something is coming from behind us." As soon as she said it, she stared down at where her thighs vanished in the fog. Dozens of pressure imprints approached from ahead of them, similar to how she could sense through the earth wherever a person stood nearby, though these didn't feel anywhere near as substantial as people. "...and something is coming from ahead of us."

"Something?" asked Beowyn. "I don't see anything. What did you hear?"

"I feel it in the ground. Lots of footsteps but too light to be people."

Everyone stood in tense silence for about ten seconds before the clatter of bones echoed off the walls in front of them. Oona drew her longsword, as did the soldiers.

"Skeletons." Beowyn yanked his great blade from his back-sheath.

"Niron..." Kitlyn turned to stare toward the canyon exit. "The horses..."

"Going." Galfred sprinted off.

Beowyn, Isha, Frith, and Keal formed a line.

A mass of skeletons rushed out of a standing wall of fog about fifty feet ahead, appearing like specters from thin air. Some wore armored helms, some had tattered fragments of clothing or armor dangling from their bones. All carried rusted blades of varying length.

Kitlyn drew a melon-sized rock out of the wall to her right and hurled it into the approaching fiends. A comet of black surrounded in brilliant emerald fire smashed through them with a rippling crunch like dozens of branches snapping in rapid succession. The stone barely slowed, punching its way out the other end of the crowd. Bones flew in random directions and a handful of skeletons blasted completely apart.

The front line of skeletal warriors crashed into the soldiers with a disharmonic ring of steel on steel.

"Not going!" shouted Galfred from behind. He ran back into view, chased by a far larger mass of skeletons, and skidded to a stop by Oona before turning to face the oncoming wave of dried bones.

One against over a hundred.

Kitlyn glanced rapidly back and forth between the two groups trapping them. *Bad to fight two armies at once.* She faced to the rear, dug her toes into the dirt, and opened the core of magic in her chest. When she'd awakened Omun, she'd been terrified. Her emotion almost reached the same peak, but rather than fear, her desperate need to protect Oona surged out in spirals of green energy.

She pictured a barrier forming and rising, growing, blocking off the entire chasm from wall to wall. Black stone rose from the fog, lifting at a ponderous pace. The skeletons charged into it, half a dozen spilling over and landing flat before the wall became too high for them to hurdle. A few more climbed and leapt to the ground, but she pushed it higher until the continuous scratching of bone on rock announced they could no longer get past it.

Galfred, Bertan, and Oona met the skeletons that made it past the wall. Oona swung her longsword in a two-handed grip, but didn't seem ready for the skeleton's speed. It dodged her strike and pressed the attack forcing her to focus entirely on defense, giving ground but not suffering a wound. The first skeleton to reach Galfred stabbed him in the thigh, but he continued swinging, driving his sword into its chest with enough force to smash it apart.

Bertan whirled into a frenzy of slashing and kicking, tearing down three skeletons in the few seconds it took Kitlyn to cease concentrating on making the wall bigger and summon another fist-sized stone. She launched it at the skeleton menacing Oona, blasting it to pieces. The second it went down, Oona lunged to her left and whacked her sword into the spine of another one attacking Galfred, shaving off a few ribs. It ignored her, continuing to swing at him. Shouts of anger, pain, and triumph arose behind her from the soldiers fighting the forward group.

Kitlyn spun, waving her arms while glowing spots of green energy formed in her hands. She raised her arms with a rapid thrust, drawing a rock spire up from the ground that smashed two skeletons trading swings with Bertan. Free of their assault, he lunged and grabbed the ribs of the next one near him and pulled it down while ramming his knee into its skull, sending it flying. The headless bones continued twitching until he stomped on its spine a few times.

Oona drew back and chopped at the same skeleton she'd been fighting again, slicing its left leg off at the hip. It careened over sideways, finally took notice of her, and began crawling across the ground at her, barely visible in the fog. Oona shrieked and jumped back while slicing downward. A hollow *clonk* with a hint of crunch accompanied her blade stopping. She swung again and again, emitting a series of war cries each time.

Galfred punched another skeleton in the sternum, knocking it back far enough that he had the room to round his blade in a solid blow that shattered it to loose bones. Bertan smashed the last one in the rear group, his attack disintegrating its spine the same instant the fiend's rusty sword clanged against Galfred's shiny one.

Oona kept chopping at the fog in a repetitive series of clanking crunches.

"It's dead, highness," said Galfred.

"Of course it's dead!" She swung twice more. "It's bones."

"I mean… It's destroyed." He sighed at his leg. "Ouch."

Kitlyn spun to face the front of the group and lobbed rock after rock, winging them around the soldiers. The enchanted stones smashed anywhere from two to four skeletons at a time, blasting bones far into the air. Between her magic and the ex-deserters' blades, in under a minute, the only skeletons still moving stood behind the wall, clawing, hissing, and scratching.

"My word, highness." A nearly-out-of-breath Isha stumbled over to her. "That was impressive."

Beowyn, sweating but grinning like a boy having the time of his life, rested his blade across his shoulder. "That's the last of them"—he stared at the wall—"what in the name of…"

"There's gotta be a hundred or more out there." Galfred pointed at the wall and collapsed to sit.

Oona finally stopped smashing the bones that had crawled after her. She stood straight, clutching the blade close and shivering, staring imperiously down as if she intended to resume swinging if so much as one bone chip twitched. The sight of Galfred clutching his bloody thigh erased her fear and she rushed to his side. "Here, let me see that."

Galfred, as if only now feeling any pain from the wound, let out a groan.

Bertan and Frith patted him on the shoulders.

"Now you're a true soldier." Isha swatted him on the head. "Even if you did take the easy path with a leg wound."

They all chuckled.

"What are we going to do about that?" Keal, nursing a bleeding arm, indicated the wall with a nod.

Kitlyn walked over to the barrier she'd made and placed her hand on it. "I have an idea."

Her sense of the skeletons walking around on the other side revealed they had spread out across the entire thirty-foot width, pressing close. With an impish smile, she liquefied a strip of rock across the bottom on the opposite face as well as a few inches in from the edges where it met the canyon face. The remaining hard stone cracked, sending the barrier toppling over onto the skeletons with a deafening *whud* and a rush of air that blasted away fog behind it. The tremor from the enormous stone slab hitting the ground knocked everyone off their feet.

Except for Galfred who'd already been seated.

"Navissa's neth—"

Oona covered his mouth.

"That is the first time I have ever seen a wall turned into an *offensive* weapon." Beowyn laughed.

Kitlyn stooped to pick up a rusty sword, tilting it back and forth to examine the edge. "They came from the mass grave. That's what spooked the wyverns." She dropped it, dusted her hands off, and stood, squinting into the wind blowing down the ravine. "May Tenebrea guide these souls to where they belong."

Isha held her hands to her mouth and made a loud, noise somewhat bird-like that echoed off along the canyon.

In response, a similar trill came from the distance.

The soldiers all seemed relieved.

"The captain's okay." Isha faced Kitlyn. "Not sure how, but that particular call means all clear."

Golden light surrounded Oona's hands. Galfred grunted.

"Orien has cleansed the wound as well. Rusty blades leave sickness." Oona smiled and squeezed his shoulder. "I think it will be sore for some time, but not as much as Niron's. The bear took quite a nip."

"Go keep watch with Niron," said Beowyn.

"I'm good." Galfred groaned and forced himself upright. "Don't need ta run off."

Beowyn folded his arms. "Walk back and forth a couple times from wall ta wall."

Galfred clenched his jaw and managed it, though with a noticeable limp. He did, at least, appear more agile than Niron.

The burly sergeant appeared about ready to order him back, but at the last minute, nodded. "We hit any nasty terrain, yer gonna stay parked and guard our backs."

"Aye." Galfred stopped walking and braced a hand on the bloody spot of armor.

Oona tended to Kael's wounded arm, as well as multiple nicks, scratches, and punctures on the rest of the soldiers. Upon seeing Kitlyn free of injury, she spent a moment clinging to her and whispering thanks to Lucen.

"Well, this is off to an interesting start." Beowyn kicked a few bones around.

"I never imagined such horrors as this possible. Moving dead..." Oona shivered.

Kitlyn rested her chin on Oona's shoulder. "There is much, I suspect, we have not seen of the world. Take comfort in how brittle they were. Perhaps this lich is the same."

"Let us hope." Oona heaved a breath and released their embrace. "We should not delay here."

"Lucen's light…" Frith eyed the collapsed wall. "Wish we had 'er at the battle of Pembrook."

Kitlyn touched foreheads with Oona for a second, then resumed walking deeper into the ravine. "Living soldiers would not have pressed so mindlessly against a wall like that. Nor do I think I would've been capable of crushing so many people. Those creatures weren't alive."

"A noble thought, highness." Beowyn considered putting his sword away, but kept it out. "But havin' a line of a couple hundred enemy comin' at ya ready ta slice yer head off has a way of changin' what a person's capable of doin'."

Oona glanced back. "The lich must know we are here and sent the skeletons after us, driving them to a specific place. Mindless. That is likely how Niron and the horses survived."

If I had crushed living people like that, those who expected me to wipe them out to the last would have driven the rest to a fervor. She cringed inside, grateful for the course events had taken.

Kitlyn walked ahead, thigh-deep fog billowing around her legs with each stride, so thick she couldn't even see her knees. Every rattle of armor or scuff of boots bounced off the black canyon walls. The quieter everyone tried to be, the more noise they seemed to make. Gradually, the walls narrowed to a width barely enough for a single rider on horseback, their massive height and squeezing proximity putting Kitlyn on edge. *I feel like a grain between millstones.* The soldiers rearranged themselves in single file, annoyingly with Beowyn right behind her in front of Oona.

Her earth sense revealed the ground hidden beneath the thick white vapor remained relatively flat and devoid of natural obstacles. The canyon bent left at a sharp turn, but zigzagged to the right after only a short distance. Another jagged S-curve came twelve paces later.

"Ach." Beowyn's voice practically fell on her back with physical weight. "This would've been murder on the horses."

"I hope it doesn't become any narrower." Oona looked side to side. "It feels like the walls will crush us."

"Ehh, don't say that." Galford chuckled.

Kitlyn relaxed somewhat a few minutes later when a widening of the passage revealed itself in the back of her thoughts, as well as a doorway-sized hole on the left. "We're almost there."

She hurried forward and stepped out from the claustrophobic canyon into a fog-filled chamber some sixty feet long by twenty wide. The wall at the end straight ahead continued well up into the clouds, part of the great mountain. Though the sides didn't reach anywhere near the same height, no one would be climbing a few hundred feet of sheer black stone.

Midway along the left, a rectangular opening stood inside a frame of carved runic symbols, all infused with a faint light from glowing mist trapped in the grooves. A stone skull with ram horns adorned the top, its eyes also emitting baleful white light.

"Lucen preserve us." Beowyn made a sacred hand motion in the air.

Kitlyn glanced back at everyone. Except for the burly sergeant whose expression said 'perhaps this is unwise,' the others all appeared to have decided they would not be going any further. Oona also seemed frightened, her eyes as wide as could be, though she walked closer to stand beside her.

"'Tis not a good idea ta go in there." Frith pointed at the door. "Did everyone forget the creature in there can steal the minds of men?"

Oona took a step toward the opening, looking around at the carvings before glancing at Kitlyn "So it shall be only us then?"

Isha cleared her throat.

"Uhh. I mean not *men*. Anyone." Frith cringed at Oona, gesturing at the air as if he wished to pull her back from the doorway.

"Then why say 'men' if you mean any person?" asked Oona.

Frith stared blankly at her.

"Lucen will protect us." Oona turned to face everyone. "The magic he has given me will shield our thoughts."

"You said it would spread thin the more people you protect." Kitlyn eyed the glowing marks on the wall, not at all liking the energy they gave off. "How many can we bring with complete confidence?"

Oona looked down. "I admit it will be difficult to protect everyone. The more at once, the less everyone receives. Like sharing a cup of water. Perhaps… two besides us."

"I'll go." Galfred stepped forward.

"Me as well." Bertan nodded.

"No, lad." Beowyn patted Galfred on the shoulder. "Your leg. You'll not be running or jumping on that for a while. Bertan and I will escort the queen."

Kitlyn looked up at Bertan. "I cannot ask you to do this. You have a wife and two children who have thought you dead. I fear if you are to tempt fate like this, their fears will become real."

"I am not afraid." He glanced at the door. "Well, perhaps there is fear but any living person would have it. We are soldiers because we do not surrender to our fears."

"Do not think I am implying you are afraid. I am thinking of your wife and children. Please, the greatest service you can do for me now is to survive to return to them." Kitlyn gripped his shoulder.

"You gotta get back to them." Isha stepped up. "I'll go."

"To the Pit with that." Keal shook his head. "You're only twenty-three."

She spun on him. "And you're only twenty-five. The queen's what, fifteen?"

"Sixteen," muttered Kitlyn and Oona at the same time.

"That she may be, but you can't raise giant walls out of the ground or throw shooting stars." Kael took Isha's hand.

"You lovebirds can stay here." Frith laughed. "I'll go."

Isha and Keal glared at him, both with a little blush in their cheeks.

"Beowyn and Isha." Oona looked up. "They have the strongest will."

Everyone stood in silence for a moment.

Frith grumbled.

"I do not call you weak of mind." Oona gestured at Bertan. "He is a large man with much strength, but can you not see Beowyn is twice his size? That does not make Bertan weak."

"Not sure about *twice* my size." Bertan chuckled, flexing his arm.

"All right then." Kitlyn faced the doorway. "It is settled."

Oona raised her hands as Isha and Beowyn moved up behind her. Scintillating blue light rings appeared like crowns, then faded to a barely noticeable azure glow in front of their foreheads. Kitlyn shifted her eyes up, but couldn't see anything, nor did she feel any different.

"Lucen protects us." Oona offered a solemn nod.

"Be aware." Kitlyn took a deep breath, and strode into the dark passage.

31

THE DEPTHS OF FEAR

OONA

Focused on her magic, Oona entered the passage at the rear of the group. The faint glow from her mind-shielding spell revealed a smooth-walled corridor of black stone. Cold, humid air hung heavy with the smell of wetness and mossy earth. Scuffs from their boots filled in the silence, traveling deep into the mountain to warn whatever may lie in wait for them.

She beckoned her orb and sent it floating a few feet above them, the light enough to see for a good distance ahead.

Isha and Beowyn cringed at the sudden illumination, but said nothing.

Kitlyn moved like a spirit at the lead, her bare feet silent upon the stone floor. Of the four, only she had put her sword back in its scabbard. Content to follow the shapes of the soldiers in front of her, Oona continued to concentrate mostly on guarding their thoughts from demonic influence.

High Priest Balais, or at least the vision of him she had dreamed, didn't know if all such creatures as Voldreth could steal minds or if this particular lich possessed that power due to his malefic magic.

"Beware," whispered Kitlyn.

Oona lifted her head, back from her momentary daydream.

"Here." Kitlyn crouched and thrust her fingers into the floor. "This is false. It only appears to be solid."

"An illusion." Beowyn poked his sword into the false stone. "Tis nothing solid about it."

Kitlyn started to stand, but thought better of it and crouched again. Green light surrounded her hands. A soft, scraping rumble vibrated the corridor, and the suspicious patch rippled like a pot of boiling grey mud. "There. We may find ourselves running out of here. That should be thick enough to hold our weight."

Isha's expression hardened.

"Is something wrong?" Kitlyn peered up at her, then stood.

"Seeing magic like that reminds me of *them*."

Kitlyn resumed walking. "Evermoor's soldiers?"

"Yes. Forgive me for scowling at you. The sav—well, the enemy took both of my brothers and my father. I was only eleven when my father went to Tenebrea. One of their root mages hurled him into the Churning Deep while he tried to defend our side."

Oona's heart sank. "You have every right to be angry and hurt."

"I grew up waiting for the day I could carry a sword over there and get revenge. Edden, my older brother, fell to an arrow not a month after I became a soldier. I fought for about a year before one of them murdered Cewyn."

"I'm sorry," whispered Kitlyn.

"He was your age, highness." Isha glowered at the wall. "Standing guard at night. They came up behind him and slit his throat. I stopped caring if I survived the war, only wanted to take as many of them with me as I could. Then... one day, my unit rushed to reinforce a smaller garrison by a little village east of Pirolen. The fighting happened in a field so close most of the homes had arrows stuck in them. Another wave of sav—Evermoor soldiers hit us without warning after we thought it ended, bunch of villagers out looking for their dead got caught in it. I saw one of the demon-worshipping savages run into a rain of Lucernian arrows to shield a small boy who'd been caught out in the field."

Oona gasped.

"That's the moment I started to question. As evil as we'd been told they were, to see one do a thing like that..."

"Too much deception." Kitlyn squatted to seal another illusion pit. "Too much death."

"They were goin' ta execute him, even after he saved that child." Isha bowed her head. "For whatever silly reason, they let him recover from his arrow wounds before hanging him. I helped him escape the night before... and left with him."

Beowyn glanced at her, both eyebrows up. "That is a little more than simple desertion."

Kitlyn stood, patting at the ground over the pit with her foot. "I was not aware that execution is how we dealt with prisoners of war."

"It shouldn't be, but my commander was bloodthirsty. He knew the villagers had been out in that field. Some of us even saw the boy, but he wouldn't order the archers to stop since he thought it would give the Evermoor forces an opportunity to charge us."

"If we survive this, you will give me the name of this commander." Oona narrowed her eyes. "I wish to speak with him."

Isha nodded.

They walked for a few minutes more until the hallway came to an end at a square chamber. A deep chasm with a gap of about twenty feet separated them from the other side. The corridor continued past an archway flanked by unlit sconces decorated in fist-sized skulls. Kitlyn approached the edge and peered down.

Oona glanced left at a grid of nine runes on the wall, the one at the top left corner glowing. "It's some manner of puzzle or code. Oh, this looks like it will be difficult."

The ground rumbled.

With a gasp, Oona spun to face Kitlyn.

Two polyps of stone exuded from the ledges on either side of the pit, growing outward until they joined in the center and formed a solid stone bridge.

"No... not really difficult." Kitlyn set out across the gently arched beam she'd made.

Beowyn laughed. He went next, with Isha behind him.

Oona gingerly approached the edge and peered down into complete blackness. *To split hairs, I am not so much afraid of heights as I am afraid of falling, or really... hitting the ground. If there isn't a ground to hit...* She swallowed dry. *It's only too deep to see. That means it's a really long fall.*

The others reached the opposite end, almost too far for her to shield their minds. Her fear of heights collapsed under the weight of her need to keep Kitlyn's thoughts safe from the lich. Heedless of the danger of falling, she raced out over the bridge at a sprint, clearing it before rational thought could catch up and point out that she'd just traversed such a deadly obstacle.

Isha caught her panicky sprint, holding her steady until she calmed back to normal. Or at least relative normal. She couldn't quite reach a state of complete calm in the lair of a demonic lich.

By Lucen's hand am I here. He shall protect us.

"What are you thinkin' we do?" whispered Beowyn.

"I rather doubt this creature is going to be in the mood to talk." Oona rubbed her hands together, shivering at the cold.

"No, probably not." Kitlyn slowed to a stop at a sharp right corner, and peered around. She paused only a few seconds before continuing.

They entered a long stretch of featureless corridor, four times as wide as tall. It offered plenty of room for a battle, which set Oona's nerves on edge. For what felt like hours, they walked down a tunnel with black walls and ceiling, the floor covered in dark grey silt.

Every so often, Oona bowed her head and offered a brief prayer to Lucen for protection. Perhaps the tenth time she did so, Beowyn and Isha no longer existed when she opened her eyes, and Kitlyn had gone quite far ahead.

"Kit!" shouted Oona, moving up to a run. "What happened to the others?"

Kitlyn ignored her, having spotted a door, finally at the end of the passage. She reached out to touch a rune on its surface — and the ground below her opened up, swallowing her before sealing.

"Kitlyn!" shrieked Oona. She skidded to a stop as the sound of her wife's scream from below faded to silence.

Oona pounded on the floor a few times before standing and slapping at the door, not caring if the ground swallowed her too. She *had* to get to Kitlyn. "Beowyn? Isha? Where are you?"

A man's distant voice yelled out as if calling to her, too far away to make out words.

"No!" She stomped on the spot of floor that ate Kitlyn.

"There she is."

Oona spun to the right.

A tall man in a grey maid's dress stepped out of the swirling darkness, dagger gleaming in his right hand. Two more men in Evermoor armor appeared behind him, also with drawn daggers.

Too frightened by the sight of the assassins who'd plagued her for years to question why they'd be deep within a mountain in Ondar, Oona screamed and ran directly away from them into clouds of black smoke. Men's taunting laughter chased her. Six strides later, the shifting darkness gave way to the curving hallway in Castle Cimril. She looked over her shoulder at the three assassins racing out the door of her old bedchamber.

"Princess," said a man in front of her.

Oona spun forward, skidding to a halt. Her heart nearly leapt into her throat at the sight of Ian. She tried to leap back, but found her wrists shackled together, connected to a chain leading to his fist.

Ian held up an evil bottle of frothing purple liquid. "You haven't touched your drink, princess."

"No!" Oona stared in horror at the shiny silver manacles. "You're dead!"

At rapid footsteps coming up from behind, she peered over her shoulder at the three assassins. Oona struggled at the metal locked around her wrists. Fear flickered to rage, but no matter how hard she pulled, the steel refused to release her.

"You're dead! You're not real." She hurled herself *at* Ian, reaching with her bound hands to swat the poison from his grip.

Her shoulder crashed against his chest, which gave way, no more solid than a cloud. The manacles evaporated with a twinkling clatter like thousands of tiny fragments of steel falling to a marble floor. Oona drew her longsword and prepared to face the assassins, but they, too, had disappeared.

She turned in place, sword held at the ready, looking around at the royal hall. "I'm not here. This is not real."

After a few minutes of telling the walls they didn't exist—and nothing changing—Oona picked a direction, sheathed her blade, and walked toward the grand stairway.

"Oona," said a high-pitched voice.

She stopped and spun. A door to a sitting room opened, revealing a willowy girl of about fourteen with blonde hair. Except for pale green eyes, Oona may as well have been looking into a mirror.

"Mama was right." Older-Evie scrunched up her nose in disgust. "How can you do those *things* with another girl? It's wretched. Why did you take me away from my home? I hate it here. I hate you! You're a disgrace to Lucen, doing that *stuff* with a girl. What's *wrong* with you?"

"Foul liar!" roared Oona, not believing her eyes for even a split second. "You are not my sister."

Older-Evie burst into laughter and ran off down the hall. Oona glared after her, furious.

A short distance away, the teen turned to face her again and shrank back into a seven-year-old, once again a total visage of loving innocence.

"Oona!" chirped Evie, raising her arms as if about to run into a hug. "I've missed you!"

Ruby appeared out of nowhere, swooping in and grabbing the little girl, who erupted in tears, screaming for help.

"She's mine, you filthy wretch!" screamed Ruby, backing away with the struggling child. "You know I'm going to take her back. And she must be punished for being so disloyal to her own mother."

Ruby spat in Oona's direction, then ran away.

Evie reached over her mother's shoulder toward her. "Oona! Help! I don't wanna go with her! She's gonna hit me! Help! Don't let her take me!"

Growling, Oona chased, surprising herself by drawing her longsword. She ran hard, but never gained any ground on the fleeing woman.

At the end of the corridor, Ruby kicked a door open, ducked inside, and slammed it. Oona crashed against the door, emitting a bark like a stepped-on goose when it failed to yield. She sheathed her blade and grabbed the door handle, growling as she turned it and ripped the door open.

She rushed into an impenetrably black chamber so cold her breath fogged before her eyes.

"Evie?"

Her voice echoed over itself four times.

"Evie?" called Oona, louder.

The echo came back six times, each repetition quieter than the last.

Squish.

Oona stopped and tried to look down at what she stepped on, but couldn't see anything past her chest. Even the glow of her light orb only radiated to about three feet. Skittering and scratching surrounded her.

"What is this place?"

The darkness vanished.

Oona stood at the center of a vast chamber filled with millions of spiders, insects, snakes, and unidentifiable bugs, some multi-legged horrors as thick as her arm and as long as her leg. She blinked in surprise, kicked a fat, black bug away from her foot, then sighed.

"What am I, six?" She shook her head. "I'm not afraid of creepy-crawlies."

A millipede the size of a sausage landed on her shoulder.

Oona screamed and swatted it away, shaking. "Okay, maybe I am a little. But bugs don't get that big."

A handful of snakes crawled toward her.

"This is not real. I haven't been petrified of spiders for years." She gazed up at a ceiling covered in webs and dead rats. "L-Lucen knows my heart. I do not bear falsehood. Not wanting to be near them isn't exactly the same as being terrified of them."

The ocean of creepers disappeared.

Oona blinked, and the large chamber became a city square in Cimril, the sky above overcast and grey.

"Abomination!" shouted a man behind her.

"Wretch!" yelled a woman.

Oona spun. A crowd of angry citizens appeared out of thin air and advanced toward her. Two large men at the center flung a battered and bloody Kitlyn to the ground at her feet, a gaping sword wound at the center of her chest. The crowd appeared intent on doing the same to her.

"An affront to the gods!" roared a teenage boy. "Burn them both!"

She fell to her knees and gathered Kitlyn's body in her arms, refusing to flee and leave her there. As the crowd of citizens closed in around her, Oona shut her eyes, thinking of Tenebrea's blessing and the gift Orien had given her.

"This is not real."

Men and women grabbed her arms, trying to pull her away from Kitlyn. Spit hit her in the face. Fists mashed into her back.

"Kill the abomination!" roared the crowd.

Oona clung with all her strength to Kitlyn's body, shaking with anger.

"This is not real. It's trying to trick me."

Someone yanked Oona's hair, pulling her head back.

She opened her eyes and stared up at the scowl of a furious, unfamiliar woman. The cold edge of a sharp blade pressed into the front of her throat.

"Not real," whispered Oona...

Before blacking out.

TOO FAR

KITLYN

The narrow passage behind Kitlyn had become too quiet.

She peered back and found herself alone. The others had all vanished.

"Oona?" She looked around. "Beowyn? Isha?"

For a few seconds after her voice stopped echoing, she stood there, not entirely sure what to do. *Did I miss a hole in the floor? No… they would've shouted if they fell. People don't simply vanish.* She turned back the way she had been walking and stared at more endless hallway.

"Wait… Oona is gone, and so is her light. How can I still see? That doesn't make any sense."

The instant the realization hit her, it brought on a strong spell of vertigo. Kitlyn lost her balance and fell to the floor, surprisingly soft for stone.

She sat up in her tiny bedroom across the hall from Oona's chambers, covered by her crude blanket and a thin nightdress. Her bare feet poked out from the other side, dirty as ever. The shelf with her spare tunics and breeches stood beside her on the right.

An overwhelming, sickening feeling crept into her mind: she'd dreamed it all. Oona loving her back, the Eldritch Heart, ending the war, being anything other than a pathetic lowborn girl. She'd had a wonderful dream that had become a nightmare. Little chance existed that Oona thought of her as anything more than a dear friend. She dare not admit her love, lest the girl recoil in horror and never want to see her again. That the princess had actually shared her love and even *married* her in Lucernia of all places could only have been a dream.

"Ending the war?" Kitlyn stared at her hands. "Me, a stoneshaper? Ugh. Time to grow up. I'm not a child anymore."

True, she could make pebbles dance around to amuse little Pim, but rocking the foundation of the castle to threaten the king? Laughable. Raising a massive wall to crush an army of skeletons? Ridiculous. Becoming queen? Preposterous.

Oona loving her back? The most absurd thought of all.

At that, Kitlyn buried her face against her knees, and wept.

Two loud bangs shook her door.

"Coming," muttered Kitlyn in a teary voice while wiping her face on the back of her arm.

She slipped out of bed and took her nightdress off, dropping it unceremoniously on the thin mattress, then spent a few seconds staring down at her nakedness, imagining Oona's hands caressing her.

With a sigh, she pulled on her breeches and tunic, then left her bedroom. After heading down to the ground floor to retrieve a bucket, soap, and a brush, she returned to the third floor royal hallway and proceeded to scrub. On her hands and knees, she pushed the brush back and forth in endless drudgery.

Oona emerged from her bedchamber in a beautiful blue dress, her handmaiden Elsbeth beside her. The two of them laughed and giggled about something banal. Upon seeing Kitlyn sprawled there, clad in rags and filthy, Oona whispered something behind her hand that made Elsbeth cackle with laughter. The two of them scurried off down the corridor, no doubt laughing at her.

Tears patted on the brush in Kitlyn's hands. When had Oona become so mean to her? She'd *never* been like that. Had she done something wrong? *Oh, no… I must've talked in my sleep. Someone heard me and she knows I love her! Everyone knows I'm an abomination.*

Kitlyn curled up, shivering, dreading the shame that would follow. That didn't bother her near as much as Oona being so cold—even cruel. The truth must have reached her ears. Her longtime friend had fallen in unnatural love with her, and Oona had reacted exactly as Kitlyn dreaded.

Expecting Fauhurst to appear at any minute, she forced herself to scrub onward, still sobbing. Minutes later when she reached the middle of the curve, the door to the king's bedchamber came into view.

She froze, staring at it. Those doors felt as though they belonged to her, not the king. Not her father. *No. He isn't my father. I had a dream. A wishful, made-up, impossible dream. Me the real princess? Of course I dreamed it. I've been wishing for a nobleman to ride in on a black horse and claim me as his daughter for years.* Minutes passed. No Fauhurst came to torment her. Still, the nagging sensation that she had moved into that bedchamber needled at her.

Abandoning the brush in a puddle of foam, Kitlyn stood, wiping her wet hands down the front of her plain servant's tunic. She padded up to the ornate doors and pulled one open. If anyone caught her going into the king's private quarters, she would face severe punishment. Yet, the castle had become strangely quiet.

The interior of the bedchamber appeared as she expected it should. She sighed with defeat and turned to leave, but caught sight of a simple crown perched upon a pillow in a locked cabinet. *What? The king would sooner die than be seen without his crown.*

She brushed a finger across her forehead. "It's silly to wear a crown into a fight. I don't need to wave my station in everyone's face."

Confused by the oddity of the crown sitting there unworn, Kitlyn pushed the door shut and jogged down the hallway. She hurried faster and faster, until she sprinted, her bare feet clapping on the smooth polished stone. Hallways and staircases blurred by on her way down to the throne room.

A constant low murmur of voices came from within.

Kitlyn grasped the handles of the great double doors and heaved them open. The instant the thick wooden doors parted, her servant's clothing exploded into an elaborate gown of seafoam green with white trim. Matching soft slippers appeared on her feet, tiny fabric roses of dark emerald above the toes. She glanced at her arms, covered to the elbows in white silk gloves. The weight of a thin crown settled upon her head.

A room full of advisors, courtiers, and nobles all stopped in mid-conversation to stare at her.

Oh, this is far too strange. Am I still dreaming? Did I dream that I had a dream of being queen, then waking up only to still be dreaming that I am queen? She emitted a nervous laugh. *I shall drive myself to madness with such circular thoughts.*

The throne sat empty, the carpeted path from door to dais unobstructed. For no particular reason, Kitlyn walked into the room. Whispers came from both sides, gossiping about how she loved another woman. Many expressed disgust at the notion. Some averted their eyes, refusing to even look at her, calling her a 'creature.'

"A shame such a pretty girl as the princess would be so vile inside," said a male voice on the right.

"They ought to make her marry that Lanwick prince." A woman with a huge beehive hairdo scowled at Kitlyn. "And toss that peasant girl back to the farm she came from. Maybe she'll wed one of the pigs."

The courtiers around the woman broke into laughter.

Kitlyn glared.

"Hmph." The woman broke eye contact, nose in the air.

"Prince Lanwick wouldn't dare touch a creature like her." A man scowled at Kitlyn and looked away. "Wretch."

"They'll never produce an heir." A portly man on the other side she vaguely recalled as a duke shook his head. "She simply cannot be allowed to rule on that matter alone. It breaks the hereditary royal family. She is not fit to wear the crown."

By the time Kitlyn reached the base of the throne dais, she found herself caught halfway between the urge to crush the entire room inward to silence the nattering harpies and wanting to find a small, dark place to hide away from everyone so she could burst into tears. How could people hate her so much only because the person she chose to love happened to be a woman, too?

"My clothes changed in an instant. I am either dreaming… or I'm not." She stooped and reached for the stone steps leading to the throne. A thin needle liquefied out and hardened at her command. She plucked her left glove off and pierced her palm with the point, wincing at the pain.

Nothing changed. The horrible, whispering crowd remained.

"I'm not dreaming." She dropped the needle and stood, hands balled to fists. "This is real. The lich is doing something to me. Making me see things I fear."

Murmuring swept over the crowd. A disturbance developed at the back, sweeping across toward her. Bodies parted, revealing Fauhurst in his advisor's robes, dragging Oona along by the hair. She'd been stripped to her smallclothes and bra, wearing more bruises and stains from rotting vegetables than fabric. Fauhurst marched up to Kitlyn and hurled Oona to all fours at her feet.

"Kitlyn," rasped Oona.

"I will see our glorious kingdom restored, purged of your impurity." Fauhurst put his foot against Oona's rear end and kicked her forward so she crashed into Kitlyn.

Kitlyn looked down into her love's eyes, both blackened and bruised.

"Wake up," said Oona. "I'm right here. Kit! Wake up!"

Pure rage welled up within Kitlyn. She roared, lashing out with her magic, and thrust her right arm forward, tearing dozens of giant bricks from the walls and commanding them all to fly inward at Fauhurst.

In that instant of absolute fury, her vision flashed completely white.

The hand she thrust forward struck something soft.

"Oof!" yelled Oona. "Kit?"

She blinked rapidly until the blinding glow faded.

Kitlyn once again found herself wearing her armor, standing in a black stone hallway, her right hand outstretched as if signaling a rider to stop his horse. Oona stumbled back, both hands clamped over her face.

"Oona!" shouted Kitlyn before bursting into joyful tears and leaping into an embrace. "You're all right! What an awful, awful vision."

"What did you throw rocks at?" mumbled Oona.

Kitlyn relaxed the hug enough to make eye contact. "Throw rocks?"

Oona mimicked the same gesture she'd used to hurl the stones at Fauhurst. "You mashed me in the face. The sorcerer affected us somehow. Not taking us over but making us see things. You were just standing there staring like a statue. I started shaking you, calling you, but it didn't help. Then all of a sudden, whack."

"Oh. I'm sorry. I thought Fauhurst..." She choked up, but swallowed it. "I was about to crush him."

Beowyn moaned.

Kitlyn glanced behind her.

Both Beowyn and Isha stood slouched against the walls like drunkards, twitching and muttering.

"They're under the spell." Kitlyn couldn't help herself and clung to Oona's arm, still trying to reassure herself that her rejection had been a lie in her mind. "Can we help them?"

Isha jumped forward with a battle cry, swinging her blade at a phantom. Kitlyn leapt aside, shoving Oona with her to the ground as the sword passed within inches of them.

"Highness!" shouted Isha. "Forgive me, I saw…"

"It's all right." Kitlyn picked herself up. "It's foul magic."

Tears streamed down the burly warrior's face. He twisted side to side as if cleaving his giant sword back and forth at an endless onrush of enemies.

Oona raised a hand toward him. Blue light formed at her fingertips. A matching light appeared in front of his forehead. Beowyn's arms stilled. Seconds later, his eyes fluttered open. He looked around at the hallway, bowed his head, and let out a relieved sigh.

"Are you all right?" asked Kitlyn.

"I am now. Trick of the mind." He attempted the manliest sniffle possible, then wiped his face.

"If you need to talk about anything, I'm here." Oona offered a reassuring smile. "But know it was only a lie. Deception."

"Aye." Beowyn nodded. "Kept seeing the innocent bein' overrun with fiends or thieves or some such… too slow to help any of them."

Isha looked up at him as if seeing him for the first time.

"There's a door." Beowyn pointed. "Let us move. I wish to leave this place as soon as we are able."

"Careful." Oona grabbed Kitlyn's arm. "There's a trap. You'll fall into the floor."

Kitlyn turned to face back the way they had been walking. Four skeletons lay on the ground a short distance ahead, covered in dust and cobwebs. Spiders as big as walnuts scurried away from Oona's light, seeking shelter within skulls or under the remnants of armor. The hallway ended a short distance beyond them at an onyx slab door covered in runes.

"Those poor sots never broke out of whatever that was." Beowyn cringed. "Must have starved on their feet."

Kitlyn stepped carefully around the bones, approaching the door. She didn't sense any voids in the ground below her, though the walls on either side contained a complex series of metal rods and gears. Since she couldn't make any sense of the mechanism, she assumed it magical in nature, something to do with the runes on the door.

"That looks a right bit complicated." Beowyn scratched his head.

Oona grinned. "It's not complicated."

"Actually, it is." Kitlyn pointed at the wall. "Lots of gears and stuff."

"So…" Oona glanced at her.

With a grin, Kitlyn sent her magic into the wall. The doorjamb softened and shrank from the onyx slab. Once only the metal locking bars supported its weight, she raised her leg and shoved the door with her foot. It fell inward, its weight bending the metal, and collapsed with a loud *whump*, one pale dusty footprint at its center.

"The mechanism is complicated… opening it isn't."

THE PATH OF TORMENT

OONA

Oona followed the others over the fallen door into a small alcove. A hollow in the wall straight in front of them held shelves of dusty books. To the left, an archway led to a much larger room littered with hanging cages, torture racks, metal brassieres filled with coal, and an array of other ghastly spiked contraptions Oona had no names for.

"This is not a fun place." Isha gazed up at a skeletal leg dangling from an overhead cage.

"All we need to do here is find a crown." Kitlyn walked forward, heading for a big door at the opposite side of the room. "But I don't think he'd keep it in here."

Beowyn and Isha drew their blades, moving up to follow Kitlyn close on either side.

A sudden, powerful sense of dread foreboding fell like icy water down Oona's back.

"Wait!" she shouted.

Everyone stopped.

Living darkness swam out of the corners of the room, gathering in a mass a few paces in front of Kitlyn. The growing pillar of shadow filled out into the shape of an enormous male humanoid that towered to a height of nine feet, its jet black skin gleaming like polished obsidian. Large orange eyes glowed from a bestial face that mixed traits of human, pig, and jackal. Great leathery wings spread out from its back, tipped with wicked horns at the bend. The creature's muscles swelled to ludicrous proportions, especially arms that made Beowyn's thighs appear tiny.

Oona cringed at its nakedness. Though she had never before laid eyes on a nude man, she highly suspected the tiny horns and spikes didn't belong there. What at first she thought to be coarse hair partially obscuring its sex moved — a legion of clinging insects. She swooned back, almost at the edge of vomiting.

Kitlyn growled. A stone spire lanced up from the floor and rammed into the demon's chest. The massive creature barely moved, the spire breaking aside as easily as if she'd stabbed an icicle into the castle wall.

Deep, resonant laughter filled the room. It lowered its gaze to Kitlyn.

Beowyn and Isha charged at it. Isha reached it first. The demon disregarded her attack, allowing her sword to rake across its abdomen before striking her with a backhand that launched her twenty feet sliding. She crashed into an empty cage with enough force to bend the slats. Beowyn rounded his greatsword in an overhead cleave, but the demon caught the blade, laughed, and threw the giant of a man aside like a toy. He slapped into the wall on the other side of the room halfway to the ceiling and fell straight down on his chest, his weapon ringing against the stone with a loud *clang* a few feet away from him.

Kitlyn called another spire. The stone spear broke to splinters, the demon walking through it.

Overcome with indignant rage, Oona ran forward and put herself between the demon and Kitlyn.

"Oona!" Kitlyn grabbed her from behind, trying to drag her back.

"By the light of Lord Lucen, you have no hold upon this world!" She drew her little orb around and held it in both hands above her head.

The glow flickered from blue to pure white.

Beowyn moaned and pushed himself up to kneel.

Roaring, the demon leaned forward, but appeared unable to move closer, its bare feet sliding over the smooth stone, clawed toenails scraping gouges.

"Foul minion of the Pit, in Lucen's name be gone!" Oona shouted in a furious tone Kitlyn had never before heard from her, far different from the petulant anger of a spoiled child. She stepped toward the demon and thrust her hands out, hurling the blinding orb at it. "You have no power to stand against the light of purity!"

The demon shrank back, the thin membranes of its wings burning away like paper held to a candle. Holes grew and merged until only bare spars remained. Snarling, the demon took another step away from the approaching ball of light. Oona advanced on it, her arms still raised. The orb shimmered, intensifying to the point it became painful to look directly at.

Kitlyn hurried over to Isha and pulled her away from the crumpled cage she'd crashed into. The woman limped to her feet, favoring her right side.

Roaring in agony, the demon fell to one knee. Its wings disintegrated. Desperate, it made a feeble claw swipe at her, but the arm disintegrated to the elbow, a vaporous stump passing within inches of Oona's face.

She spread her hands out to the sides in a sweeping gesture before bringing them together in front of herself. A ray of blue-white energy shot forth from her fingers and pierced the demon's chest, striking the wall behind it.

With a final belabored groan, the massive fiend fell like a rain of liquid shadows. Oona guided her light orb down near the floor until the black puddle had fully evaporated.

Beowyn bowed his head. "Lucen's grace be upon us."

"Praise Lucen," whispered Isha, also bowing her head.

Kitlyn stared in awe at Oona. "Lucen guides us."

"And in his name we shall drive every last fiend back to the Pit." Oona bowed her head. A moment later, she looked up and turned to face the others. "The fiend is gone."

The once-again-blue light ball glided down and settled into an orbit around them, its little eye spots tilted in a way that made it appear to be smiling.

"Isha's hurt." Kitlyn helped the woman over to where Oona stood.

Within a second of looking at her, Oona knew the woman had suffered a dislocated shoulder and several broken ribs. She rested her hand over the break, and concentrated on her request that Orien send his aid. In time with the golden light appearing, a disconcerting *crunch* came from Isha's chest.

"Ngh," groaned Isha, hanging on Kitlyn.

Oona moved her hands up to the shoulder, invoking her magic. A soft *pop* followed. Isha's unconscious weight pulled Kitlyn to the ground.

Beowyn rushed over. "What happened?"

"I believe she fainted from pain." Oona crouched and rested her hand on Isha's cheek. "Are you hurt?"

"Just my pride." Beowyn leaned on his sword. "Wasn't ready for anything that strong."

"A true demon." Oona patted Isha's cheek until she came to. "Probably a Pit Archon."

Kitlyn gasped.

"That's a bit much for the likes of us." Beowyn rolled his left shoulder.

Isha woke about half a minute later with a cough. "Thank you, highness."

"Praise Orien." Oona stood and looked at Beowyn. "And a demon's strength means nothing to Lucen."

Kitlyn stared at her with an odd mixture of confusion and love. "What?"

"I'm having a little trouble believing the same girl who hid under her blanket from an assassin turned into that radiantly confident figure of light who stared down a demon almost twice her height."

Oona's cheeks warmed with blush. "With Lucen guiding me, I am not afraid of demons. Assassins are much scarier. And spiders. But I'm not as afraid of spiders as I used to be when I was small."

Beowyn raised a finger. "Spiders *are* scary."

"*You* are afraid of spiders?" Kitlyn blinked at him.

"Screams like a four-year-old girl." Isha chuckled. "One crawled onto his leg at the camp when he squatted ta unburden himself o' the prior night's dinner."

Beowyn feigned shock. He grabbed Isha in a playful headlock. "I'll show ya four-year-old…"

"Ow." Isha gasped.

He froze, then gingerly eased her back to her feet. "Sorry. Forgot."

"It's all right." She rubbed her side. "Merely a bit of soreness, praise Orien."

Kitlyn stepped around the area where the demon melted despite the floor appearing clean, and headed for the door at the far end of the torture room. Oona sensed no taint in the stone, so she went over it.

The door opened into a corridor that extended off in two directions with multiple branching passages on both sides. Other than the occasional tall vase or dusty bench, it appeared the lich lacked in interior decorating skills.

Oona looked left and right. "It's like a maze."

"Give me a moment." Kitlyn closed her eyes and stood in silence for a short while before proceeding onward, her eyes still shut. "Warn me if I'm going to walk into something."

"You see it?" asked Oona.

"There's a large chamber to the left. Feels like a library. Lots of tall stone shelves. Most of the rooms in here are small."

Isha hurried over in front of Kitlyn, blade drawn, on guard for threats. Whenever she reached an intersection, she paused and waited for Kitlyn to pick a direction, then moved in front again. Oona followed with a hand on Kitlyn's shoulder. Beowyn brought up the rear, clutching his blade in both hands while keeping most of his attention to the rear in case anything tried to sneak up on them.

Kitlyn navigated a series of turns and long corridors as if looking at a map only she could see. Oona cringed at the mostly featureless hallways, pale grey in the light of her orb. Already, she felt hopelessly lost.

Glowing spectral hands reached out from the walls, but burned away to mist as soon as they entered the radiant light. Isha paled at the sight of it, for the first time appearing truly frightened. However, her fear showed mostly in her wide-eyed stare, her hands not shaking nor her posture weakened. The spirit in the wall tailed them, constantly testing its ability to withstand the light.

Some minutes later, Kitlyn took a right turn into a short hallway that led to a fancy pair of double doors, together no wider than a normal single door. A glowing arcane pattern of silver light covered the upper half, inscribed within a circle. She reached toward it.

"Be wary, that looks like a glyph." Beowyn pointed his sword at the door.

"Glyph?" Kitlyn hesitated, her fingers inches from contact.

"Ran into a few of them when we hit enemy camps." He made an explosion gesture. "They do magic if you disturb them. Never saw one this big before though."

Kitlyn backed up. "I'm starting to suspect this lich doesn't want guests."

A nervous laugh came from Isha.

Oona glanced at luminous fingers swiping at them from the wall. *Hmm.* She hurried back a few steps, pulling the light with her before dimming it to almost off. The faint fist-sized circle hovered next to her, its eye spots tilting upward in confusion.

"Gah!" cried Kitlyn in the dark. "Oona? Are you okay?"

The glowing apparition of a cloaked figure glided out of the wall. Rather than legs, the tatters of its cloak trailed off into a wispy tendril of spiritual energy. Beowyn and Isha both slashed at it, though their blades didn't appear to do anything. The spirit reached a clawed hand toward Kitlyn, but before it could touch her, Oona commanded the orb back to full brightness.

Shrieking a keening wail, the phantom recoiled directly away from her, crossing its arms in a defensive gesture. The instant it attempted to pass through the glyphed door, a blinding cascade of lightning erupted in a sizzling crackle that ended in an explosion of hot, transparent slime. Oona coughed on the stink of ozone and burned dust.

The formerly-glowing lines on the door had turned black and smoking.

Beowyn, who bore the brunt of the slime blast, turned to face her, dripping head-to-boot in a thick layer of glistening, clear goo. "May I ask what we just witnessed?"

Kitlyn cringed, slinging the same ooze off her arms. "I believe, the destruction of a malign spirit… and the glyph."

"Is this stuff dangerous?" Isha raked her hands down her arms, scraping slime away.

"No, merely disgusting." Oona flashed a weak smile, as she'd been standing far enough away to have avoided the spatter.

Beowyn chuckled, shaking his head. He swiped his hands at his face to clear his eyes, but otherwise ignored the residue dripping off him. The narrow twin doors opened at the behest of his boot. He led the way into a huge rectangular room with a two-story vaulted ceiling. Twenty massive bookshelves lined both sides of a central aisle, all packed with as much dust as books. Random baubles such as skulls, candles, small boxes, bottles, and unrecognizable metal contraptions also littered the shelves.

This place looks familiar. Like I've been here before. She gazed around at the shelves, remembering a man in a black cloak walking among them. *The vision!*

"Search for anything that looks like a crown." Kitlyn hurried forward.

"Be careful," whispered Oona. "He's close. I've seen this place before. Lucen gave me a vision of it."

They split up, dividing the great room into quarters. Oona dared not touch anything, though upon sensing *bad* feelings from a book bound in black leather, she drew her light close to examine it. The tome burst into dark crimson flames.

She narrowed her eyes, focusing Lucen's wrath on the demonic writings until nothing remained of it but ash. One after the next, she made her way around the shelves, incinerating fourteen more books until she became aware of eyes staring at her.

Kitlyn, Beowyn, and Isha stood at the end of the shelf, giving her looks as though she'd belched in public.

"Is something wrong?" asked Oona.

"What are you doing?" Kitlyn gestured at a pile of ashes.

"Oh. Demonic books. I can't leave them here."

The look of confusion on Kitlyn's face became understanding. "Oh. The crown isn't in this room. We're close to another large chamber."

"Let's hope it's in there. It'll take us days to search all the little rooms." Isha faced to the right and headed off.

Oona glanced around, sensed nothing else of particular evil, and followed. Kitlyn walked straight toward a large double door at the opposite end of the library from where they entered. At the halfway point, a giant pedestal on the left supported a book four feet tall and about a foot thick. Recognizable human face patterns suggested the dark black leather binding it had been taken from people.

Horrified—and positive it radiated demonic energy—Oona raised her arms and beckoned Lucen's light. Her beam melted a hole all the way through the tome in an instant. The giant book burst into flames and flipped into the air, flapping its covers like a bird. Emitting a shriek, it flew in circles, but didn't climb too far before the fire overwhelmed it and it fell to the ground with a loud *slam*. Seconds after fire consumed it, several indistinct spirit forms appeared around it, bowed in thanks, and faded.

Kitlyn, Beowyn, and Isha, all jumped away, swords drawn and pointed at it.

Answering screeches came from everywhere. Hundreds of normal sized books leapt off the shelves, filling the air with flapping pages and demonic wails. The tomes hurled themselves at everyone, more annoying than deadly, but a few had enough heft to do damage.

"Go!" shouted Kitlyn while slashing a diving book in half before it could hit her in the face.

Oona raised her arms to guard her head, emitting grunts and squeaks under the pelting coming from every direction. Isha cut several down before taking a hard bonk to the side of the head that knocked her over. Another hit Beowyn in the back of the head, but stopped cold, not moving him at all. He grabbed it, pulled it around in front, and ripped the squirming book in half. The instant it came apart, a flash of sickly lime green light blasted out and the pages ceased moving. With a grunt, he tossed each half aside.

Isha rolled upright and sliced another passing book out of the air.

A giant tome slammed into Oona's back, knocking her flat on her chest, unable to breathe. Beowyn leapt after it, but his huge sword rounded too slow and missed by an inch. A low-flying one crashed into Kitlyn's shins, taking her off her feet. She landed as if doing a push up, and leapt into a sprint.

Beowyn stooped to grab Oona's hand and hauled her into the air, tucking her under his left arm like an ordinary-sized man carrying a child. Rather than try to chop down the unending barrage of tomes, he weathered their strikes, showing little if any reaction to the pelting as he ran.

Kitlyn reached the exit first. She opened the right side of the stone double doors and slipped through. Beowyn set Oona down, using his body as a shield while she ducked into the next room. After Isha darted past him, he jumped in and pulled the door closed.

Books kept pounding against the stone, but lacked the power to do any damage.

"Whew…" Oona backed up, staring at the doors. "We're safe."

"Umm." Kitlyn's voice quivered. "I'm not so sure about that."

Isha sucked in a sharp breath.

Oona turned her head, then the rest of her body to face the room behind her. Large tables on either side of the chamber held books, bottles, various body parts, and bowls of glowing substances. More shelves behind them contained an array of dusty objects.

She ignored all of that.

A throne at the opposite end of the room about fifty feet away held a figure in a billowing black robe with a large hood obscuring its features. Rotting semi-skeletal hands covered in bejeweled rings clasped the armrests.

The figure raised its head, revealing a dusty skeletal face adorned with a thin golden crown. Eerie yellow energy glowed within otherwise empty eye sockets.

Oona's heart nearly stopped beating. She clutched the amulet of Lucen at her chest and focused on reinforcing her mind shield spell.

"Lucen help us."

DARKNESS, LIGHT, AND STONE

KITLYN

Foggy thoughts circled Kitlyn's mind. One moment, she gazed upon the lich as if she loved him more than anything. The next second, she wanted to scream and run. Oona's soft whispering pushed into her consciousness, displacing both the overriding fear and the need to adore the undead creature.

The same instant she realized her thoughts remained her own, Voldreth emitted a dark, growling hiss. He raised an arm as a billowy black breath blasted over his rotten teeth, coalescing into a cloud that gathered low to the ground in front of his seat.

Kitlyn gathered a lump of stone from the floor, levitating it within a shroud of green light. After growing it to the size of a human head, she launched it at the lich. A shadowy arm reached out of the growing gloom, intercepting the stone, deflecting it off to the side. Another demon, somewhat smaller than the last, reached a second arm out from the hole that had formed in the floor, and started to pull itself up into the world.

"Away!" shouted Oona. Her light brightened. "Lucen shall suffer not the presence of demons here!"

Brilliant white light washed over Kitlyn from behind, disintegrating the demon back into wisping shadows. Voldreth snarled and thrust his arm out. The rattle of a heavy chain preceded a strangled gurgle. Kitlyn whirled around.

Oona dangled off the floor, suspended by a chain around her neck that had burst out from the ceiling. Squarish spiky links of black metal radiated demonic energy. Beowyn ran to her, tall enough to reach her neck and grab the constricting chain. Kitlyn focused on the ceiling, liquefying the stone where the metal links emerged, but it didn't help—the chain came straight down from… nowhere.

The light orb flickered, and the chain burst into shadows, dropping Oona onto all fours, coughing and gagging. She looked up with more anger than fear in her eyes, raised her arms, and projected a wide bolt of blue light. The beam hit the lich like a punch to the chest, but didn't appear to have much effect other than blasting dust off his robes.

Isha charged. Voldreth leapt from his throne, unfurling a black skull-headed flail. He swung it in an upward arc to block; her blade bounced off the spiked metal skull with a flash of pale yellow light. The magical burst nearly threw her sword from her grip. Isha staggered, pulled by the force with which her weapon ricocheted off the flail. The lich drifted after her, swinging in a downward arc. Isha let herself fall, avoiding the attack while somersaulting backward onto her feet.

Oona coughed again and stood. She raised her hands as if preparing to do something… but waited.

The lich isn't a demon. Her magic isn't that strong against people… or skeletons.

Kitlyn shoved her arm out, calling a rock spire from the ground behind the lich. Her stone lance slammed into him with a *crunch*, flinging the undead mage clear across the room. The lich slapped chest first into the wall above the tall bookshelves with a clatter like a bundle of broomsticks. He fell on the shelves, bounced off, and crashed flat on his back atop the giant tables, knocking numerous bottles to the ground where they exploded in flashes of violet, red, or green light.

Beowyn roared and raced at him. Another chain shot out of the ceiling and wrapped around the big man's head, pulling him up on tiptoe. He stopped short, blood dribbling down his cheeks from the spikes. Oona pointed a hand at him while Isha ran at the lich. Voldreth grabbed a bottle from the table and hurled it at the charging soldier. She instinctively swung her sword at it. Fearing disaster, Kitlyn called to the stone under the woman's feet and dragged it to the side, pulling Isha off balance. She fell on her butt, her defensive slash at the flying bottle going wild, missing. The bottle sailed past her and exploded on impact with the wall, setting off a fireball that spanned the height of the room.

Kitlyn shielded her face from the blast of greasy, sulfurous smoke and painfully hot air. Somewhere on the other side of the haze, Beowyn snarled. Loose chain links clattered to the stony floor. The lich glared at Kitlyn, the yellow energy in his eye sockets brightening with anger. Two swirling portals of violet and black appeared in midair on either side of her. Ink-black arms with clawed hands reached out. She tried to leap back, but the hot, leathery hands seized her by the wrists, receding into their portals until she dangled from her arms, feet off the ground.

Tenebrea's tits! Kitlyn stared at the approaching lich, straining to stretch her legs and touch the floor. *He knows...* Boots interfered with her connection to the earth, but being held completely off the ground probably broke it entirely. She pointed her right leg at him, trying to call a stone, but managed only to raise a pebble like the ones she amused Pim with. It bounced off the lich's skull with a hollow *clonk*.

Voldreth didn't appear impressed. He stepped closer, raising his skull-headed flail. Beowyn rushed to get in the lich's way, swinging his greatsword in a wild sideways arc. The lich snapped his flail into the sword's path. Both weapons bounced off each other with a yellow flash and loud *bang*. Beowyn grunted, knocked back on one leg, though he held his ground. Voldreth swung at him, but the surprisingly agile big man leaned out of the way, twisting himself to pull his blade into the lich's side, a weak swing with his hands close to his body. Hissing, Voldreth took a step from the force of the blow. Beowyn continued the twist into a spin and a follow-up swing at full force. The giant sword smacked into the undead's chest with a dull *thud*, knocking Voldreth a few steps away from Kitlyn.

She kicked her legs at the air, grunting, but couldn't escape the demonic grip around her wrists.

Isha grabbed a bottle of glowing blue liquid from the table and threw it at the lich. Voldreth pivoted and caught it with his free left hand, then threw it back at her. Isha dove for cover a second before a blast of ice covered the floor and wall. The racing blue stain passed under Beowyn's feet. His boots shot out from under him and he landed flat on his back, wheezing.

Kitlyn gasped in pain, staring up at the evil limbs emerging from swirling portals. Any second now, she expected they would pull her arms straight out of her shoulder sockets.

Strong white light washed over her. Oona stepped out of the fireball smoke, glaring in her direction. The orb cradled in her hands radiated an intense—and warm—light that blasted the demonic arms away to smoke.

Kitlyn dropped. The instant her feet touched stone, a tingle of energy rode up her legs into her chest. Grinning, she gathered a melon-sized rock from the floor, scooping it up like clay. Enraged, the lich whirled on Oona, grabbing at empty air with his left hand.

A thick book leapt off a stand on the largest table, flying into Oona's head from behind. She let out a clipped squeak and collapsed unconscious. Kitlyn launched the huge stone at the lich, a comet wrapped in emerald light. Distracted by Oona, Voldreth twisted his skull toward Kitlyn a mere second before the big stone smashed into his chest. It ripped clear through him, pulling bits of robe out behind it, a spray of bone chips flying.

Voldreth glanced down at the near-perfect hole in his body, then looked back at her like an affronted nobleman after a carless servant girl spilled wine on his shirt. Kitlyn's blood chilled. He tilted his head, gazing at her.

The walls blurred. Beowyn and Isha pulled themselves back to their feet but stood as still as statues, staring at the lich. She couldn't quite recall what Voldreth was or why she came here. After a moment, she remembered that the unconscious blonde girl sprawled out on the floor had to die. That girl had done something to make Master Voldreth furious, and he needed Kitlyn to make sure that awful girl never did anything like that again.

Kitlyn drew her longsword, smiling at the wicked sharp edge. Stabbing the girl in the chest would be too fast. She should cut off her hands first, then the rest of her arms. Maybe an ear or two... then ram the blade straight into her heart.

She padded over to the limp form, put her bare foot against the girl's shoulder, and kicked her over onto her back, her arms flopping limp. Long, beautiful blonde spilled out like liquid, framing a pale, angelic face. Kitlyn grinned with delight that Master Voldreth would be so happy with her, and crouched to rest the edge of her blade over the girl's delicate wrist.

Something felt wrong.

No. She wouldn't cut the girl's hand off. That would probably cause enough pain to wake her up and she'd do more of that nasty light magic that ruined the master's demons. Master Voldreth folded his arms, flail dangling from his right hand. He gave her a nod of approval. Beowyn and Isha stood as blank as zombies, gazing into nowhere.

Kitlyn got to her feet and pointed her sword at Oona's throat, about to thrust it in.

Something still felt wrong.

She repositioned the tip over the girl's heart.

Master Voldreth wanted her dead.

Kitlyn clenched her jaw and tensed her arm, but the tip of the sword shook. It took her a second to realize the shaking came from her hand, as if her body refused to obey her. Again, she rested the tip of her blade at Oona's heart. Something still didn't feel right about doing that. Why couldn't she kill this girl? She looked up at Master Voldreth in confusion.

"Where should I—?"

"Kit," muttered Oona.

She looked down. *Oh, no. She's awake. Master Voldreth is going to be—*

Oona's eyes bulged as she stared up the length of the blade hovering at her heart. Blue light flashed in Kitlyn's vision.

Why am I pointing my sword at Oona? She jumped back with a gasp, horrified.

"He's in your thoughts!" shouted Oona.

Voldreth hissed. A leathery hand came out of nowhere and closed around Kitlyn's right ankle before yanking her off her feet. She twisted back, screamed in anger, and hacked at the ebon limb emerging from a swirling portal. One swipe of her longsword blade severed it at the wrist. Cringing in disgust, she kicked at the air until the disembodied hand went flying.

Oona scrambled to her feet.

Beowyn and Isha turned toward her, raising their blades. The instant they began to charge at her, Kitlyn created a waving ripple in the floor that knocked them both flat on their fronts. Oona started to concentrate on the two soldiers, but another portal hand reached out and grabbed her by the hair, dragging her up on tiptoe, screaming in pain.

Kitlyn jumped at her, slashing the hand loose from the arm. Oona landed flat on her feet and stumbled backward. The severed hand tumbled out of her hair, disintegrating to smoke before striking the floor. Demon claws sank into Kitlyn's shoulders. Another pair of disembodied portal-arms pulled her off the ground.

Voldreth — and the two possessed soldiers — approached Oona.

Kitlyn leaned her head to the right, trying to saw at the clawed hand embedded in her shoulder. Oona turned her light on them, and the arms disintegrated. Kitlyn dropped back to the floor, cringing from the pain in her shoulders. Beowyn bellowed and swung his greatsword to take Oona's head off.

"Stop!" shouted Kitlyn, raising a narrow earthen lance straight up from the ground in front of her wife.

Steel rang against stone, the massive sword severing the top few feet of it, but the pillar stopped the strike from reaching Oona. Kit knocked Isha over with another ripple in the ground. Oona backpedaled, one hand clutching her Lucen amulet, the other pointed at Beowyn.

The big man blinked a few times and the lifeless look left his eyes. Isha leapt upright and ran for Oona, but Beowyn knocked her blade aside and swept her up in his arms, holding her off the ground in a bear hug.

Voldreth glowered and grabbed at the air as if pulling something toward him.

Oona gasped, wide-eyed at the familiar gesture. She ducked an instant before another flying book could knock her out. It sailed over her head and slapped into Beowyn's chest before flopping to the floor.

Kitlyn raked her hand at the air, separating a large piece of ceiling from the rock around it. The several-hundred-pound chunk crashed straight down on top of Voldreth, the *boom* of it landing so loud it masked the crunch of bones. A blast of white vapor raced away in all directions, causing every bit of glassware on both tables to explode in a dazzling cascade of fire, ice, lightning, and black vapor. In seconds, the reek of burned, decaying flesh filled the air.

Isha stopped struggling.

Thin wisps of eerie white vapor continued exuding out from under the slab.

Kitlyn gasped for breath, staring at the hunk of ceiling.

"Well, that's one way to kill a lich." Beowyn chuckled.

What did I almost do…? The longsword fell from her hand with a *clank*. She turned toward Oona, lip quivering, about to burst into tears.

Oona ran to her, grabbing on in a tight embrace. "The lich took over your mind. My spell stopped working when it knocked me out." Golden light flickered on the walls from somewhere behind her and the stinging pain in her shoulders lessened to a dull soreness. "It's not your fault."

"I almost… almost…" Kitlyn sniffled into her shoulder.

"You didn't. The sorcerer wanted you to, but you didn't. You *couldn't*." Oona leaned back out of the hug far enough to kiss her on the lips. "The part of you that remained *you* fought back."

"I love you so much, I couldn't bear to lose you… or even hurt you." Kitlyn rocked her side to side.

"Please stop crying. There's nothing to be sad about." Oona smiled, her eyes sparkling blue. "No magic exists dark enough to break how much I love you."

Beowyn glanced away, wiping a tear.

Kitlyn breathed deep a few times, collecting herself. "That was so scary. All I wanted to do was make him happy."

"It's mind control." Oona shot a dirty look at the giant rock. "Oh, by Lucen… I hope he wasn't wearing the Nimse's crown."

35

UNRAVELING

OONA

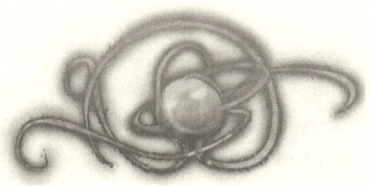

*I*sha approached. Hundreds of pieces of broken glass stuck out of her cheek.

"Oh… ouch." Oona cringed and guided her to sit on one of the tables. "This is going to be uncomfortable."

"Can't hurt more than it did going in." Isha clenched her jaw.

While Kitlyn and Beowyn rummaged around the room, Oona plucked glass from Isha piece by piece. The woman never once flinched.

"Don't touch it," said Beowyn several minutes later. "I'm about as magical as a lump of rock and even *I* can feel something ain't right with that thing."

Kitlyn sighed. "I know."

After plucking the last piece of glass, Oona held her hand over Isha's bleeding face. Orien's cleansing light enshrouded her fingers and all the tiny cuts closed.

"One of the innkeeps I talked to said he heard liches can't be killed." Isha pulled a rag of scrap cloth from a satchel and wiped at her face. "Something about they'll eventually get back up. Destroy the body but the umm… animating force or something goes off to the Netherworld to get power, then comes back and repairs the body."

"How long does that take?" Kitlyn walked over, rubbing at her shoulder.

"Not sure, highness." Isha shrugged. "He didn't say. Could be hours, days, years…"

"Well…" Beowyn kicked the giant rock. "We'll be long gone by then."

Kitlyn faced the slab. "Lucernia is facing enough problems at the moment. We don't need an ancient lich wanting revenge. Can we burn it?"

"Destroying the bones might work, but it could always find a different body." Beowyn pressed against the slab, unable to budge it. "That is a robust stone."

A sudden inspiration came to Oona. She walked over to the huge chunk of ceiling. "Kit, can you please move this?"

"All right." Kitlyn bowed her head in concentration. Seconds later, green light swam around her arms.

Four stone shafts rose out of the ground, lifting the enormous rock off the pulverized remains of the lich. Only a bit of jawbone, a few teeth, and some pieces of skull remained recognizable as bones, the rest had been reduced to dust. An ooze of fetid, rotting flesh had squeezed out from rips in the robe.

"Kinda looks like a jelly-filled sweet bread someone stepped on." Beowyn chuckled.

Isha gagged.

The broken mass of rock rose on the lifting shafts until it settled into the opening from which it had fallen. Dozens of cracks around it unwound as if breaking in reverse. After a moment, the ceiling appeared as though it had never come apart. Kitlyn lowered the four spires into the floor.

Oona raised her hands over the remains. Her light orb glided down in front of her, its little eye spots angled in a manner that made it appear angry. "Lucen, as you provide the light in our darkest moments, I ask that you banish this tainted soul into the care of your daughter so that he may atone for his vileness and no longer plague the living."

The orb vibrated, flickering and sputtering tiny streams of blue light.

Voldreth's bones smoked, blackened, and dissolved to fine ash.

"Lucen does not suffer demons to walk his land, nor those who traffic with them." Oona bowed her head in reverence. "Voldreth shall plague the living no longer."

"I think we found it." Kitlyn pointed at a shelf on the left. "But it's giving off bad energy."

Oona followed her around the long table to a huge bookshelf that held little in the way of books. Various containers the size of jewelry boxes, crystal orbs, skulls, and broken jars oozing unidentifiable substances covered it. Near the floor on the bottom shelf, a thick child-sized crown of bronze, gold, and silver sat upon a violet pillow. Large rectangular rubies encircled the base with lines of pea-sized sapphires ascending ten decorative points.

A copious carpet of dust covered everything on the shelf except for the crown and a bit of pillow around it, as if the energy within had been so vile even dirt wanted to avoid it. Merely looking at it sent a chill over Oona.

"I am inclined to agree. That crown is most assuredly cursed."

Kitlyn squatted for a closer look, but didn't touch. "Perhaps I could encase it in stone so we can carry it?"

"That would be quite heavy; we don't know that the curse wouldn't pass through the stone; and we would still need to find a way to break the curse." Oona rubbed her chin. "Let me try something."

She guided the orb closer and poured magic into it, brightening the usual blue light that served only to illuminate into the searing white purifying glow of Lucen. The gems gleamed in response, but after a few minutes of concentrating on her desire to remove the curse, the crown still radiated malice. Oona gave up and slouched with a sigh. "It's too powerful for me."

"What about smashing it?" Beowyn hefted his blade. "Would that break the curse?"

"Somehow I doubt it." Kitlyn folded her arms. "And the queen might be upset with us if we destroy it. I got the feeling she wanted it back."

"It looks expensive." Isha leaned closer. "I'd want it back, too."

"Feels like it's filled with death." Kitlyn shuddered. "The curse drew the life out of the Na'vir."

Beowyn patted Oona on the shoulder. "Well, she's got the attention of Orien, god of Life." He paused, evidently realizing he'd just touched the queen consort, and pulled his hand back, whistling innocently.

Oona smiled and leaned against him with a brief hug. "It's all right."

He bowed.

"Oh, please stop being so formal. We all nearly died to an ancient lich, there's no one from the court to see us, and... and... we're not as stuck up as the last queen." Oona sighed out her nose.

Isha gasped, blinked, then laughed.

"She is far too kind, sweet, and caring to be a queen of Lucernia."
Kitlyn winked. "You know she even thinks the chamber maids ought to
learn how to read. Oh, the scandal of it."

Oona glanced at her. "I know you are joking, but it's awful that some
would find it inappropriate. And I am still quite new at receiving Orien's
blessing. I don't think I have the skills to break a curse like this with life
energy."

"Maybe someone from, uhh, Evermoor could help?" Beowyn
quirked an eyebrow. "Their lifecallers are incredibly annoying."

"Annoying?" asked Kitlyn.

"What else would you call it when a soldier you thought you killed
gets back up?"

"Horrifying..." Kitlyn blinked at him.

"Not as an undead." He waved his hand as if declining an offer of
food. "All back to rights, alive. I mean, the men weren't all the way
dead, just close. But their lifecallers get them back up right quick like."

"Hmm. Well." Oona regarded the crown. "The Nimse are attacking
both sides, so the people of Evermoor would have reason to help us
beyond it merely being the right thing to do."

Kitlyn put a hand on her shoulder. "Wait a moment. I'm no lifecaller,
but I know I have a connection to the Alderswood. I could try to ask it
for help or energy while you bathe the crown in the light of Lucen's
purity?"

"That sounds like a reasonable idea since we are already here." Oona
knelt in front of the crown, which sat on the bottom shelf only two
inches off the floor. "It's infuriating to me that this creature destroyed
the entire civilization then tossed the crown here like it's some triviality
in his collection."

"Probably because that is exactly how he thought of it." Kitlyn
squatted beside her. "I've never done this before so I have no idea if it
will work. I suppose you should wait to see if anything happens, then
call the light."

Oona nodded.

Kitlyn pressed her hands on the floor in front of her toes and closed
her eyes. Oona watched in silence. Nothing happened for a few minutes,
but right as she prepared to give up on anything occurring, a faint
cracking came from the shelf. She bit her lip, staring at the crown,
hunting for the source of the noise. Another faint *crack* happened.
Seconds later, a thin green leafy vine grew up from behind the pillow.

The floor in front of the shelf split open with a small six-inch fissure. More bright green vines emerged, leaning toward the crown. One by one, hundreds of them appeared, forming a verdant wreath around the pillow.

Oona held her hands out over the crown. Blue light glowed over her fingers. Her little orb raced down to hover above the ring of still-growing plants. As if in response to it, the vines glowed with swirls of emerald magic.

Crunching came from the wall behind the shelf. More and more vines burst out from the stone, engulfing the bookshelf in life energy. Oona intensified her light, calling upon the purity of Lucen. She pictured the wretched Nimse, forced to suffer as barely-intelligent creatures for no reason other than they had refused to help a maleficar.

"Lucen," said Oona, "the Na'vir may not revere you as I do, or as the people of Lucernia do, but they were punished for trying to stand against one who sought power from demons. Please bestow your purity upon this crown and banish the corruption."

Kitlyn grunted as if trying to lift something heavy. She gave off a surge of energy. An answering resonance of magic rose within Oona's chest and raced down her arms. Brilliant white light radiated from under her hands. The mass of tiny vines shot inward, engulfing the crown and turning black as pitch.

The energy flowing through her burned. Oona clenched her jaw and pushed past the pain. *Lucen guided me here. I will help the Na'vir.* Her arms shuddered from the effort. Kitlyn emitted a belabored groan.

The faint tinkling of a tiny crystal shattering broke the silence.

Before Oona even had time to think it an odd noise, a blast of force blew outward from the crown. In an instant, she found herself crumpled against the wall at the opposite corner of the room, legs in the air, ears ringing from a *boom* she couldn't remember consciously hearing.

Kitlyn lay at the end of a streak of dustless floor, slumped in the opposite corner to Oona's left. A matching smear of clean floor led from Oona to the shelf, which hid behind a dense cloud of mist.

"Did that work?" asked Kitlyn in a moan.

Oona peered into the glimmering blue-white fog. The sense of malice that had been emanating from the crown no longer tainted the air. "I think so? It did *something.*"

"Ugh." Kitlyn unfolded herself and sat up. "It tossed us across the room. That's something."

Oona laughed. "Yes, I suppose it is."

A large arm rose out from a pile of rubble about halfway between her and Kitlyn, one finger pointing at the ceiling.

"Ouch," declared Beowyn, then lowered his arm.

"Isha?" Kitlyn looked around.

A groan came from above.

Oona looked up. Isha lay flat atop the shelf beside her, about twelve feet off the ground. "By Lucen... are you hurt?"

"I..." Isha grabbed the edge and peered down at her. "Thought for sure I heard my leg break but it's not hurt. Maybe I imagined it."

Kitlyn grabbed the wall and pulled herself standing. "The Alderswood sent a great amount of life energy. Maybe it *did* break but the tree healed you."

Beowyn sat up, stone chips and broken pieces of shelf falling away from his chest. Other than covered in dust, he appeared uninjured. Oona crawled back to where she'd been kneeling. The Na'vir crown glimmered with a definite magical light, though it gave off no sense of darkness. Nothing of the vines remained other than the cracks they'd left in the walls and floor. She reached out with both hands to cradle the small crown, blinking in surprise at finding it warm.

She lifted it from the pillow and rocked back onto her feet, turning to face the room. Beowyn helped Isha down from the shelf.

Kitlyn stumbled over and looked at the crown. "It does feel different now. Let's bring it back where it belongs."

Oona gently placed the crown in her satchel. "Please tell me you can find your way back out of that maze."

"That's the easy part." Kitlyn headed for the door. "Unless there are more ghosts."

36

FORMAL INTRODUCTIONS

KITLYN

*N*iron and the horses met them at the end of the canyon, unhurt.

"Was the weirdest thing I'll ever see." He whistled. "Hundreds of skeletons just rushed by like I didn't even stand here with no chance at all of holding them off."

Kitlyn patted his arm. "They had specific orders."

"Captain." Beowyn saluted him. "Under your command again."

Niron returned his salute before looking at Kitlyn. "What now?"

"Now, I'd ask you and your men to ride with me back to Cimril. We have a rather demanding deadline to return this crown, but we can spare the time needed for me to officially reinstate you all."

"We should be in good hands provided we stay by your side. If you are pressed for time, we shall accompany you to Underholm." Niron glanced off to the west. "How long do you have?"

"Only about ten years." Kitlyn chuckled. "I think the Na'vir queen has a strange idea of time after being alive so long."

Niron laughed. "Very well then, highness. To Cimril."

"To Cimril!" shouted the other soldiers in unison.

THEY SPENT THE NIGHT ONCE MORE AT THE SAME INN IN IMBREC.

Everyone took the liberty of a bath, Kitlyn devoting over an hour to scrubbing before she managed to rid herself of all the tomb dust under her toenails. The next day, they set off to the south. With Niron guiding the way, they arrived at the actual Valor Pass rather than the highland route Kitlyn had stumbled across. The Ondari military garrison at the gate paid them little attention, likely because their direction of travel took them away from Ondar.

The Lucernian counterpart on the other side stopped them, curious at a group of nine people in armor that made them look like soldiers without any prior notification that a scouting mission would come by. Unfortunately, the commander there recognized Niron.

"Deserters!" The white-haired older captain drew his blade. "Drop your weapons... or don't. Better you die with the honor you abandoned."

"Stand down," said Kitlyn.

"Quiet, girl." He glanced at her. "You don't look familiar. You're with deserters, so you must be one as well... though you do seem a bit young. What unit are you from?"

Kitlyn glowered at him. "Cimril."

A few men and women in the ranks behind him gasped.

"Are you sure I don't look familiar, Captain Andren?"

He stepped closer, looking her over. "Cimril, you say? Who is your commander... or *was* your commander."

A red-haired woman hurried up beside him. "Umm, sir..."

Captain Andren glanced at her. "What?"

"That's the queen," whispered the woman before giving Kitlyn a 'please don't kill me' stare.

"Are you pulling my leg?" roared Andren. "That's preposterous. That's—"

Kitlyn lazily flopped her hand to the side, summoning a small rock to leap up from the ground and spiral around it.

"Oh dear." Captain Andren lowered his sword. "That *is* the queen."

Kitlyn tossed the rock aside. "These soldiers with me are reinstated. While I appreciate the need to have a severe punishment for desertion, they did not flee for cowardice. Whether by Lucen's guidance or their own perception, they saw the truth beneath the lies of the war and refused to wage an unjust slaughter. Those who desert for cowardice, continue to punish as appropriate."

"Very well." The captain bowed his head. "Forgive me for not recognizing you, highness. Your attire…"

"I am aware of that, Captain Andren. Being discreet made my journey simpler. Now if you don't mind, we shall continue back to the city."

"Of course, highness." He sheathed his weapon, backed up, and sent the other soldiers once more to their duties.

Kitlyn sighed. "We've got a lot of work ahead of us."

"Yes. But it is good work." Oona smiled. "Our nation needs to learn how to exist without war going on."

Since Oona's estate would be over an hour detour further north away from Cimril, they spent the night in the city of Gwynaben at a nice inn called the Sleepy Rooster before making haste south along the road. After one more night spent in a roadside inn at the midway point between Gwynaben and Cimril, they arrived in the castle city early evening.

Kitlyn headed straight for the royal study and stared at the papers all over the desk, not knowing where to start. Within a minute of her rear end touching the seat, all five advisors rushed in.

"Good timing." She looked up at them and explained the situation with Niron and the others. "What letters do I need to send to who in order to reinstate them?"

Beredwyn and Lanon guided her through the process. They wrote out twenty-one notices, three copies each of seven, which she signed. Each soldier received one to carry around in case they needed proof, another went to the castle archives, and the last copy would make the rounds among generals.

That done, she invited the former deserters to have dinner at the castle in two hours—enough time to take a decent bath and change. Also, to satisfy the insistent questions from the advisors, she instructed them to arrange the dinner in one of the larger halls so the advisors could join them as well.

"I shall explain everything over our meal. Right now, I am going to bathe and put on something more comfortable than this armor." She grabbed Oona by the hand and whisked her out of the study.

THE ADVISORS AND SOLDIERS ALL APPEARED AT THE APPOINTED TIME, and over a pleasant meal, Kitlyn went over the details of everything that had happened. Despite the wonderful food and good company, she did, however, look forward to later that night, when she'd be back in her bedchamber for some time alone with Oona. Even if they only cuddled.

It's good to be home.

TWO DAYS FOLLOWING THEIR RETURN TO THE CASTLE, KITLYN, OONA, and a group of twenty soldiers rode up to the gates of Underholm. She and Oona once again wore their armor, though this time, she also decided they should wear their crowns… and she kept her boots on.

Kitlyn dismounted long enough to press a hand to the giant doors and urge them open.

Since the tunnels of Underholm had plenty of room and they had quite a distance to cover, they rode the horses down into the depths. While Apples didn't appear to care one whit at the darkness, Cloud responded with much less dignity, shifting and whinnying the whole way to the main chamber. Oona's light orb led the way, trailed by twenty lanterns.

Nimse peeked out here and there, though they appeared to recognize them and held back their aggression. A few scurried along the walls and ceiling, keeping pace with the riders. Upon reaching the underground city, Kitlyn steered to the right. The soldiers all whistled in awe. A few whispered nervously, unsettled by the shapes of Nimse gliding back and forth across the ceiling like silent phantoms.

Darn. Maybe we didn't *break the curse. Hopefully, the queen will know what needs to be done.*

They rode past the large pit that had once been a pool and brought the horses to a stop in the plain open courtyard in front of the Na'vir queen's palace. Kitlyn dismounted with a modest amount of grace, but still had to grab her head to keep her crown from falling off. Oona flowed to her feet with ease.

"How do you manage that so easily?" Kitlyn looked her up and down. "Every time I get down from the saddle, I expect to land on my chin."

"Only practice." She sighed. "I've been riding for ten years. You've only been on a horse three times until recently."

Kitlyn grumbled at the castle staff. "Do you think that wretched woman fainted when she learned who I am?"

"Miss Dunbrook?"

"Is that the name of the witch who thought 'the common whelp' would damage the horses merely by touching them?" Kitlyn stormed toward the doors.

"Yes. I haven't seen her in a while." Oona peeked into her satchel, then sighed with relief and patted it.

By the time she passed the bejeweled columns, she'd already stopped caring about that horrible woman. So many people had treated her so poorly that any attempt to remain angry at them would consume her entire day. She pushed the door open and entered the grand hall, striding up the middle into the dark toward where she remembered the throne dais.

Oona followed, as did about ten soldiers.

The withered queen looked like a long-forgotten doll slumped in the throne. She raised a hand to shield her eyes from the glaring orb. Dozens of Nimse swarmed in, collecting behind the humans, though they gave off curiosity more than threat.

"You are back so soon? You only just left." The queen leaned closer, her glimmering amethyst eyes widening. "That's not my crown. You are wearing the wrong crown." She jabbed a finger at Oona. "So is that one. Not the right crown." Her lips opened in a snarl, bearing tiny, sharpened teeth.

"Good queen of the Na'vir, I bid you a moment's pause." Kitlyn gestured at Oona.

"This belongs to you." Oona pulled the miniature crown out from the satchel and held it up.

The small woman with wrinkled ink-black skin twitched and emitted a raspy squeal, her eyes wide and glowing pale pink-purple. "Give it here! Give!"

Oona hurried forward to hand it over.

A tad ungrateful... Kitlyn bit her lip, wondering if perhaps the curse overwhelmed her manners.

"My crown!" squealed the Nimse Queen, turning it over in her hands, eyes brimming with tears.

The mass of Nimse filling the room emitted a collective, awed, "ooooooh" in a chorus of high-pitched voices.

Shaking, the wrinkled little woman scooted back on her throne, raised the crown, and set it down upon her wild grey-white mane.

Two orbs of pale spirit light emerged from the crown and whirled around, rising into the air, spinning faster and faster until they became a solid circle. After a few seconds, the energy ring burst outward, expanding across the whole room and vanishing into the walls.

Color washed down from the woman's head, turning her hair a beautiful shade of metallic copper. Her skin changed color, becoming the pale near-white of someone who hadn't seen the sun in centuries. Wrinkles faded to the smooth contours of a woman not quite thirty. Though she had the physical size of a ten-year-old human child, her shape left no doubt as to her adulthood. Her amethyst eyes brightened to a purplish magical glow.

The Na'vir queen shuddered and slumped back against the throne, gasping for breath.

A high-pitched scream fell from the ceiling. Kitlyn whirled, barely catching sight of the Nimse that fell. The sea of tiny black bodies keeled over as if ill. One by one, clouds of silvery-white light burst around them. The mist soon faded, revealing a mass of naked people roughly half the size of humans. A sea of startled, glowing eyes in dozens of hues gazed back at her.

Kitlyn gasped and whirled away from several hundred tiny, nude — and highly confused—Na'vir. *Of course... the Nimse were feral creatures. They didn't have anything on.*

"By Ximren's quill, I will need to replace this gown." The Na'vir queen regarded herself. Pale skin showed from numerous holes in the rotting, once-grand dress.

The soldiers stifled snickers at watching the overjoyed, but embarrassed crowd scramble to cover themselves.

"It seems quite a bit of new clothing is needed here." Kitlyn managed a smile.

"After a thousand years, there's barely a scrap of fabric in Underholm that hasn't rotted." The tiny woman eyed her dress, seeming afraid to move lest it fall apart. "Our gardens are likely dead and will need to be cultivated. Our conjurers can produce some garments, but the magic is not permanent. You have done a service beyond measure for my people."

Outside the great hall, joyful cheers, mortified screams, and sorrowful wails at the destruction echoed.

The patter of bare feet approached behind them, and a small voice cleared her throat.

Kitlyn and Oona turned toward each other, glancing down at a dark-haired woman who barely stood taller than their belts. Her eyes radiated a soft cobalt blue light and a rather large bruise covered her right side from armpit to hip.

"I am Xira." The small woman bowed at them, some pain evident in her expression. "I apologize for attacking you. Thank you for sparing my life."

"You…" Oona took a knee, still blushing.

"Yes. You spared my life and let me crawl back into the burrow. The curse compelled me to eat and kill."

Kitlyn found it uncomfortable to look at her between guilt at almost killing her, awkwardness at her lack of clothing, and fighting the urge to be condescending and think of a tiny person as cute or childlike. The woman appeared to be around eighteen, which for a Na'vir, would equate to roughly 180 years of age, well older than her. "Please forgive me for the Nimse that I've hurt."

Oona bit her lip, blushed brighter red, but placed her hand on the woman's side. Orien's light glowed in a bloom of golden warmth. When it faded, the bruise shrank to a sixth of its former size.

Xira gasped, nearly losing her balance. Her eyes fluttered and a dazed smile parted her lips. "Ooh! The pain is much less. What did you do?"

A man nearby spoke rapidly in the indecipherable language.

"Oh, yes. Orien." Xira curtsied. "You are so kind and generous to heal me after I tried to harm you. Thank you."

The queen stood, clutching her disaster of a gown, and stepped down from the throne. "The curse compelled my people to be monsters. We cannot blame you for defending yourselves. Even I had difficulty resisting the urge to devour. You have given us back our lives." The queen flashed a broad smile, revealing normal—unpointy—teeth. Tears gathered in her eyes. Overcome with joy, she lurched forward, grabbing Kitlyn and Oona in an embrace around their hips.

"Would it be insulting if I picked you up?" asked Kitlyn. "The temptation is overwhelming."

The queen stepped back, fists on her hips. "That is one thing about surface dwellers I will never understand. Why do they all have an urge to do that to us?"

"I think it would be a little insulting, yes." Oona glanced at Kitlyn. "She's not a child."

"Let us start this over." The small woman struck as regal a pose as her tattered gown allowed. "I am Lady Xorana of the house Nazadur, Queen of the Na'vir and ruler of Underholm."

Kitlyn offered a nod of greeting. "I am Lady Kitlyn Talomir, Queen of Lucernia. This is Lady Oona Talomir, my wife." She hesitated a second. "Queen Consort of Lucernia."

Oona also nodded in greeting. "It is a pleasure to make your acquaintance, Queen Xorana."

A roar of applause rose up behind them.

Kitlyn glanced back—a few hundred Na'vir abruptly ceased clapping to cover themselves with their hands.

Queen Xorana's eyebrows went up. "Your wife? I am impressed. I did not think humans, *especially* Lucernians, would tolerate a love like yours at all, much less for their royals. Perhaps much *has* changed in the past thousand years."

"The old doctrines were misinterpreted." Kitlyn took Oona's hand. "The gods themselves have smiled upon us, and for that, I will ever be grateful."

Oona beamed.

"You have done my people and me a great service. I declare you friends of Underholm. It will, however, take us many years to rebuild. It is also likely that many of my people may take quite a long time to trust humans again, though your actions give us hope. In time, we may re-open the gates of Underholm to trade."

"As soon as you feel the time is ready, I would be honored to receive your emissaries." Kitlyn squeezed Oona's hand. "However, I believe some early trading may be in order. I can send wagons bearing food, fabric, and thread as soon as I return to my home."

Queen Xorana fidgeted at her dress. "Perhaps, in that case, it would be wise to hasten the re-establishment of trade, yes. We have gems and precious metals we can offer as payment. Once we have repaired Underholm to a proper state, I will invite you as honored guests for a celebration. You will, of course, forgive me as we are... not ready for such a visit yet."

Kitlyn twisted to peek behind her, letting out a relieved sigh at the empty room no longer wall to wall with nakedness. "I understand. We shall bid our leave then."

Once more overcome with emotion, Queen Xorana moved in to hug them. Kitlyn hastily squatted, accepting the embrace at eye level, as did Oona.

"Farewell, Queen Kitlyn and Lady Oona." Queen Xorana bowed her head, her almost floor-long hair falling over her like a curtain of coppery strands. "Travel with safety and honor."

Oona held out her hand, beaming a huge smile. Kitlyn took it, and walked with her out of the great hall.

SMALL TORMENTS

OONA

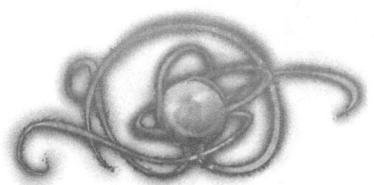

Oona found herself awake.

Ordinarily, that wouldn't have bothered her if not for it being quite late at night. She snuggled close to Kitlyn's warmth under the covers in the vast softness of their bed in Castle Cimril. Neither of them had bothered to put a nightdress on once they'd finished experimenting with some of those 'things' Ruby had so feared they'd done before marriage.

Unable to explain why she'd snapped out of sleep, she closed her eyes again.

Fingertips brushed across her cheek.

"Wake," whispered a feminine voice.

Oona opened her eyes and rolled to her left, peering up at a pale girl of about fifteen. Long slate-grey hair hung past her knees, the last foot or so metallic silver. She wore a simple black dress, bare toes peeking out from under the hem. A strong melancholy presence wafted from her, though she regarded Oona with a faint smile.

Her sleep-fogged brain took a few seconds to realize she stared up at someone who looked exactly like Tenebrea. She blinked. Her eyes shot open wide.

The girl-who-looked-too-much-like-Tenebrea gestured toward the wall, a note of warning in her expression. Before Oona could open her mouth to say a word, the young girl disappeared into thin air, nothing but a semi-luminous silver fog clinging to the floor where she'd been.

Eep! She didn't 'look like' Tenebrea. She was *Tenebrea.* Oona stared at the wall, noting nothing more alarming than a bookshelf. She sat up out from under the blanket and shook Kitlyn's shoulder until she woke.

Kitlyn scrunched up her face and twisted to peer up at her.

Click.

That bookshelf swung inward at a slow creep, like an opening door.

Kitlyn sat up.

A wild-haired man in dingy cream-colored robes liberally stained with dirt edged around the bookshelf. He clutched a dagger in one hand, the other gripping the bookshelf/door, but at the sight of four bare breasts staring him in the face, he froze. The odor of whiskey drifted by.

Tenebrea warned me. Oona's jaw hung open. "He means to kill us."

Kitlyn leapt out of bed, naked as a newborn babe, and grabbed her longsword from its sheath leaning against the wall. "Fauhurst…"

"What?" Oona looked back and forth between them. "That's Fauhurst? I thought he was a beggar?"

"I'd recognize those cruel eyes anywhere." Kitlyn pointed her blade at him.

"Kit. Put something on," whispered Oona.

"This wouldn't be the first time I've killed a man while not wearing pants."

She locked stares with Fauhurst. He squeezed and relaxed his grip on the dagger, a manic look in his eye.

Feeling more trapped by the bedding than embarrassed, Oona chose mobility and scrambled to her feet. Scarlet-faced, she grabbed her longsword and tried to put on an air of authority. "What do you mean this wouldn't be the first time?"

"I told you about that man in the keep… yanked my breeches down to trip me up."

"Oh." Oona padded to the end of the bed and glared at the former advisor. "You came here to kill us."

"How did you get in here?" Kitlyn stepped closer to him, no trace of fear or hesitation.

Fauhurst gazed between them, a bit of manic drool rolling down the beard he hadn't shaved in weeks.

"As an advisor, he knows all the secret passages. He ran off after we confronted the king and never came back to have his keys taken away." Oona let anger keep her from being mortified, and also took a step toward him. "The castle hasn't been haunted with a ghost. It was him!"

"Wretches," hissed Fauhurst. "The two of you. Impure! Dare you stand before a man not your husband in a state of undress?"

Kitlyn took another step. "What do you call a man who sneaks into a young woman's bedchamber at night?"

"If you kill me, it will show everyone your true intentions." Fauhurst backed away from the secret door, making jabby twitching motions with the knife. "They'll all know you mean to force your abomination on the kingdom. Soon, it will be the pure love between man and woman that's viewed as a crime against Lucen."

"You've completely lost your mind." Kitlyn stalked toward him. "The people will think nothing of the sort, or did you forget that sneaking into the queen's room in the middle of the night with a dagger makes you a wretched cur of a coward assassin?"

"It's obvious you are a coward. You hoped to catch us sleeping. Two small women our size, not even dressed, and you still fear coming anywhere near us." Oona edged closer. "Put down that dagger or I'll be forced to show you everything Guard Lorne has taught us."

Kitlyn raised her sword. "Drop that dagger or try to use it, cur."

A metal candleholder rose up behind Fauhurst.

He pointed at them. "Stay back! Don't bring your abom—"

The candleholder came down on his head with a dull *clonk*. He emitted a weak whimper of a moan and collapsed, mostly unconscious. Piper stood behind him in a nightgown, the slender girl struggling with the weight of her improvised mace.

Oona blinked at her. "Where did you come from?"

"He's not the only one who knows all the secret passages." She pointed at a half-height opening in the wall below a small table between two bookcases, then set the candleholder down on the table with a pronounced *thud*. "I used to be a spy, after all. I sleep pretty light and heard you talking." Piper crouched and pulled the dagger away from Fauhurst's hand. "Shall I fetch the guards or send him to Tenebrea?"

Kitlyn tossed her sword on the bed and grabbed her nightdress from a nearby chair. "Please fetch the guards."

Piper stood, still holding the dagger, but looking relieved. "Okay." She ran to the actual door, unlocked it, and ran off down the hallway.

Oona stared at the arch until the patter of running feet faded to silence.

"My love, you should put something on. The guards will be here soon." Kitlyn let her nightdress fall around her, then walked over to the muttering Fauhurst, squatted, and punched him in the eye.

"Oh. Yes." Oona grabbed her nightdress and slipped into it.

Piper returned less than a minute later with five guards. One of them carried the dagger.

"That is Fauhurst." Kitlyn pointed at him. "He attempted to kill us in our sleep. He is also charged with plotting sedition. Please look into how a drunk managed to infiltrate the castle's secret passageways and stay there for weeks undetected, even if he *did* have a key."

"Right away, highness." The guard with the dagger tucked it in his belt, bowed at them, and helped carry Fauhurst out.

Oona hugged Piper. "Nice move with the candle."

She curtseyed. "I didn't think you wanted to kill him, or you would've just run over and done it. Probably the best choice. He'd have haunted you for years."

Kitlyn glanced at Oona with a raised eyebrow.

"Well, I'm not going to be able to go back to sleep." Oona sighed, crossed the room, and put her sword back in the scabbard, which she leaned against the wall.

"We could stay up all night talking." Kitlyn fell seated on the edge of the bed. "Though this mattress has strong magic. It may yet lull us into slumber."

"You could tell me about going to Ondar, and the Nimses." Piper bounced on her toes.

"Nimse, not Nimses. It's the same word for one or more than one." Oona wagged a finger at her. "And they're the Na'vir now."

"Ooh. Please tell me what happened?" Piper leapt up and sat cross-legged at the foot of the bed.

"It's less than four hours until dawn." Kitlyn glanced at the window.

Oona smiled and crawled into bed. "Well, we can tell as much story as we can before we drift off."

Piper grinned.

Oona reclined in the bathtub with Evie planted beside her.

She washed her sister's hair while Piper, kneeling outside the tub, worked on hers.

"Do I have to wear a big dress?" Evie looked up at her, squinting at the soap. "I don't like the big dresses 'cause I can't breathe."

"I hate them, too." Oona poured water over the girl's head. "You can wear one that's comfortable but a little fancy."

"Okay," chirped Evie.

Once they finished bathing, they toweled off and padded past the curtain to the bedroom. Oona put on a light set of underpinnings, skipping the hose and the burdensome crinoline, and selected a crushed blue velvet dress with silver trim. It had back lacings and frilly sleeves, but no boning in the corset area. The soft material didn't limit her breathing and would be quite comfortable.

Evie sat there wrapped in a towel, watching Oona dress and laughing at Piper muttering oaths to Navissa while fighting with the back lacing. When her turn came, she stood on the bed as Piper and Oona dressed her in a small gown of similar comfort and style.

"So, what happened after you returned to Underholm?" Piper snugged the last lace, knotted it, and lifted Evie off the bed to set her on the floor. "I may have fallen asleep."

Oona laughed, imagining the scandal that would've erupted had one of Queen Solara's handmaidens been found sleeping in the same bed, like a pack of common young girls inviting friends over for the night. She stuck her tongue out at the stodgy old people who'd faint over such a thing. "The Na'vir are free of the curse. In a few years, they may send an ambassador here."

"Will you tell me the story, too?" Evie smiled up at her.

"Of course. But later. We have matters to attend." Oona patted Evie on the head.

Kitlyn glided in and hastily changed from a plain dress to a satin one slightly more elaborate than Oona's. While standing there suffering Meredith's assault on the back lacing, she smiled at Evie. "Oh, you are adorable!"

Evie beamed, swishing side to side to show off how her dress fluffed around.

Oona waited until Kitlyn appeared ready. "Come then. Time to deal with the dreadful."

"What?" Piper tilted her head. "You don't like being queen?"

"I hated being princess because I thought I would have to destroy

Evermoor. I don't mind being the queen consort, but sitting in a room full of old men quibbling percentages of taxation is absolute *torture*."

Kitlyn, Evie, Piper, and Meredith laughed.

It's not as bad as sitting in a room while Aodh tried to auction me off to a foreign prince. She took Evie's hand and followed Kitlyn down the hall to the stairs for another day at court.

AS EQUALS

KITLYN

*P*erched upon her throne, Kitlyn once again felt as though time decided to go on holiday.

In all likelihood, she'd only been there for about fifteen minutes thus far, but it felt like hours. The endless murmuring din of advisors, nobles, and courtiers reminded her how little sleep she'd had the night before. She couldn't wait for nighttime to return so she could crawl back into bed. Any minute now, the advisors would line up and present whatever list of matters that they felt worth elevating to her direct attention that they couldn't decide for themselves.

If she managed to survive the day without passing out on her feet in front of a packed room, she'd consider it an act of the gods.

Evie sat on a little chair between the two thrones, occasionally holding their hands, but more often than not fidgeting and bouncing.

Oona reached over to adjust the girl's floral crown, whispering, "Please try to sit a little more still. This is dreadfully boring, I know, but it won't be long."

"Okay," whispered Evie, nodding.

Kitlyn looked down the length of her dress at the tips of her matching emerald green shoes poking out from under it. She raised and lowered her big toe, amusing herself by watching the fabric move. *Beredwyn said I will not find this quite so dreadfully boring when I grow older. Am I too young to be queen?*

She let her thoughts drift to Oona telling her that Tenebrea had appeared in person to warn them of Fauhurst. *What have we done to be worthy of such direct intervention of the goddess?* For a moment, she felt tiny and insignificant, like some little beggar girl the richest person in the land had decided to randomly adopt.

It cannot be simply me, or even Oona. The gods must be acting for the all of Lucernia, and we are somehow important to that.

Beredwyn cleared his throat.

Kitlyn lifted her head, not having realized she'd slumped forward. The advisors all stood in a line to the right of the carpet leading away from the throne dais. A line of people: a few nobles, a handful of merchants, and a couple dressed in commoners' garb waited to speak to her.

"Someone fell aslee-eep," singsonged Evie in whisper.

Kitlyn didn't bother holding back the laugh. She stood and moved to the top of the dais stairs. "Before we begin, I have a short decree to announce."

The room fell quiet.

Beredwyn tilted his head, one eyebrow up.

"My father proved that too much power concentrated in too small a place leaves too much room for cruelty, greed, and capriciousness."

A few murmurs came from the court.

"I do not wish to become or be viewed as a tyrant. To that end, I hereby declare that my wife is an equal. No longer queen consort, but a regent equal in standing to me. Henceforth, we shall both bear the title of queen." At an upsurge in muttering, she raised her hand, quieting it. Noticing an urgency in Lanon's eyes, she nodded at him. "Advisor?"

"Highness." He waved his hand about, trying to collect his thoughts. "Queen Solara had no real power. This is an unusual precedent."

"I am aware of that. At least, that is what I have been told. I was quite young when she was murdered. My father craved power. He loved having authority and status more than anything. My mother accepted being politically weak to soothe his ambitions. She satisfied herself with the luxury of life as a queen. I only crave two things, and power is not one of them. My bloodline and the people have given me power, and I accept it for what it is—a responsibility. The two things I crave are..." She twisted to smile at Oona. "My wife, Oona... And for the people of Lucernia to prosper in a much-overdue time of peace."

A few hesitant claps started, then more, growing to a reasonable level of applause. Though she wouldn't call it deafening, it reached enough of a volume to make her smile.

"That is all. Shall we proceed with the matters of state?" Kitlyn backed up two steps and took her seat.

Beredwyn nodded, his tall hat wobbling. "In the matter of the traitor, Fauhurst. You must decide his sentence."

Kitlyn emitted a 'must I deal with this now?' sigh, and glanced at Oona.

Oona uncovered her mouth, the grin she'd been hiding long gone. "Let him scrub floors for the rest of his days in the dungeons."

"I agree." Kitlyn looked at Beredwyn. "Life imprisonment, and he shall be tasked with cleaning the floors."

Beredwyn barely managed to conceal a smile and scribbled something on his record scroll. "Now on to the matter of Lord and Lady Fenmeer and their land claim."

Evie let her head fall back against the seat, looking up at Oona. "Is this going to take long?"

fin

THE STORY CONTINUES

Kitlyn and Oona's story will continue in *The Sapphire Soul.*

ACKNOWLEDGMENTS

Thank you for reading The Cursed Crown!

I had been considering doing a sequel to The Eldritch Heart for a while, but it kept finding itself bumped back by other projects. Well, when I heard from a mom that her daughter made a specific request from her hospital bed that I write a sequel, I knew there was no possibility of refusing such a request.

And so, here we are at the end of The Cursed Crown.

Thanks to Lee Hargrove for editing.

Additional thanks to Dianne, Gwen, and Daniel Cox (no relation) for beta reading.

And of course, my most sincere appreciation goes out to Amalia Chitulescu for the beautiful cover art. - www.amaliach.com

ABOUT THE AUTHOR

Originally from South Amboy NJ, Matthew has been creating science fiction and fantasy worlds for most of his reasoning life. Since 1996, he has developed the "Divergent Fates" world, in which *Division Zero, Virtual Immortality, The Awakened Series, The Harmony Paradox, and the Daughter of Mars series* take place. Along with being an editor at Curiosity Quills press, he has worked in IT and technical support.

Matthew is an avid gamer, a recovered WoW addict, Gamemaster for two custom RPG systems, and a fan of anime, British humour, and intellectual science fiction that questions the nature of reality, life, and what happens after it.

He is also fond of cats.

Visit me online at:
    Facebook: https://www.facebook.com/MatthewSCoxAuthor
    Pinterest: https://www.pinterest.com/matthewcox10420/
    Goodreads: https://www.goodreads.com/author/show/7712730.Matthew_S_Cox
    Email: mcox2112@gmail.com

OTHER BOOKS BY MATTHEW S. COX

Divergent Fates Universe Novels

Division Zero series

- Division Zero
- Lex De Mortuis
- Thrall
- Guardian
- Harbinger
- The Shadow Fixer

The Awakened series

- Prophet of the Badlands
- Archon's Queen
- Grey Ronin
- Daughter of Ash
- Zero Rogue
- Angel Descended

Daughter of Mars series

- The Hand of Raziel
- Araphel
- Ghost Black

Virtual Immortality series

- Virtual Immortality
- The Harmony Paradox

Prophet of the Badlands Series

- Prophet's Journey

Divergent Fates Anthology

(Fiction Novels - Adult)

The Roadhouse Chronicles Series

- One More Run
- The Redeemed
- Dead Man's Number

Faded Skies series

- Heir Ascendant
- Ascendant Unrest
- Ascendant Revolution

Temporal Armistice Series

- Nascent Shadow
- The Shadow Collector
- The Gate to Oblivion
- The Queen of Discord

Vampire Innocent series

- A Nighttime of Forever
- A Beginner's Guide to Fangs
- The Artist of Ruin
- The Last Family Road Trip
- The Phantom Oracle
- How Not to Summon Demons
- Ordinary Problems of a College Vampire
- A Vampire's Guide to Surviving Holidays
- An Introduction to Paranormal Diplomacy
- A Vampire's Guide to Adulting

Standalones

- Wayfarer: AV494
- Axillon99
- Chiaroscuro: The Mouse and the Candle
- The Spirits of Six Minstrel Run
- Sophie's Light
- The Far Side of Promise anthology
- Operation: Chimera (with Tony Healey)
- The Dysfunctional Conspiracy (with Christopher Veltmann)
- Of Myth and Shadow
- The Girl Who Found the Sun

Winter Solstice series (with J.R. Rain)

- Convergence
- Containment
- Catalyst
- Catacomb

Alexis Silver series (with J.R. Rain)

- Silver Light
- Deep Silver
- Silver Quarrel

Samantha Moon Origins series (with J.R. Rain)

- New Moon Rising
- Moon Mourning
- Haunted Moon

Vampire For Hire series (with J.R. Rain)

- Moon Master
- Dead Moon
- Lost Moon

Maddy Wimsey series (with J.R. Rain)

- The Devil's Eye

- The Drifting Gloom
- Dark Mercy

Samantha Moon Case Files series (with J.R. Rain)

- Blood Moon

Immortal Operative (with J.R. Rain)

- Broken Ice

Four Elements series (with J.R. Rain)

- The Elementalist
- The Black Rose
- The Wakefield Curse

Young Adult Novels

The Eldritch Heart Series

- The Eldritch Heart
- The Cursed Crown

Evergreen Series

- Evergreen
- The World That Remains
- The Lucky Ones
- Nuclear Summer

Standalones

- Caller 107
- The Summer the World Ended
- Nine Candles of Deepest Black
- The Forest Beyond the Earth
- Out of Sight

Middle Grade Novels

The Adventures of Ubergirl series

- My Dad is a Mad Scientist
- Aliens Ate My Homework
- The End of all Halloweens

Tales of Widowswood series

- Emma and the Banderwigh
- Emma and the Silk Thieves
- Emma and the Silverbell Faeries
- Emma and the Elixir of Madness
- Emma and the Weeping Spirit

Standalones

- Citadel: The Concordant Sequence
- The Cursed Codex
- The Menagerie of Jenkins Bailey